A TIME TO FORGIVE

MARTA PERRY
A Time to Forgive

Promise Forever

Steeple
Hill®

Published by Steeple Hill Books™

STEEPLE HILL BOOKS

Steeple
Hill®

Recycling programs
for this product may
not exist in your area.

ISBN-13: 978-0-373-65138-2

A TIME TO FORGIVE AND PROMISE FOREVER

A TIME TO FORGIVE
Copyright © 2002 by Martha Johnson

PROMISE FOREVER
Copyright © 2003 by Martha Johnson

www.SteepleHill.com

Printed in U.S.A.

CONTENTS

MARTA PERRY

has written everything from Sunday School curricula to travel articles to magazine stories in more than twenty years of writing, but she feels she's found her writing home in the stories she writes for the Love Inspired lines.

Marta lives in rural Pennsylvania, but she and her husband spend part of each year at their second home in South Carolina. When she's not writing, she's probably visiting her children and her six beautiful grandchildren, traveling, gardening or relaxing with a good book.

Marta loves hearing from readers, and she'll write back with a signed bookmark and/or her brochure of Pennsylvania Dutch recipes. Write to her c/o Steeple Hill Books, 233 Broadway, Suite 1001, New York, NY 10279, e-mail her at marta@martaperry.com, or visit her on the Web at www.martaperry.com.

Speaking the truth in love, we will in all things grow up into Him who is the head, that is, Christ.
—*Ephesians* 4:15

This story is dedicated to my son,
Scott, and his wife, Karen,
with love and thanks.
And, as always, to Brian.

Chapter One

Adam Caldwell stared, appalled, at the woman who'd just swung a sledgehammer at his carefully ordered life. "What did you say?"

The slight tightening of her lips indicated impatience. "Your mother-in-law hired me to create a memorial window for your late wife." Her gesture took in the quiet interior of the Caldwell Island church, its ancient stained-glass windows glowing in the slanting October sunlight, its rows of pews empty on a weekday afternoon. "Here."

He'd always prided himself on keeping his head in difficult situations. He certainly needed that poise now, when pain had such a grip on his throat that it was hard to speak. He put a hand on the warm, smooth wood of a pew back and turned to Pastor Wells, whose call had brought him rushing from the boatyard in the middle of a workday.

"Do you know anything about this?"

The pastor beamed, brushing a lock of untidy graying hair from his forehead. "Only what Ms. Marlowe has been telling me. Isn't it wonderful, Adam? Mrs. Telforth has offered to fund not only the new window, but the repairs on all the existing windows. God has answered our prayers."

If God had answered Henry Wells's prayers in this respect, He'd certainly been ignoring Adam's. Adam glanced at the woman who stood beneath the largest of the church's windows, its jewel colors highlighting her pale face. She was watching him with a challenge in her dark eyes, as if she knew exactly how he felt about the idea of a memorial to Lila.

She couldn't. Nobody could know that.

He summed up his impressions of the woman— a tangle of dark brown curls falling to her shoulders, brown eyes under straight, determined brows, a square, stubborn chin. Her tan slacks, white shirt and navy blazer seemed designed to let her blend into any setting, but she still looked out of place on this South Carolina sea island. Slight, she nevertheless had the look of a person who'd walk over anything in her path. Right now, that anything was him.

"Well, now, Ms.—" He stopped, making it a question.

"Marlowe," she said. "Tory Marlowe."

"Yes." He glanced at the card she'd handed him. Marlowe Stained Glass Studio, Philadelphia. Not far from his mother-in-law's place in New Jersey. Maybe that was the connection between them. "Ms.

Marlowe. Caldwell Island's a long way from home for you." His South Carolina drawl was a deliberate contrast to the briskness she'd shown. A slow, courteous stone wall, that was what was called for here. "Seems kind of funny, you showing up out of the blue like this."

She lifted those level brows as if acknowledging an adversary, and he thought her long fingers tightened on the leather bag she carried. "Mrs. Telforth gave me a commission. I'm sorry Pastor Wells didn't realize I was coming. I thought Mrs. Telforth had notified him. And you."

"Also seems kind of funny that my mother-in-law didn't get in touch with me first."

Actually, it didn't, but he wasn't about to tell this stranger that. Mona Telforth blew in and out of his life, and his daughter's life, like a shower of palm leaves ripped by a storm—here unexpectedly, gone almost as quickly.

"I wouldn't know anything about that, but she spelled out her wishes quite clearly." The overhead fan moved the sultry air and ruffled the woman's hair. "She said she'd been thinking about this for some time, and she wants me to create a window that will be a tribute to her daughter's life and memory."

Pain clenched again, harder this time. Mona Telforth didn't know everything about her daughter's life. She never would. He'd protect her memories of Lila, but he wouldn't walk into this sanctuary every Sunday and look at a window memorializing a lie.

He inhaled the mingled scent of flowers and

polished wood that always told him he was in the church. A place that meant peace to him had turned into a combat zone. "You have some proof of this, I suppose."

A soft murmur of dismay came from Henry. "I'm sure Ms. Marlowe is telling us the truth, Adam."

The woman didn't even glance toward the pastor. She was quick—he'd give her that. She'd already sized up the situation and realized he was the one she had to deal with, not Henry.

"I'm not a con artist, Mr. Caldwell. This commission is real. Take a look." She pulled an envelope from her oversize shoulder bag and thrust it toward Adam. If the paper had been heavier, she'd probably have thrown it.

The letter was definitely from Mona, written in the sprawling hand he recognized. And in spite of straying from the point a time or two, she made her wishes clear. She was aware of the deteriorating condition of the existing windows, and she'd fund all the repairs if she could have one window to honor her daughter's life. She'd even added the inscription she wanted on the window. *Lila Marie Caldwell, beloved daughter, wife, mother.*

If his jaw got any tighter, it would probably break.

Tory Marlowe seemed just as tense. Her hands clenched, pressing against her bag, as if she wanted to snatch the letter back. "Satisfied?"

"Ms. Marlowe, it's not a question of my being satisfied." He tried to identify the look in her velvet brown eyes when she wasn't actively glaring at him.

It took a moment, but then he had it. Loneliness. Tory Marlowe had the loneliest eyes he'd ever seen.

A vague feeling of recognition moved in him. "Have we met before? You seem familiar to me."

She withdrew an inch or two. "No. About the commission—"

He tried to shake off the sense that he should know her. "My mother-in-law is a person of whims. I'm sure she was interested when she wrote this, but she's probably gone on to something else already." He could only hope. "You'd best go back to Philadelphia and look for another commission. This one isn't going to work out."

He saw the anger flare in her face, saw the effort she made to control it.

"It almost sounds as if you don't want a memorial to your late wife, Mr. Caldwell."

Now he was the one struggling—with grief, anger, betrayal. How could this woman, this stranger, cut right to the pain no one else even guessed at?

"Of course he does." Henry sounded scandalized.

The woman glanced at the pastor, startled, as if she'd forgotten he was there. Adam had almost forgotten Henry, too. He and Tory Marlowe had found their own private little arena in which to fight.

He shoved his emotions down, forcing them behind the friendly, smiling mask that was all his neighbors ever saw from him. "Pastor, you don't need to defend me. Ms. Marlowe is entitled to her opinion."

"But she didn't know Lila," Henry protested.

"Why, Adam and Lila were the most devoted couple you could ever want to meet. Everyone loved Lila."

Everyone loved Lila. Including, Adam supposed, the man she'd been running to when the accident took her life. For one insane moment he wondered what they'd say if he blurted the truth.

Speaking the truth in love, we grow up in all things into Christ... The Bible verse Grandmother Caldwell had given him on his baptism flitted through his mind, and he shook it off with a quick glance at the carved wooden baptismal font that stood near the pulpit. The truth couldn't be told about this. He might somehow, someday, be able to deal with Lila's desire to be rid of him. He couldn't ever forgive the fact that she'd been ready to desert their daughter.

Jenny. Determination hardened his will. Jenny idolized the mother she barely recalled, and she must never learn the truth. He had to keep his secret for her sake.

He rallied his defenses. "Both Ms. Marlowe and my mother-in-law are forgetting something, even if Mona does mean to go ahead with this."

Tory's long fingers closed around Mona's letter. "What's that?"

He managed a smile, knowing he was on firmer ground. "It's up to the church council to decide if they want a new window." He gestured toward the stained glass on either side of the sanctuary. "As you can see, we have a full complement of windows. I don't think they'll want to destroy one in order to build something different, no matter how generous the gift."

"They're going to lose one anyway, regardless of whether I replace it." She shot the words back. "Have you taken a good look at the second one on the left?"

"Such bad shape," Henry murmured. He walked to the window with the image of Moses and the burning bush. "It's one of the oldest ones. Is it really beyond hope?"

"It would probably shatter if we took it down for repair. I could rebuild it the way it is, but that wouldn't meet the terms of the commission." She moved to the window and outlined a fragment of rose glass, her finger moving as lovingly as if she touched a child. "It might be possible to save some of the pieces and incorporate them in the new window."

"Do you really think so?" Henry's eager tone sounded a warning note to Adam. Henry's enthusiasm would sweep the rest of the board along if Adam didn't find some way of diverting this project.

"You're being premature."

Henry and the woman swung around to face him, and for an instant they seemed allied against him.

Nonsense. This church was built and maintained by Caldwells, had been since the first Caldwell set foot on the island generations ago. Henry would side with him, not with a stranger.

"We can't do anything until I talk to my mother-in-law and find out if she really intends to pursue this project." Adam tried to smile, but his lips felt too stiff to move. "Frankly, I think you're here on a wild-goose chase, Ms. Marlowe. Naturally, if she has changed her mind, we'll cover your travel expenses back to Philadelphia."

Tory took a quick, impulsive step toward him, and again he had that sense of familiarity. Then she stopped, shaking her head. "That's very generous of you. But I don't think I'll be needing it."

"We'll see." He managed to smile and offer his hand. Hers was cool, long-fingered, with calluses that declared her occupation.

"Yes. We'll see."

He caught a trace of resentment in her tone as she dropped his hand and took a step away from him. She probably thought he was being unfair. Maybe so.

But the bottom line was that he had trouble enough living a necessary lie as it was. If he had to contend with this memorial—

He wouldn't. Which meant that Tory Marlowe, with her determined air and her lonely eyes, had to go back where she belonged.

He hadn't recognized her. Once both men were gone, Tory sank down in the nearest pew, hands clutching the smooth seat on either side of her. Adam Caldwell hadn't recognized her.

Well, of course not, some rational part of her commented. It was fifteen years ago, after all.

She'd seen a brief flicker of vague query in Adam's face when he'd looked at her. He'd asked if they'd met. Her response had been out of her mouth before she'd considered, but it had been the right one. If he didn't remember, she wouldn't remind him of that night.

It was silly for her to look back, sillier yet that Adam Caldwell sometimes drifted through her dreams like a Prince Charming she'd encountered once and lost.

She stared across the curving rows of empty pews, then focused on the window in front of her. In an example of stained-glass artistry that made her catch her breath, Jesus walked on the water of a glass sea, holding out His hand to a sinking Peter. Her gaze lingered on the gray-and-green glass waves.

Real waves had been slapping against the dock the night she'd pushed open the yacht club door—a fifteen-year-old visitor on her way to a dance, knowing nothing of the Caldwells for whom the island was named. One of her stepfather's golfing buddies had thrown out a casual invitation, probably because he'd wanted to make a favorable impression on a wealthy visitor.

She'd stood for a moment, watching couples move on the polished floor and be reflected in the wide windows that overlooked the water. The strains of music flowed over her, and her hands clenched nervously. She was an outsider, as usual.

Then someone tapped her lightly on the shoulder. She turned, heart thumping, to find a tall stranger holding out his hand.

"Dance?"

She looked into sea-green eyes in a boyishly

handsome face. He smiled, and her heart turned over. Holding her breath, afraid to break the spell, she took his hand and followed him onto the dance floor. When his arms went around her, she felt as if she'd been waiting all her life for that moment.

They'd danced; they'd talked. They'd gone onto the veranda and watched the moonlight on the water. Adam had plucked a white rose from a table arrangement and tucked it in her hair, calling her Cinderella, because she was the one unknown at the dance. It had been a fairy tale come true.

Right up until the moment she'd called to ask permission to stay later. She'd heard her mother weeping, her stepfather shouting. She'd raced out, hoping to get to them in time to avoid the inevitable. She hadn't.

She leaned back in the pew, staring dry-eyed at the window. That night had cut her past in two as cleanly as any knife, but she didn't cry about it any longer.

Probably she remembered Adam because she'd met him that particular night. She didn't believe in love at first sight or fairy-tale endings—they were for dreamy adolescents. Life had taught her that love, any kind of love, inevitably came with strings attached.

Adam didn't remember her, and that was for the best. If he had, it could only have led to an awkward conversation.

Of course, we danced together one night, didn't we? Whatever happened to you?

No, she certainly didn't want to have that conversation with an Adam Caldwell who was considerably more imposing than the seventeen-year-old he'd been then. Imposing, that was definitely the word. She glanced at the spot where he'd stood, frowning at her as if he didn't believe a word she was saying.

The friendly voice she remembered had deepened to an authoritative baritone, and Adam's hair had darkened to chestnut brown. He seemed broader, stronger. Life had given more wariness to his open face, added a few lines around his ocean-colored eyes.

But he still had that comfortable-in-his-own-skin air that said he was sure of himself and his place in the world. He was a Caldwell of Caldwell Island. And he still had that honeyed drawl that could send shivers down a woman's spine.

Maybe she'd better concentrate on the reasons she'd come back after all these years. With this commission, her fledgling stained-glass business was on its way. She'd never have to work for someone else or let another take credit for what she'd done.

For an instant her former fiancé intruded into her thoughts, and she pushed him away. Her engagement to her boss had confirmed a lesson she should have learned a long time ago—love always came with strings attached. Jason Lockwood had shown her clearly that he'd only love her if she did what he wanted.

Forget Jason. Forget everything except the reason you've come here. This memorial was her chance, and she wouldn't let it slip away because Adam Caldwell was, for some inexplicable reason, opposed to it.

More important, being here would let her fulfill

the promise she'd made last year when her mother was dying. She'd finally erase the shadow Caldwell Island had cast over both their lives for too long. She wouldn't fail.

She focused on the image of Jesus' face in the window, the silence in the old church pressing on her. Fredrick Bauer, her teacher, had always said a person couldn't work constantly in sanctuaries without being aware of the presence of God. Somehow she'd never been able to move past an adversarial relationship with the One Fredrick had insisted loved her.

Still, she knew God's hand was at work in bringing her here. Why else would she have found Mrs. Telforth's ad when she'd needed a reason to be here? Why else would her talents have been just what Mrs. Telforth needed?

You brought me here. If this is Your will, You'll have to give me a hand with Adam Caldwell. I don't know why, but I know he'll stop me if he can.

Tory was ready to take on Adam Caldwell again. She looked over the items she'd spread across the round oak table in the Dolphin Inn's small sitting room that evening. Her credentials, photos of windows she'd designed, the four-page spread in *Glass Today* magazine featuring a project she'd worked on.

Miranda Caldwell, who'd been working at the desk when Tory checked in, had insisted she use the sitting room for this meeting with Adam. The Caldwells who owned the island's only inn turned out to be Adam's aunt and uncle, making Miranda his cousin. The sweet-faced woman had been only too happy to talk about Adam.

He and Lila were so happy—her death devastated him.

Was that the reason for Adam's reluctance about the memorial window? Did he find his memories too painful? She paced restlessly across the room, stopping at the window to brush aside lace curtains and stare at boats rocking against a dock. Across the inland waterway, lights glowed on the mainland.

Adam's a real sweetheart, Miranda had said. Everyone's friend, the person the whole community relies on. And the family peacemaker, as well.

Tory didn't have much experience with family peacemakers. Her family could have used one. But she didn't think Adam intended to use his peacemaking skills on her.

A firm step sounded in the hallway. He was coming. She moved quickly to the table.

"Ms. Marlowe." Adam paused, filling the doorway.

She hadn't been as aware of his height and breadth in the high-ceilinged sanctuary. Here, there was just too much of him.

Her hands clenched. Concentrate on the work.

"I have some materials I thought you might be interested in." She gestured toward the table.

He didn't move. Instead he glanced around, as if it had been a while since he'd been in this room. His gaze went from sofa to mantelpiece to bookshelves. His eyes looked darker in the twilight, like the ocean on a cloudy day. He'd changed from the white shirt and khakis he'd worn earlier to jeans and a gray pullover that fit snugly across broad shoulders.

"My cousin Miranda must like you, if she's letting you use the family parlor."

"I didn't realize." She followed his gaze, suddenly off balance. Now that she looked around, it was obvious this was the family's quarters. She'd been too caught up in herself to notice. Photos of babies, children riding bicycles, fishermen holding up their catch, weddings—a whole family's history was written on these walls. Everything about the space was slightly faded, slightly shabby and obviously well loved. "I didn't mean to impose."

"Miranda wouldn't have told you to use the parlor unless she wanted you to." He crossed to the table, moving so quickly that she took an automatic step back and bumped into its edge. He reached out to flip through the photos she'd spread out. "You've had a busy afternoon."

Her efforts to impress him suddenly seemed too obvious. "I thought you might like to see projects I've worked on."

"Trying to convince me of your abilities?" His smile took the sting out of the words.

"Not exactly." She took a breath, trying to find the best way to say this. It was too bad diplomacy wasn't her strong suit. "This is an awkward situation. Your mother-in-law hired me, but it's important that you be satisfied with my work. After all, you knew your wife better than anyone."

The strong, tanned hand that flipped through the

photos stopped abruptly. He pressed his fingers against the table until they whitened.

She'd made a mistake. She shouldn't have mentioned his wife, but how else could they discuss the memorial?

An apology lingered on her tongue, but that might make things worse. She forced herself to meet his gaze. "I'm sorry if—"

He cut her off with an abrupt, chopping gesture. "Don't." He seemed to force a smile. "It's irrelevant, in any event. My mother-in-law chose you from all the people who answered her ad. She must have been satisfied with your ability to do what she wants."

"You've talked with her, then." She couldn't imagine that conversation.

"Yes." His lips tightened. "She's very enthusiastic about this project."

She might as well say what they both knew. "But you're not."

He shrugged. "Let's just say you caught me by surprise today and leave it at that. All right?"

There was more to it, but she wasn't in any position to argue. Not if the battle she'd anticipated was unnecessary.

"All right. I hope I can come up with a design that pleases both of you."

His gaze lingered on her face, as if he assessed her. She steeled herself not to look away from that steady gaze.

He frowned. "My mother-in-law has asked me to take care of all the details about this project."

"I see." She kept her voice noncommittal. "So you'll be supervising my work."

"I would in any event, since I'm chair of the church's buildings and grounds committee."

This wasn't any ordinary church business they were talking about, but a memorial to his late wife. She had to show a little more tact.

"Perhaps you'd like to take with you some of my designs." She put the folder in his hand. "They might give you an idea of what would best memorialize your wife."

He dropped the folder, spilling photos onto the table. "No. Not now. Pastor Wells and I feel it best if you do the repair work first."

She stifled the argument that sprang to her lips. "Of course." She could only hope she sounded accommodating. "But I'll need to have some idea of what you want."

"Later." His tone didn't leave any room for argument. "We'll talk about it later."

The customer is always right, she reminded herself. Even when he's wrong.

"I'll start the analysis of the existing windows tomorrow then."

"I can be reached at the boatyard if you need me." He took a quick step away from the table, and she suspected only his innate courtesy kept him there at all.

"Mr. Caldwell, I..." What could she say? "I'm glad you've decided to go ahead with the project."

"It's my mother-in-law's project, not mine."

Again she had the sense of strong emotion, forced down behind his pleasant, polite facade. "We'll both have to try and make her happy with it." He held out his hand, and she put hers into it. "Welcome to Caldwell Cove, Ms. Marlowe."

His firm grasp had as much ability to flutter her pulse now as when she'd been fifteen. Her smile faltered.

Don't be stupid, she lectured herself. The man means nothing to you. He never did.

Now if she could just convince herself of that, she might get through her second encounter with Adam Caldwell a little better than she had the first.

Chapter Two

At least Adam hadn't shown up yet with another reason she should leave the island and forget this project, Tory thought as she studied the church's east window the next morning. She half expected to hear his step behind her, but nothing broke the stillness.

She'd had an early breakfast at the inn, a place that seemed overly full of Caldwell cousins, all curious about her project. Then she'd hurried through the village of Caldwell Cove to the church, eager to begin but half-afraid she'd find another Caldwell waiting for her.

Adam had given in, she reminded herself. He'd agreed to his mother-in-law's proposal. So why did his attitude still bother her?

His face formed in her mind—easy smile, strong jaw, eyes filled with integrity. He had a face anyone would trust.

But Tory had seen the flash of feeling in his eyes

every time the memorial to his late wife was mentioned. She hadn't identified the emotion yet, but she knew it was somehow out of place.

Lila Caldwell had died four years ago. One would expect to see sorrow on her husband's face at the mention of her name. The feeling that darkened Adam's eyes was something much stronger than sadness.

Maybe the pastor and Miranda had it right. Perhaps Adam had loved his beautiful wife so dearly he still couldn't bear to discuss her. If so, that made her job more difficult.

The next time she saw him, she had to confront the subject. It was all very well to say she could begin with the repair work, but she should be working on the design for the new window. She had to get him to talk to her about it.

She moved up the stepladder to touch the intricate detail of the twined floral border around the window of Jesus and the children. Someone with pride in his craftsmanship and love for his subject had done that, choosing flowers to echo the children's faces instead of a more traditional symbol. A hundred years from now, she hoped someone might touch a window she'd created and think the same.

I can do this, can't I? She looked at the pictured face, longing for the love she saw there welling inside her. *Please, Lord, let me create something worthy of this place.*

If she did… How hard it was not to let self-interest creep in, even when she was planning something to

God's glory. But she knew that success here could establish her business. For the first time since she was fifteen, she wouldn't have to scrape for every penny. She'd be able to pay her mother's final expenses and get a suitable stone to mark her grave. And she'd never have to rely on anyone else again.

The wooden outside door creaked. Tory's grip on the ladder tightened as she listened for Adam's confident tread. Instead, the patter of running feet broke the stillness. She turned.

The little girl scampering toward her had a tumble of light brown curls and a confident smile. A bright green cast on her wrist peeped out from the sleeve of a sunny yellow dress. She skidded to a stop perilously close to the ladder, and Tory jumped down.

"Hey, take it easy." She reached a steadying hand toward the child. "You don't want to add another cast to your collection, do you?"

The child smiled at her. Sunlight through stained glass crossed her face, and Tory saw that the cast matched her eyes. "I fell off the swing and broke my wrist," she said.

"You jumped off the swing." Adam's words quickly drew Tory's gaze to where he stood in the doorway. With the sun behind him, Tory couldn't see his expression, but she heard the smile in his voice. "And you're not going to do that again, are you, Jenny?"

This was his daughter, then, Tory's employer's granddaughter. Jenny needs this memorial to her mother. Mrs. Telforth's words echoed in her mind. She does.

The emphasis had seemed odd at the time. It still did.

Jenny sent her father an impish grin, then turned to Tory. "I got to be off school all morning to get my cast checked. Did you ever break anything?"

Adam reached the child and clasped her shoulders in a mock-ferocious grip. He was dressed a little more formally today than the night before, exchanging his khakis for dark trousers and a cream shirt. "Jenny, sugar, that's a personal question. You shouldn't ask Ms. Tory that when you don't even know her."

His daughter looked at him, brow wrinkling. "But, Daddy, that's how I'll *get* to know her."

Tory's lips twitched, as much at Adam's expression as the child's words. "I think she's got you there." She bent to hold out her hand to Adam's little girl. "Hi, I'm Tory. Yes, I broke my leg when I was nine. It wasn't much fun."

Jenny shook hands solemnly, her hand very small in Tory's. "But why not? Didn't you get a present for being a good girl when they put on the cast, and a chocolate cake for dessert, and an extra story?"

Tory's mind winced away from the memory of her stepfather berating her all the way to the emergency room for upsetting her mother while she lay in the back seat and bit her lip to keep from crying. "No, I'm afraid not. You're a lucky girl."

"She's a spoiled girl." But Adam didn't look as if the prospect bothered him very much. He smiled at his daughter with such love in his face that it hurt Tory's heart.

"I'm not spoiled, Daddy. Granny says I'm a caution." She frowned at the word, then looked at Tory. "Do you know what that means?"

"I suspect it means she loves you very much."

The frown disappeared. "Oh. That's okay, then."

"Jenny, love, let me get a word in edgewise, okay?"

Jenny nodded. "Okay, Daddy. I'll put water in the flowers. Don't worry, Granny showed me how." She scurried off.

"Sorry about that." Adam watched his daughter for a moment, then turned to Tory. "I really didn't come so Jenny could give you the third degree."

"She's delightful. How old is she?"

"Eight going on twenty, I think. I never know what she's going to come out with next."

His smile suggested he wanted it that way. Jenny didn't know how lucky she was. Tory realized she was seeing the Adam Miranda had described—the man everyone liked and relied on.

"That must keep life interesting." She wanted to prolong the moment. At least when they talked about his daughter they weren't at odds. They almost felt like friends.

"It does that." He glanced at the window. "Are you finding much damage?"

They were back to business, obviously. "Some of the windows are worse than others." She traced a crack in the molding around the image of Jesus and the children. "Settling has done this, but I can fix it."

Adam reached out to touch the crack. His hand brushed hers, sending a jolt of awareness through her. He was so close, the sanctuary so quiet, that she could hear his breath. He went still for an instant, so briefly she might have imagined it.

"Let me know if you need any equipment. We might have it at the boatyard."

She nodded. She had to stop letting the man affect her.

"Look, Daddy. I brought the water." Jenny put a plastic pitcher carefully on the floor, spilling only a few drops, then skipped over to them. "You know what? I know what you're doing, Ms. Tory."

"Ms. Tory's fixing the windows for us, sugar."

She shook her head, curls bouncing. "Not just that. Everybody knows that. But I know she's gonna make a window for Mommy."

Tory happened to be watching his hand. It clenched so tightly his knuckles went white.

"Who told you that?"

"I did."

Tory blinked. She hadn't heard the church door open again, maybe because she'd been concentrating too much on Adam. A small, white-haired woman marched erectly toward them, a basket filled with bronze and yellow mums on her arm. The striped dress and straw hat she wore might have been equally at home in the 1940s.

"I told Jenny about the memorial window, Adam." She peered at him through gold-rimmed glasses. "Do you have a problem with that?"

"Of course not, Gran." Tory thought the smile he gave his grandmother was a little forced, but he bent to kiss her cheek. "I was just surprised news traveled that fast."

"You ought to know how the island busybodies work by now." She turned to Tory, holding out her hand. "I'm Naomi Caldwell. You'd be the lady who's come to do the stained glass. Ms. Marlowe, is it?"

"Tory Marlowe. I'm pleased to meet you, Mrs. Caldwell."

The elderly woman must be in her seventies at least, if she was Adam's grandmother, but she had a firm grip and a bright, inquisitive gaze.

"I hear tell you're going to replace the Moses window."

"Does that bother you, Gran?" Adam sounded as if he hoped so.

His grandmother shook her head decidedly. "Never was up to the rest of the windows. If something's good, it'll improve with age."

Adam's expression softened. "Like you, for instance."

She swatted at him. "Don't you try to butter me up, young man."

She turned away, but Tory saw the glow of pleasure in her cheeks. For an instant she felt a wave of envy. If she'd had a grandmother like that, how different might her life have been?

"Jenny, child. Come help me with these flowers." Naomi Caldwell ushered Adam's daughter toward the pulpit, handing her the basket. "We'll put them on the dolphin shelf."

Tory tensed at the words. "The dolphin shelf?" She glanced at Adam, making it a question.

"That bracket behind the pulpit. A wooden carving of a dolphin once stood there. Gran likes to keep flowers in its place." Adam nodded toward the shelf where his grandmother was placing a vase.

I never meant for the dolphin to disappear. I didn't. Her mother's voice, broken with sobs, sounded in Tory's mind.

If she asked Adam about the dolphin, what would he say? Tory's mind worked busily. She had to find out more about the dolphin's disappearance if she were to fulfill her promise to her mother, but the last thing she needed was to stir up any additional conflict with Adam.

"What's this new window going to look like?" Mrs. Caldwell's question interrupted her thoughts before she could come up with an answer.

"That's really up to the family." Maybe she'd better stay focused on the window for the moment. "Usually I try to come up with some designs that reflect the person being honored, then let the family decide."

"How do you do that?" The woman paused, head tilted, her hands full of bronze mums. "Reflect somebody in a design, I mean." She seemed genuinely interested in the design, unlike everyone else Tory had met since she'd come to the island.

"Well, first I try to find out as much as I can about the person—her likes and dislikes, her personality, her background. Then—"

Carried away by the subject, she glanced at Adam.

His expression dried the words on her tongue. He stared at her, his eyes like pieces of jagged green glass.

"No." He ground out the word.

"What?" She blinked, not sure what he meant.

"I said no. You'll have to find another way of working this time."

Before she could respond he was calling the child, saying goodbye to his grandmother and walking out of the sanctuary.

The heavy door swung shut behind him, canceling the shaft of sunlight it had let in.

"I'm sorry about that." Adam's grandmother shook her head. "Reckon Adam's a bit sensitive about Lila."

"I see."

She'd made another misstep. She should have been more careful. But how on earth could she possibly find any common ground with Adam if he wouldn't even talk to her?

"I can't do this." Adam had arrived at his office at Caldwell Boatyard after dropping Jenny at school, his stomach still roiling. He'd found his brother, Matthew, waiting for him.

"Can't do what?" Matt perched on the edge of Adam's cluttered desk, toying with the bronze dolphin paperweight Lila had given Adam in happier times. Matt looked as if he had all the time in the world.

"Help that woman design a memorial window for

Lila, of all things." Adam slumped into the leather chair behind the desk. Matt was the only person in the world he'd speak to so freely, because Matt was the only one he'd told the whole story to. A good thing he had his brother, or he might resort to punching the paneling. "If my mother-in-law wanted a window, why didn't she put it in her own church instead of saddling me with it?"

"Maybe because St. Andrews was Lila's church," Matt offered helpfully.

Adam glared at him. "Don't you have work to do? Or doesn't running a weekly paper and being husband and stepfather for two whole months keep you busy enough?"

"Actually, I am working." Matt smiled, his face more relaxed than Adam had seen it in years. Marriage seemed to agree with him. "Sarah and I want to do a story for the *Gazette* about the church windows."

"Great. That's just what I need." Adam rotated his chair so he could stare at the sloop he was refitting for an off-island summer sailor. "Maybe you can satisfy Tory Marlowe's curiosity."

He glanced at his brother, wondering how much he wanted to say about Tory. Everything, probably.

Matt lifted an eyebrow. "Curiosity?"

"She wants to talk about Lila." His throat tightened. "She wants to get to know her so she can create a fitting memorial."

Matt whistled softly, obviously understanding all the things Adam didn't say out loud. "What are you doing about it?"

"Not telling her the truth, that's for sure." He rubbed his forehead as if he could rub the memories away. He and Lila had married too quickly, too young, and he faulted himself for that as much as Lila. He hadn't realized until later, carried away as he was, that Lila had had totally skewed ideas of what their married life would be like. She'd hated the island, and everything he'd done to try and make things better only seemed to backfire. Even their beautiful baby hadn't made Lila want a real family.

She'd craved excitement, and eventually she'd found that with a man she'd met on one of her frequent trips to visit friends who, she claimed, were living the life she should have had.

He frowned at Matt. "I certainly can't tell her the truth. I'm not telling her anything, if I can help it."

"Sounds like a mistake to me."

"Why?" He shot the word at his brother like a dare, but Matt looked unaffected.

"You'll just encourage her to go to other people for what she needs."

"No one knows the truth."

Matt shrugged. "You're probably right. But what if you're not? Better answer her questions yourself than have her asking around town."

Unfortunately, that sounded like good advice. He lifted an eyebrow at Matt.

"How did you get to know so much about women, little brother?"

Matt grinned. "My wife's training me." He sobered. "Seriously, Adam. Just get through it the best you can. Give the woman a few noncommittal details and say you trust her artistic sense to come up with the design. She'll get busy with the design and stop bothering you."

"I hope so." But somehow he didn't think Tory was the kind of person to do anything without doing it to perfection.

He got up slowly, letting the chair roll against shelves crammed with shipbuilding lore. "Guess I'd better go back to the church and make peace with her, if I can."

Adam slipped in the side door to the sanctuary and stopped in the shadows. Tory, on the ladder, didn't seem to hear him. He could take a minute to think what he'd say to her.

Unfortunately he wasn't thinking about that. Instead he was watching her, trying to figure out what it was about the woman that made it so hard to pull his gaze away.

She wasn't beautiful. That was his first impression. At least, she wasn't beautiful like Lila had been, all sleek perfection. But Tory had something, some quality that made a man look, then look again.

Those must be her working clothes—well-worn jeans, sneakers, a T-shirt topped by an oversize man's white shirt that served to emphasize her slender figure. She looked like what she was, he supposed. An artisan, a woman who worked with her hands and didn't have time or inclination for the expensive frills that had been so important to Lila.

Tory's hair, rich as dark chocolate, had been pulled back and tied at the nape of her neck with a red scarf. The hair seemed to have a mind of its own, as tendrils escaped to curl against her neck and around the pale oval of her face.

Oh, no. He'd been that route before, hadn't he? Intrigued by a woman, mistaking a lovely face for a lovely soul, thinking her promises meant loyalty that would last a lifetime. With Lila, that lifetime had only lasted five years before she'd lost interest in keeping her vows.

His hands clenched. He wouldn't do that again. He had his daughter, his family, his business to take care of. That was enough for any sensible man.

The smartest thing would be to avoid Ms. Tory Marlowe entirely, but he couldn't do that. Thanks to Mona's bright idea, he and Tory were tied inextricably together until this project was finished.

Something winced inside him. He had to talk to her, and it might as well be now.

He took a step forward, frowning. Tory had leaned over perilously far, long fingers outstretched to touch some flaw she must see in the window.

"Hold it."

She jerked around at the sound of his voice, the ladder wobbling. His breath caught as she put a steadying hand on the wall. He hurried to brace the ladder for her, annoyed with himself for startling her.

She frowned at him. "Are you trying to make me fall?"

"Sorry. I didn't mean to startle you. I'm trying to

keep you from falling." He gave the elderly wooden ladder a shake. "This thing isn't safe."

She jumped down, landing close enough for him to smell the fresh scent that clung to her. "I do this all the time, you know. Scrambling around on rickety ladders comes with the territory."

"You might do that elsewhere, sugar, but not in my church."

Her dark eyes met his, startled and a little wary. The red T-shirt she wore under the white shirt seemed to make them even darker. "What did you call me?"

"Sorry." But somehow he wasn't. "Afraid that slipped out. It's usually Jenny I'm lecturing about dangerous pastimes."

Her already firm jaw tightened. "I'm not eight, and I'm doing my job."

She reminded him of Gran, intent on doing what she wanted to no matter how well-intentioned her family's interference was. The comparison made him smile.

"Are you always this stubborn?"

"Always." Something that might have been amusement touched her face. "I'm not your responsibility."

"Well, you know, there's where you're wrong. In a way, you are my responsibility."

She lifted level brows. "How do you figure that?"

He patted the ladder, and it shook. "Everything about the building and grounds of St. Andrews is my responsibility. Including rickety ladders."

She grimaced. "I've been on worse than this one, believe me."

"You shouldn't be up on a ladder at all." An idea sprang into his mind, and it was such a perfect solution he didn't know why it hadn't occurred to him sooner.

Steel glinted in Tory's eyes. "If you think I'll give up the project because I have to climb a ladder, you have the wrong impression of me, Mr. Caldwell."

"Adam," he corrected. "I think my impression of you is fairly accurate, as a matter of fact. But I was referring to the ladder, not your personality, Ms. Marlowe."

A faint flush stained her cheeks, and she fingered the fine silver chain that circled her neck. "Maybe you'd better make that Tory. What about the ladder?"

"It's not safe. I'll have a crew come over from the boatyard to put up scaffolding so you can inspect the windows safely. That's what we should have done to begin with."

He was taking charge of the situation. That, too, was what he should have done from the word *go*, instead of letting himself get defensive.

"You don't need to—"

"As far as working on them is concerned—" he swept on "—we'll take the panels out completely. That way we won't have to worry about St. Andrews getting slapped with a lawsuit."

He thought her lips twitched. "Is that what you're worried about?"

"Definitely."

She nodded. "Well, in that case, since you're being so cooperative, I will need a workroom, preferably with good light, where things won't be disturbed." She glanced around. "Is there a space in the church that would do?"

"Nothing," he replied promptly. Ms. Tory didn't know it, but she was walking right into his plans. "We have just what you need at the house, though. It's a big room with plenty of light and a door you can lock. We'll move in tables or benches, whatever you need."

He could see the wariness in her face at the idea. "I don't think I should be imposing on you."

"It's not an imposition. It's my responsibility, remember?"

"Having me work at your home sounds well beyond the call of duty. I'll be in your way."

"You haven't seen our house if you think that. It's a great rambling barn."

"Even so…" She still looked reluctant.

"You don't want me to bring up the big guns, do you?"

"Big guns?"

"Pastor Wells and my grandmother. They'll agree this is the best solution. You'd find them a formidable pair in an argument."

The smile he hadn't seen before lit her face like sunlight sparkling on the sound. "Thanks, but I think you're formidable enough. All right. We'll try it your way."

"Good." He was irrationally pleased that she'd

given in without more of a fight. "I'll have a crew over here later this afternoon to set up scaffolding, so you can inspect the rest of the windows tomorrow. Don't climb any ladders in the meantime."

She lifted her brows at what undoubtedly sounded like an order. "Are you always this determined to look after people?"

"Always."

She turned to grasp the ladder. He helped her lower it to the floor. Her hair brushed his cheek lightly as they moved together, and he had to dismiss the idea of prolonging the moment.

Just get through it, Matt had said. Okay, that's what he'd do. He'd take control of this project instead of reacting to it. And the first step in that direction was to have Tory's workroom right under his eyes. Of course that meant that Tory herself would be, as well.

He could manage this. All right, he found her attractive. That didn't mean he'd act on that attraction, not even in his imagination.

Chapter Three

"Well, what do you think? Will this be a comfortable place to work?"

Adam looked at her for approval. Light poured into the large room he called the studio from its banks of windows. On one side Tory could see the salt marsh, beyond it the sparkle of open water. At the back, the windows overlooked a stretch of lawn, then garden and stables. Pale wooden molding surrounded the windows, and low shelves reached from the sills to the wide-planked floor. Anyone would say it was an ideal place to work.

"This should do very nicely." She couldn't say that his home had taken her by surprise. This wasn't a house—it was a mansion. And she didn't want to say that she'd lived like this once, before her mother's downward spiral into depression, alcoholism and poverty.

She took a breath. She'd been handling those recollections for a long time. She could handle this reminder. Besides, being here was a golden opportunity to find out what she needed to about the Caldwells. She just had to get Adam to open up.

"Why do you call it a studio?"

He shrugged. "We always have. My mother used it that way. Dad turned the space into a playroom for us kids after she died." He pointed to a small easel in the corner, the shelves behind it stacked with children's books, paints and crayons. "Jenny likes to paint in here when she's in the mood."

The room seemed uncomfortably full of his family with one notable exception. He hadn't mentioned his wife. "Was your mother an artist?"

"She painted, did needlework, that kind of thing." Sadness shadowed Adam's face for a moment. "I can remember her sitting in front of the windows with some project on her lap. She died when I was eight."

"I'm sorry." Tory had been five when her father died. She hesitated, torn. If she told Adam about it, that might create a bond that would encourage him to talk, but she didn't give away pieces of herself that easily.

She walked to the long table that held the first of the panels they'd removed from the church that morning. Everything she'd asked for was here, ready and waiting for her. She longed to dive into the work and forget everything else. If Adam would leave—

"What about you?" Adam leaned his hip against the table, crossing his arms, clearly not intending to go anywhere at the moment.

She looked at him blankly, not sure what he meant by the question.

"Family," he added. "You've met Jenny and my grandmother, heard about my mother. What about your family?"

It was the inevitable question Southerners put to each other at some point. She'd heard it before, phrased a little differently each time, maybe, but always asking the same thing. Who are your people? That was more important than what you did or where you went to school or even how much money you had. Who are your people?

"I'm alone." That wouldn't be enough. She had to say more or he'd wonder. "My father died when I was quite young, and my mother last year. I don't have any other relatives." At least, not any relatives that would like to claim me.

"I'm sorry." Adam's eyes darkened with quick sympathy. "That's rough. They were from this part of the world, weren't they?"

The question struck her like a blow. "What makes you think that?"

He smiled slowly. Devastatingly. "Sugar, you've been slipping back into a low-country accent since the day you arrived. You can't fool an old geechee like me."

Geechee. She hadn't heard that word since she'd left Savannah, but it resounded in her heart. Anyone born along this part of the coast was a geechee, said either affectionately or with derision, depending on the speaker. Apparently she couldn't leave her heritage behind, no matter how she tried.

Tory managed a stiff smile in return. "I'm from Savannah originally, but I've been up north so long I thought I passed for one of them."

"Not a chance." He pushed himself away from the table, the movement bringing him close enough to make her catch her breath, making her too aware of the solid strength of him. "Welcome back home, Tory Marlowe."

She wanted to deny it, to say she didn't have any intention of belonging in this part of the world again. But his low voice, threaded with amusement, seemed to have taken away her ability to speak. Or maybe it was his sheer masculine presence, only inches from her.

Adam wasn't the boy he'd been at seventeen. That boy had been charming enough to haunt her dreams for a good long time. Grown-up Adam was twice as hard to ignore. He was taller, broader, stronger. The lines around his eyes said he'd dealt with pain and come away cautious, but he had an air of assurance that compelled a response.

A response she didn't have any intention of making. She wouldn't let fragments of memory turn her to mush. She'd better get back to business, right now.

She cleared her throat, dismissing its tightness. "One thing about working in the studio concerns me."

He lifted an eyebrow. "Only one?"

She would not return that attractive smile. "Glass slivers fly around when I'm working. And the lead I use is dangerous to children."

He nodded, face sobering. "I've told Jenny she

must never come in unless you invite her. To be extra safe, I have a key to the studio for you." Adam held out a key ring. "And a house key, in case you ever need to come in when no one is here."

It was as if he handed her a key to the Caldwell family. Everything she was hiding from him flooded her mind. "I won't need that."

He took her hand and put the ring in her palm, his fingers warm against hers. "Just in case." *We trust you,* he seemed to be saying.

You can't. You can't trust me.

"Looks as if you're getting all set up in here." A tall, silver-haired man paused in the doorway, his interruption saving her from blurting something that would defeat her goals even before she started.

Adam took his hand away from hers, unhurried. "Tory, this is my father, Jefferson Caldwell."

"Mr. Caldwell." He came toward her, and she shook his hand while she tried to ignore the voice in her mind.

Jefferson and Clayton Caldwell. Her mother's words had been disjointed and hard to follow. *They were brothers, just a year apart.* Her mother's co-quettish giggle had sounded out of place in the hospital room. *They were both sweet on me, you know.*

Tory could easily imagine that. She'd seen pictures of her mother at fifteen, before alcohol and sorrow had weighed her down. Emily had been a golden girl, far more beautiful than Tory could ever dream of being.

If she mentioned Emily Brandeis's name to Jefferson Caldwell, would he remember that long-ago summer? Her mother had certainly remembered it. Rational or not, she'd traced everything that had gone wrong in her life to the events of that summer.

Jefferson surveyed the setup that had changed his studio into her workroom, then turned to her. "Welcome to Caldwell Island, Ms. Marlowe. I hope you're finding everything you need for this project."

Jefferson's beautifully tailored jacket and silky dress shirt gave him an urbane, sophisticated air that seemed out of tune with the down-home impression she received from his brother, Clayton, whose family ran the inn.

"Yes, thank you. I hope it won't inconvenience you to have my workshop here."

"Not at all." He waved his hand as if to encompass the entire estate. "Twin Oaks is a big enough place to accommodate all of us."

"It's a beautiful house." She said what he no doubt expected.

"Yes, it is that." Jefferson smiled with satisfaction at her words.

A cold house, she thought, but who was she to judge? No house could be more frigid than her grandmother's mansion in Savannah.

The hospital where she'd sat beside her mother's bed hadn't been far from her grandmother's Bull Street mansion, but there'd been no contact. Neither of them had expected it. Amanda Marlowe had long since cut all ties with her embarrassing daughter-in-law. Probably losing touch with her granddaughter had seemed a small price to pay.

Her mother had moved restlessly on the bed, shaking her head from side to side. *I didn't mean for him to take his family's heirloom. I didn't mean it, Tory. I didn't want anyone to get hurt.* Tears had overflowed. *You have to find the dolphin and put it back. Promise me.* Her thin hand had gripped Tory's painfully. *Promise me. You have to promise me.*

I didn't mean for him to take it. Her mother had felt responsible for the disappearance of the carved dolphin from the island church. For reasons Tory would never understand, that guilt had haunted her during her final illness. Someone had been hurt, but who?

I didn't mean for him to take it. One of the Caldwells, obviously, but which brother? Jefferson or Clayton?

She searched for something to say to drown out her mother's voice in her mind. "I'm staying at the Dolphin Inn, you know. So I've become acquainted with your brother and his family."

Jefferson's face froze as a chill seemed to permeate the air. "I suppose they're making you as comfortable as they can. When the new Dalton Hotel is finished, we'll be able to offer visitors something better than Clayton's little operation."

The spurt of malice in his words silenced her. Had he really just insulted his brother to a stranger?

Luckily Jefferson didn't seem to expect a response. "I'll let you get on with your work. Please ask if there's anything else you need." He turned and left the room before she could find a response.

When Jefferson's footsteps had faded down the hallway, she gave Adam a cautious look. "Did I say something I shouldn't?"

He shrugged, but she could almost feel the tension in his shoulders. "Nothing you could have known about, so don't worry. My father and his brother have been on the outs for a long time. The rest of us have learned to take it for granted."

The silence stretched between them, broken only by a bird's song drifting through the open window. How long a time, she wanted to ask. Since they were teenagers? Since Emily Brandeis came to the island and the dolphin vanished from the church?

But she couldn't ask because she wasn't ready for these people to know who she was yet. Until she knew how they'd respond, she couldn't risk it.

"I'm sorry for putting my foot in it," she said carefully. "Family feuds can be devastating." Nobody knew that better than she did.

"I'm used to it."

Was he? Or was that merely a convenient thing to believe?

One thing was certain. Her job on the island wasn't just another commission or a step toward the independence she longed for or even a chance to keep her promise.

Like it or not, her history and Adam's history were interwoven in ways he couldn't begin to imagine.

What was she thinking? Adam leaned against the heavy oak table, watching Tory's face. Light from the bank of windows made her hair glint like a raven's wing.

He forgot, sometimes, how odd the Caldwell family feud must seem to an outsider, especially since he had no intention of telling this particular outsider anything else. She didn't need to know that his father's drive for success at any cost had created a wedge between him and the rest of the family, who thought he'd left his honor behind along the way.

She also didn't need to learn that Adam's peacemaker role had grown increasingly difficult over the years. He'd been peacemaker between his father and brother, between his father and the rest of the family—maybe the truth was that the buffer always ended up battered by all sides.

"It must bother you." Her eyes went soft as brown velvet with sympathy.

That look of hers would be enough to melt his heart if he didn't watch out. "I suppose it does, sometimes." She was a stranger, he reminded himself. Furthermore, she was a stranger whose presence here threatened his secret.

Get through it, his brother had said. Matt charged at problems headlong, shoving barriers out of his way. Adam wasn't Matt.

He'd come up with another way of dealing with the trouble represented by Tory Marlowe. His gaze was drawn irresistibly to her. What was she thinking?

Apparently assuming he wasn't going to say anything else, she bent over the window panel, her fingers tracing the pieces as lovingly as he'd touch his daughter's hair. Her dark locks were escaping from the scarf that tied them back. They curled against her neck as if they had a mind of their own.

Deal with her, he reminded himself. Not gawk at her as if you've never seen a woman before.

He didn't want her wandering around Caldwell Cove, digging into a past that was best forgotten. So the best solution, until and unless he could find a way to derail this memorial window altogether, was to move Tory into Twin Oaks.

"I've been having second thoughts about this arrangement."

She looked up, startled. Apparently while he was watching the way her hair curled against her skin, she'd forgotten he was in the room. "What do you mean? I thought you wanted me to work here."

Would he ever get things right with this woman? He reminded himself that it didn't matter—all that did was her leaving Caldwell Cove.

"Of course I want you to work here." He almost put his hand on her shoulder, then decided that would be a bad idea. "In fact, I think you ought to stay here at the house while you're in Caldwell Cove."

A frown line appeared between her brows. "Is this because of the feud between your father and his brother?"

He should have realized she'd think that. "Absolutely not," he said. "I get along fine with Uncle Clayton and everyone else in the family."

"Well, you would." Her lips curved in the slightest of smiles. "Miranda says you're everyone's friend. That everyone in town relies on you."

"I wonder if she meant that as a compliment." That was him, all right. Good old reliable Adam.

"Of course she did. Anyone would."

"Sounds sort of stodgy, don't you think?"

"It sounds good." She looked startled, as if she hadn't intended to say that. "Anyway, if it's not that, then why should I move here from the inn? I'm comfortable there, and I can drive over every day."

Because I want to keep tabs on you. He could give her any reason but the real one.

"We have plenty of room for you."

"They have room for me where I am."

"Yes, but you won't have to pay for a room here."

She blinked at that, face suddenly shadowed. The look opened up a whole new train of thought. Was money a problem?

"I don't know what advance my mother-in-law has paid you," he said cautiously. Tory obviously had an independent streak a mile wide. "But it stands to reason we should pick up your expenses while you're here."

"That doesn't mean I should be your houseguest."

"It doesn't mean you shouldn't." He suspected he sounded the way he did when he tried to coax Jenny into eating her collard greens. "If you move into Twin Oaks, you'll be close to your work. That will certainly be more convenient."

Her lips pursed as she considered, and he found himself wondering how it would feel to kiss those

lips. He shook off the speculation. Not a good idea,
Caldwell.

"If you're worried about propriety, you needn't
be. As my father said, it's a big house. Miz Becky,
the housekeeper, lives in, and we often have business
colleagues of my father's staying."

"That isn't what I'm worried about." She looked
up, eyes dark and serious. "I might even find it
helpful—giving me a better sense of the kind of
person your late wife was."

It felt as if she'd punched him, and he could only
hope his expression didn't change. Naturally she'd
think living in Lila's house, talking with the people
who'd been closest to her, would help her know Lila.

*Nobody here will tell you the truth, Tory, because
nobody knows it but me.*

Well, Miz Becky might have guessed some of it.
The Gullah woman who'd taken care of the family
since his mother died often knew things no one had
told her. But Miz Becky would never betray his trust,
no matter what Tory asked. She understood loyalty.

He managed a smile. "What's holding you back?"

"Your father."

"Dad?" That startled him. "Why on earth?"

"I didn't get off to a good start with him. I can't
imagine that he'd want me living under his roof."

"Now that's where you're wrong. He's the one
who suggested it."

Get her out of Clayton's place, for pity's sake, his
father had said irritably. *That's the last impression we
want to make on the woman—that Caldwells are*

back-country hicks with no more ambition than to rent out a few rooms and go fishing.

"Is that true?"

"Cross my heart," he said lightly. "Dad would like you to stay here."

"And you would like me to leave the island and never come back." Her eyes met his.

She wouldn't be convinced by a polite evasion. His natural instinct was to say as little about Lila as possible. As long as he didn't talk about her, he could forget. At least, that's what he told himself.

Tory's gaze was unwavering. He felt a surge of annoyance. No one else in his life pushed him on this. They respected his grief and kept silent.

Or maybe that was the pattern of his relationships. He was the listener, the shoulder to cry on. He wasn't supposed to have tears of his own.

"All right." He blew out a frustrated breath. "I'm not crazy about this idea of Mona's."

"That's been clear all along. But I don't understand why. A memorial to your wife…"

"Exactly. A memorial. Something that brings back memories." He swung away from her, not wanting her to discover what kind of memories they were.

"I'm sorry." Her voice softened, filled with sympathy for the grief she imagined he was expressing. "I don't want to hurt you, and I'm sure that's the last thing on your mother-in-law's mind."

"Thank you." She shamed him with her quick sympathy. For an instant he imagined the relief he'd feel at telling her the truth.

Horrified, he rejected the thought. He couldn't tell anyone, least of all a stranger working for Lila's mother. Mona, like Jenny, would never know the truth from him. He turned toward her.

"Look, this will work out. Just give me time to get used to the idea. All right?"

Tory nodded. Her dark eyes shimmered with unshed tears, and he felt like a dog for accepting the sympathy he didn't deserve.

"All right. And if you're sure about this, I'll take you up on your offer of a room."

Relief swept through him. "I'm sure."

Tory squeezed his hand, the gesture probably intended to express sympathy. He felt the touch of her fingers right up his arm.

His eyes met hers. Her dark eyes widened, and her lips formed a silent *oh*. She felt what he did. And she didn't know what to do with it, either.

This is a mistake. The voice inside his head was deafening. You won't risk feeling anything for a woman again. And if you wanted to, it wouldn't be Tory. She's complicating your life enough just by being here.

Good advice. That was his specialty, giving good advice to other people. Why did he feel that following his own advice was going to be next to impossible where Tory Marlowe was concerned?

If she'd thought living at Twin Oaks would bring her any closer to her goals, Tory had been wrong. She hadn't found out a single thing about Lila or the disappearance of the dolphin in the three days she'd been there.

She leaned against the back porch post, sketch pad on her lap. The lawn, greening again after summer's heat, stretched under live oaks draped with Spanish moss that looked like swags of gray-green lace. Bronze and yellow chrysanthemums spilled over the flower beds along the walks.

Jenny lazed away a Saturday afternoon, pushing herself back and forth in a wooden plank swing suspended from a sturdy branch. Her sneakers scraped the ground with each arc, and her curls bounced.

Tory looked from the child to the sketch that had grown under her fingers. Jenny swung on the page, face lifted to the breeze she was creating.

"That's good, that is."

Tory glanced up. Miz Becky, the woman who ran Twin Oaks and apparently everyone in it, settled in the bentwood rocker.

"Thanks." Tory flexed her fingers and stretched, lifting damp hair off her neck. Even in fall, the air was sultry here. "I can't sit without doodling."

Miz Becky's smile warmed her elegant, austere face. With her hair covered by a colorful scarf wound into a turban, she looked like royalty. "Know what you mean about that." She lifted the strainer of fresh green beans. "I got to keep my hands busy, too."

It was the first time she'd been alone with Miz Becky, her first opportunity to ask her about Lila Caldwell if she wanted.

"How're those windows at the church coming along?" Miz Becky asked.

"Not bad." Tory wrapped her arms around her knees, wishing she could find a tactful way to broach the subject. "The repairs are moving along. Unfortunately, the new window isn't."

The woman popped the ends off the beans with a decisive snap. "Why's that?"

"I really need to find out more about Mrs. Caldwell's life if I'm going to come up with a design to honor her. So far—"

"So far Adam's not talking." Mix Becky tossed a handful of beans into a sweetgrass basket.

"That's about the size of it." She thought of the darkness that crossed Adam's open, friendly face whenever the topic was raised. "I don't want to intrude on his grief, but I'm afraid I'll have to."

"Grief?" Miz Becky seemed to consider the word. "I'm not so sure that's what's keeping him close-mouthed about her."

Tory glanced up, startled. That almost sounded as if…

Before she could respond, Jenny ran toward them.

"Miz Tory, could we go for a walk on the beach?" The child hopped onto the first step and balanced on one foot. "Please?" She gave Tory the smile that was so like her father's. "I can't go by myself."

She couldn't resist that smile. "If Miz Becky says it's okay."

"Get along." Miz Becky flapped a hand at them.

She held Tory's gaze for an instant. "Just might answer a few questions for you."

Was the woman suggesting that Jenny could be a source of information? Adam would definitely disapprove of that.

Jenny grasped Tory's hand and tugged her off the step. "Come on. I'll race you."

Grabbing the sketch pad, Tory followed. She wouldn't ask the child. If Jenny volunteered anything, that was different.

They crossed the lawn. Jenny skipped ahead of her down the path toward the beach. Palmettos and pines lined it, casting dense shadows littered with oversize pinecones and palmetto fans stripped by the wind.

They emerged from tree shadows into bright, clear light, the ocean stretching blue, then gray, then blending into the sky at the horizon. Tory tilted her head back, inhaling the tang of salt and fish and seaweed washed up by the tide and baking in the sun. It filled her with an irrational sense of well-being, nostalgic for a time she could barely remember.

Jenny trotted across beige sand and hopped onto a fallen log, bleached white by the sea. She patted the smooth space next to her. "Sit here, Miz Tory. I want to talk to you."

Smiling at the serious turn of phrase, Tory sat. The log was smooth, sun-warmed, a little sandy. "About what?"

"My mother," Jenny said promptly. "I want to talk about my mother."

"Listen, Jenny, I don't think your daddy would like that."

Jenny's frown resembled her father's, too. "The window you're making is for my mommy. I can tell you lots of things that will help." She pointed to the small purple and white flowers blooming close to the ground among the sea oats in the dunes. "See those?"

"Beach morning glories, aren't they?" She hadn't expected to, but she remembered the tiny, trumpet-shaped flowers from those early childhood holidays when her father was alive and the family summered on Tybee Island. Her fingers automatically picked up the pencil.

"Those were my mommy's favorite flowers." Jenny said it firmly, as if to refute argument.

"They're very pretty." Beach morning glories began to grow on the paper under her hand.

"I remember lots of things." A frown clouded her small face. "Like how Mommy smelled, and what she liked to eat. And—"

"What are you doing?"

Tory's heart jolted into overdrive. Adam stood at the end of the path, glaring. There wasn't any doubt that his sharp question was aimed at her.

Chapter Four

A rush of anger threatened to overwhelm Adam. Tory was talking to his daughter about Lila. He clenched his fists. He'd avoided her questions so she'd turned to his child. How dare she?

Jenny's stubborn pout reached through his anger to sound a warning note. Careful. Don't make too much of this in front of her.

"We're talking, Daddy." Jenny tilted her chin. "About Mommy."

"I see." He crossed the sand toward them, put one foot on the bleached log, tried for a casualness he didn't feel. "That's nice, sugar, but Miz Becky's looking for you. She has your snack ready."

"But, Daddy, I don't want to go yet. I'm not done telling Ms. Tory about Mommy."

He pushed down another wave of anger at Tory, took Jenny's hands and swung her off the log. "Maybe not, but Miz Becky's waiting for you. Get along, now."

Jenny pouted, then glanced at Tory. "I'll see you after a while. We'll talk some more." At his warning look, she darted toward the path.

The smile Tory had for his daughter slipped from her face once Jenny was gone. She planted her hands against the log on either side of her, seeming to brace herself for battle. "Is something wrong?"

"I think you know something's wrong." Anger drove him, so intense he almost didn't know where to begin. "First off, Jenny's not supposed to go to the beach without asking, even with a grown-up."

Tory lifted her level brows. "Miz Becky gave her permission. Surely you don't think I'd take Jenny anywhere otherwise."

"I don't know what you'd do." Being blunt might be the only thing that would work with the woman. "You were probing Jenny for information about her mother." He flung the words at her like missiles. He wanted her to admit she'd been wrong. More than that, he wanted her gone.

She didn't give any sign of being struck. "I wasn't probing. Jenny brought it up. She wanted to talk."

His heart seemed to wince at that, and for a moment there was no sound but the rustle of sea oats bowing in the wind. Then he found his voice. "That's ridiculous. Jenny was only four when her mother died. She barely recalls her."

"Maybe that's the point. She wants to remember." Passion flared in Tory's face, vivid and startling. "Don't you realize that?"

Her question flicked him on the raw edges of

emotion, and he wanted to hit back. "I realize it's none of your business."

Her mouth tightened, as if acknowledging his right to say it. "You can't stop the child from remembering." Her voice softened, and she put up one hand to brush windblown hair from her eyes. "Why would you want to?"

It was safer not to stare into brown eyes that seemed to know too much about loneliness. He looked beyond Tory, focusing on the inexorable movement of the waves rolling into shore. A line of sandpipers rushed importantly along the wet sand. He struggled, trying to find the right words.

"I don't. But I don't want her to be stuck in grieving. Jenny needs to look forward," he said. "There's nothing to be gained by dwelling on the past."

"Are you talking about Jenny or about yourself?" The question was like a blow to the stomach, but before he could react, she was shaking her head. "I'm sorry. I shouldn't have said that."

"No." He had to force the word through tight lips. "You shouldn't." She had no right.

"I just want…" She let the words trail off, then held her sketch pad out to him. "Look. This is what I'm trying to do."

He took the pad, frowning at a sketch of beach morning glories trailing along the page. "You're drawing flowers. What does that have to do with questioning my daughter?"

Tory's sigh was audible. "I wasn't questioning her. Coming down to the beach was Jenny's idea. She brought me here because she wanted to show me something—the morning glories. She says they were her mother's favorite flower."

"I don't think so." Lila hadn't even like the beach. She'd longed to return to her native Atlanta almost from the day they'd married. The beach was always too windy or too hot or too cold for her.

Tory stood, the movement bringing her close enough that her wiry hair, escaping from its band and caught by the breeze, brushed his arm. "Look." She touched the drawing. "Don't you see? I could work this into the design for the window."

"The window." Back to that again. Or maybe they'd never left it. "I told you we'd decided to do the repairs first."

She wasn't listening to him. Her gaze focused on the pad, and she pulled it from his hands. She sat back on the log as if she'd forgotten he was there, her pencil flying across the paper.

He watched, bemused. Tory had withdrawn into some other world where nothing could touch her. He doubted she heard the screech of the gulls or the rustle of the sea oats. Only the breeze drew a reaction from her as she pushed her hair back impatiently and smoothed the paper flat.

"There," she said at last, looking at him, eyes alight with passion. "See? This is what I can do with it." She thrust the sketch pad at him.

He took it, sitting down next to her on the log. How was he going to get through to the woman if she wouldn't even listen to what he said?

"This is the window's shape." Her finger traced the arched rectangle she'd drawn. "That's a given. The border can go all around."

She'd turned the morning glories into a twining design that made a frame for whatever would go into the center. He didn't want to be intrigued, and he fought the feeling.

"As I said, we want you to do the repairs first. We're not ready to plan the window yet."

Her gaze probed for what lay behind the words. "I know. You've told me, several times. But you don't understand. It takes time to create a new design and order the materials. I have to work on this now, while I'm doing the repairs, or I won't be ready when the time comes."

How did he argue with that? Did he tell her the truth—that she'd never come up with a design he'd approve of because such a thing could never exist?

He concentrated on the page, trying to ignore the wave of energy coming from Tory. But he couldn't do that, either.

This mattered to her. Maybe she brought this kind of passion to all her work. Did she have any of that passion left over for anything or anyone else?

Not a question he had the right to wonder about, he told himself quickly.

"All right." He gave in because he didn't know what else to do, and it didn't really matter, anyway. "This looks fine, although I think Lila preferred hothouse orchids." Now, how had that slipped out? He didn't intend to tell her anything.

Dismay filled Tory's eyes. "But Jenny said her mother loved the morning glories."

He shook his head. "Maybe Jenny's confused. Or it's just her imagination."

She reached out as if to take the pad. "I can change the design."

"No." His grip tightened. "Leave it. It's more important that Jenny feel a part of this project."

Tory's rare smile lit her face, making his breath catch. "That's true. I'm glad you see it that way."

See it that way? What on earth was wrong with him? He didn't want this window. The last thing he should do was encourage Tory. But he had the uneasy feeling her smile could make him forget his decision, if he let it.

What was Adam thinking?

For a few minutes Tory had been totally absorbed in the idea that was taking shape under her fingers. She'd forgotten Adam was next to her.

Now he seemed uncomfortably close, and even through the distraction caused by his physical presence, she knew he was hiding something. Some alien emotion roiled beneath his calm facade. She didn't know what it was, but it had to do with his wife. Lila.

Adam flipped through the sketch pad as if to distance himself from any discussion of the window. She watched his hands move over her drawings and wondered how he'd react if he ever saw the sketch in her old pad from that long-ago summer—the one she'd drawn of him after that night at the yacht club. She'd almost thrown it away a dozen times, but something always stopped her.

He wouldn't see it, she assured herself. He'd obviously forgotten that night, and she'd never remind him. Their relationship was complicated enough without that.

Adam stopped, turned back a page to something he must have missed the first time through.

"When did you do this?" His voice had changed as he tilted the sketch of Jenny toward her. Maybe the current battle was over, if not the war.

"This morning. She looked as if she were trying to go into orbit on that swing."

His lips twitched. "She does do that, doesn't she? She scares me half to death sometimes." He quirked an eyebrow at her, green eyes smiling, and her heart turned over. "May I have this?"

Apparently they'd declared a truce for the moment. "Of course, if you really want it." She felt the heat come up in her cheeks. "It's not that good. I'm not an artist, just a craftsman."

His tanned fingers touched the drawing lightly. "Looks pretty professional to me. Anyway, you caught that sense of adventure in her face. That's wonderful, even when it terrifies me."

"You wouldn't want her to be any different." She thought about her mother and stepfather, who'd always wanted her to be different. About her grandmother and Jason, who'd have loved her if she'd been willing to change.

"Of course not." He looked surprised, as if the thought had never occurred to him. "Jenny is herself. I wouldn't change her for the world." He smiled. "But I thank God every day that I have plenty of people to help me with her—family, Miz Becky. I don't know what I'd do without them."

"Caldwell Island is filled with Caldwells, isn't it?" And Adam Caldwell belonged here, in a way she'd never belonged anywhere.

"We are kind of thick on the ground," he agreed. He seemed to relax now that they were away from the subject of the window. "Especially since my brother and my cousin Chloe came home. We never thought those two wanderers would settle down. At least, nobody thought it but Gran."

She pictured the erect elderly woman with her obvious pride in her family. "I take it the Caldwell clan was among the first settlers on the island."

"Oh, yes." He stretched, his arm brushing hers and sending a trickle of warmth along her skin. He nodded toward the mainland, shimmering green against the blue water to the west. "The island doesn't seem far from the mainland now, but before the bridge was built, this was wild country. The first Caldwells date back to the eighteenth century, and they lived pretty isolated for a long time."

"Sounds like there's a story in that." She put a question in her voice. Her mother had said that the carved dolphin was somehow related to the Caldwell family's history. Maybe if Adam talked about it…

He shrugged. "Lots of stories, but I'm not the

best one to tell them. Get Gran going on it sometime. She's a real sea island storyteller. Nobody knows the legends like she does."

"I'll bet you know them. After all, you grew up here, while I—"

She stopped that thought before it could spill out, appalled at her carelessness. She'd almost said she'd only been here twice.

"While you?" He smiled, watching her, and her heart seemed to lurch. There was something about his interested gaze that made a person want to confide in Adam. He focused on her with such flattering attention that it drew the words out. Maybe that was why, as Miranda had said, everyone depended on him.

She managed a smile in return. "While I'm a newcomer," she said firmly. "A visitor, isn't that what you'd say? I notice no one says tourist."

"We think visitor sounds nicer. Anyway, we've never had what you'd call hordes of tourists on the island. Just as well, as far as most of us are concerned. Mostly we get the summer residents who own or rent those houses down by the yacht club."

The last place she wanted to discuss was the yacht club. It brought back too many memories—dancing in the moonlight, the scent of white roses, the feel of Adam's strong arm around her waist.

"I understand a new hotel is going up," she said hurriedly.

He nodded, but he seemed distracted, too, as if chasing down a vagrant thought. Because he was recalling a moonlit night that was better forgotten?

"It'll mean changes," he said. "Good or bad, I guess we'll see. More nightlife, probably. Lila would have liked that." He stopped abruptly, as if surprised at his words.

"She enjoyed going out?" Tory was so glad to be off the dangerous topic of the yacht club that she asked the question without thinking.

He snapped the sketch pad closed, and his face closed, too. "Yes." He clipped off the word. "But I don't see how you can incorporate that into your design."

"I wasn't…" *I wasn't trying to get you to talk about her. I just wanted to change the subject.*

Obviously she couldn't say that. Before she could think of something noncommittal, he stood.

"I'd best get back."

He didn't give her a chance to say she'd walk to the house with him. He spun away from her and strode up the path as if something were chasing him.

Memories, she thought. *Memories are chasing you, Adam, and you don't want to let them catch up. Is it because you grieve for your wife so deeply? Or do you have some other reason?*

Well, she was certainly the last person he'd confide in. She tilted her head, letting the breeze tangle her hair. She'd have done a better job of handling that conversation if she hadn't been so worried about her own secrets.

She frowned at the sketch of the beach morning glories. She could create something good from that, if Adam would let her. If.

Where is this going, Lord?
There didn't seem to be an answer.

Tory hadn't, in her wildest imaginings of being on Caldwell Island, expected to be standing next to Adam in the front pew on Sunday morning, sharing a hymnbook as the pastor announced the last hymn. Adam flipped to the song, his hand brown against the white page, and she stilled the by-now-familiar tingle at his nearness.

She'd been startled at his automatic assumption they'd go to church together. When she'd met him at the bottom of the stairs and waited with him for Jenny and Miz Becky, it had been almost as if they were family.

No, not that. She hurried away from that notion and focused instead on the window of Jesus and the children. She and Adam had worked late with his crew the evening before, wanting to put the repaired panels back before this morning.

Last night, she'd felt as if they were on the same team. But they weren't. She had to remember that. She had an undeclared purpose here, and she had the strong feeling that Adam was hiding something, too.

Sunlight slanted through the old glass, casting rays of ruby and amethyst across the faces of the worshipers. She found herself drawn to the image of Jesus. The light behind the window made the face glow with an inner peace.

You brought me here, she prayed silently. *Show me what to do.*

She had to succeed. The thought sent a shiver through her. Because if she didn't, she'd spend her life thinking she'd failed her mother one last time. She couldn't be in this sanctuary without seeing that shelf and knowing what she had to do.

Show me, she said again. *Please.*

"Eternal Father, strong to save, whose arm has bound the restless wave…" She sang the words with the congregation, sensing the emotion that rippled through the sanctuary. These people lived lives surrounded by the ocean. They knew what it was to beg God's mercy for those in peril on the sea.

Her gaze moved to the dolphin shelf behind the pulpit, filled with the late chrysanthemums Adam's grandmother had put there. Was that why the dolphin had been so important to them—because of its connection with the ocean?

She had to know more. And Adam was the one who could tell her, if he would. If she had the courage to bring it up.

She slanted a sideways glance at him. As if feeling her gaze, he looked at her, eyes crinkling in a smile, and her hand tightened on the hymnal.

The amen sounded, and Pastor Wells lifted his hands. "Before we leave today, I'd like to draw your attention to the window of Jesus and the children. The repair work has already been finished on it, and I'm sure you'll want to say a word to the stained-glass artist who will be with us working on the windows, Tory Marlowe."

He nodded toward her, smiling, and she didn't

know where to look. She hadn't expected that. She was here to do a job, not become a part of this community.

Pastor Wells launched into his benediction, and the moment passed. But she soon found that wasn't all there was to it. Once the organist began to play the postlude, everyone in the sanctuary seemed intent on speaking to her.

By the time she'd shaken hands a dozen times, nodded and smiled and said whatever she could about the windows, Adam had slipped away.

Fine, she told herself. She hadn't expected him to wait for her. Not when she was just someone he had to put up with for the duration. She could easily walk to the house.

"You did a fine job with that." Adam's grandmother paused next to her, navy bag clasped in white-gloved hands.

"Thank you." She joined Mrs. Caldwell in looking at the window. "The cleaning really brought out those beautiful colors."

"Always has been one of my favorites." The elderly woman reached up to settle her navy straw hat more firmly. "Which one do you reckon to do next?"

Tory nodded toward the image of Jesus feeding the five thousand. "That one. But I'm not sure I'll have it finished by next Sunday." She frowned, worrying. "If they can get it to me quickly…"

Mrs. Caldwell patted her hand. "You talk to Adam about it. He'll work it out." She moved away.

Talk to Adam. Yes, she'd do that.

And she had to talk to Adam about the dolphin. She traced a glass flower, wondering. Maybe the time had come to level with him about who she was. That might be the only way she'd gain his cooperation. Without that, she stood little chance of finding out what had happened to the dolphin. Still, she couldn't help cringing at the thought of telling him.

"Are you planning your strategy?"

She jumped at the baritone voice so close behind her, her heartbeat accelerating. Adam hadn't gone, after all. Was he reading her mind?

Chapter Five

Tory tried to catch the breath his words had stolen. Adam was in the nearest pew, apparently gathering discarded bulletins. It took a moment to convince herself he wasn't reading her mind. With a wave of relief, she realized he was talking about the window, not her search for the dolphin.

"Something like that. I'd like to get started on the next one." She paused. "I thought you'd already left."

He lifted an eyebrow. "My daddy always told me if you bring a lady somewhere, you take her home again."

"Going to church isn't—" *A date.* She didn't want to say that. "I could easily walk back to the house. It's not far and it's a beautiful day."

Adam nodded, scooping the bulletins into a neat stack. "October weather is perfect on the island. I never have figured out why the visitors don't seem to know that." He grinned. "Not that I'm complaining about it, you understand."

"I can see why you want the place to yourself, if that's what you mean." She glanced around. It was disconcerting to be suddenly alone with him when a few moments earlier the church had been full. "Is Jenny outside?"

"Miz Becky took her on home. She wanted to get started on lunch. The buildings and grounds chair always gets stuck with last-minute chores after the service."

That sounded like an invitation. "Can I help?"

"Sure." He looked around the empty sanctuary as if picking out a job for her. "You might take those flowers from the dolphin shelf. We'll drop them off for one of the shut-ins on our way home."

Tory moved slowly past the pulpit, her gaze on the bracket where the carved wooden dolphin had once stood. She inhaled the spicy aroma of the chrysanthemums, then ran her hand along the shelf. Her fingertips touched the border of seashells, incised by a careful hand generations ago. Someone had put a great deal of love into the shelf to hold the dolphin.

Her throat tightened. The disappearance of the dolphin had messed up several lives. Returning it couldn't erase the damage, but it was the last thing she'd ever do for her mother. Maybe that would make up for all the times she'd failed—failed to understand, failed to keep her mother from drinking again, failed to somehow save her from herself.

"Tell me about the dolphin." She tried to keep her voice casual, not wanting Adam to guess it meant anything at all to her.

"My gran would tell it better." He shoved a hymnal into the pew rack.

But she wanted to hear it from him. "I'm sure you know it by heart."

"Nobody knows how much truth there is to the story," he warned.

"I'll take it as legend." She smiled, trying to disguise how keyed up she was.

He shrugged, as if giving in to her whim, and leaned his hip against the pew back. "It's said the first Caldwell on the island was a shipwrecked sailor. Supposedly he was close to drowning when an island girl and her dolphins rescued him. 'He took one look and knew he'd love her forever,' that's what Gran always says." Adam's voice deepened on the words. "He carved the dolphin as a symbol of their love. Tradition says those who marry under the dolphin's gaze are especially blessed."

She thought he was moved more than he wanted to admit by the story. Her throat had certainly tightened. *He took one look and knew he'd love her forever.* What woman didn't long for that, even though she knew it was a fantasy? The silent sanctuary seemed to murmur of the hundreds of vows that had been uttered there.

"What happened to the dolphin?" she asked when she could speak again.

Adam walked toward her, mounting the single step to the chancel. His sleeve brushed her arm as he touched the shelf, and she resisted the urge to step backward. He traced the carving as she had done.

"The carving stood here for generations. My dad was around when it disappeared. He was in his teens then."

I know. "Did they ever find out who took it?"

He was close enough that she could see the change in his eyes at the question. Some strong emotion showed for a moment and was quickly suppressed.

"No." His voice was colorless.

He knew more, she was sure of it. "They must have had some idea."

Adam's hand tightened on the shelf until the knuckles whitened. "There were stories. They say some rich girl—a summer visitor—was involved."

Grief had a stranglehold on her throat, but she forced the words out. "Why would she do that?"

"Who knows? A whim, maybe." He let go of the shelf suddenly, as if he didn't want to touch it while he spoke of it. "Something to do on a lazy summer day. It didn't mean anything to her. Obviously she didn't care what it meant to us."

Contempt filled Adam's voice, and her heart contracted. She'd wanted the dolphin story, and he'd given it to her. But she'd gotten something she hadn't bargained for.

He blamed her mother. She struggled with that unpalatable truth. He apparently didn't know who the rich girl was, but he held her responsible. She should have realized that would be the case. Probably the whole Caldwell clan felt the same way about her mother.

The brief thought she'd had of telling Adam the truth about herself suddenly seemed very foolish. She couldn't. He resented her presence because of the memorial window. If he knew who she was, he wouldn't tolerate her for another instant.

That knowledge hurt more than it had any right to.

He was spending too much time watching Tory, Adam decided. Maybe it was Miz Becky's fault for seating her directly across from him at the dinner table that Sunday evening. How could he help noticing the way the candlelight reflected in Tory's dark eyes and the sheen of her hair against the white dress she wore?

All right, he was drawn to her. He'd already admitted that to himself. And it wasn't just the way she looked. He'd seen the passion in her eyes when she talked about her work and he'd glimpsed her caring heart in the drawing she'd done of Jenny.

Unfortunately the bottom line was that he hated her reason for being here. He'd stop her if he could.

With a spurt of determination, he focused on his father, seated as always at the head of the oval mahogany table. Dad had been talking for the last ten minutes about his latest business trip. A trip that had, as always, been extended so he didn't get back in time for the Sunday service.

Had Tory wondered about his father's absence from worship this morning? Probably not. She hadn't been around long enough to know it was habitual.

He fingered the heavy silver knife, letting it clink against the china plate. Tory also didn't know he hadn't told her the whole truth about the dolphin's disappearance. He hadn't told her the most significant part—that his father had taken it.

Miz Becky's pecan pie turned tasteless in his mouth. Matt had been the one to learn about Jefferson's involvement. According to Matt, Dad claimed he'd borrowed the dolphin to impress a girl. The party they'd been attending was raided, and when all the confusion cleared, he'd never seen either the girl or the dolphin again.

Too many questions remained unanswered about that night—questions Adam had never asked. He'd accepted what his brother told him. He hadn't ever so much as brought it up with his father. Maybe it was time he did.

Adam slanted a glance at his father. Jefferson was being charming to Tory at the moment. The courtly Southern gentleman was a role he liked to play, as if it canceled out the ambitious businessman he really was.

Jefferson picked up his coffee cup. "If you'll excuse me, there are some contracts in the study I must put away."

"I'll join you." Adam's chair scraped as he shoved it back. For a moment he wondered what he was doing. He was the family peacemaker, wasn't he? He was about to stir up trouble. "I need to discuss something with you."

His father lifted an eyebrow slightly, then nodded.

With a murmured excuse to Tory, Adam followed him next door to the study.

The book-lined room was dim and still. His father crossed to the desk where a single brass lamp cast a circle of light. He started shuffling together the papers that littered the surface.

He glanced at Adam. "What is it, son? Something about the boatyard?"

"No." As always, his father's first concern was business. "I've come about the dolphin."

Jefferson's manicured hands froze on the papers, and his face looked old. "You know all there is to know from your brother. I don't see any benefit to discussing it again."

"You talked to Matt about it." At some level, that rankled. Why had Matt—the rebel, the wanderer—been the one his father confided in? Why not him, the good son who'd always been there for his father?

"Only because he didn't give me much choice." His father frowned.

Adam didn't move. After a long moment Jefferson slumped into the leather chair behind the cherry desk. A breeze from the French doors ruffled the papers on the desk and brought the scent of the salt marsh into the room.

"All right," his father said finally. "What are you wondering?"

He'd been holding his breath. He let it out slowly. "I want to know why. Just why. Why did you take the dolphin?"

His father leaned back, rubbing his temples as if

to massage away memories. "I was sixteen. It was a girl. Your brother must have told you that."

"Not just any girl." Why, Dad? Why would you betray everything your family held dear?

"No." The lines in his father's face deepened. "Not any girl. Emily Brandeis."

"A summer visitor."

Jefferson shook his head with sudden impatience. "I can't make you understand what it was like then."

"Try." It might be the first time in his adult life he'd pushed his father.

Jefferson stared at him, his face tightening. "They looked down on us—the yacht club people with their fancy boats and fine houses. They thought we were dirt beneath their feet."

Bitterness etched his father's voice. Was that where his drive to succeed at any cost had come from? "Including the girl?"

"Emily was different." His voice softened. "She was—a golden girl. Different from anyone I'd ever known. It was like having a princess step out of a fairy tale. And she wanted to be with us, Clayton and me."

So Uncle Clayton was part of this story. "The three of you were friends."

"More than that. Puppy love, I suppose it was, but I've never felt anything like it before or since. I'd have done whatever Emily wanted. And when she teased us about getting the dolphin for her—"

He stopped, his lips twisting. "Clayton wouldn't. Mr. Goody Two-shoes would never do anything like that. I wanted to show her I cared for her more that he did. I'd have put it back the next day, and no one the wiser."

Oh, Dad. "You didn't."

"No. We were having a clambake out on Angel Isle. The island kids and some of the summer visitors. We weren't supposed to hang out together, but we did. I showed Emily the dolphin." He stopped.

"And then?" Adam prodded.

His father made a chopping motion as if to cut away the rest of the story. "We quarreled. I left. Later a bunch of yacht club parents raided the party. Emily's father must have been upset that she was hanging out with geechees like us. Her family left the next day."

"That's it?" He sensed things unsaid, things his father would probably never say.

Jefferson's mouth formed a tight line. "Believe it or not, I never saw her or the dolphin again."

Tory took a soundless step away from the open French doors, then another. She backed up until she hit the railing that separated the veranda from the salt marsh. Raising her hand to her cheek, she discovered it was wet with tears.

She hadn't meant to eavesdrop. Their voices had come floating out the open door into the darkness on the veranda. She'd heard her mother's name and she hadn't been able to move away.

Tory wiped tears away with the back of her hand. She couldn't change the past. She had to decide.

What was she going to do with the knowledge she'd been hiding?

A footstep sounded, and Adam came through the French doors. The room behind him, lit only by the small desk lamp, was empty. His father must have left while she'd stood there crying. She pressed her hands against the railing, trying to regain control.

Adam took another step, then stopped abruptly. "Tory. I didn't realize you were out here. You look like a ghost in that white dress."

"I'm sorry if I startled you. I came out for a breath of air." To her dismay, her voice was thick with tears.

Adam was at her side in a moment. "What is it? What's wrong?"

She'd asked herself what she should do with her knowledge, but there was really only one possible answer. She had to tell him. But how?

Maybe the only way was to blurt it out.

"I heard you and your father talking."

He stiffened as if she'd struck him. "Eavesdropping, Tory?"

"I didn't mean—" She could hardly claim that. "I'm sorry. I didn't intend to listen."

"Then why did you? You could have walked away." Contempt edged his voice.

She took a breath. She should have known from the beginning that this foolish plan of hers would never work—that she would fail her mother in this, too. "Because you were talking about my mother."

Adam's silence was probably shock.

"Your mother was Emily Brandeis."

"Yes."

The evening was so still she heard the intake of his breath, caught the faint splash of something moving out in the marsh. Then the breeze picked up again, fanning her hot cheeks and rustling the spartina grass.

"I don't understand." At least there wasn't anger in his voice, not yet. He took a step closer, his hand on the rail, his gaze intent on her face in the dim light. "Did you know the connection when you came here?"

"I knew."

"Why didn't you tell me?" Anger spurted through his words, scalding her.

"I'm telling you now."

"You should have told me the day we met."

Of course he'd think that. "It was all so complicated. What was I supposed to do that first day in the church? Announce that I was here to repair the windows and, by the way, my mother was involved in the disappearance of the dolphin?"

"That would have been better than hiding it from all of us."

"I didn't know enough, don't you understand that?" She wanted to grasp him and make him believe her, but she couldn't. "I had to try and find out where you stood before I could tell you anything."

He shook his head. "This is crazy." Something sharpened in his tone. "Did you talk my mother-in-law into this commission just so you could come here?"

"Of course not." She should have realized he'd

assume the worst. "She'd already decided on the window. I had nothing to do with that. But when I saw her ad for someone to work at the Caldwell Cove church, I felt as if it was meant."

"Meant." He repeated the word heavily. "Why? What possible reason could you have for coming to the island? Don't tell me you've finally decided to give the dolphin back."

Her nails bit into her palms. He'd never believe her, and he'd probably use this as an excuse to stop work on the windows. She couldn't blame him.

"You have to understand." She said the words slowly, hoping against hope he'd hear the truth in them. "I can't give the dolphin back. I don't have it. I never did. My mother didn't take it off the island."

There was silence again, but this time sheer disbelief emanated from him. It hurt more than she'd have thought possible.

"How can I believe that?" Adam flung out his hand toward the study door. "You were listening. You heard what my father said."

"She didn't take it away." She searched for the words that would convince him. "All I can tell you is what I believe to be the truth. When my mother was dying, she seemed to become fixated on that time. It was as if she thought all the problems in her life stemmed from the events of that summer." She couldn't stop the tremor in her voice. "Maybe knowing you're dying does that to a person."

Some of the anger seemed to go out of him at her pain. "I'd forgotten she died so recently." He touched her wrist, his sympathy light as a gull's wing. "I'm sorry."

Her tears tried to surface again, and she fought them back.

"I hadn't known about the dolphin before, but it seemed to haunt her. She kept saying, 'I never meant for him to take it.' I didn't know then who she meant."

"I guess we know now." His voice was dry, but his father's actions had to have cut him deeply. They were both trapped by their parents' behavior.

Her hands clenched. "It doesn't seem to lead anywhere. Your father says he gave her the dolphin. But she didn't take it away."

The clouds cleared from the moon, showing her his face, intent and frowning. To her relief, his antagonism faded as he focused on the problem.

"Didn't she tell you what happened to it?"

She shook her head slowly. It all sounded so improbable, but she knew it was true. "She kept drifting in and out of consciousness those last days. I had to piece it together. One thing was clear—she blamed herself for what happened, but she didn't take the dolphin away."

"How do you know she was telling the truth?" He sounded as frustrated as she felt. "You said yourself she was confused, incoherent."

"She wasn't lying." Tory knew that, bone deep.

"All right, not lying." He frowned, obviously trying to come up with something to explain. "She was just a kid at the time. Maybe she took it, pawned it, even threw it away. Then she was ashamed and didn't want to admit it. Did you look through her papers for any clue?"

"Of course I did. There was nothing." She reached out to grasp his sleeve, intent on making him believe her. She could feel the warmth of his skin through the fine cotton, and she had to take a breath before she could go on. "I know she didn't take the dolphin. I know because of what she asked me to do."

"What do you mean?" His hand closed hard over hers. "What did she ask you to do?"

He was listening. He wasn't dismissing her out of hand.

"That was my mother's dying wish." She forced away the tears she was determined not to shed in front of him. "She begged me to find the dolphin and put it back in the church where it belongs."

Chapter Six

It was true, then. Adam wanted to reject Tory's words, but he couldn't. Her determined, passionate face convinced him he couldn't deny them, no matter how much he wanted to.

His gaze traced her features, turned toward him in the moonlight. His father had described Emily as a golden girl, but Emily's daughter was the opposite. The dim light silvered her skin, as if she were a pen-and-ink sketch of a woman.

He had to say something. "It's over then. The dolphin is lost for good." His sense of relief surprised him. He'd have said they all wanted it back, but maybe he didn't feel that way. As far as he was concerned, raking up the past only seemed to bring pain. "Now we can stop wondering what happened."

"It's not over." The passion in her voice caught him off guard. "It can't be over."

"Tory—" He shrugged, feeling helpless in the

face of her reaction. "What do you expect to do? The dolphin's been gone for forty-some years. There's no way we can find it now."

You. He should have said *you.* He shouldn't align himself with her.

"There has to be." Tory's lips tightened. "Don't you understand? This was the last thing my mother ever asked of me. I made a promise."

"An impossible promise. It's not your fault if you can't keep it."

"You wouldn't say that if you were the one who'd made it."

"I'd face reality." He couldn't help the exasperation that filled his voice.

"No, you wouldn't." She shook her head, her cloud of black hair flying rebelliously. "I didn't have to know you ten minutes to see what mattered to you. You wouldn't give up if you'd made a promise. Loyalty is too important to you for that."

Loyalty. The word lodged in his heart, and he couldn't speak. How could she know that about him? The thought of Lila flickered through his mind, and he pushed it away. Protecting the memory of the wife who'd betrayed him didn't have anything to do with loyalty. He was doing it for his daughter.

"What I would or wouldn't do isn't the question." He had to fight to maintain a detached tone. "Why did it mean so much to your mother? You'd think she'd have forgotten the dolphin."

Matt had said that Emily Brandeis had died in poverty. What had happened to his father's golden girl?

"She never forgot. That night—I don't know, it was as if something broke in her that night." Tory's eyes clouded with pain, and he fought a ridiculous urge to comfort her. "She felt guilty for involving your father and his brother. Apparently her father was so furious that he took her away the next day. He pushed her into the life he'd planned for her— the right schools, the right friends, the right marriage."

The bitterness with which she said the last words tipped him off. "I take it the marriage wasn't so right, after all."

She shrugged, but the casual gesture couldn't hide her pain. "I don't remember much about my father, but by all accounts it wasn't a happy marriage. She remarried after his death. The situation with my stepfather wasn't much better. Maybe it would have lasted a little longer, but the summer we came here—"

She stopped abruptly, her lips tightening as if to keep back the words.

"I thought you'd never been to the island before." Suspicion sharpened his voice. He'd been too quick to believe her.

"I..." She looked at him, maybe considering another lie. Then she shook her head. "I was here once." The words came out reluctantly. "A long time ago, when I was fifteen."

"We met then." His sureness surprised him. He hadn't remembered her before, but now he knew. There'd been that sense of familiarity that plagued him from the first day at the church.

"We met," she agreed. "I came to a dance at the yacht club, and you were there."

He stared at her, memories stirring. The yacht club terrace, music playing in the background, the scent of roses. A girl wearing a white dress, standing in the moonlight.

"You wore a white dress. You had a white rose in your hair."

He thought she flushed, although he couldn't be sure in the dim light. "That's right. It was nothing. Just a dance."

"A dance." He frowned at her, remembering. "You turned into Cinderella, as I recall. You ran off and you didn't bother to leave a glass slipper behind."

Something quick and pained crossed her face. "I had to leave."

"Why?" He wouldn't let her get away with less than the whole story.

"My mother." She looked past him, toward the spartina grass waving in the marsh, but he wasn't sure she saw it. "When I called home to ask if I could stay later at the dance, my mother was crying. Hysterical. I knew what that meant."

A dozen possibilities raced through his mind. "Your stepfather—"

"No, he wasn't abusive, not physically, anyway. But he didn't understand her. When something upset her, she couldn't help it." She seemed to be begging him to understand. Or maybe she was trying to understand herself. "She'd start down into depression. I always thought if I just got to her soon enough, I could stop it. But I never could."

He saw. "You think it was because she'd come back to the island."

"I know it was. This place haunted her. I promised I'd put that to rest for her. I have to try." Her eyes were wide and dark in the moonlight. "Will you help me?"

If she'd asked him that ten minutes ago, he might have been able to resist. He didn't want to do this.

But he'd seen how much it hurt her. Like it or not, his family shared the responsibility. He couldn't say no.

"All right," he said finally. "I don't know what I can do—what either of us can do. But I'll try."

The smile that blossomed on her face would have made any amount of effort worthwhile. "Thank you, Adam. My mother would be grateful."

"I'm not doing it for her. I don't even think I'm doing it for you."

Her brows lifted. "Then why bother, if you don't believe we're going to get the dolphin back?"

He thought about what Tory must have faced when she'd run out of the yacht club that night. Regret shimmered through him. She'd been a kid, and by the sound of it, she'd had to be a parent to her mother. She hadn't deserved that.

"I guess I'm doing it for that girl in a white dress with a rose in her hair," he said.

Tory brushed at her hair a little self-consciously. "Maybe I should wear a rose in my hair more often."

"Maybe you should." He touched the springing hair at her temple. He intended it for the lightest of gestures, a relief from the emotion of the last few minutes.

But a lock of her hair twined around his finger, almost as if clinging to him. He brushed the fine skin at her temple.

"Did I kiss you that night?"

She swallowed, and he felt the effort through his fingertips. "I don't remember."

"Hard to believe I wasn't more memorable than that." He tried to keep it light, but something deeper than memory was driving him. "Maybe we should try it again."

"I'm not sure—"

He stopped her words with his kiss. Her eyes closed. He made no move to hold her, and nothing touched but their lips. It should have been the simplest of gestures.

A wave of longing swamped him. He wanted that feeling again—wanted to see the future stretching ahead of him, ready to be explored, clean as a fresh page in Tory's sketch pad.

But he couldn't have that again. Probably neither of them could. He drew back reluctantly, not quite able to regret that he'd kissed her.

"I guess I should apologize."

Tory shook her head quickly. "It's all right. It doesn't mean anything."

She spun and hurried toward the door, the white dress fluttering in the evening breeze. In an instant she was gone.

There was no fresh page. They couldn't go back

and become teenagers kissing in the moonlight again. Too much had happened to both of them.

He'd committed himself to helping her in an undoubtedly futile attempt. He'd try, but somehow he didn't think any of this was going to turn out the way Tory wanted. And he couldn't disregard the sense that they were headed for trouble.

Each time she thought about the night before, Tory's stomach tightened. It was a wonder she'd been able to eat any of the mouthwatering she-crab soup Miz Becky had fixed for lunch.

She frowned at the sketch pad in her lap. She'd been sitting in the bentwood rocker on the front veranda since lunch. It was certainly safer to sit here than on the side of the house overlooking the salt marsh. There, she'd have been reminded with every breath of confiding in Adam. Of kissing Adam.

Her stomach quivered as she saw Adam's face in the moonlight. She felt the featherlight touch of his lips, and a wave of longing swept through her. If only—

No. She drowned the longing with anger, but it was anger at herself, not Adam. She'd wasted too many dreams over the years on the Adam she remembered. She wouldn't do that to herself again. She set the rocker moving with a push of her feet. Its creak was oddly comforting. She could be rational about the situation with Adam.

He'd promised his help. That was all she wanted. Other than that, their relationship was strictly business, nothing more.

She was still staring at the page a half hour later when she heard the crunch of tires on the shell-covered driveway. Adam was back from the boatyard, and she hadn't accomplished a thing. She smoothed the cover of the pad over the design.

He came toward her, his step assured, giving her that endearing smile as he mounted the front steps. Her stomach quivered again.

"Hey, Tory." He glanced at the pad in her lap. "Are you busy?"

"Not terribly," she said cautiously. If he brought up last night…

"Come for a ride with me, then. There's something I want to show you."

Her preservation instincts told her that being alone with Adam in a car was not a good idea. "What is it?"

He lifted an eyebrow, the effect devastating. "Don't you like surprises?"

"No." She didn't have to think about that one. All the surprises in her life had been unpleasant ones.

He studied her for a moment, then nodded as if he understood. "All right. No surprises. I was able to find the house your mother's family rented when they came here that summer. I thought you'd want to see it."

She had to catch her breath. He'd promised to help, but she hadn't expected anything so concrete already. "That was fast."

"It wasn't that hard. There's only one rental agency that handles houses suitable for wealthy summer visitors. Their records go back a hundred years." He nodded toward the car. "Shall we go?"

Tension gripped her, but she couldn't back out. She dropped the sketch pad on the rocker as she stood. "Am I dressed all right?"

"Since I have the keys and no one is renting it, you won't meet anyone but me." His gaze swept her chinos and cotton sweater with what seemed to be approval. "And you look good to me."

Warmth flooded her cheeks. She really hadn't been asking for a compliment. "Let's go, then."

She followed him to the car. He opened the door and took her arm to usher her in. Her skin tingled where he touched it.

Stop it, she lectured as he went to the other door and slid behind the wheel. Just stop it.

Adam turned the car, swung out through the pillared wrought-iron gates to the road, and Caldwell Cove spread out in front of them. From Twin Oaks, situated at the end of the village, a crescent of houses and shops faced the inland waterway. The docks, busy with boats, fringed the water.

Tory's gaze traced the outline of the village, bisected neatly by the church spire, and her fingers itched for her pencils. If she didn't include the few cars along the street in a sketch, the scene might have been today or a century ago.

Adam turned away from town onto the road that swung around the heel of the island. The breeze through the open window freshened as they drove along the shore, lifting her hair. Unfortunately it couldn't blow away the lump that had formed in her throat.

"You're sure you found the right house?" She asked the question more for the sake of saying something than because she doubted him.

"Positive." He glanced at her, creases forming between his brows. "Having second thoughts?"

"No." She couldn't. "But there won't be anything left to find there after forty years."

Adam shrugged, frowning at the narrow road. "I don't expect to find anything, period. Not after all this time. But I said I'd help, and this was the only place I could think of to start."

"I guess you're right." She discovered she was watching his hands on the wheel and averted her eyes as if afraid he'd catch her. "I was so worried about getting here that I didn't spend a lot of time thinking about how I'd look for the dolphin."

That sounded stupid, and she half expected him to say so. Instead he pointed toward the waves. "Speaking of dolphins, there they are now."

She followed the direction of his hand. At first she saw nothing but ocean. Then a silver crescent arced through the waves, followed by another and another. She couldn't stop a gasp. "They're beautiful."

"Yes." His voice was soft. "Seeing them is just as exciting the hundredth time as it is the first."

She glanced at him, moved by the tenderness in his voice. "You said the legend was that the dolphins saved the shipwrecked sailor. Can that part of it possibly be true?"

"Sure. There are plenty of stories about dolphins interacting with people."

"I've seen trained ones, but in the wild, that has to be different."

Adam smiled. "You should see my cousin Chloe. She'd make a believer out of you. She talks to them, and when you watch them, you're convinced they talk back to her."

Adam spoke easily, without the tension that had marked every conversation they'd had since she came to the island. Her gaze followed the dolphins as they headed toward the open ocean. If she could talk to them like his cousin Chloe, she'd thank the dolphins for that.

Adam turned into a shell-covered drive opposite a deserted stretch of beach. The car bounced over ruts, then came to a stop. "There it is."

She looked, and everything in her froze. She was still sitting, hands pressed against the dashboard, when he came around and opened the door.

"Tory? Is something wrong?"

She turned her head slowly, forced herself to focus on his face. "You're sure this is the right house? The one my grandfather rented when my mother was a girl?"

"Of course." He looked puzzled. "Why?"

She swallowed hard. "Because this is also the house my stepfather rented when I was fifteen."

She watched him absorb that, his face troubled.

"It's not so unusual, when you stop to think about it," he said finally. "There are only so many houses of this size to rent now, and there were even fewer then." His gaze rested on her face, sympathetic. "Are you sure you want to go in?"

She wouldn't be a coward about this. "Yes."

They went up the steps to the porch, and Adam put the key in the lock. She looked around, trying to remember their arrival that summer. She couldn't. That had been wiped out by the way the vacation ended.

But she had probably run up the steps, excited and happy at the prospect of staying at the shore. The weathered gray shingles would have been the same, as well as the beach roses climbing the porch rail.

Adam pushed open the door, then looked at her, eyes questioning. "Okay?"

She nodded. "I'm fine." She took a breath and walked into the house.

He followed her to the hallway, then went into the living room, footsteps echoing on the uncarpeted floor. "I'm sure it's been refurnished since you were here."

"Yes." She stood in the archway, scanning the room. New furniture, fresh paint, different pictures on the walls. It was a pretty room, with its pale walls and floral upholstery. Nothing was left of the past.

But the view from the large windows was familiar. She'd stood in the archway looking at her mother sobbing on the sofa and her stepfather shouting in anger and frustration.

"They'd have replaced the mirror." The words came out before she thought about them. "He threw a glass at it and broke it."

Adam touched her shoulder—a brief, sympathetic stroke of his hand. "I'm sorry."

"It's all right." She took a breath, sought for calm.

"How long did you stay?" He was probably trying to help her by talking.

"Just a few days. I remember my mother was brittle, too excited, almost feverish the whole time." She shook her head. "I should have known something was wrong. I shouldn't have gone out that night."

"You were a kid." The anger in his voice startled her. "It wasn't your responsibility."

"I was all she had." She pressed her fist against her stomach as if that would push away the sick feeling of remembering. "I guess I understand now."

"What?" He moved a step closer, as if he wanted to protect her.

But she didn't need protecting. She'd been taking care of herself all her life.

"Why that trip sent my mother over the edge. It's affecting me, being here, and I'm strong. She was fragile. She was always fragile. Being back in the same house, being flooded by memories and guilt—it's not surprising she fell apart. We never should have come here. She didn't want to, but my stepfather didn't listen. He never did."

It was so quiet she heard the intake of his breath. "What happened? After that, I mean."

She tried to concentrate—to separate what really happened then from what she'd learned later. "She was hospitalized for depression, I know. And my stepfather filed for divorce. I stayed in his house until she got out of the hospital, but then I found a place for the two of us."

"You were too young for that." Again there was suppressed anger in his voice. "Wasn't there any family who could help you? What about your father's family?"

"They'd washed their hands of us a long time before that. We did all right on our own."

"You shouldn't have had to."

She tried to force a smile. "Ancient history. It doesn't matter anymore."

She'd never told anyone most of what she'd poured out to Adam. She saw why Miranda said he was everyone's friend. That sympathetic voice had pulled far more out of her than she'd intended to say.

"Well." She tried to sound brisk. "Shall we take a look at the rest of the house?"

He shrugged. "If you want." He studied her face for a long moment. "Are you sure you're okay?"

"Fine." Despite Adam's sympathy, she knew he had his own agenda in all of this. She had to remember that. His family was involved, too.

"You know, it's funny," he said slowly, his gaze still fixed on her face.

"What is?"

"The way things ended, both times. It almost seems as if history repeated itself."

Something shivered inside her. Her mother had been snatched away from her summer love in traumatic circumstances, and she'd never really stopped regretting that.

Years later, Tory had been snatched away just as suddenly.

Nonsense, she told herself sternly. The two things had little in common. Adam hadn't been a summer love. She'd only known him for a single evening. He didn't mean anything to her.

You dreamed about him for years, a little voice whispered in her mind. How long will you dream about him when you leave this time?

Chapter Seven

Tory hadn't shaken off the feelings roused by their visit to the beach house when she entered the dining room that night. Being in this place didn't help. Each time she entered the gracious room with the rice-carved mahogany furniture that was unique to the low country, she was reminded of that other life, just as the rice carving was reminiscent of the rice plantations that had once thrived here.

The mahogany-framed mirror over the sideboard reflected her pale face at her. Paler than usual? She wasn't sure.

"Tory." Jefferson Caldwell rose from his seat and pulled out her chair before Adam could move. "Good evening."

She slipped into the chair, glancing at Jefferson's urbane face as he resumed his seat at the head of the oval table. Adam must have told him who she was. What did he think about having the daughter of the woman he'd once been infatuated with in his house? Her tension jerked up a notch. Was this going to be unpleasant?

Jenny bounced into her chair. "Is it my turn to say the blessing?"

Adam nodded, and Jenny lowered her head and clasped her hands. She raced through the words so quickly Tory barely got her head bowed in time. When she looked up, Adam was frowning at his daughter.

"Jennifer Ann, I don't believe that's an appropriate way to ask the blessing. You sound as if you're in a race to get finished."

She wiggled. "But Daddy, you know cousin Andi's coming to spend the night tonight. I want to be done with supper when she gets here so we can play."

"You know perfectly well that Andi will wait if you're not finished with your meal."

"But, Daddy…"

Miz Becky pushed through the door from the kitchen carrying a steaming platter of fried chicken. Tory suspected the distraction was well timed, before Jenny managed to talk herself into any more trouble with her father.

Jefferson offered her a bowl of sweet potatoes. "Andi is my son Matthew's oldest girl," he said, as casually as if explaining his family to any stranger instead of to an interloper who'd hidden her identity from him. "These two young ladies will be giggling all night if we don't watch out."

Jenny looked up from her drumstick. "We'll be good, Grandpa. Honest."

He smiled indulgently at the child. "We'll believe that when we see it. Or when we don't hear it, as the case may be."

Tory was still smiling at Jenny's expression when Jefferson turned to her. "Adam has told me about your mother."

She nearly choked on the sweet potatoes. What was he going to say? He couldn't be happy with the situation. She put her fork down carefully on the silver-trimmed edge of the plate.

"I was sorry to hear of her passing." The words were formal, but sorrow touched his face. "I remember her well."

"Thank you." She hesitated, wondering if she should say more. "She remembered you, too. She… she regretted what happened."

He nodded gravely, his white hair glistening in the light from the chandelier. "I appreciate knowing that, Tory. I wish—" He stopped. "Well, there's little point in revisiting the past." The lines of his face deepened, making him look very different from the young man her mother had talked about.

Did his words mean Adam hadn't told him she wanted to recover the dolphin? She couldn't imagine he'd welcome that. He'd apparently kept his involvement secret for most of his life. She glanced toward Adam for a cue.

He seemed to pick up instantly on her unspoken question. "My father doesn't feel there's much hope of finding it after all these years."

He shot a look toward his daughter, and Tory

understood. He didn't want to talk about this in front of her.

"Finding what, Daddy?" Jenny, of course, had picked up on what he might want her to miss.

"Nothing, honey. It's just something that was lost a long time ago."

"I lost my green barrette on the playground last week, and Andi helped me find it. She's good at finding things."

"It sounds as if you're lucky to have a cousin like her," Tory said. Obviously she never should have said anything at the dinner table. Still, Jefferson had been the one to bring it up.

The doorbell rang, and Jenny leaped from her seat. She bounced up and down on her toes, fingertips resting on the edge of the table "That's Andi. May I be excused, Daddy? Please?"

He looked from her half-finished plate to her excited face and sighed. "All right, go ahead. I expect Miz Becky's going to have a snack for you two later."

Jenny darted from the dining room before he finished the sentence, and her high voice echoed from the hallway as she greeted her cousin.

"I'm sorry." Tory glanced from one male Caldwell to the other. "I shouldn't have discussed the subject in front of her."

Jefferson's face darkened with sudden emotion. "Sometimes I wish we'd never heard of that dolphin. We'd be better off forgetting the thing ever existed, legend or no legend."

Well, she'd wondered what he thought. She couldn't blame him for telling her.

"I'd like to forget it, but I can't." She met his gaze squarely. "I made a promise to my mother, and I have to try and fulfill it, even if it seems hopeless." She tensed, waiting for him to suggest she pack her bag.

"Hopeless is the right word. Everything about that situation is hopeless." For an instant Jefferson looked startled at his own emotion. Then he tossed his napkin on the tablecloth. "Excuse me." He went quickly out of the room.

She bit her lip. Her return to Caldwell Cove seemed destined to bring nothing but grief. "I'm sorry. I didn't mean to upset him."

"Forget it." Adam managed a smile, but she could see his tension in the way his hand gripped the fork. "You had to tell him the truth."

"I could have been more tactful. I'm not very good at that." At least it didn't look as if she'd be kicked out. Yet.

"It's all right, Tory."

But it wasn't, and they both knew it. Too many emotions swirled, and no matter what she did, somebody was going to be hurt.

This was what she needed, Tory decided the next morning. A few hours away from anybody named Caldwell and from all the complications associated with their mutual past. She walked down the narrow main street of Caldwell Cove, enjoying the breeze off the water and the salt tang of the air. It was cooler today, with just a hint that autumn must come, even here. She zipped the light windbreaker she'd thrown on when she left the house.

The channel between the island and the mainland was busy with boats of all sizes and descriptions. An elegant sailboat skimmed past a bulky shrimper that drew in toward the public dock. Gulls swooped around it, probably hoping for lunch.

Glancing away from the water, she saw canopies dotting the open lawn between the bank and the café. A few feet closer and she could read the sign. Gullah Market Today.

She hesitated. She ought to get to work, but the windows weren't going anywhere, and she deserved a break. She stepped off the sidewalk and started down the grassy space between the canopies.

Booths offered everything from fresh fruit to baskets to brightly woven cloth. She turned toward the display of baskets and found herself standing next to Miranda Caldwell.

"Hey, Tory. Nice to see you. How are the windows coming along?"

So much for her assumption that she could avoid the sprawling Caldwell clan anywhere in Caldwell Cove. At least it wasn't Adam.

"Fine, thanks. I was ready for a break from them."

Miranda's green eyes sparkled with amusement. "Same here. My mother announced it was time for fall cleaning at the inn, so I decided I needed to come to market."

"These baskets are lovely." Tory picked one up, hoping it would be a safe subject of conversation. Adam had told his father who she was. Had he passed the information on to the rest of his family? She hoped not.

She probably should have asked him, but things had been strained enough between them after that uncharacteristic display of emotion from his father.

"Sweetgrass," Miranda said, touching the intricately woven strands of the basket. "This is Josepha Green's work. She's a local Gullah basket weaver."

"How can you tell?" Her artisan's curiosity won out over her desire to end the conversation quickly.

"Every Gullah weaver uses the same tools and techniques that have been used for hundreds of years, but each one has his own little trick." She traced the rim of the basket. "See this strand of bulrush woven in? Nobody else does that."

"The artist's personal touch. I guess each of us wants to put our own stamp on things."

"Yes." Miranda's voice was soft. "Like you with your window design, trying to find a way to say who Lila was."

Startled, she met Miranda's gaze, oblivious to the moving, colorful crowd around them. Was she imagining it or was that a hint that Miranda would talk about Lila?

Before she could find a response, someone stopped close behind them. Her pulse thudded, notifying her that it was Adam even before she turned.

"Sharing secrets, ladies?" His words were casual,

his eyes guarded. She didn't think he liked finding her in conversation with his cousin.

"Just talking about baskets, sugar." Miranda smiled. "What brings you away from the boatyard in the middle of the day?"

He shrugged. "The chance I'd run into my favorite cousin talking to Tory, maybe."

She studied him as he bantered with Miranda, switching between English and Gullah, the mixture of dialect native to the sea islands. He should look casual and relaxed in his khakis and faded denim shirt. But the tension lines around his eyes gave him away.

Why didn't he want her to talk to Miranda? Was he afraid of what Tory might say or what Miranda might tell her?

Before she could decide, he turned to her. "If you're done here, I'll give you a ride to the house."

"Sugar, she hasn't even bought anything yet." Miranda linked arms with Tory, her voice gently teasing. "What's wrong? Don't you want to turn your guest loose at market with me?"

"I probably should be getting back to work." Tory felt vaguely uncomfortable, as if she'd been caught gossiping on the boss's time.

"Come on, now," Miranda coaxed. "My daddy's back at the food stand munching on sweet-potato fries. Let's join him."

Adam frowned, and she could feel his tension. "Miranda, if Tory wants to get back to work—"

"Here comes Gran," Miranda interrupted, turning

to greet the erect elderly woman who marched toward them through the crowd, nodding or speaking to practically every person there.

Tory took advantage of Miranda's momentary distraction to speak to Adam. "Is there some reason you don't want me to talk with your cousin?" she said quietly.

"Of course not. Why would there be?"

If that were true, he probably wouldn't have spent so much time on his answer. But there was no chance to discuss it. Mrs. Caldwell had reached them.

She zeroed in on Tory. "Miz Tory, you're just the person I want to see. Are you coming to the beach picnic tonight?"

Tory blinked. "I'm sorry. I didn't know about it." Was this something someone had mentioned and she'd forgotten?

Mrs. Caldwell poked Adam's arm. "Well, young man? Why haven't you invited Tory to the picnic yet?"

He caught his grandmother's hand in his. "Stop poking me, Gran. I'm not six anymore. Next you'll be asking if I've brushed my teeth and said my prayers."

His light answer didn't disguise his annoyance. From the sharp look she gave him, it didn't fool his grandmother, either. She turned to Tory.

"Since this grandson of mine didn't remember, I'll do the inviting. The Caldwells are having a picnic on the beach tonight. We want you to come."

She could practically feel Adam willing her to say no. "I don't think I…"

"No excuses, now. You come along with Adam and Jenny, you hear? I'll see you there."

She made it sound like a command. Tory seemed to have no choice but to nod agreement.

But when she looked from Adam's face to his grandmother's she knew she wasn't imagining things. Mrs. Caldwell wanted her there. Adam didn't. He couldn't very well say so, but taking her to this family event was the last thing he wanted to do.

Thanks to Gran, he didn't have a choice about the picnic. Adam paused in the kitchen to pick up the cooler Miz Becky had left ready on the table. He'd best collect Jenny and Tory and be on his way.

His father wouldn't be going, of course. As usual, Jefferson had found a pressing business meeting that took priority. Any other time, Adam might have tried to talk him into going, but with Tory there…

Balancing the family's need to have the dolphin back against Tory's promise and his father's wishes wasn't just difficult—it was impossible. All his instincts told him that having Tory attend the picnic was a bad idea.

As he swung the cooler off the table, he heard the low murmur of voices from the back porch. He moved quietly to the screen door. Tory and Jenny sat on the top step, probably waiting for him.

"Well, I think it was mean." Jenny's pout was visible from where he stood. "Andi didn't have to go home yet. I wanted to play some more."

"If her mother needed her, she probably had to

listen." Tory was clearly trying to be the voice of reason for his strong-willed little daughter.

"Her mama would have let her stay if she'd asked. I wanted to cut out paper dolls, but Andi didn't. So she went home. And I'm not going to play with her anymore."

Knowing Jenny's habit of trying to boss everyone around, he suspected there was more to it than that. He should intervene, but she'd chosen to confide in Tory, not in him.

"Well, I've never had a cousin, so I don't really know what that's like," Tory said. "But I do know what it's like when somebody you love disappoints you."

"It's mean," Jenny burst out, and he realized she was on the verge of tears.

"I'll bet Andi didn't intend to be mean. Of course, sometimes we can hurt other people's feelings even when we don't mean to."

Something about Tory's words must have caught Jenny's attention. She was looking at Tory's face, her resentment seeming to slip away.

"I wouldn't do that," she said self-righteously.

Tory smiled at his daughter with such gentleness it clutched his heart. "I know you wouldn't want to. But don't you think sometimes it happens anyway?"

Jenny's lower lip came out. "Maybe."

"Maybe," Tory agreed. "It isn't easy to forgive someone you love when they've hurt you." She touched the front of Jenny's T-shirt. "But I bet you'll feel better in here if you do. I know when I hold on to being mad at someone, it hurts me more than it does them."

The soft words reached inside him and grabbed his heart in a vise. From the little he'd learned of her family in the last few days, he knew Tory had plenty of reasons to hold on to resentment against them. Apparently she'd found a way to let that go.

Jenny rubbed the front of her shirt. "You mean it makes my heart hurt when I'm mad at someone?"

Tory nodded, lips curving in a smile. "Don't you think you might be able to forgive Andi if you tried?"

Jenny seemed to ponder that. Finally she heaved an elaborate sigh. "Well, I guess it would be more fun at the picnic if we weren't being mad at each other."

"That's a very sensible way to look at it," Tory said solemnly. She touched Jenny's curls lightly. "I'm glad you see it that way."

Forgiving. Adam leaned against the kitchen counter, not quite willing to join them. It was probably just as well Jenny hadn't come to him for advice on that particular subject. It wasn't one he'd dealt with very successfully.

His father and Uncle Clayton hadn't forgiven each other for the differences between them. He couldn't forgive Lila for what she'd done to him and to Jenny. The truth seemed to be that his side of the family wasn't very skilled at forgiving.

And Tory's presence, no matter how he looked at it, seemed to make that worse.

Chapter Eight

"I don't think I should be here." Tory followed Adam and Jenny down the path toward the beach, her footsteps making no sound on the carpet of pine needles. Her sense of not belonging grew stronger by the minute. Adam didn't want her here. She knew that even if he'd never say it.

"Why not?" She detected a faint note of frustration as he switched the cooler he carried from one hand to the other. "My grandmother invited you. Look, they've already started the fire for the crab boil."

They emerged from the shadow of the pines to the dunes, and Jenny darted toward the group gathered on the beach. Some people fed a fire while others unpacked hampers. Children bicycled around them on the hard-packed sand, looking like so many seabirds darting in and out. The orange glow of the fire matched the orange sunset to the west, over the mainland. It was a beautiful, peaceful scene. She didn't belong.

Tory tried to find the words for her uneasiness. "It's a family thing. I'm sure your grandmother just invited me because I'm staying at Twin Oaks."

Adam stopped and smiled at her, the sun lines around his eyes crinkling. Whatever reservations he had about this, he was managing to suppress them. "You don't know my grandmother very well if you think that. Relax, Tory. You'll have a good time."

A good time? She wasn't so sure of that. But maybe it could be a useful time. Adam had said his aunt and uncle would be at the picnic with the rest of their family. This might be her best chance to talk to Clayton about the dolphin.

She'd heard Jefferson's version of events. She wanted to hear Clayton's. Maybe she also wanted to have a glimpse of her mother through his eyes. Did he perceive Emily the same way Adam's father did?

She glanced at Adam, who was lifting his hand to wave to the group on the beach. He belonged to this place and these people. With his faded jeans and his white sweatshirt, he looked like what he was— a man who worked hard, played hard and was at peace with his world.

Or was he? The only chink in his facade was his relationship with his late wife, and that she had yet to figure out. After ten days of working on the sanctuary windows and living in Adam's house, she was no closer to understanding the woman she was supposed to memorialize. Adam wasn't just reticent about Lila—he was a blank wall.

They reached the hard-packed sand where walking was easier, and she paused to shake the loose sand from her shoes. Adam paused, too, looking at her with a hint of a frown in his eyes.

"There's something I should mention before we join the others."

She found herself tensing. The feeling couldn't be shaken off the way the sand could. "What?"

He hesitated, as if wondering how to say whatever it was, and her tension doubled.

"I've told them who you are," Adam said. "They know you're Emily's daughter."

She froze, staring at him, hoping she'd heard wrong. "You what?"

His face tightened. "They're my family. It wasn't something I felt I could keep secret from them. After all, they all know about the dolphin."

"You might have warned me before this." Anger sharpened the words. She should have known he'd tell them. All that loyalty of his was directed toward his family, not her.

"Would you have come if I had?" His gaze challenged her.

"Probably not, but I think I had the right to decide for myself."

"Look, you may as well get used to the situation. No one here is going to blame you for—" He stopped as if realizing where he was headed.

"For something my mother did?" Her fists clenched so hard her nails bit into her palms. "My mother didn't take the dolphin."

"No." Something bleak appeared in his eyes. "My father did."

"But everyone thinks she took it away. You said so yourself."

He put the cooler down and stood looking at her. Was that sympathy or pity in his eyes? She didn't welcome either. "That was before you told me what she asked you to do. I believe you."

"Do they?" She jerked a nod toward the others, still out of earshot.

"I can't answer that." His jaw tightened as if in exasperation, a small muscle twitching. "You asked me to help you. I'm trying to."

She wanted to flare out at him—wanted to tell him she didn't need his help.

Unfortunately that wasn't true. She did need his help, and she needed the cooperation of those people around the fire. The question was, how likely were they to cooperate with the daughter of the woman they blamed for the disappearance of their family heirloom?

"All right." She bit off the words. "It's too late to change that now. Maybe since your uncle already knows who I am, it will be easier for me to speak with him about that night."

"My uncle—" Adam's expression froze. "I don't think that's necessary."

She blinked. "But he's the only one who might have some clues as to what happened after your father left the party."

"Don't you think my uncle would have spoken up years ago if he did?"

She could hear the anger under his words, but she didn't understand it. "Look, don't you see that this is the next logical step? And there must be other people who were there that night we can talk with."

Adam planted his hands on his hips. "You've already heard my father's account," he said stubbornly. "As for other people—everyone on the island knew by the next day that the dolphin was missing. If they knew anything, they'd have spoken up."

Suddenly she knew what was going on here and why Adam hadn't invited her to this event. He wanted to keep her away from his uncle.

"This is because of the feud between your father and your uncle, isn't it?"

His expression got even more forbidding. "What if it is?"

"I thought you said that didn't affect your relationship with the rest of the family."

She saw the anger flare in his eyes, saw him fight it and control it.

"Fine." He ground out the word. "You want to talk to Clayton, go ahead and do it. Talk to anyone you want. I can't stop you." He picked up the cooler, dangling it from one strong hand. "Let's go." He stalked toward the fire.

Tory followed him, her stomach quivering as they approached the others. That unexpected quarrel with Adam had shaken her confidence, and the fact that everyone was watching them didn't help.

No, not them. Everyone watched *her*, with expressions she could only call guarded. Tension tightened her muscles until it took an effort to walk naturally.

They came up to the cluster of people. For a moment no one spoke. Adam's cousins stopped feeding the fire. His nieces and nephews stopped circling. Everyone looked at her.

Then his grandmother marched toward them.

"'Bout time you two were getting here. You don't want to miss the food, do you? Tory, I'm right glad you decided to join us."

Tory's tension ebbed in the warmth of the elderly woman's smile. "Thank you for inviting me, Mrs. Caldwell."

"Might as well call me Gran. Everyone else does. Make yourself at home. If you don't know somebody, just ask. They all know who you are."

Tory looked for malice in that last sentence but found none in Gran's sharp old eyes. She took a deep breath. She may as well put her cards on the table.

"I understand Adam told you who my mother was."

The elderly woman nodded. "Can't say I'd have recognized you otherwise. You don't favor your mother much, do you?"

The casual question knocked her off balance. She'd forgotten that Adam's grandmother would probably have seen her mother during that long-ago summer.

"No, I guess I take more after my father." That much was easy to say. The next question wasn't. "Did you know her?"

"Not to say *know.* I knew who she was."

Of course she would. Of all the people here, Naomi Caldwell had the most cause to blame Tory's mother for what happened to her sons.

But Adam's grandmother didn't seem to be carrying any resentment. She nodded toward Adam's uncle, bending to put a piece of driftwood onto the fire. "I reckon Clayton's the one you need to see."

Tory felt Adam's tension as surely as if they were touching instead of inches apart. He didn't welcome the idea from his grandmother any more than he'd welcomed it from Tory. Would he tell Gran so?

"Guess I'll go help with the fire," he said, and moved off quickly.

Obviously he wouldn't.

Tory looked at Clayton Caldwell. The lean, gray-haired man walked around the fire, limping slightly. He hadn't so much as glanced in her direction, and her heart sank. "It doesn't look as if Clayton wants to talk to me."

Mrs. Caldwell frowned toward her son, then transferred her gaze to Adam as she assessed each of them. "We don't always get to do what we want to do. Besides, seems to me that this family's been keeping too many secrets for too many years. Secrets aren't good for anyone. That's the verse I gave Adam, you know."

Tory felt as if she'd missed a step in the dark. "Verse?"

The elderly woman shook her head. "Forgot you wouldn't know about that. All my children and grandchildren—the Lord gave me scripture verses for them when they were baptized. Adam's is from Ephesians. 'Speaking the truth in love...'" She paused, looking expectantly at Tory.

Tory was irrationally glad she didn't have to disappoint. "We will in all things grow up into Him who is the head."

That earned her an approving nod. "Maybe it's time for some truth speaking. Maybe that's why you're here." She patted Tory's arm as if she were one of the grandchildren who'd done well.

The touch was disarming. Tory felt a ridiculous urge to pour out all her concerns—about her mother, about Adam, about fulfilling her promise. She pushed the sensation down with a spurt of something like panic. She didn't confide in people. She didn't lean on people. That wasn't how she was.

"I hope you're right." She managed to speak.

Mrs. Caldwell patted her arm again. "Looks like Adam's filled a plate for you. You go on and have your food now. You'll have a chance to hear Clayton's story. Don't you worry about it. He'll get together with you before the evening's over."

She could only hope the woman knew what she was talking about. Mrs. Caldwell walked off, calling the children to come and eat, and Adam approached her, a laden plate in each hand.

"Sorry. Guess I overreacted. Did Gran make everything okay?"

She took the plate he held out to her. "Well, she convinced me that the family isn't planning to run me out of town on a rail, if that's what you mean."

Adam's face relaxed. "Gran's good at reassuring people. Among lots of other things." He took her arm. "Looks like there's room on that blanket. Come and meet my brother and his family."

She let him steer her toward a place to sit. If Adam wanted to make up for his hasty words, she would let him. As she'd told Jenny, it didn't pay to hold a grudge.

The man she knew was his brother looked up at their approach. He smiled and pulled a chubby blond toddler onto his lap to make room for them.

All right, the Caldwells were more welcoming than she had any reason to expect. Apparently Adam hadn't ruined things by telling them about her, but he still should have asked her first. As far as talking to his uncle was concerned, she probably couldn't count on Adam to help her with that.

A question of loyalty, she thought again, glancing at his face as he exchanged banter with his brother. With Adam, things would always come down to that. She knew perfectly well that his loyalty would never be directed to her.

Adam put down his dessert plate and leaned back on his elbows on the blanket. The warmth of the sand lingered even though it was getting dark.

Who'd have guessed he'd find such enjoyment in a family picnic with Tory Marlowe sitting next to him? He watched her lean over to tickle the baby who sat on his sister-in-law's lap. Tory, prickly and uncomfortable at first, had thawed under the influence of Sarah's warm interest. Sarah seemed to have that effect on everyone. She'd certainly warmed up his brother, turning Matthew from a globe-trotting loner into a contented family man.

It was Sarah who'd produced a windbreaker for Tory to put on. Adam should have thought to warn her it would get chilly after the sun went down. In Sarah's Pirate Days jacket, she looked like a real islander.

Adam looked from one familiar, fire-lit face to another. The children had settled onto blankets around the fire, the younger ones drifting off to sleep, the older ones pointing out constellations in the star-studded sky or toasting one last marshmallow. Jenny huddled close to Andi, their quarrel apparently forgiven and forgotten, as Adam's cousin David started to play the guitar. Under cover of the music he leaned close to Tory.

"I see Uncle Clayton's gone over on the dock to smoke his pipe," he murmured. "Maybe we ought to join him."

She flashed him a look that mingled surprise with apprehension. Then she nodded and got to her feet.

They picked their way through sprawled grown-ups and children and started down the beach. The sound of music and voices faded. Darkness closed, and Tory hugged her borrowed jacket tight. The muted, incessant rumble of the waves accompanied the rustle of the sea oats.

"I thought you didn't want to do this."

He shrugged, then realized she couldn't see the gesture in the dark. "I made you a promise. Guess

I got a little derailed there for a moment, but I plan to keep it."

They took a few more steps before Tory spoke. "Do you think he'll speak to us? He didn't look especially welcoming."

He heard the tension under her question. "I think he will. Looked to me as if Gran had a few words with him. You're never too old for a talking-to from Gran."

He caught her hand in what was meant to be a reassuring gesture. Her long fingers curled around his, and his skin tingled.

How long had it been since he'd held a woman's hand while they walked? Too long, certainly. He hadn't had either the time or the inclination for dating since Lila left.

He shouldn't let Tory get her hopes up. "The thing is, if Clayton had any answers, he'd have spoken up long ago." He grimaced, knowing the darkness protected his expression. "He wouldn't keep something like that secret to protect my father. Guess you've already figured that part out."

She'd probably also guessed how Adam felt about it. He sensed her searching gaze.

"I understand they don't get along. You never did tell me just what went wrong between them."

It wasn't any of her business, was it? And yet their histories were so entangled it made little sense to try and keep it from her.

"My father uses words like lazy and shiftless to describe his brother," he said, his voice dry. "And

Uncle Clayton's been known to say that my father would sell his honor for success. You might say their values are polar opposites."

Tory was silent for a long moment. "You'd think there must be something more personal that started it."

She meant the dolphin, of course. In spite of what he knew, he wasn't quite ready to admit that. "The way I understand it, they always fought, like brothers do. But now..." Now the breach seemed wider than ever. "Maybe we'd better concentrate on hearing his version."

The string of lights that outlined the dock sent an amber glow over his uncle. Clayton sat with his back to a post, his bad leg stretched stiffly in front of him. His pipe made an orange spark in the darkness as he puffed on it.

"Kind of thought y'all would be along." He took the pipe out of his mouth and cradled it in one hand. "Seems like Tory would want to see me."

"You know who I am." Tension radiated from Tory, passing to Adam as if they were connected.

Clayton nodded. "The whole family knows. Pull up some dock and sit. I'm not sure I can help, but I'll try."

Tory sank to a cross-legged position opposite him, and Adam sat next to her. He didn't have a good feeling about this. He couldn't stop it.

"You don't favor your mother much."

Tory's hands clasped each other tightly. Was she tired of being compared to her beautiful mother or was there more going on?

"No." Her voice had tightened. "I look like my father."

The incoming tide shushed softly against the weathered wooden boards of the dock, and the breeze lifted Tory's hair. The silence stretched. Probably neither of them knew where to start.

Adam leaned forward, planting his palms against the warm, rough planks. Looked as if it was up to him, like it or not. "My father already told us everything he knows about that night. Tory was hoping you might remember something else."

Clayton frowned absently at his pipe, then glanced at Adam with an expression he couldn't interpret. "He told you everything?"

Adam nodded. They all knew what his father had done.

"Well, I don't have much else to add, but I'll try. There were a bunch of folks there on Angel Isle that night. We'd had a crab boil." He jerked his head toward the fire that shone on the beach. "Sort of like tonight, 'cept it was all kids, mostly islanders, a few summer folk."

"Did you see my father when he came? Did you know he had the dolphin with him?" Adam found it harder to say the words than he'd expected.

"Not then. I didn't learn that until the next day, when they found out it was gone. Then I knew."

"You didn't tell." Tory's voice was soft.

"He's my brother." Clayton didn't seem to think it required more explanation than that.

"But did you see him?" Adam frowned, trying to

picture what it had been like. "Was it dark when he got there?"

"Just dusk. I saw his boat come in, but I was busy with the fire. Emily was in the house, fixing something in the kitchen. Guess he went in to see her."

His hands pressed down so hard he felt as if he could launch himself off the dock. "Did you see him leave?"

"Nope, just noticed later his boat wasn't there. Emily never said anything about what passed between them, and I never spotted the dolphin that night."

"It must have been there."

Clayton shrugged. "Maybe so, but after Emily's father heard what Jefferson had to say, he and a bunch of his yacht club friends came storming in like the marines landing."

Adam was concentrating so hard on the sequence of events he almost missed it. Then he looked at his uncle, and dread hardened into a ball in his stomach. "My father told? That's how they found out?"

Clayton looked stricken. "Son, I thought you knew. You said he told you everything about that night."

"I guess he left that part out." He wanted to say his father couldn't have done that, but he knew it wasn't true. He could have. If Emily had turned him down, had scorned him for taking the dolphin, Jefferson might very well have done that.

His father had betrayed his own brother. Pain tightened around Adam's heart.

Tory made a small, distressed sound and reached toward him in sympathy. He pushed her hand away with a quick gesture. He didn't want her sympathy. He didn't want anything except to forget what he'd just learned.

But he couldn't. He had to find out everything. He swallowed hard. "Didn't Emily explain what happened with the dolphin?"

He could feel Clayton's reluctance. He shook his head slowly.

"But why?" Tory's voice sounded choked. "Surely she'd tell you what happened."

The lines in Clayton's weather-beaten face looked carved in stone. "Guess she never had the chance. I was outside, y'see, and I climbed on the lumber we had piled up for the addition to the cottage. Had this dumb idea I was going to get everyone's attention, try to calm them down."

Adam pictured a young version of his uncle clambering up, waving his arms, trying to take charge of an out-of-control situation. Something bad was coming, he could feel it.

"What happened?"

"I saw her daddy pulling Emily along. She was crying. I tried to jump down and get to her, but the wood shifted. Whole thing collapsed, came down right on top of me."

The sick taste of dread filled Adam's mouth. "You were hurt."

Clayton rubbed his bad leg. "Felt this snap—turned out it was broke in a couple of places. I heard Emily screaming as her daddy dragged her away." He shook his head. "Reckon I passed out then."

Tory rocked back and forth, hugging herself as if she couldn't stand that last image of her mother. Adam didn't know how he was going to get the picture out of his mind. Or how he'd forget his father was responsible.

His instincts had been right. The past was better off buried. Tory's determination to uncover it would lead to a lot of heartache for all of them.

Chapter Nine

"Are you sure you want to do this?" Tory stood on the dock late the next afternoon, watching as Adam pulled the covers off the boat's seats. He didn't look happy to be taking her to see Angel Isle, the site of the dolphin's disappearance. And after the shock they'd received the night before, she could hardly blame him.

"It's no trouble."

Adam's words were his usual response to helping someone. She'd heard him say that a dozen times since she'd been in Caldwell Cove. No trouble, he'd say with that boyish smile, regardless of the request.

Unfortunately taking her to Angel Isle was a problem for him, and they both knew it.

Clayton's revelation had blown up in their faces. She suspected Adam still hadn't come to terms with the idea that his father had not only taken the dolphin, he'd also informed on his brother.

Jefferson couldn't have foreseen the results of that angry act. It wasn't his fault that Clayton had climbed on that woodpile, but still, in some way, he must feel responsible. Clayton had to deal with a lifelong disability, and as for Tory's mother—she winced at the image of young Emily, screaming, being dragged away after seeing the boy she loved lying hurt, probably fearing he was dead.

It was small wonder Emily had never been able to forget. They all still felt the repercussions of that night, fair or not.

She leaned against the dock railing, looking at the water and letting the sun dazzle her eyes, making a reasonable excuse for any unwanted tears.

That night had changed her mother's life. She tried to shrug the tightness out of her shoulders at the thought of Emily, dragged from her summer romance, feeling guilty over what happened with the dolphin, grieving the loss of Clayton.

Was that the seed that had sprouted into drinking and depression? Or would something else have precipitated her mother's problems if that hadn't? Tory would never know.

Adam pressed the lever that lowered the boat into the water, and Tory tried to let the whir of the motor drown out all the voices in her head. The boat settled gently, rocking with the tide, and he shut the motor off. The screech of a laughing gull broke the momentary silence, and she realized she had to try again.

"Adam, I'm sure you have other things you need

to do. I can get someone else to run me out to Angel Isle. Or we can go another time."

His brows lowered in annoyance. "If you're going, I'm taking you," he said shortly. "Hop in."

That seemed to be that. She stepped onto the catamaran's seat, then the deck, trying to keep her stomach from misbehaving at the rocking movement. She hadn't been on a boat since her childhood, and she didn't want to disgrace herself in front of Adam. Although it hardly seemed likely he could regard her as more of a nuisance than he already did.

"Daddy, Daddy!" Jenny's voice, accompanied by the sound of running feet, stopped his hand as he reached toward the starter. The child raced toward them along the tabby path from the house, Miz Becky behind her. "Stop. I want to go."

Adam leaned on the windscreen, watching his daughter as she reached the dock. "Jenny, I've already told you that you can't go this time. Ms. Tory and I have work to do."

Jenny grabbed the dock railing, teetering as if about to jump into the boat. "Dad-dy!" It was a plaintive wail. "Take me."

"Jenny." His tone was a gentle warning. "We've had this conversation before."

Her bottom lip came out. "I don't want you to go with Miz Tory. You went with her last night."

He frowned. "What are you talking about? We all went to the picnic."

Jenny's lips trembled. "You went for a walk with

her all by yourselves. And my mama was lots prettier than she is."

The child's words seemed to hit Tory right in the heart. Surely Jenny didn't think...

She backed away from the rest of that thought. Her cheeks had to be scarlet, and all she wanted to do was climb right out of that boat and disappear.

But Adam pinned her in place with a single glance. He swung onto the dock, and the power of his push set the boat rocking. He squatted to bring his face level with his daughter's.

"Jenny, there is never a good reason to make a guest in our house feel uncomfortable. I'm embarrassed by your behavior."

His voice was firm, sounding a note of regret and disappointment. He took both the child's hands in his, the touch loving.

"I know my girl doesn't like to behave that way, does she?"

"No, Daddy." Jenny's voice dropped to a whisper. "I'm sorry."

He put his arm around her. "It's Miz Tory who deserves your apology, sugar."

Jenny looked at her, blinking back tears. "I'm sorry, Miz Tory."

She wanted to protest, wanted to explain that Jenny was wrong, that her daddy wasn't interested in Tory in any way that required a comparison with the child's mother. But she couldn't.

"It's all right, Jenny," she said softly, and blinked back a tear.

Adam nodded toward Miz Becky, who waited at the end of the dock. "Go on back to the house with Miz Becky, now. We'll go out in the boat together another day."

Jenny threw her arms around his neck in a throttling hug. Then she ran to the waiting housekeeper.

So that was what a father was like. Tory turned away so Adam couldn't see her tears as he dropped into the boat. That was how a real father handled his child when she disappointed him—with love, with fairness, without blame. A sudden longing for something she'd never had filled her, so intense it almost made her gasp.

By the time she'd gained control of her emotions, Adam had started the motor and begun easing the boat away from the dock.

"Adam—"

He shook his head. "Leave it, Tory."

She had no choice but to obey as he turned the boat seaward. His hands were tight on the wheel as he eased through the no-wake zone near the docks. Once clear of the area, he accelerated.

The speed pressed Tory back on the bench, and the motor's roar drowned anything she might have found to say. Adam was taking his frustration and embarrassment out in typical male fashion—speed and noise.

She settled a little more comfortably on the bench seat. She might as well enjoy the ride. Adam probably wouldn't slow down until he'd gotten the emotions out of his system.

The boat rocketed around the curve of the island, passing the long, low yacht club with its cluster of white boats at the dock. Her gaze traced the steps she'd gone up with such anticipation the night she'd met Adam. There'd been nothing but dread filling her when she'd run down them hours later.

She shook her head, lifting her face to the wind that whipped her hair into tangles. Let the ocean breeze blow the ugly thoughts away. She couldn't go back and change the past. She could only try to make amends by fulfilling her promise.

The boat bounced over waves as Adam took the turn into the sound between Caldwell Island and the fringe of barrier islands that protected it from the open ocean. He eased back on the throttle. The roar of the motor softened to a purr, and Tory's stomach seemed to catch up with the rest of her.

"Dolphin Sound," he said, and he pointed to the waves. "And there are the dolphins it's named for."

She leaned forward, seeing nothing but the shimmer of sun on water at first. Then a silver shape lunged into the sunlight only feet from the boat. The dolphin balanced on its tail, seeming to smile at her. "He's beautiful." She grabbed her sketch pad.

"Yes." He let the boat rock gently. The dolphin slipped beneath the waves, then surfaced farther away. "I never tire of watching them."

"You couldn't." The graceful shape, water sheeting from its back, formed under her pencil. "I can't do it justice."

Adam left the wheel, coming to look at the sketch.

He braced one hand on the seat back behind her, his arm brushing her shoulder and sending waves of warmth through her. He was wearing shorts and a T-shirt, and his tanned strength stole her breath.

"I think you've captured the essence, the way you did with Jenny on the swing. You're very talented, Tory."

She shook her head, reminded of the wooden dolphin and all it meant. Had its carver been satisfied he'd captured that grace and power in his work? He must have been, if he'd been willing to give his creation to the church.

She glanced at Adam, wanting to say something about the dolphin carving. He was frowning at the sketch pad.

"What is it? Did I get it wrong?"

"You got it right." He shook his head. "I was thinking about Jenny. I'm sorry about the way she behaved. She obviously thought…"

She could understand why he didn't want to finish that sentence. "She misunderstood what was happening, that's all."

"I'll talk to her. Make her see that we don't have that kind of relationship."

And what about the night you kissed me, Adam? What did that mean?

Nothing, obviously.

"I think that would be a good idea," she said carefully. "She needs to understand the situation between us so she won't be upset when we need to spend time together."

He straightened, standing between her and the sun. "She shouldn't be upset in any event. Just because I haven't dated in the last four years doesn't mean I won't sometime."

She wanted to say she understood how Jenny felt. Wanted to say she'd been there. But if she started talking about her reactions to her father's death and her mother's remarriage, where would it end? She might give away more of herself than she'd bargained for.

"You'll make her understand," she said finally. "You're a good father."

Adam looked at her for a long moment, his gaze probing. Then he managed a half smile. "I try."

He turned to the wheel and started toward the small island across the sound. The moment she could have opened up to him was gone.

The dolphins were gone, too. A sense of loss touched her as she watched them move toward open ocean. They seemed—she struggled to formulate the thought. Somehow the dolphins symbolized this place and these people, living off the sea, moving in tune with the tides. The carved dolphin had been a fitting symbol of God's providence for the people of the island.

The small island on the horizon grew as they approached it, changing from a smudge against the sky to a mosaic of green and gold.

"Angel Isle." Adam slowed the boat as they approached a tangle of lush green undergrowth jutting into the water. He rounded it. Beyond the junglelike growth stretched a crescent of sandy beach backed by loblolly pines, live oaks and crepe myrtle, untouched and unspoiled.

Tory's breath caught at the sight. "It looks like Eden."

He cast her an approving glance. "I've always thought so." He cut the motor, and the catamaran bumped gently against a mossy dock. "Angel Isle has belonged to the family for generations."

"You're lucky."

"We are." Some emotion shadowed his face briefly. Was he thinking that Angel Isle hadn't been lucky for the Caldwell brothers one particular night? Whatever it was, he seemed to shake the feeling off as he tossed a rope around the dock's post.

"Come on." He climbed out with that deceptively easy grace and reached down to help her. "Let's have a look at the site of the infamous party."

Her determination to come here suddenly seemed as foolish as looking at the rental house. "There won't be anything to see after forty years."

"No, I suppose not." He led the way off the dock and started up a path through the undergrowth. "Still, not much has changed. You'll be able to see what it was like." He paused, nodding toward the dock. "That hasn't changed. Unless they came in something small enough to pull onto the beach, they tied up there."

She tried to visualize it. Young people—kids, really—scrambling out of their boats with towels, blankets, hampers, intent on nothing more than a good time. Probably for her mother the excursion had been even more exciting because she'd known her father wouldn't approve.

"Does your family come here often?" Did his father come back? That was what she really wanted to ask, but she couldn't quite.

Adam shrugged, and she suspected he knew what was in her mind. "In the olden days, the Caldwell clan summered here. Before air-conditioning everyone headed for the outer islands if they could."

Her father's family had summered on Tybee Island, off Savannah. Those must have been happy times, but she could barely remember.

Adam brushed a gnat away from her face. "Let's go inside before you get bitten." He led the way around a last clump of crepe myrtle. "Here's the cottage."

She stopped next to him. It wasn't a cottage at all, not that she'd expected it to be. The long, two-story building, its gray shingles merging into the gray-green background of trees and Spanish moss, stretched out a welcoming porch to them.

"I guess from what Clayton said the house was here when they had the party."

Adam nodded. "It's sat in that spot since the mid-1800s. Added onto and propped up now and then, but otherwise just the same. A summer haven for all the Caldwells. Uncle Clayton actually owns the island, but we all use it."

Her imagination peopled the porch with a young version of her mother, the golden girl, and the two boys who'd loved her.

"Your uncle said Emily was in the kitchen. If

that's where she and your father talked, that must be where the dolphin was at the time."

"Let's have a look." The words sounded casual, but she could feel the tension in his hand as he touched her elbow to lead her up the steps. He unlocked the door and ushered her inside.

"You're welcome to look around the kitchen all you want." He moved away from her quickly to throw open a shutter. "But there have been a few thousand meals cooked in there, probably, since that night. You won't find anything."

A shaft of sunlight pierced the window, touching the wide plank floor, the hooked rug, the massive fireplace. Chintz-covered couches sat in front of crowded bookcases. The warm, welcoming room seemed to say that people had been happy here, despite the disturbing events of one particular night.

"Adam—" What could she say? That she had to see for herself? He must already know that.

The swinging door probably led to the kitchen. She pushed through it and found herself in a square, open room. The counters were topped with linoleum, faded from years of scrubbing. White wooden cupboards, glass-fronted, showed off a mismatched assortment of enough dishes to feed an army. Probably every time someone in the family bought something new, the old set went to the cottage.

"I'm afraid there's no place here where something could be hidden." Adam leaned against the door frame, his easy smile saying he'd gotten his momentary irritation under control.

She flipped open a bottom cupboard door at random to display neatly arranged pots and pans. The Caldwells kept a clean cottage, regardless of how much or how little time they spent here.

"I guess you're right. If it had been here, someone would have found it by now." She glanced at him, raising an eyebrow. "You're sure there are no secret passages or hidden cupboards?"

His face relaxed. "We spent some time looking for one on rainy days when we were kids, believe me. We were inspired by all those Hardy Boys and Nancy Drew mysteries on the shelves. Never found a thing."

"What's back here?" She pushed open the door on the other side of the kitchen to reveal a long room whose walls of windows seemed to invite the outdoors in.

"Game room, I guess you'd call it." Adam came to stand behind her, nodding to the table-tennis outfit and card tables. "I don't think this addition had been finished that summer, though. Maybe that's what Clayton meant when he talked about the lumber pile." Pain flickered in his eyes, and he seemed to force it away. "The kids are in and out of the closets all the time for games and toys, anyway."

"What was here before?"

"Nothing, as far as I know." He frowned. "I'm sorry, Tory. Judging from what Clayton said, most of the party must have centered outside. I'm afraid there's nothing to find here. Except—"

"Except what?"

He shrugged, still frowning. "I guess I just look

at the place with different eyes after hearing about that night."

"I can see how that would be." She hesitated, wondering if she could say anything that would make him feel better about what they'd learned. "I'm sorry. About what your uncle said last night, I mean. I know it wasn't an easy thing to take."

"Easy? No." His lips tightened. "I've always known what my father's like, though. I love him, but I know he doesn't have the..." He shook his head as if he had to struggle to go on. "He doesn't have the same standards as the rest of the Caldwell clan."

"As you do," she said softly, knowing that was true. Adam was an honorable man all the way through.

He shrugged. "Funny, isn't it? My brother dealt with his feelings by rebelling. Before he left for college, our family life seemed to be one long shouting match for a while."

"You don't handle things that way."

"Nothing so dramatic for me. I was the buffer between Matt and our father. Between Dad and the rest of the family, for that matter."

She was almost afraid to breathe, afraid to disrupt the flow of his words.

"You still are, aren't you?" she said softly.

The lines around his eyes deepened. "Someone has to be."

"I guess so." Pain laced her words. "Or else the family just blows apart."

Adam put his hand lightly on her shoulder, his

intent gaze focusing on her as if he looked into her heart and saw the hurt there. "That sounds like personal experience speaking."

She wanted to back away, make some excuse, change the subject. But he'd opened up to her, and that couldn't have been easy for him. She knew more about the skeletons in Adam's family closet than anyone else did. It wasn't fair to shut him out of hers.

"My father's family never approved of my mother. After his death, they wanted her to let them raise me." She tried to swallow the lump in her throat. "When she wouldn't, they washed their hands of us."

He blinked. "They must have kept in touch with you even if they didn't like Emily."

"Not a word. Not even a card on my birthday." She shrugged, trying to pass it off casually, as if it didn't still hurt. "I guess they figured losing me was a small price to pay for getting rid of her."

His grip on her shoulder tightened. "There may have been things at work you didn't understand as a child."

"You think I haven't thought of that?" The anger flared suddenly, startling her. "I wasn't a child when I graduated from high school. My grandmother came to see me. She made me an offer. They'd pay my university expenses and bring me into Savannah society. All I had to do was promise to stay away from my mother."

He didn't respond for a long moment. Was he embarrassed? She never should have said anything.

"She was stupid," he said finally.

Surprise brought her gaze up to meet his. "Why do you say that?"

He touched her cheek, the sensation featherlight but filled with a power that stole her breath away. "If she'd known anything about you, she'd have known what your response would be. She'd have known that someone who'd agree to her bargain wasn't worth anything."

"She didn't see it that way." Tory could still see her formidable grandmother, eyes cold as a glacier when she'd announced her terms. "Funny. I guess I knew even then that I wasn't going to be able to save my mother from herself. But I sure wasn't going to abandon her for the sake of that woman's money and position."

Love with strings attached, that was what her grandmother offered. There were always strings attached. She might not have known a lot about people then, but she'd known she wouldn't settle for that.

"I'm sorry." His palm flattened against her cheek, cradling it. "I shouldn't have brought it up. I didn't mean to bring back hurtful memories."

She tried to smile, but the pressure of his skin against hers seemed to have paralyzed the muscles. "We seem destined to do that to each other."

He shook his head. "We shouldn't." He barely breathed the words as he leaned closer.

He was going to kiss her. She should move, back away, say something. This wasn't a good idea. But she couldn't move. No matter how foolish it was, she wanted to be in his arms.

He was going to kiss her. Adam had a brief, rational instant when he knew this was a mistake. Then common sense was swamped by the need to hold her in his arms. He tilted her face up. Her eyes were dark with conflict, but she didn't pull away.

He drew her closer and covered her lips with his. Her mouth was warm and sweet and willing, and the sensation filled him with longing and need. He felt her hands slip up his back to his shoulders, holding him more fully. He was dizzy with wanting her, but he knew, bone deep, that it was more than that. He'd never felt such a need to protect, to comfort, to love.

The thought set alarm bells clanging in whatever was left of his mind. This was a mistake, a big one. He couldn't let himself think about loving any woman. He'd been there, he'd done that and he'd paid the price. And even if he could love again, it wouldn't be Tory. Too much complicated history stood between them.

He drew back slowly, reluctantly. Tory's eyes were dazed, and she braced her hands against his forearms as if he were her anchor.

He should say he was sorry, but he wasn't. Even if there could never be anything between them, he wasn't sorry he'd kissed her once.

Twice, a little voice in his brain reminded him. Three times, if you count the night you kissed Cinderella at the yacht club dance.

All right, she had an effect on him. He'd recognized that from the start, hadn't he?

Still the emotion had blindsided him as much as it had her. He brushed a strand of dark hair from her cheek. "I didn't see that coming."

She blinked, and her eyes no longer seemed dazzled. "No, I... It's all right." She tried to smile, seemed to gather her armor against rejection.

He couldn't let her think— "Tory, it's not you. I just can't get involved." He couldn't explain to her what he didn't understand himself.

"I know." Her voice was soft. "You're not ready for anyone else. You're still in love with Lila."

Her innocent words struck him like a blow. The truth beat at his brain as if demanding to be let out.

It had been one thing to let Tory believe a lie when she'd walked into his life. He'd been acting purely out of self-preservation. But now—now that he knew her, now that she'd opened up her own painful secrets to him—now it wasn't right.

"I have to tell you something," he said abruptly before he could talk himself out of it. "About my wife."

She blinked again. Whatever she'd been expecting to hear, it wasn't that. "What about her?" She took a step back and bumped into the door frame.

"You think I oppose this memorial window because of grief." He forced the words out. *You think that's why I can't let myself care for you.*

"I know." Pain darkened her eyes. "I'm sorry."

His jaw clenched. "It's not grief. I don't want a window to memorialize a lie." The words he'd held back demanded to be said. "Lila was leaving us when she died. She was leaving Jenny and me to go with another man."

Tory stared at him, eyes wide with shock. "But everyone I've spoken with thinks—"

"Everyone thinks what I've let them think. Everyone thinks Lila and I were madly in love. Just like I did."

The harsh words tasted of bitterness. He walked away from her because he couldn't be still, ending up with his hands braced against the worn kitchen counter.

It was silent in the old house, so silent he could hear the trill of a mockingbird in the distance. Then Tory's footsteps crossed the floor behind him. Stopped.

"Why didn't you tell anyone the truth?" She sounded as if she struggled to understand. "Isn't it hard to pretend?"

"Hard? I'll tell you what would be hard." He swung to face her. "Hard would be letting my daughter know her mother was willing to give her up so she could run off with another man."

"Jenny." He heard her breath catch on the name.

"Jenny," he repeated. "She can't know that, ever. If that means I have to let all of Caldwell Cove grieve with the heartbroken widower, that's what I'll do."

Tory lifted one hand as if she wanted to touch him, comfort him. Then she let it drop. Maybe she realized how futile that effort would be. Nothing could comfort this. "Lila's mother doesn't know, does she?"

"I don't think so. If she did, I don't think she'd want to have the memorial here in Caldwell Cove."

"I'm sorry." She sounded helpless. "I understand. But what can we do about it?"

"I don't know." For the last four years he'd known what he had to do and he'd gone on putting one foot in front of the other. Now, suddenly, because of Tory, he didn't know.

"I don't know," he said again. "I just know I can't walk into church every Sunday and look at a window memorializing a lie. I can't do it, Tory."

Chapter Ten

"This hurts too much." Tory said the words aloud
in the empty sanctuary. They seemed to linger under
the arched wooden ceiling, almost as visible as the
dust motes in a shaft of jewel-toned sunlight through
the stained glass. "It's not fair."

When had love ever been fair? As soon as she
thought the word, she wanted to cancel it. She
didn't love Adam. And he certainly didn't have
those feelings for her. He'd proved that when he'd
backed away from her after those moments at the
cottage on Saturday. He'd been distant ever since,
even yesterday when he sat next to her for the
Sunday service.

She leaned against the scaffolding, trying to get
a handle on the hurt that felt as if a whale lay on her
chest. She put her hand on the spot, willing it to go
away. That didn't work.

On the window above her, Jesus walked across the

waves of a storm-tossed sea. From the water, Peter reached out to him in an agony of fear.

That was how she felt. Lost and afraid.

"This isn't going to work, don't You see that?" She said the words, then realized that for once in her life, her prayer wasn't filled with antagonism. "It just isn't going to work. I can't help him."

She shut her eyes. The light from the window dazzled on the blackness of her closed eyelids. If she gave up the window project—

That was what Adam wanted her to do. He hadn't asked it directly even when he'd told her the truth about Lila. But she'd known.

She opened her eyes to look at the pictured face again. The image projected calm and peace even in the midst of the storm.

"Should I give it up?" She asked the question simply, without bargaining. "Should I?"

If she did, would that help Adam? She tried to look at it without letting thoughts of her business, her success or failure, intervene. Would giving up the project help Adam?

One thing had become crystal clear that day at the cottage. Adam carried a heavy load of bitterness against his late wife. He didn't want to be reminded of those feelings every time he walked into the sanctuary that had been his place of worship all his life.

Understandable. But how could either of them get out of fulfilling this commitment?

"I just don't know what to do." That was honest, at least.

"About the new window? Or about that grandson of mine?"

The question startled Tory away from the scaffolding. She spun to face the woman who stood inside the door to the Sunday school rooms.

"Mrs. Caldwell." She had to catch her breath. "I didn't realize anyone was here."

The elderly woman came closer. "Thought you were going to call me Gran. And there's always Someone here, child. You know that."

Tory felt the wave of warmth in her cheeks. "I was talking to myself."

"You were talking to the Lord," Adam's grandmother corrected. "Nothing wrong with that. I do it myself, all the time."

It was impossible to go on feeling embarrassed when the woman looked at her with such understanding. "I'm afraid mostly I argue with Him."

"Nothing wrong with that, either. I've done my share of arguing over the years, especially over the dolphin. Is that what's troubling you?"

Tory rubbed her forehead, trying to ignore the stinging in her eyes. "I wanted to find it for my mother's sake. I thought if I could do that one last thing for her…" She trailed off. She couldn't talk about the weight she felt for Adam, for her mother's memory.

"I know." The elderly woman patted her hand. "We all have regrets, child. Things we wish we'd done differently, things we want to make up. But maybe, however much we want it, we're not meant to find the dolphin now."

"Then what good has all this been?" The question burst out. "Why did I come here?"

"We can't always know what God has in mind. Don't you lose faith in what He has for you." She gripped Tory's hand tightly, her own firm and strong. Suddenly, surprisingly, she leaned forward and kissed Tory's cheek. Without saying another word, she turned and went out.

Tory sank down in the nearest pew. *Were You speaking to me through Adam's grandmother, Lord? Were You?*

She leaned forward to grasp the pew in front of her and closed her eyes. In the stillness, she listened.

Nothing about the situation with Tory had gone as he'd expected. Adam frowned at the invoices scattered over his desk. He should be working, and instead he kept obsessing about Tory.

After baring his soul to her at the cottage on Saturday, all he'd wanted to do was withdraw. He couldn't stand seeing the pity in her eyes. He'd managed to avoid being alone with her. By Monday night, ashamed of his behavior, he'd looked for her, hoping to get things back to normal between them.

But Tory had closeted herself in the workroom immediately after dinner, making it clear she didn't want to be disturbed. Because she had work to do or because she just plain didn't want to see him? He didn't know the answer to that.

He tossed his pen onto the blotter and swiveled his chair, looking out the window at the boatyard, busy with new orders now that the summer rush of repairs had passed. Beyond the yard, October sunlight sparkled on the water. The sight reminded him that he was lucky to be doing work he loved in the place where he belonged. Today it seemed to have lost its power to soothe him.

What was he going to do about Tory?

One thing he wouldn't do was kiss her again, no matter how much he wanted to see the loneliness disappear from her eyes. No matter how much he wanted the comfort of holding her in his arms.

He wouldn't go down that road again. He'd have to handle doing without a relationship with her.

If Tory pursued the memorial window, he'd have to handle that, too. He rubbed the back of his neck, trying to erase the tension that sat there.

Maybe he'd known all along he didn't stand a chance of stopping this memorial without creating still more questions about Lila. The best he could hope for was that Tory would create some standard biblical portrayal. He could try to look at that on its own merits without thinking of Lila at all.

Yeah, right.

The door opened behind him, and he spoke without turning around. "Tina, whatever it is, can it wait?"

"It's not your secretary." The door closed. "It's me."

He spun the chair around, trying to beat down the wave of pleasure he felt every time he looked at Tory.

"Hey. What brings you here?" And how could he gracefully tell her that maybe they shouldn't be alone together?

"I need to talk with you." She slipped the strap of her leather portfolio from her shoulder. "Do you have a few minutes?"

He made a point of glancing at his watch. "Actually, not many. Jenny's being dropped off here after school. I promised she could go out on the trial run of a new boat."

"This won't take long." Tory seemed immune to his hint. She was dressed a little more formally than usual, wearing pressed khakis instead of jeans and a scarlet sweater that made her hair look darker in contrast. He couldn't deny that he liked having her in his office even if it was a bad idea.

She propped the portfolio on the visitor's chair opposite his desk and fumbled with the catch. "I have something to show you."

Her tension leaped the few feet between them to needle him, and he guessed why she was there before she could speak. The design for the memorial window, it had to be that. His fists clenched in spite of his effort to stay detached.

Tory pulled out a large pad. "I've come up with a design."

He took a breath. Okay, he had to do this. He held out his hand. "Let me see."

She gave him the pad, then clasped both hands in front of her like a child waiting for approval. He'd just—

Tory's design swam in front of his eyes. There was the border of beach morning glories, the space at the bottom for the inevitable inscription.

But Tory hadn't put a scriptural scene in the center. Instead, a silver dolphin leaped from a glass sea.

A vise clamped his throat, shutting off speech. The drawing was beautiful—a perfect depiction of the Caldwell dolphin. And Tory proposed putting that in a window dedicated to the woman who'd betrayed him.

He dropped the drawing as if it burned his fingers. "No." He glared at her. "No."

Her throat moved as she swallowed, but her gaze didn't falter. "I know what you're thinking. But hear me out first."

"Tory—" He shot to his feet, unable to sit still any longer. "What are you thinking? After what I told you, you ought to know I can't live with this."

"It's because of what you told me." She fired the words at him, leaning forward, her face intent and passionate. "Don't you understand? Any design I came up with would hurt you, I knew that. But if there's going to be a window, isn't it better to make it something that honors your family?"

He planted both fists on the desk. "Is this about my family or yours?"

Tory flushed as if he'd scored against her, but she stood her ground. "It's both. You told me all along we wouldn't find the dolphin. I guess you were right. There's no place left to look." She spread her hands, palms out, empty. "But this is something I can do to make up for whatever part my mother played in its loss. I thought it might make your family happy. Wouldn't it?"

"Maybe." Gran would be pleased, certainly. She'd have something to point to as a symbol of the Caldwell heritage. "But I'd still have to look at that inscription." His jaw was so tight it felt ready to shatter. "I'd still have to think about how Lila betrayed everything that heritage stands for."

She took a step forward so only the width of the desk separated them. Her hands went out pleadingly. "Adam, think about this instead. Lila gave you Jenny. Whatever wrong she did in the end, she gave you that beautiful, perfect child to carry on your name. Doesn't that make her part of the Caldwell heritage, too?"

He wanted to say no. He wanted to forget this whole thing and return to the days before he met Tory, back to keeping his secret and carrying his burden. It had been painful, but easier.

He turned away from the drawing, rubbing his neck again. The tension had taken up permanent residence.

"I don't know," he said finally. "I just don't know." He forced himself to meet her gaze. "Can I think about this?"

"Of course."

Running feet sounded in the outer office. "That'll be Jenny." He reached for the drawing, but Tory beat him to it, slipping it into the portfolio.

"It's all right." She gave him that rare, brilliant smile. "We'll talk about it later."

"Thank you." His voice roughened on the words, and he took a deep breath, trying to regain his composure. No emotional involvement, remember? Unfortunately strong feelings, whether they were negative or positive, seemed built into every encounter he had with Tory.

A wave of relief swept over Tory. Adam hadn't rejected her idea out of hand. He'd listened to her arguments in favor of the memorial.

If only he could accept it. The idea had felt so right when she'd sat in the quiet sanctuary with his grandmother's words ringing in her ears.

Please. That would be a step toward healing for him, wouldn't it? I know creating this window would help to heal me, too.

The door burst open, and Jenny danced through, clearly excited. She saw Tory, and Tory braced herself for a repeat of the scene on the dock.

But the little girl's smile didn't falter. "Hey, Miz Tory. We're going out in the new boat my daddy made. Did you know that?"

"I heard something about it." Obviously, Adam's talk with his little daughter had borne fruit. She'd better not push her luck, though. She picked up the portfolio. "I should be getting back to work."

A look flashed between Jenny and Adam, a look of understanding without the need for words between father and daughter.

"You don't have to go yet, do you, Miz Tory? Can't you come out on the boat with us?"

The longing to do just that startled Tory with its strength. Frightened her, too, just a little. She had no future with these people, and she shouldn't create bonds that were bound to break.

"Please," Jenny wheedled. "I want you to come, honest."

"We both do." Adam's smile dissipated the lines of strain around his eyes. It went right to her heart and lodged there. "Please."

She shouldn't, should she? But Adam's asking seemed a peace offering. Besides, she wanted to.

"If you're sure I won't be in the way."

"Not at all." Adam ruffled his daughter's light brown curls. "Let's go, ladies. The *Terrapin* is ready for her maiden voyage."

"Yes!" Jenny clapped once, then raced ahead of them. They were going for a boat ride.

Walking beside Adam as they left the office, Tory tried to find some nice, neutral topic of conversation that would steer clear of anything painful.

"Jenny seems to know her way around."

He pulled the door shut behind them. "She's had the run of the boatyard since she was four. After Lila died, I wanted her with me as much as possible, so I brought her down often."

She'd managed to stumble into the wrong subject again. Still, Adam had said Lila's name with an ease she hadn't heard from him before. She'd like to interpret that as a good sign.

"So you're training the next generation to take over the family business." She fell into step with him as they went down the passageway to the docks.

He looked startled at that. "I never thought of it that way. Whatever Jenny wants to do is fine with me. I don't believe in putting pressure on kids to be what parents want."

That struck her in the heart. "More parents should feel that way."

Adam took her arm as they walked through a tangle of tools and cables. "I feel like I'm playing it by ear most of the time."

"Then you must have perfect pitch. Jenny's a delightful child."

His eyes crinkled. "You can't say anything a father wants to hear more."

They stepped into the sunlight, and he gestured to the docks ahead of them, lining the wharf in front of a cavernous building. "We do a lot of storage and repair work here. But creating a boat from design to launch—that's the best part."

Jenny had stopped on one of the docks, chattering excitedly to an elderly man who leaned on the rail of what appeared to be— Tory blinked.

"Is that a pirate ship?"

Jenny heard the question and swung toward her, face animated. "It's our very own pirate ship, the *Jolly Roger.* This is Thomas." She gestured to the man on the deck. "He's helping us get it ready for Pirate Days. I'm going to wear a patch over my eye and sail it all the way around the island."

"The pirate ship, not the patch," Adam clarified, a note of laughter in his voice. "And I think she might have a little help with the sailing part."

Tory looked at the masts towering above them. "I'd hope so. You're really going to sail this?"

Adam grinned. "Sounds a little silly, I guess."

The gray-haired workman shook his head. "Nothin' silly about remembering." He grinned widely. "Or havin' a good excuse for a shindig after all the summer folk are gone."

"You need any help getting her ready?" Adam rested a hand on the black wooden hull. "I could spare a few hours this week."

"That'd be a help." Thomas nodded toward Tory. "We surely do want everything up to snuff if we have a guest on board."

"I'm not…"

"But Miz Tory, you have to come." Jenny grabbed her hand, jumping excitedly on one foot. "It's so much fun to play pirates."

"Give Miz Tory time to think about it," Adam said, detaching her. "Right now we've got a boat to launch, remember?"

"The *Terrapin*!" Jenny shouted, and raced down the dock.

Adam lifted a hand to Thomas as they followed. "Enthusiastic little thing, isn't she? Still, I'm pretty proud of it myself."

They passed the bulk of the pirate ship and caught up with Jenny, teetering on the edge of the dock next to a gleaming white boat. Black trim and shiny fittings completed the image of a craft fresh from the builder's hands.

Tory stopped, admiring the sleek lines. "It's beautiful. You actually built it?"

Adam climbed aboard, swung Jenny onto the deck and held out his hand to Tory. "Planed every board. Nothing mass-produced comes out of the Caldwell Boatyard. You want a custom-designed boat, that's what you get."

She took his hand, preparing to step on board, but he caught her by the waist and swung her on as he had Jenny. She stumbled, catching her breath and trying to stop the racing of her heart.

"You must be very proud of it." She hoped her voice sounded normal.

"We all are."

He nodded to the men who gathered on the dock. Two of them unfastened the lines, tossing them on board, and Jenny raced to coil them as if she'd been doing it all her life.

"Start her up, captain." Thomas grinned, and Tory couldn't mistake the look of pride and respect on his face—in fact, on all their faces.

Adam started the motor, and the *Terrapin* edged away from the dock. The men clapped, grinning. An odd shiver went down Tory's spine. Adam must feel the way she did when she'd completed a window. But he had people cheering for him, sharing his satisfaction.

She settled onto the seat behind him as he turned the new boat into the channel. "You're really an artisan, aren't you?"

Jenny wiggled onto the seat next to her. "What's an artisan?"

"Someone like me, who makes things with their hands. I make windows, and your daddy makes boats."

Jenny tipped her head to one side, considering. "I

think I'd like to be an artisan, too. But I don't know what I want to make."

Adam flashed Tory an amused glance. "You have plenty of time to decide that, sugar."

They moved into the waterway, the boatyard and its buildings growing smaller behind them. Sunlight glittered on the water and turned the marshes to gold. The breeze lifted Tory's hair, the sun warmed her skin, and Jenny pressed against her arm in unconscious acceptance. The tension she'd felt since she'd walked into Adam's office slid away, like the boat slipping its moorings.

Adam glanced at her as if measuring her satisfaction. "Feels good, doesn't it?"

"I can understand why you'd never want to live anywhere else." She tipped her head back, enjoying the sunlight on her face. "It's perfect."

"Look, Miz Tory." Jenny leaned across her, pointing to a buoy in the channel. "That's an osprey's nest."

"You're quite the naturalist, aren't you?" Jenny really was an islander born and bred.

"And a sailor." Adam leaned back and reached out a long arm for his daughter. "Come on up here and help me steer her, sugar."

"Can I, Daddy?" Jenny scampered to him, and he wedged her onto the seat next to him.

"Sure you can. You're my first mate." His large hands covered his daughter's small ones on the wheel. "Keep her between the channel markers."

There was a lump in Tory's throat the size of a

baseball. The relationship between Jenny and her father was a beautiful thing to see. Adam might not realize it, but if Jenny ever did find out the truth about her mother, he'd already given her enough love and acceptance to deal with it. Jenny would never doubt that she was loved unconditionally, no strings attached.

They rounded the end of the island and made the turn into the sound. Jenny wiggled around to look in her father's face.

"We should let Miz Tory have a turn. She didn't get to steer yet."

Adam dropped a kiss on her curls. "That's a nice idea, sugar."

"I can't," Tory said hurriedly, sure she didn't want the fate of what had to be an expensive boat in her hands. "I don't know how, and there's not room for both of us on that seat."

But Jenny had already slid out, and Adam stood, hand still on the wheel, freeing the seat.

"You just slip in here," he said. He gave her a reassuring smile. "Don't worry. I'll stay right behind you."

"Promise you won't let go of the wheel," she bargained, sliding reluctantly into the seat and tilting her head to see his face.

"I promise." He smiled, so close it took her breath away.

"I...I still don't think this is a good idea." Probably because she couldn't think straight with him so near.

"Sure it is." He bent down so his face was next to hers, barely an inch away. His arms brushed against hers as he held the wheel. "Look right through the windscreen as you steer. It's like driving a car."

"I don't risk beaching a car."

He tapped a gauge on the dash. "That shows you the bottom depth. As long as you keep her between the buoys, we're safe."

"And if I don't?" His nearness was doing odd things to her heart, and it took an effort to sound natural.

Adam turned to look at her, and she felt his breath warm against her cheek. "If you beach her, we'll wait for the tide to come in and float us off." His voice grew husky, as if he thought about being stranded. Together.

Her heart was beating so loudly the noise drowned everything else out. If only... The longing in her heart took form. If only she really could belong here. With him.

"I love being on the boat, don't you, Miz Tory?" Jenny sounded as if she thought she'd been out of the conversation long enough. "Isn't it just the best thing?"

"Yes." Tory's gaze tangled with Adam's, and she couldn't see anything beyond the emotion in his eyes. "It's the best thing."

"My mommy never liked it," Jenny went on. "That's funny, isn't it?"

Adam stiffened, his hand tightening over hers so hard it hurt. But it didn't hurt as much as seeing the pleasure fade from his eyes or recognizing the truth in her heart.

Adam was still all knotted up inside over his wife's betrayal. And as long as he was, he remained tied to Lila just as surely as if she were still alive and here next to them.

Until Adam found a way to forgive the past, he'd never be free to give his heart to anyone else.

Chapter Eleven

She'd been waiting since the day before for Adam to give her his answer. She was still waiting.

Tory curled up on the overstuffed sofa in the downstairs sitting room after dinner Wednesday night. She'd discovered the small room almost by accident—it was tucked behind the formal living room. Tory found its faded chintzes and soft colors soothing in comparison to the elegance of the rest of Twin Oaks. The jewel colors of the worn Oriental carpet glowed in the lamplight.

The room didn't seem to be exuding its usual peace at the moment. She frowned at the sketch pad in her lap, reluctant to open it. She'd shown the design to Adam the day before. He'd promised to consider it and give her his answer. But the hours ticked away, and he hadn't responded. Maybe he never would.

She saw again the bleakness in his face when

Jenny had innocently mentioned her mother. Adam's bitterness bound him to his late wife even more firmly than grief. How could Tory hope he'd agree to any design? How could she hope he'd be able to feel something for her?

I'm not hoping that. I'm not. But a small voice in her heart whispered that she was.

She pressed her hand against her chest as if to silence that voice. She wouldn't think about it. She'd think about the design she'd completed, about the pleasure she'd taken in choosing the glass, about the intensive labor involved in creating the life-size pattern she'd work from on the window.

All that work was worthwhile if Adam would only agree. She had to talk with him about the memorial, whether he wanted to or not.

And there was another subject on which they had to talk—one where she was the reluctant party. Should she show him? Her fingers clenched the frayed old notebook that lay under her sketch pad.

Should I, Lord? Is this the right thing to do?

She heard Adam's step in the hall, and her breath caught. "Adam?" His name was out before she thought it through.

Maybe that was for the best. God might be pushing her into this decision.

"Tory. You're so quiet I didn't realize you were back here." He lingered in the doorway, bracing one hand against the frame. He'd rolled up the sleeves of the dress shirt he'd worn at dinner, and his hair was mussed as if he'd been roughhousing with his daughter.

"Is Jenny all tucked in?"

Adam's face softened as it always did at his daughter's name. "She had to have three bedtime stories before she'd settle tonight. She's so excited about the Pirate Days celebration that she's probably dreaming about it right now."

"I know you've been busy with preparations." *Is that your excuse for not getting back to me?* "Do you have a couple of minutes? I'd like to talk with you."

She felt his tension from across the room. He undoubtedly thought she wanted to talk about the window, and he seemed to be searching for any excuse. And she did mean to, of course, but something else came first.

"I have some work—" It didn't sound convincing.

"This will only take a moment." The tattered notebook felt warm under her fingers, and she knew she'd made the decision. "I'd like to show you this."

He shrugged, looking harassed, then crossed the room to sit beside her on the sofa. Tory swung her feet to the floor and sat up straight, putting a few inches between them. It didn't help. She was still far too aware of his nearness.

"More sketches?" There was an edge to his words that didn't bode well for her project.

"In a way." She tried to smile and couldn't. "But not mine this time."

That caught his attention. He lifted his eyebrows. "Whose?"

She slipped the notebook from under her sketch pad. "My mother's." She took a breath, willing herself not to let her emotions show.

"The book was your mother's?" His tone had gentled, as if he was acknowledging her grief.

"She had a couple of old trunks I had to go through after she died." She caressed the faded cover. "I found this. It's the only thing that dates from the summer she spent here."

Adam's tension was back, vibrating across the inches between them. He leaned closer. "Does she say anything about the dolphin?"

"Not in words." She opened the navy blue cover carefully, mindful of the fragile pages. "But she did this."

She handed it to him, her throat tightening as she looked at the faded drawing—the wooden dolphin on its shelf in the church, its sleek body curved almost as if in prayer.

Adam took the notebook, his hand gentle. "She did this that summer? Are you sure?"

She pointed to the bottom corner. "Yes. She dated it."

He studied the drawing. "She was a talented artist. No one ever mentions it when they talk about her."

"No, they don't." She pushed down a wave of anger. "All anyone seemed to notice was her beauty. She was much more than the way she looked."

His gaze lifted to her face as if he was assessing her emotions. "Clayton and Jefferson were teenage boys then. Teenage boys think with their hormones, I'm afraid."

"I know." She touched the page lightly. "It's only—it makes me angry that she saw herself the same way. She never tried to develop her talent or make it on her own. She let herself be defined by what other people thought." She stopped, her voice suddenly choking.

Adam's hand closed strongly over hers. "Tory, what happened to your mother wasn't your fault. You were the child, not the parent."

His words went right to the center of her pain and lodged there. How could he see so clearly what she felt? She didn't open her heart that way.

It was far better to focus elsewhere. She nodded toward the notebook. "There's another one you should see."

Adam turned the page, and his hand seemed to freeze. Lamplight cast a golden glow over the pictured faces.

Tory looked at the drawing, trying to see it through Adam's eyes. Two teenage boys, similar features, arms thrown across each other's shoulders. Jefferson's head was tipped back in laughter, and Clayton looked at his brother with a smile.

Adam cleared his throat, and his eyes were suspiciously bright. "We should show this to Dad."

Dismay flooded her. "I don't think that's a good idea. I'm sure your father feels I've interfered in your family business enough."

Adam's hand closed over hers again, warm and

compelling. "Tory, this is important. He has to see this, even if it's uncomfortable."

Her gaze met his. His usual low-key, relaxed manner had been transformed into something determined and passionate that willed her agreement. She could no more resist than she could take wing and fly away.

And that was a sad comment on just how far beyond control her feelings for Adam had become.

Adam stood and held out his hand to Tory, wondering at himself. Tory was right to feel apprehensive. Interfering in the feud between his father and Uncle Clayton was playing with dynamite.

What had happened to his being the peacemaker? Peacemakers didn't set off dynamite.

Maybe he was tired of being the buffer in the family. Or maybe feeling Tory's pain over her family rift drove him. Whatever caused it, he felt compelled to do something—anything—that might make a difference.

They reached the study door. Tory hung back, her reluctance palpable. "I'm an outsider. I shouldn't be involved in this."

He didn't have to think about it. He drew her close to his side. "You're already involved. Our families were intertwined before either of us was born. Please, Tory."

She looked at him, her dark eyes huge. Then she nodded.

He tapped lightly, then opened the door. His father glanced up from the papers spread across his desk. When he saw Tory, he quickly removed the glasses he wore for reading.

"Adam. Tory. What can I do for you?" Jefferson's gaze seemed to soften as it rested on Tory, and Adam knew he was right to bring her in. Somehow, when his father looked at Tory, he saw Emily. It made him vulnerable in a way Adam had seldom seen.

"Tory has something I think you ought to see." Grasping her hand, he drew her across to the desk. He held out the notebook. "This was her mother's. From the summer she was here."

He sensed his father's withdrawal. It wasn't surprising Jefferson preferred to ignore that time in his life.

Determination stiffened in Adam. He wouldn't let his father pretend any longer.

"Look at it." His words probably came out a little more peremptory than they should, but they worked. His father took the notebook.

"I'm not sure what all the—" The sketch of the dolphin confronted him, silenced him.

Tory's fingers clenched Adam's tightly, and he gave them a reassuring squeeze. This was the right thing to do. He was sure of it.

His father didn't move for a long moment, and Adam suspected Tory held her breath just as he did. Finally Jefferson touched the page.

"I remember when she drew this." He sounded very far away. "I found her sitting on the church steps, sketching. She said she wanted to draw the dolphin. I knew where the key to the sanctuary was, so I took her inside."

They stood silent, listening.

"She was so entranced with the dolphin. I'd never

seen her like that. Why should she care about something in a little church on a little island? After all, she had everything."

The words touched Adam's heart. Had that encounter been the beginning of his father's need for success at any cost? His feeling that the girl he loved had everything while he had nothing?

Adam cleared his throat. "Maybe you ought to look at the next page."

Jefferson turned the sheet over carefully. His hand froze. Nothing broke the silence but the tick of the grandfather clock.

Adam willed his father to speak, sensing that Tory felt the same. They seemed linked through their clasped hands, or maybe through something more elemental that he didn't comprehend.

At last Jefferson put the notebook on the desk. He touched the pictured faces lightly with his fingertips.

"So long ago." He shook his head. "I remember. We were so close, long ago."

"You could be again." Adam forced the words out. "You could be, if you want it enough."

His father's mouth worked as if he tried to hold back emotion. "It's too late for that. We've said too many painful things."

"It's not too late." Adam leaned forward. "It doesn't have to be. You need to make the first move."

A sudden flare of anger chased the sorrow from his father's face. "Why should I do that?"

Adam held his gaze, knowing he was about to say something that could create a breach between them.

Knowing, too, that he had to say it. "Because you were wrong. You know you were wrong."

Jefferson glared at him for a moment. Then, quite suddenly, tears welled in his eyes. He shook his head, blinking. "I know. I was wrong. But I don't know how to make up for it."

Adam could breathe again. "You can find a way if you really want it. Just take one small step toward him, that's all."

One step. He held Tory's hand, knowing he should take his own advice. He needed to take one small step that would set things right between them.

It wasn't Tory's fault his wife had betrayed him. It wasn't her fault his mother-in-law had unwittingly given her an impossible job.

He had to take one small step. The trouble was, he didn't know if he could.

Tory turned off the soldering iron and pushed her protective goggles to the top of her head. She stretched, trying to get the kinks out of her back, and looked with satisfaction at the window of Jesus walking on the water, touched by the last rays of the setting sun.

It was finished. Each piece had been painstakingly cleaned and the damaged pieces replaced. The fresh look of the new lead would quickly fade. The window was as lovely as it had been a hundred years ago. She only wished she could feel as happy with her original work.

She stretched again, then moved slowly to the

workroom's other table. She'd done everything she could to prepare to work on the new window. Everything except begin.

She looked longingly at the full-size design, carefully smoothed and taped to the tabletop. Unfortunately being ready didn't do her any good. Nothing would, unless and until Adam gave his approval.

She gripped the edge of the table. She'd thought, after the way they'd opened up to each other the previous night, that it would make a difference in Adam's attitude. Apparently she'd been wrong.

Father, is this going to work at all? She touched the design longingly. *I think I could do something beautiful to Your glory, if only Adam would let me.*

She closed her eyes, trying to listen to her heart. She didn't hear an answer.

"Tory? May I come in?"

She whirled at the sound of Adam's voice. He lingered in the doorway, as if the workroom belonged to her instead of to him. With his creased chinos and white knit shirt, his hair wet from the shower, he looked ready for an evening out.

She wiped her hands on her jeans, then pushed her hair from her face. She probably looked ready to clean the trash cans.

"Of course, come in." She moved quickly to the repaired window, not sure she wanted him looking at the new window she'd laid out. He might think she'd started work on it in defiance of his wishes. "This window is ready to go back whenever your crew can take it."

He stood next to her, looking at the window. He smelled of soap and sunshine, and his nearness sent a little shimmer of pleasure across her skin.

"You've done a wonderful job. I didn't realize how dim the window had become until you cleaned it." He touched the stained glass reverently. "This has always been my favorite."

"You have good judgment. The artistry in this one is special." She stopped, shaking her head. "The waves are so real, you can almost feel Peter's fear."

"Maybe that's why islanders love it so much. They know what the sea can do."

Was he thinking of that shipwrecked ancestor of his? Or of more recent storms?

"It was a joy to work on. I almost felt in touch with the artisan who created it." She smiled. "That's a good feeling, believe me."

"I guess it would be. Sort of like working on a good boat. You know that your labors are worthwhile."

"Exactly." She smiled at him, feeling in tune for a moment.

He touched her arm lightly, and his expression was very serious. "I've been wanting to tell you. You did a good thing last night, Tory. Thank you for showing me your mother's drawings. And thank you for going with me to my father."

"I hope—" She hesitated, not sure she should say what she was thinking. "I believe my mother saw restoring the dolphin as a means of repairing the damage caused by what happened that summer." She chose her words carefully. "I don't mean just the harm to the church, but the trouble between your father and his brother."

His jaw tightened, the movement barely perceptible, but she saw it. "She wasn't the only cause of their problems, as far as I can tell. Their quarrel over her was just the latest in a string of incidents."

"Regardless, she felt responsible. She wanted the dolphin returned, but it doesn't look as if that's going to happen." She felt her throat tighten. "There's no place left to look, we both know that."

His hand closed over her wrist, and she felt his sympathy flow through it. "Tory, I'm sorry. I wish we'd had a happier outcome."

"You tried. I appreciate that."

"It was a pleasure." His voice roughened on the words, and she looked at him, startled. His eyes had darkened, and he seemed to search for words. "I didn't expect to, but I've enjoyed the time we've spent together."

"That almost sounds like goodbye." She tried to say it lightly, but she was afraid her voice betrayed her.

"Goodbye?" Surely that was genuine surprise in his voice. "Why would I say goodbye?"

She nodded toward the stained glass. "That's the last of the repair work. If you don't want me to start on the new window, then I guess I'm done here."

"No." He shook his head irritably. "I mean, no, I don't want you to leave. I want you to go ahead with the dolphin window."

A spurt of joy shot through her, but it was quickly tempered by the way he'd expressed himself. Apparently Adam still couldn't refer to it as the memorial window. That fact sent warning bells clanging in her mind.

"Are you sure?"

He turned away from her and looked at the design she'd spread on the other table. She studied the rigid line of his shoulders, wishing she could ease the tension away and make him happy.

"I'm sure," he said finally. He tapped the table. "You have a good design here, Tory. This window is as much for Jenny as for anyone. I want her to see the Caldwell dolphin in the church one way or another."

He still wasn't mentioning Lila. Maybe she should say something, but she couldn't. If he intended to let her go ahead with the project, that was the best she could hope for. She'd have to be content.

"Thank you, Adam. I'm glad. I'll try not to let you down."

He swung toward her, and she had the sense that his tension eased as soon as he wasn't looking at the design. Would he really be able to cope with the finished product?

His smile flickered. "You won't let us down," he said. "Your dolphin will be beautiful."

"Will it make up for coming here and prying into your family's past?" Into your past, she'd almost said, but she'd caught herself in time.

Adam leaned against the table, his long-limbed figure seeming relaxed now that he'd made the decision. "I think, in the long run, a little prying will make things better. Maybe we can put this stupid feud behind us, once and for all."

"I hope that's so." She probably wouldn't be here to see it, but she hoped he was right.

He braced his hands behind him on the table edge, careful not to touch the design. "That wasn't the only reason I came in to see you, by the way."

"Then why?"

He smiled. "You've been ignoring Pirate Days. And that's not easy to do when all of Caldwell Cove is caught up in the excitement."

"I've noticed. But I don't belong to Caldwell Cove, remember?"

He shrugged that off. "You have as much reason to be part of the celebration as anyone. Jenny and I want you to join us."

"Join you?"

"Sail on the *Jolly Roger* with us for Pirate Days. Everything starts a week from Saturday, with the regatta. There's a dinner and dance that evening, then a church service with the blessing of the boats on Sunday."

"It sounds lovely. But isn't sailing the ship just for your family?"

"Family, friends. We're inviting you, Jenny and I. We want you to be a part of the *Jolly Roger*'s crew."

"But…" A dozen objections leaped into her mind. "I don't know anything about sailing a pirate ship."

He grinned. "You don't have to. You can be the royal maiden kidnapped by the pirates."

"I don't think I brought any royal maiden dresses with me."

He brushed that aside with a quick gesture. "We have years' worth of costumes around. We'll find something for you. Come on, say you'll do it. You don't have to work all the time, you know."

"Well, I..." She couldn't believe how appealing it sounded to take part in something that made him so happy. "Are you sure Jenny wants me to come?"

"She does." He took both of her hands in his, and their warmth seemed to flow right up her arms and touch her heart. "We both do."

He didn't mean anything by it, she knew that. As long as she knew it, she'd be safe from letting him bruise her heart again.

And she'd have a lovely memory to take with her when she left Caldwell Island.

"All right. I'd love to."

Chapter Twelve

"I thought you said I got to be the royal maiden." Tory swung the paintbrush against the mast of the *Jolly Roger* and glanced at Adam, who was doing the same thing on the other side of the mast. "You didn't mention anything about being a painter's assistant."

He grinned, looking relaxed and happy in his paint-daubed jeans and T-shirt. "You were working too hard. I thought you needed a break."

"Are you saying this isn't work?" She bent to dip her brush in the can of black paint.

"At least you're using different muscles."

How would you know what muscles I use on the windows, Adam? How would you know anything about it? You haven't been in the workroom for the last week.

He hadn't done more than thrust his head into the room when he came to urge her to help with some last-minute painting to ready the pirate ship for the following day. All week, since the night he'd told her to go ahead with the window, he'd avoided the workroom as if it pained him to be near it.

Well, maybe it did. She should be glad her work was going well. She didn't have the right to expect Adam to be happy about it.

Certainly the congregation had seemed pleased with the repair work at church on Sunday. Pastor Wells had thanked her again from the pulpit, and most of the church members had stopped to add their words of appreciation after the service.

"Everyone's happy about the windows, you know." Adam seemed to be reading her mind. "I can't tell you how many people have commented about your work."

She knelt to touch up some chipped places at the base of the mast. "I enjoyed being there Sunday to hear what they thought of it. Usually when you work in a church, you're not around long enough to see people's reactions to what you did."

"Is that mostly what you do?" He looked at her, seeming genuinely interested. "Church windows?" It was the first time he'd mentioned her work other than in the context of the problem between them.

"My last employer did all sorts of projects, but he ran a big studio. I'd like to specialize in church projects—both repair work and new designs."

She half expected him to tense at the mention of new designs, but he didn't seem distressed. "Why church works, especially?"

She couldn't say this to just anyone. But she could

to him. "The other work is satisfying, but church windows give me the chance to express my faith in my designs. What is better than that?"

He nodded. "I guess I feel that way about the boatyard. We have to do repairs—that's the bread and butter. But creating our individual boats for customers who want quality craftsmanship is where the joy comes in."

"Exactly. Joy is just the right word." They were connecting at a level she hadn't expected on a subject that had to be touchy where Adam was concerned.

She sat on the sun-warmed deck, finding it easier to paint that way. Adam had been right—this did use different muscles. But at least here at the boatyard she could feel the sun beat on her back and smell the mingled aromas of salt air, fish and paint.

"So what made you start your own business? Weren't you able to do what you wanted with the last studio you worked for?"

His question made her feel she was the one being pushed into a touchy area. She could evade the truth, but Adam had been honest with her. She owed him the same. And they were alone, with every other worker out of earshot.

"I liked the work, all right." She took a breath, then forced herself to look at him. The sunlight dazzled her eyes. "The problem was, I was engaged to the firm's owner. When our relationship fell apart, I didn't fit in any longer. It seemed time to go out on my own."

Adam's brush paused in its even strokes. He

squatted on his heels across from her, face intent. "What happened to your engagement?"

She wanted to resent the question but she couldn't, not when it was filled with such caring.

"I thought Jason and I were a team," she said carefully. She hadn't said this to anyone, but she was going to tell Adam. "We'd done a big project—the one I showed you in the magazine spread. I was the designer on that job, but when the project began to get some attention, Jason made it clear that he expected to receive all the credit for the designs."

The realization didn't hurt as much as it had once, but it still stung.

"I saw that wasn't the kind of relationship that would make for a good marriage."

She studied the black-and-white label on the paint can as if it fascinated her, so she wouldn't have to look at Adam. "That was when I decided to strike out on my own."

"And you ended up in Caldwell Cove." He reached out to touch her paint-stained hand. "I'm glad."

Are you, Adam? Her breath caught. Could she possibly believe he meant anything by it?

Then he stood, putting the lid on the paint can, and the moment was over. Maybe that was just as well. She shouldn't be reading anything into the kindness Adam dealt out to everyone who crossed his path. It didn't mean he had feelings for her.

"Here comes Jenny." He shaded his eyes, looking toward the road. "We're about to get some help." He smiled. "That's why I closed the paint can."

"Wise man." Keep it light, remember? That way nobody got hurt.

"Trust me, I learned my lesson the hard way. You don't want to know what happened when we painted the barn last year. It took six months for Jenny's pony to look normal again."

She stood, taking the rag he tossed her and wiping her hands. "You're right, I don't want to know." She glanced at her watch. "Isn't it too early for her to be out of school?"

"You really haven't caught on to how seriously we take Pirate Days, have you? Even school dismisses early so the children can help get ready. They consider it an educational event."

He seemed to be serious.

"You're not telling there were actual, historical pirates, are you? I thought this was just an excuse to have a little fun."

"Hey, Daddy. Hey, Miz Tory. What can I do?" Jenny skidded to a stop perilously close to the paint can.

Adam grabbed her. "Hey, yourself. Take it easy. You just got your cast off, remember? You don't need another one."

"I'm always careful, Daddy." Jenny didn't look especially impressed with the warning. "What can I do? Can I paint?" She reached eagerly toward a wet brush, and Adam caught her hand.

"You can tell Miz Tory about the pirates. She doesn't think they were real."

"Not real?" Jenny's eyes widened. "We learned

all about them in school, Miz Tory. It's real, honest. The pirates used to hide around the sea islands. Some people even say they buried treasure here. Why, one time somebody even found a gold Spanish coin in an old log."

Tory looked from Jenny to Adam. Both of them certainly seemed to be taking it seriously. "So this parade with the boats tomorrow—"

"It's to remember when a pirate named John Law took over the island in 1802." Jenny rattled the facts off as if she'd memorized them. "His ship was called the *Jolly Roger,* and ours is meant to look just like his."

"Very good." Adam ruffled her hair, then smiled at Tory. "We do have a few modern innovations, though. The pirates storm ashore at the yacht club, for instance, which obviously wasn't there in 1802. And nobody really walks the plank."

"I'm relieved to hear it."

"I have a costume like Daddy's, Miz Tory. Did you get your costume yet?"

She glanced at Adam. "Actually, I forgot all about it. Was I supposed to look for one?"

"Nope. It's all taken care of." He caught Jenny's hands and swung them back and forth, making her giggle. "Miz Tory is going to look like a princess."

"I get to be a pirate," Jenny declared. "With an eye patch and everything. That's better. But you'll make a nice princess, Miz Tory," she added generously.

Tory felt a slight tremor of apprehension. What exactly was this costume? "I've never considered myself the princess type."

"Oh, I don't know." Adam's face crinkled with amusement. "I seem to remember a time when you were Cinderella."

"That was a long time ago," she said firmly. "I'm a craftsman now, not a princess."

She realized suddenly that they were talking easily, even joking about the night that had haunted her for such a long time. She wouldn't have thought that possible before she'd come back to Caldwell Cove.

Maybe she and Adam were moving toward accepting the past. If so, this trip had been worthwhile even without finding the dolphin.

Jenny grabbed her hand. "Miz Tory, can I come see the window you're making for my mommy? Miz Becky keeps saying I have to wait, but I want to see it now."

Jenny's sudden change of subject caught her off guard. "If it's okay with your daddy."

"No." The word came out with explosive force. She looked at Adam to find his eyes suddenly as gray and bleak as a storm on the ocean. "It's not okay."

Her heart stuttered. She'd been wrong. The knowledge was a physical pain that cut through her. Adam wasn't accepting the past at all.

Now where had that come from? Adam shook his head, hoping he could shake off the feelings that had erupted with Jenny's innocent question. His response had been instinctive, but it hadn't been fair to either Jenny or Tory.

"Sorry, sugar." He touched his daughter's cheek lightly. "I didn't mean to sound like a bear."

Jenny pouted. "Well, you did. A growly bear. I don't see why I can't look at the window."

"Nobody's looking at it until it's finished." That was the first reasonable excuse for his behavior that popped into his head, and he could only hope it sounded good to both of them. "I'm sure Miz Tory will be finished with the window soon, and then you can see it before anybody else, okay?"

"It'll be ready in just a couple more days," Tory said quickly. "I'll tell you when."

"Okay." Jenny's smile reappeared. "Now can I help paint?"

The tension inside him eased. "We're finished with the painting, but Uncle Matt's about ready to swab the deck. How about helping him?"

"I can do that." Jenny whirled and darted toward the stern. "Uncle Matt, I can help you," she called.

Jenny was easily distracted, and just as easily forgiving. Tory was something else again. He turned to her, trying to find an excuse for his behavior. There wasn't one.

"I'm sorry." He spread his hands, palms up. "That was stupid."

Her mouth was tight. He might have thought it expressed anger, but he could see the hurt hiding in her eyes.

"You have a right to do what you want." She turned away. "But she'll have to see the window sometime."

"I know. Tory…" His voice trailed off. What else could he say?

His gaze traced the pale skin of her nape, the tension in her shoulders, the curve of her back. Vulnerable. He'd seen it that first day when he'd looked into Tory's dark eyes and recognized loneliness.

Tory put on a good front of being determined and independent and depending on nobody. But he knew better. He knew just how tender she was inside.

She wasn't the only one. He tried to look honestly at his feelings. He was drawn to Tory in a way he'd never been drawn to another woman, even Lila. Lila had been youthful infatuation masquerading as reality. Tory was real. Tory had somehow reached him through all the defenses he'd erected after Lila's betrayal.

But they were both too wounded to love again. That was the bottom line. He had to be careful.

"I'm sorry," he said again finally. "I want Jenny to see the window. I know she'll be happy with it."

And I'm sorry I hurt you, Tory. That was what he felt, but he didn't think he could say that. At least not out loud.

Tory stood before the oval mahogany mirror in her bedroom the next day, mentally ticking off all the ways she didn't resemble any princess she'd ever heard of.

Princesses didn't wear faded sweat suits and sneakers. They didn't have a tangle of dark hair. They didn't look ready to scrub the floor. Cinderella, even before the fairy godmother dusted her off, had undoubtedly been a blond-haired, blue-eyed beauty.

Like her mother.

She pressed her fist against her midsection. She might as well tell the truth, at least to herself. This sudden panic wasn't over whether she did or didn't resemble a princess. She was afraid because she didn't belong.

Adam Caldwell, with his flock of relatives and his self-assured, confident air, couldn't possibly understand that. He'd always known he belonged here. She'd never belonged anywhere.

A rap on the door interrupted the morbid turn her thoughts had suddenly taken. Straighten up, she told herself sternly. You can pretend you're part of this, at least for one day.

She opened the door. Miz Becky stood there, her arms filled with a frothy confection in emerald green.

"Time's a-wasting, child." She bustled into the room, spread the gown on the bed and looked at it with satisfaction. "We got to get you ready."

"That's for me?" Tory felt a wave of light-headedness. "I didn't expect anything like that. Adam just said there were some old costumes around."

"He must have been joking. He rented this gown special from the costume shop in Savannah where they got the pirate outfits." She stroked the silk once, then crossed to the dressing table and picked up a brush. "Come on, now. Let's get your hair fixed first."

Tory's hands flew to her unruly mop. "I don't

expect you to do my hair. I'm sure you have lots to do getting ready yourself."

Miz Becky's eyes crinkled in amusement. "Nobody's getting me on a pirate ship, I can tell you that. So I got plenty of time to dress for the party. Right now, all I want is to see you turn into a princess. Come on now. Don't be giving me any excuses."

Tory took a seat reluctantly at the dressing table, and Miz Becky began brushing her hair from her face. "I still don't think—"

"Don't think, then. Just enjoy." She swept Tory's mane up, pinning it into place with clips she took from her apron pocket. "I tell you the truth, it does my heart good to see Adam so excited about this day. He hasn't been this pleased about the celebration since I don't remember when."

Tory's gaze caught Miz Becky's in the mirror. "Really?"

The housekeeper nodded. "Honest." She picked up the curling iron and began taming Tory's curls. "Ever since Lila left, he's been going through the motions. It's good for him to be looking forward to this day. He's been unhappy about that for too long. It's time he got over it. Time he moved on with his life."

"I'm not sure he can move on when he's still grieving," Tory said cautiously.

"I don't reckon it's grieving he's been doing all this time."

Apparently Miz Becky did know. Did Adam

realize someone who knew him as well as Miz Becky did had guessed?

"Maybe not grieving," she conceded. "But he's—" She bit her lip. She shouldn't be talking about him this way. But Miz Becky loved him. "He's still bitter."

The woman nodded, as if Tory had given the right answer. "That woman's got him tied to her by that. It's high time he got free."

She didn't seem to expect an answer, just concentrated on putting the finishing touches to Tory's hair. Tory hardly noticed, she was so busy wrestling with Miz Becky's words.

She was right. Adam's bitterness tied him to the memory of Lila's betrayal. He hadn't forgiven her. That was why he couldn't look at the window in her memory. Not because it reminded him of her, but because it reminded him of his inability to forgive.

Is that it, Lord? Is that why Adam has been confronted with this window—because he has to forgive?

"Now you just stand still and let me put the dress on you." Miz Becky's deft fingers adjusted the layers of petticoats.

She lifted the dress, and Tory felt the whisper of silk as it fell into place. Miz Becky fastened it, then twitched the skirt until it hung to her satisfaction.

"There," she said, turning Tory toward the mirror. "Now look."

Tory blinked. The elegant stranger looking back at her certainly wasn't plain, workaday Tory Marlowe. "Is that really me?"

Miz Becky threw back her head and laughed. "Sure is. You do look like a princess today." She pressed her warm cheek briefly against Tory's. "You go down there and do us proud. Adam's waiting for you."

Adam. Her heart skipped a beat. What would Adam think of this?

She let herself be hustled out of the bedroom to the stairs. She stopped at the top of the sweeping stairway for a moment, clutching the polished rail. It wouldn't do a thing for the elegant getup if she tumbled all the way down, would it?

"Keep your head up and hold your skirt with one hand," Miz Becky advised. "How women ever did anything at all in an outfit like that is beyond me, but you surely do look beautiful."

She wanted to reject the words. She hadn't been beautiful a day in her life. But maybe she could pretend, just for today.

That thought gave her the courage to lift her chin, grasp her skirt and walk slowly down the stairs. As she came around the curve of the stairway, she saw Adam waiting at the bottom. He watched her with open admiration, and her heart skipped again.

No man had any right to look like that. Adam's boy-next-door good looks had been transformed by the black pants, high boots and white buccaneer shirt. A black eye patch gave him an unexpectedly dangerous look.

She reached the hallway without incident. Adam took her hand, swept her a bow.

"You look wonderful." He lifted her hand, and the brush of his lips on her skin sent shivers racing up her arm. "Wonderful."

Jenny, wearing an identical pirate outfit, ran to her. She pirouetted. "I'm a pirate, too, just like Daddy."

"You're a very convincing pirate," Tory said.

"You look like a princess, Miz Tory." Jenny grabbed her hand.

"She looks like Cinderella."

"But Daddy, Cinderella should have glass slippers." Jenny seemed prepared to argue the point.

"Cinderella," Adam said firmly, tucking Tory's hand into the crook of his elbow, "Shall we go?"

It's pretend, she told herself desperately. Just pretend. We're all pretending.

It didn't feel like pretence to have her hand clasping Adam's strong arm. Or to have Jenny clinging to her other hand. It felt like belonging. And that was a dangerous thing to start believing.

Chapter Thirteen

It wouldn't be hard to convince herself she'd fallen into a fairy tale, Tory thought as she leaned back in her deck chair. White sails billowed in the breeze, and the pirate pennant above her head snapped. The *Jolly Roger* moved into the channel to the accompaniment of seagulls squawking and bells clanging.

Adam stood at the wheel with Jenny in front of him, his strong hands covering her small ones. His gaze found Tory's across a deck crowded with Caldwells and their friends, and he gave her a smile of such pure pleasure her breath caught. He should look that carefree and happy always.

"Reckon Adam likes being a swashbuckler for a day." Adam's grandmother, seated next to Tory, watched him with approval in her sharp eyes. "It's good for that boy to cut loose once in a while."

"He doesn't cut loose often, does he?"

"Land, no." Mrs. Caldwell shook her head.

"Maybe that's how he wants it." Adam's loyalty to his family, even to his late wife—well, it was admirable, wasn't it?

The elderly woman regarded her, and Tory felt as if her heart and soul were being carefully examined. "I s'pose he does. Guess you'd know that, since you're one of the responsible ones, too."

"Me?" The idea startled her. "I'm on my own. Responsible to no one."

Adam's grandmother shook her head. "You can't deny your nature, child. No one can. You came here because you felt responsible, though you weren't even born when the dolphin disappeared."

She hadn't thought of it that way. She'd only known that recovering the dolphin was one thing she could do for her mother.

"Responsible or not, I didn't succeed." Her throat tightened. She'd failed to fulfill that last promise. "I didn't find it."

Mrs. Caldwell smoothed the gray lace of her dress. "I'd like to see that dolphin back where it belongs, too, but you know things happen in God's own time, not ours."

"Gran, you're not harping on that dolphin again, are you?" Miranda Caldwell settled into the chair on the other side of Tory. With her bronze hair and her Civil War era dress and hat, she reminded Tory of Scarlett O'Hara. "I know you miss it, but we're doing all right even without the dolphin there for weddings."

"I don't see you settling down to happily-ever-after, young lady." Her grandmother's voice was tart. "Seems like you need to find somebody to love."

Miranda snapped open a lace fan, and it hid her face for a moment. "Could be that's not meant to happen, Gran. Dolphin or no dolphin." The smile she gave Tory seemed strained. "You have to forgive Gran. She's got this notion that Caldwells are supposed to be married under the dolphin."

"It's not a notion." Her grandmother leaned forward in the chair as if she'd jump up and set things right if she could. "There's a lot more truth in legends and such than you young folk want to believe."

"All right, Gran," Miranda said hastily. "I believe you."

"That dolphin belongs in the church, and things won't really be the way they're supposed to be till then." She looked from Miranda to Tory. "And that's the truth."

Tory clenched her fists against the green silk. "I wish I'd been able to make that happen." She looked at Adam again, her gaze tracing the lines of his strong face. A good face, one meant for more happiness than he'd found. "For all of you."

Mrs. Caldwell reached over to clasp her hand in a firm grip. "Don't you blame yourself, now. It's all in the good Lord's hands. We just have to trust it will work out the way He plans. Besides, maybe you're here for another reason altogether."

Tory's heart seemed to stutter. "I don't know what you mean." What did those wise old eyes see in her?

Miranda had turned away to say something to her

young son, and Adam's grandmother leaned closer, her words just for Tory. "Seems to me maybe you and your window can help Adam put the past behind him."

For a moment she couldn't speak. But such honesty seemed to demand honesty in return. "I haven't done such a good job of ignoring the past in my own life."

Gran patted her hand. "Not ignore, child. Forgive. If you've got a ways to go, maybe you'll help each other. Nothing wrong with that."

"I don't think—"

"Don't think so much." Gran's wise old eyes twinkled. "That's the trouble with you young ones, you think too much. Just let your heart guide you."

Tory let the words sink in, her gaze on Adam. If she listened to her heart right now, what was it telling her? Maybe it was saying to relax and enjoy this day without worrying so much about tomorrow.

Adam looked at her and smiled again, and her heart fluttered. He couldn't possibly have heard what they'd said, but he seemed to be communicating directly with her. He held out his hand.

"Come along and help me steer this thing, Tory," he called.

She could almost feel Adam's grandmother pushing her out of the chair. She crossed the deck, mindful of the unaccustomed long skirt, and joined him.

Adam had shoved the eye patch back, but he still had a devastatingly dangerous look in that pirate outfit. She had to clamp down on a rush of longing.

"I don't think you really want my help," she said. "I don't know a thing about boats, remember?"

"Just stand here and talk to me, then." He gave a quick, experienced glance at the sails, then turned his smiling gaze on her. "My first mate deserted me to play with her cousins."

Tory looked at the crowd lining the rails and sitting on the deck. Jenny had linked arms with her cousin Andi and seemed to be attempting a jig. "Looks like quite a group of Caldwells."

He nodded. "The family always sails the *Jolly Roger*, and we take turns being the captain. This is my lucky year." He gave Tory a look that might mean, if she really let herself imagine things, that meeting her again was part of that luck.

She suspected her cheeks were red. "Seems as if the whole island gets in on the act."

"You bet." He nodded toward the clutch of small boats that bobbed along in the ship's wake, escorting the *Jolly Roger*. "Watch what happens. Each time we pass a dock on our way around the island, we'll pick up more boats. By the time we reach the yacht club, half the islanders will be with us, and the other half will be waiting there."

"So there is something the islanders and the yacht club crowd do together."

He frowned briefly, then shrugged. "I guess you're right. I hadn't thought about it, but this is the one time of the year that all the barriers come down."

It would be nice to believe those weren't the only barriers that could fall. But what kept her from Adam was far more elemental than the money and tradition that separated the islanders from the summer people. She ought to remember that.

It wasn't easy when Adam caught her arm and drew her closer. "Put your hands here on the wheel and feel how she responds."

The *Jolly Roger* wasn't the only female who responded. With Adam's hands covering hers, his breath warm on her neck, her heart swelled.

"Like this?" The polished wheel felt smooth beneath her fingers, and Adam's grip was firm and sure. "I don't want to run us aground."

"You won't." His breath caressed her cheek. "I'll take care of you."

Something that might have been hope blossomed inside Tory. Maybe it was time to stop telling herself this couldn't work—and to follow her heart.

Adam didn't want to let her go. Glancing at Tory, next to him as she had been for most of the trip, Adam knew he was in trouble. This woman had taken possession of his thoughts and feelings, maybe of his heart.

That jolted him right down to his soles. He couldn't let himself feel this way. He couldn't give his heart to another woman.

Tory isn't Lila, a small voice whispered in his mind. Tory is honest, forthright, caring. She wouldn't trample on your love.

He frowned, automatically checking the sails as he made the last sweeping turn around the curve of the island. Was that really what he was doing—letting Lila's betrayal sour him on any other woman?

The yacht club, its dock crowded with people, came into view. His gaze traced the wide white steps. He'd hurried down those steps looking for Tory that night, when he'd realized she wasn't coming back. But all he'd found was the white rose she'd worn in her hair, lying forgotten on the walk.

What would have happened if Tory hadn't disappeared that night? His heart clenched. How different would their lives have been?

He couldn't let himself think that way. No matter how much Lila had hurt him in the end, she'd given him Jenny. His daughter was worth any price. Even if he could go back and change things, knowing what he knew now about how they'd end up, he wouldn't.

Not change the past, no. But what about the present? What about seizing the present?

The swashbuckler he was portraying would do that, but Adam was pretending. A costume didn't turn him into a different person.

"I didn't realize there were that many people on the island." Tory's voice interrupted his thoughts before he could argue that he was really a swashbuckler at heart. "There's quite a crowd to greet you."

Adam glanced at his crew, making sure they were all at their stations. "The whole island's watching us bring the *Jolly Roger* in. It's not a time when you want to miss the dock. Or worse, crash into it."

Tory took a step back as if to give him more space.

"I'm not worried." Her voice was filled with confidence. "You'll do it."

He could only hope her trust wasn't misplaced. He gauged the current, the wind and the rapidly narrowing space between the prow and the dock. He called out his orders, knowing he could trust his brother and cousins to move quickly.

The *Jolly Roger* seemed to curtsey on the waves. There was a moment of tension when he wondered if he'd judged it right. Then the prow kissed the dock as smoothly as if he did this every day of the week.

He heard the cheers and clapping, but they were background music. All he could think about was the delighted expression on Tory's face when he turned to look at her.

"That was wonderful."

"Not bad," he said.

She leaned closer, and he caught the faint scent of roses that seemed to surround her. It reminded him of playing in the shade of his grandmother's flower beds on a warm afternoon.

"What happens next?"

He nodded toward the crew as they swarmed ashore. "Our pirates are going to take control and raise the Jolly Roger flag. Then we all adjourn to the yacht club for dining and dancing."

She smiled. "Undoubtedly what the original pirates did."

"Oh, I don't know. They did celebrate when they found a safe haven. But I promise you a better dinner and a better dance floor than they'd have had."

He glanced up, realizing the crew had raised the flag and he hadn't even noticed. He took Tory's arm. "Let's see if I'm right."

"Lead on, Captain."

He stepped to the dock, then reached back to grasp her by the waist and swing her over. His hands fit neatly around her, and she clasped his arms for support.

"You didn't need to do that." She sounded slightly breathless. "I could have gotten out myself."

"Just trying to stay in character." He offered his arm. "Don't you think that's what your typical pirate would do?"

"Never having met one, I couldn't say." She slipped her hand into the crook of his arm. "I'll try and act the princess, but I'm not sure how gracefully I can manage this skirt."

"That was the first thing I thought when I saw you." The words came out without conscious consideration. "That night at the yacht club dance. You had on a white dress, and when you walked across the floor, you moved like a dancer."

She shook her head, and he thought she flushed a little. "You must have been dreaming."

"Maybe I was." They started up the steps. "But if so, it was a nice dream."

She glanced at him, her face very close to his as he opened the door. Her dark eyes were serious. "The trouble with dreams is that you have to wake up."

He pulled open one of the white double doors and ushered her inside. "That doesn't mean you can't enjoy them."

Swashbuckler or not, that was what he intended to do. He'd leave all his native caution behind and, at least for tonight, enjoy the moment.

Jenny raced to them, cheeks flushed with excitement. "Aunt Sarah says can I sit with them for dinner? We're going to have sweet corn and watermelon and all the chicken we can eat. And afterward we're going to dance."

Matt and Sarah were probably matchmaking by taking Jenny off his hands, but at the moment he didn't care. "Okay, but you be good, you hear? And don't forget Miz Becky's going to take you home at eight o'clock."

Jenny pouted. "Can't I stay longer? I bet my cousins get to stay longer than that."

"I bet they don't." He ruffled her hair. "I know your Aunt Sarah and Uncle Matt too well to buy that. You run along now and have a good time."

She scampered off, and he turned to find Tory looking apprehensive. "You mean I have to eat sweet corn and watermelon in this dress? I wouldn't dare."

He couldn't help but laugh at her expression. "Sugar, it doesn't matter in the least if something gets spilled on that dress. But I expect they have more grown-up food, too. This is one time they try to satisfy everyone."

"If you say so." She looked doubtful.

"Take a look around." He gestured toward the crowd thronging through the double doors. The polished floor echoed to the sound of pirate boots, and the usually sedate yacht club echoed with laughter. "This party's for the whole island, and we're all set to celebrate together."

"A time when barriers come down," she said softly, and nodded toward the corner. "Do you see that?"

He followed the direction of her gaze, and his heart jolted with shock. His father and Uncle Clayton stood together. Alone together. Talking.

"I don't think I've ever seen that in my whole life," he said quietly, knowing his voice had roughened with telltale emotion. "None of us has."

"They look uncomfortable."

Tory sounded so anxious he squeezed her hand and then didn't want to let go. "I know they don't look like they did in that picture your mother drew. But just the fact that they're talking—" He stopped, knowing he could never make her understand how important this was. "Thank you, Tory. If you hadn't come, this might never have happened."

"You're the one who told your father to take that first step," she said. "It looks as if he listened to you."

"Yes, it does." He'd have said it was impossible, but it had happened. Maybe this was a time for miracles.

Tory pushed open the door to the ladies' room after dinner and paused, not sure whether to advance or retreat. It sounded as if someone was crying. A child. She moved quickly around the corner.

Jenny huddled in the corner of a wicker love seat, her shoulders shaking with sobs. Tory flew across the room.

"Jenny, what is it? Are you sick?"

Jenny's small face was blotchy from crying. "No," she muttered. "I want to go home!" A sob punctuated the word.

What had happened to the excited child who'd so looked forward to this evening? Tory's heart clenched. If someone had hurt Jenny...

She slid onto the couch and gathered Jenny against her. "Hush, now." She rocked her. "It'll be all right. Just tell me what happened."

Jenny sniffed, shaking her head.

"Come on, sugar," Tory coaxed, realizing she'd used Adam's pet name for his daughter. "You don't want me to bring your daddy in here, do you? He'd get in trouble for coming in the ladies' room."

That earned a watery giggle, and Jenny pulled back an inch so she could see Tory's face. "They were mean."

"Who was mean?" She stroked tangled curls from Jenny's face.

"We were dancing, me and Andi. We practiced and everything. We wanted to do a jig, like pirates do."

Tory nodded, remembering the girls dancing on the deck. "Well, that's a nice idea."

"It wasn't nice!" Jenny said, her lip trembling. "There were some bigger boys watching us, and they made fun of us. They laughed at us!"

Something in Tory relaxed. Bruised pride was bad enough, but there were worse things. "Honey, you were right. They were mean."

"But I thought we danced right. I don't want people to laugh at me."

Tory drew her close. "I know, Jenny. People do that sometimes, and it hurts. Then you have to remember that what other people think doesn't matter all that much. It's what's in your heart that's important."

Jenny snuggled against her. "But I wanted to dance." Her voice was soft.

"And you will." Tory knew exactly what would make Jenny happy right now, because it was the same thing that would make her happy. "Come on, let's wash the tears away. Then you're going to dance with the handsomest man in the room."

A few minutes later they went, hand in hand, into the ballroom. Tory spotted Adam instantly. She seemed to have radar where he was concerned. She led Jenny to him.

"Captain, there's a young pirate here who really needs to dance with you." She put Jenny's hand in Adam's.

Adam sent one searching glance at his daughter's face and seemed to understand all the things Tory didn't say. In an instant he'd swept Jenny onto the floor.

Tory watched them, irresistibly reminded of that night so many years ago. She'd probably looked about as woebegone as Jenny did, coming into the dance all alone.

Now Jenny was smiling, eyes sparkling as she looked at her father. Adam twirled her around and around the floor. By the time the music ended they were both laughing.

Adam spun to a stop in front of Tory and caught Jenny in his arms for a kiss. "Thank you, Miz Jenny. That was the best dance of the night."

Jenny wiggled her way down. "I'm going to go tell Andi I was dancing. I think you should dance with Miz Tory now."

She darted off, and Adam held out his hand. "May I have this dance?"

It was what he'd said fifteen years before. And her heart seemed to be fluttering just as it had then.

No, she decided as she stepped into his arms. This Adam wasn't like the boy he'd been that night. He was a hundred times more exciting, and she was a hundred times more vulnerable.

"Thank you," he murmured, his breath stirring her hair. "Whatever it was, thank you."

"Jenny didn't tell you?"

He smiled. "I asked. She said I wouldn't understand. It was girl stuff. She said you made everything better."

"I suspect it was dancing with you that made her world all right."

He drew her closer into his arms. "Let's see if it has the same effect on you," he murmured, his lips brushing her cheek.

Her hand tightened on his shoulder as he swung her around. She felt strong muscle and warm skin through the fine fabric of his shirt. Warmth. Strength. Those words described Adam perfectly. He was a man a woman could depend on. Unfortunately, the woman who'd betrayed him still had those qualities entangled in the memory of that betrayal.

Tory wouldn't worry about that tonight. Adam's cheek was against hers, canceling out anything negative. She would follow her heart just this once.

Adam drew back an inch or two, enough to see her face. His gaze, mysterious as the ocean, lingered on each feature as if memorizing it, and her skin warmed.

"Remembering the last time we did this?" he asked softly.

"No." His lips were only a breath away from hers. "I'm just...enjoying the moment, that's all. Not thinking about the past. Just now."

His arm tightened around her. "That's what I've been telling myself all day. Seize the present. Don't worry about the past or the future."

"Can you do that?"

"I don't know." His eyes met hers honestly. "But I can try."

She tried not to let herself hope, but she couldn't seem to help it. "Maybe that's all any of us can do."

He didn't answer with words, but he drew her closer again. Their feet moved in perfect unison to the music, and she didn't know or care whether there was another person on the dance floor. Being here, with Adam, in this moment—that was enough.

The music stopped. She took a step back, disoriented, as if she'd wakened in a strange place from a very real dream.

Adam held her hand tightly. "Let's get a breath of air. This way."

The silk of her skirt whispered as they crossed the floor. Was anyone watching them, noting that Adam Caldwell was taking her onto the veranda? She didn't know, didn't care.

He swept her around him onto the dimly lit veranda, then closed the French doors. A patch of light, cross-hatched by the small panes, fell onto wide boards. Still holding her hand, Adam led her toward the railing, where the only illumination was the pale moonlight.

He paused for an instant, picking up something from the wrought-iron table. Then he held it out to her—a white rose.

"I know we said we wouldn't think about the past." His voice was a touch rueful. "But somehow this seemed a fitting gesture."

Her heart was too full for words when she took the rose. She inhaled the sweet aroma and brushed velvety petals against her cheek. "That's a good memory." Her voice came out breathless. "I think we can hang on to that, can't we?"

He nodded. "You wore it in your hair. I'd try to put it there, but if I pricked you with a thorn, it might ruin the romantic gesture."

"I can manage." Her laugh was unsteady. She tucked the rose into the cluster of curls Miz Becky had pinned up what seemed an eon ago, knowing she wouldn't care if she did prick herself. "There."

"Beautiful." He touched the rose, then her cheek, his hand so gentle. "You're beautiful, Tory."

An automatic denial sprang to her lips. She wasn't beautiful, not like her mother. But she held the words back. Maybe it was time to give up that hurtful comparison for good.

Adam didn't seem to expect an answer. He cupped her chin in his hand, lifting it. He was going to kiss her.

A momentary panic swept her in a cold wave. She wasn't the Cinderella he remembered. And he wasn't ready, hadn't dealt with his feelings about his wife. They shouldn't.

Then his lips claimed hers, and her rational mind shut down entirely. Nothing remained but the moonlight, the faint strains of music and the strength of his arms around her. This wasn't about the past. This was about now.

Chapter Fourteen

This was just another part of the fairy tale, Tory told herself when she joined Adam's family at the public dock the next day after church. Being here, feeling a part of their clan, was a fantasy, not her ordinary life.

The warm Carolina sun beat down on her bare head, and she lifted a hand to shield her eyes. Philadelphia was probably cold and rainy, but here the weather insisted on apparently endless summer. It was all part of the fantasy.

The entire congregation of the Caldwell Cove church must have made its way to the dock. Some people carried flowers that fluttered in the breeze off the water. It should have been a festive scene, but people's expressions were serious, in contrast to yesterday's frivolity.

Jenny pressed close to her, slipping a small hand into hers. She smiled at the child, her heart warmed by the little sign of acceptance. She and Jenny seemed to have moved to a new place in their friendship since the incident at the yacht club.

"What happens next?" she whispered.

Jenny nodded to the water. "The boats will come. Watch for my daddy."

The crowd shifted a little, faces turning as if they'd received some sort of signal. Tory turned, the skirt of her dress fluttering in the breeze, and saw the first boat round the curve of the island and arrow toward the dock. Another followed it, then another, until the waterway was white with dozens of boats.

Jenny tugged at her hand and pointed. "See, there's Daddy," she whispered.

Adam was at the helm of the boat they'd taken the day they went to Angel Isle. He eased into the dock just below where they stood and cut his motor. Moving with that easy grace across the deck, he tossed a rope to the dock. His father caught it and made it fast.

Adam stood, his gaze seeming to search the crowd until he found them. He sketched a salute to Jenny. Then he gave Tory a small, private smile that made her heart tremble.

A fairy tale, she reminded herself desperately. It's just a fairy tale. But she was afraid her vulnerable heart wasn't listening.

One after another the boats moved in. She saw Adam's brother, then the Caldwell cousins, moor next to him. When every spot at the dock was taken, the boats formed a second row beyond the first, all of it accomplished with no sound but the creaking of timbers, the slap of the waves and the cries of the gulls.

When the last of the boats had been made fast, Pastor Wells stepped onto a makeshift platform at the end of the dock. As he lifted his hands to lead them in an opening prayer, Tory realized this really was a worship service. The blessing of the boats was an important part of the spiritual life of the island.

Everyone stood silent on the dock or in the boats as Pastor Wells began to read. A shiver made its way down Tory's spine. He was reading the names of all the islanders who'd died at sea.

She held Jenny's hand a little tighter. On the other side of the child, Adam's grandmother stood. Her face was strong, but tears filled her eyes as the names tolled on. With each name, those who carried flowers tossed them onto the water. The scent of the blossoms mingled with the salt air.

Her throat tight, Tory sought Adam's face again. He stood straight, almost at attention, his expression grave. This was a part of him she hadn't seen before—a part of island life she hadn't seen before. When he'd told her the family story about the shipwrecked sailor, she hadn't realized just what it meant. These people had lived, and died, by the sea for generations.

At last the reading of the names ended, and Pastor Wells lifted his hands again, facing the gathered boats. As he prayed for God's blessing on those who trod the sea, her heart seemed to overflow with her prayers and her almost incoherent longing to be a true part of this loving community.

Promptly after the amen, the choir began to sing the hymn she'd heard more than once since she'd been on the island.

"Eternal Father, strong to save, whose arm has bound the restless wave…"

As the crowd joined in the hymn, those on the boats climbed onto the dock to join their families. Adam joined them, sweeping Jenny into his arms as he took his place between Tory and his grandmother. He reached down to clasp Tory's hand, holding it strongly as the hymn came to an end. The final amen floated over the water.

People started to move away, but Tory couldn't, not until she'd blinked away the last of the tears. Adam put Jenny down, said something quietly to his grandmother, then turned to her.

"It's okay to cry, you know." He brushed a tear from her cheek. "I always do."

"I didn't realize what it was like." She swallowed hard, trying to get her voice to sound normal. "All those names."

He nodded, seeming to understand. "Even though I know it's coming, it still always hits me. How many we've lost over the years—some of them caught in storms, some through taking foolish chances. Some far away, like my grandfather's brother. He died on his ship at Pearl Harbor, but he's buried here."

She had trouble swallowing. "No wonder this place means so much to all of you."

"Gran says Caldwells are meant to come back to Caldwell Island no matter how far away they wander."

He looked at the waterway, and she followed his gaze. The flowers had floated into the center of the channel, carried by the tidal current. They formed a multicolored carpet on the green water.

"Did you ever think about going away?"

Adam shrugged. "I suppose every kid thinks once in a while of going out into the wide world to make his fortune. But I realized soon enough that all my dreams were here. My place, my family, my craft— everything I could want I found here on the island."

Still holding her hand, he began walking toward the street. Tory fell into step with him, wondering. Everything he could want, he'd said. Did he include his marriage in that list?

She couldn't ask. His bitterness toward Lila hadn't surfaced lately, and she hoped that meant he was coming to terms with it.

"What about you?" He looked at her with a question in his eyes.

"What about me what?"

"Your dreams," he prompted. "What are they, Tory?"

She could hardly say she thought her dreams were coming true when he kissed her the night before. It had been a kiss. No promises—just a kiss.

"Not very grand dreams, I suppose. Just the chance to do the work I love." She shrugged, thinking about it, and felt a wave of longing. "I guess I don't belong to a special place in the way you do with the island. My mother considered herself a Savannahian no matter where she lived. I like the city, but it's never felt like home to me."

"Maybe you haven't found the right place yet." Their linked hands swung between them as they walked.

"Maybe," she agreed, but something in her heart cried. She'd found a place she wanted to call home. She'd found her soul mate.

She couldn't kid herself that she was pretending. She might not be Cinderella, but she'd found her Prince Charming.

Unfortunately, Adam didn't act as if he wanted anything deeper than a casual relationship. That would be fine, if not for the fact that she'd gone and fallen in love with him.

Adam couldn't deny the truth to himself. He was on his way home from the boatyard earlier than usual on Monday because he wanted to see Tory. Somehow she'd managed to flood his mind with memories of her face, her smile, her touch.

He didn't know where their relationship was going, and that was the honest truth. When Tory finished working on the window—

That was like running into a brick wall. When Tory finished the window, he'd have to face looking at it. And she was nearing that point. He'd heard her on the phone with Mona, talking about the progress she'd made.

He pulled through the gates of Twin Oaks and

parked, then sat for a moment, staring through the windshield without really seeing. Okay, he could do this thing. It wouldn't be easy, but he'd find a way to cope with the memorial to Lila.

After all, he'd gotten through the years of sympathy, of people tiptoeing around his feelings because of the grief they assumed he bore. He'd get through this, too.

When Tory finished the window, she'd go away. The depth of his reaction to that startled him. He didn't want her to leave.

But he also wasn't prepared to ask her to stay. What that said about his emotional state he didn't want to consider.

He got out of the car and headed toward the house. He'd have to figure it out soon, or Cinderella would run out of his life again, just as she had before.

Jenny hurried to meet him on the porch, and he swung her up in his arms, planting a kiss of her soft cheek.

"How's my girl today?"

"I'm fine." She wiggled free and grabbed his hand, tugging at it. "Come on, Daddy. You have to come, right now."

He grinned, teasing her by hanging back. "Why do I have to come, sugar? What if I don't want to?"

She stamped her foot. "You have to, Daddy. Miz Tory wants us to come to the workroom."

He could feel the grin fade from his face. "Why does she?"

"The window!" Jenny practically bounced with

excitement. "It's almost done, and she says we can see it. I wanted to go in already, but she said I had to wait until you got home. Now come!"

His stomach roiled. He'd known this moment was coming. He'd tried to fool himself that he was ready for it. He wasn't.

So much for his idea that he could live with this. He didn't want to see the window Tory had created for Lila, and he especially didn't want to see it with Jenny.

Resentment burned along his nerves as Jenny tugged him toward the stairway. Couldn't Tory have been a little more thoughtful? Didn't she realize how hard it would be to look at the window for the first time with Jenny?

Apparently she didn't. His jaw tightened until it felt ready to crack.

Tory stood outside the studio, waiting. She wore her usual jeans, this time with a cobalt-blue sweater. Her hands held each other tightly.

"Can I go in? Please, Miz Tory?"

Tory nodded, and Jenny darted into the room.

"Don't touch anything." He stopped next to Tory and lowered his voice. "Did you really have to set it up so that Jenny and I see this window at the same time?"

She whitened as if he'd hit her. "I think you've forgotten," she said evenly. "You were the one who told Jenny she'd be the first one to see it, as soon as it was ready."

The fact that he knew he was in the wrong

didn't make him feel any better. He ought to apologize. He couldn't.

"All right. Let's get this over with." He steeled himself for the inevitable.

Tory gave a curt nod. She turned and walked across the studio to the table, her back straight, her shoulders stiff.

He'd hurt her. He didn't know if he was angrier with her, with himself or with his mother-in-law for precipitating this.

Jenny stood on the opposite side of the table, hand hovering over the window as if she longed to touch it but knew she couldn't. "Look, Daddy," she breathed. "Just look."

He looked. The first thing he saw was the inscription at the base of the window.

In memory of Lila Marie Caldwell, beloved daughter, wife and mother.

Anger and betrayal burned in his heart like a physical pain. He'd thought he was over what Lila had done to him. He'd thought he was ready to try having a relationship with Tory.

How could he, when he was still filled with so much resentment?

"Oh, Daddy, look here. Isn't he beautiful?" Jenny clasped her hands together. "It's our dolphin."

He saw the joy on his daughter's face and finally looked at Tory's design. His breath caught.

The silver-gray dolphin soared from the waves, body curving in a perfect arc against the sky. The sensation of movement was so strong he could hardly convince himself the creature was made of glass. It was real, and yet somehow it was also the same dolphin carved by that first Caldwell so long ago.

"Yes," he said finally, choking out the word. "You're right, sugar. It is our dolphin." He managed to look at Tory, wanting to wipe the hurt from her eyes. "It's beautiful."

Relief swept across her face. Then Jenny hurtled into Tory's arms.

"I love it, Miz Tory. I just love it. Now everyone will be able to see the dolphin again."

Tory hugged her. "I'm glad you like it, sweetheart. I just have to finish the last few details, and then we'll be ready to put it up in the church."

"I'm going to tell Grandpa and Miz Becky about the window." Jenny danced to the door. "They'll be really happy, too."

Then she was gone, and he was alone with Tory and the memory of his harsh words. He had to apologize, had to tell her—

"Are you all right?" Her eyes, deep as brown velvet, assessed him.

For an instant his mind showed him how she'd looked in the moonlight when he kissed her. He had to force the image away so he could concentrate on the present.

"I think so." He swallowed, knowing he couldn't get through this easily. "I'm sorry. I did tell Jenny she could be the first to see it. I had no right to react the way I did."

She shook her head. "It's not a question of rights. I know how hard it must be. I just—" She spread her hands wide. "You had to see it sometime."

"You were right."

"I was?" She looked confused. "About what?"

"When you first showed me the design. You said that it was as much for Jenny as for Lila. You said you thought it would honor the family." He nodded toward the dolphin. "Jenny saw that as soon as she looked at the window. It just took me a little longer."

Tory stared at him steadily, as if assessing whether or not he really meant his words. "You said once that you couldn't walk into the church every Sunday and look at a memorial window for Lila. Has that changed?"

He tried to be honest with her, as well as with himself. "I guess I'm not going to know exactly how I'll feel until it happens. The dedication will be hard."

"People will expect you to talk about her."

"Yes." That would be the hardest thing. "But once it's over—" He looked at her, trying to find the words that would tell her how he felt. "Once it's over, I can forget about the dedication. I can concentrate on your beautiful dolphin, and just be thankful for it."

The joy that flooded her eyes rewarded him. "Thank you, Adam." Her voice was barely more than a whisper. "I'm glad."

He looked at the dolphin again, not letting his gaze stray toward the words. Tory should be able to feel pride in her work without being hampered by the emotions he couldn't seem to control.

"It really is beautiful, you know. I should think clients would be lining up with commissions for you." As soon as the words were out, it occurred to him that it sounded as if he wanted her to leave.

She glanced away. "I'm afraid it's not so easy as that. People have to know the kind of work you can do. But it's a start. Now I have something all my own to show prospective clients."

"Back in Philadelphia."

She looked at him, startled. "Of course."

He shouldn't say anything. He didn't know where they were going or whether anything could come of this. But he couldn't let her walk away again.

"Do you have to go back? Couldn't you work somewhere else? Like here?"

Tory's heart seemed to stop beating as Adam's words penetrated. He wanted her to stay.

Careful, she thought, careful. Don't jump to conclusions that could hurt and embarrass both of you. Find out what's on his mind.

"I…I don't know what you mean." She hated the fact that she sounded so hesitant. What had happened to her prized independence?

Adam looked as if he were struggling with what he meant, too. Before he could speak, quick footsteps sounded in the hallway.

"Adam, dear! Ms. Marlowe! I just couldn't stay away any longer. Once Tory told me it was nearly finished, I had to see the memorial for myself." Adam's mother-in-law fluttered into the room and threw her arms around him.

Mixed emotions flooded through Tory. Of course her client had every right to see the window she'd commissioned. The natural apprehension as to whether the woman would be pleased with her work mingled with a dread of what this might do to Adam's precarious acceptance of the memorial. Was he going to be able to handle this?

"Mona, I didn't expect…" Adam seemed to censor his words. "It's good to see you. If you'd let me know you were coming, I'd have met you at the airport."

Mrs. Telforth took a step back, patting his cheek. "My dear, I didn't want to trouble you."

She spun to Tory, holding out both hands. "Tory, dear." She looked as she had each time Tory had seen her—elegant and expensive from the top of her carefully tinted ash-blond hair to the tips of her handmade Italian shoes.

"Mrs. Telforth, how are you?" Why didn't you warn us you were coming? And will your presence complicate an already difficult situation?

"Fine, fine." She glanced around the room. "Is it finished? Can I see?"

Adam's smile was so stiff it looked as if it would break. "It's almost finished. I think you'll be pleased with what Tory's accomplished." He took her arm and led her toward the table.

Tory followed, an incoherent prayer forming in her heart. *Please, please.*

Adam and his mother-in-law stopped at the edge of the table. For a long moment no one said anything. Then Mrs. Telforth clasped both hands together in a gesture that reminded Tory of Jenny.

"It's beautiful. Oh, Adam, isn't it just beautiful? Wouldn't Lila have loved it?"

From where she stood, Tory could see the muscle twitching in his jaw. "Yes," he said evenly. "I'm sure she'd have been pleased."

Mrs. Telforth blotted tears with a lace handkerchief. "I wanted so much to have a memorial to her here, on the island, where her life was. Read the inscription for me, dear."

His pain reached across the distance between them to grasp Tory's throat as she read aloud.

His gaze met Tory's over his mother-in-law's bowed head, and whatever hope had lingered in her heart turned to dust. All the light had gone out of him. He looked as stern and unforgiving as the sea.

Chapter Fifteen

Tory crossed the workroom hours later to stare out the window at the darkening sky. Streaks of pink and purple, painted across the horizon, bathed the island in the gathering dusk. Soon it would be full dark.

Soon it would be time for her to leave. Her throat tightened. The window was finished. Once it was installed in the church, there was no reason for her to be here.

A few hours ago she'd stood in this room and heard Adam ask her to stay. She shook her head. That had been real, hadn't it?

She pressed her hand against her heart. Adam had shut down at the sight of his mother-in-law. She didn't think he was going to open up again. Whatever he'd intended to say to her had been wiped out.

"Tory."

At the sound of his voice, her treacherous heart

persisted in filling with unreasonable hope. She turned to find him crossing the workroom toward her.

"Why did you disappear from dinner so quickly?"

Because it hurt too much to see you. "Well, I…I thought it was a time for family."

A shadow crossed his face as he stood next to her at the window. "Mona's arrival was a surprise."

Not a welcome one, to judge by his expression. "You said once she acted on whim."

He shrugged, managing a smile. "That's Mona. Still, it's good for Jenny to spend a little time with her, I guess."

"Of course." Jenny had been obviously entranced with the arrival of her grandmother, and she'd spent the entire dinner hour filling her in on everything she'd done in the last month.

"She won't stay long," he said. "She never does."

The last thing she wanted to do was have a casual conversation with Adam about his late wife's mother. Or anything else, for that matter. She wanted to know what he'd been going to say before Mona had come fluttering into the studio. She couldn't ask.

Adam shook his head, as if to chase away his thoughts. "We never got to finish our conversation this afternoon. About you not leaving."

"I don't…" She stopped, collected her thoughts. Adam would have to be clearer than that. "My job is almost finished. Why would I stay?"

He looked uncomfortable at the direct question. "You've been working hard. Don't you deserve a little vacation?"

She tried not to let disappointment show on her face. Adam was being kind. Everyone knew he was always kind.

"Whether I deserve it or not, I don't think I can afford it. I've got a struggling business to get on its feet, remember?"

Struggling was certainly the word. The amount she'd receive from this job would about cover the final expenses she owed from her mother's illness and death without much left over to pay the rent. "I have to start looking for my next commission."

"Is there any reason you can't do that from here? As far as I can see, your business is pretty much in your own hands."

She turned toward the window. It had gotten darker in the last few minutes, and she hoped the darkness hid her face. Adam was more right about that than he probably knew. Marlowe Stained Glass Studio consisted of her business cards, her small cache of equipment and her own two hands. She could work from anywhere.

But there was a very good reason that anywhere shouldn't be here. She'd done the last thing she should have done—she'd fallen in love with a man who wasn't ready to love again.

She couldn't let him guess that. Unfortunately, she'd never been especially good at hiding what she felt.

"I guess it's true that I can take my work anywhere." She wasn't any good at beating around the bush, either. She swung to face him. "Why would you ask me to stay? Given the reason I came, I should think you'd be glad to see the last of me."

His expression softened, his lips slipping into a rueful smile. "Come on, Tory. You know that's not true. With you around, I'm starting to feel seventeen again. You can't tell me you're not feeling that way, too."

"I guess not, but…" She'd begun to hope until Mona Telforth had fluttered into the workroom. "I had the sense Mona's arrival changed things."

Adam's jaw tightened. "I can't deny seeing her threw me. But after the initial shock passed, I realized it didn't have to change anything. Mona is Jenny's grandmother, so she'll always be part of our lives, but the past is past. Maybe it's time to move beyond it."

Could he? Or was he fooling himself? And her.

Adam's step covered the space between them, and he took both of her hands in his. "We can't go back to our past, either. But I'd like for us to have a chance to get to know each other again."

The fluttering began in the pit of her stomach and spread to her heart. How could she answer that?

Unfortunately she was way ahead of him. She didn't need time to get to know Adam again. She felt as if she'd already known him forever—known him and loved him. If he didn't feel the same, was any amount of time going to change that?

"Please." His voice deepened, and the tone set her nerves vibrating in response. "That's what happened before. You left, and we never had a chance to find out what might happen between us. I don't want it to be that way again."

She took a breath, trying to think beyond the clamor of her emotions. Trying to stifle the voice that said she should grab this opportunity and hold fast because it wouldn't come again.

"I guess." She steadied her voice. "I guess I can stay until the new window is dedicated, at least."

And after that?

She'd probably find herself leaving Caldwell Island with a broken heart. But that was a sure thing anyway, wasn't it?

"Okay, I think that's going to do it." Tory stepped back from the frame for the new window, nodding to the carpenter who'd spent the morning working in the church with her. "I'll see you tomorrow to install it."

As the man gathered his tools, she heard a quick step behind her. She turned to find Miranda Caldwell crossing the sanctuary toward her.

"Hey, Tory." Miranda gazed at the empty frame. "Is the new window really ready to go up?"

"Just about." Tory's nerves jumped to attention. Did Miranda wonder why she was still here, in that case? What would the rest of the Caldwell clan think about her staying on at Twin Oaks? They might already be speculating about it. "We'll put it in tomorrow. That's always the scary part, when you visualize hours of work shattering. Pray that it goes well."

"I will. I have been." Miranda's green eyes, so like her cousin's, focused on Tory's face. "I hear you're staying around for a while."

The island grapevine must work very efficiently. "I thought I'd stay until the dedication, anyway."

Miranda clasped her hand warmly. "I'm glad, Tory. You're good for him, you know."

She couldn't pretend not to know what Miranda was talking about. "I hope so."

"I know so. Believe me, I know my cousin."

Tory glanced upward, her gaze focusing on the image of Jesus walking on the water. Unconditional love shone in His face as He reached toward Peter.

Is that what I've come here to find, Lord? That kind of love?

"Maybe," she said aloud.

"Trust," Miranda said softly. "Just trust."

Tory blinked back sudden tears. She and Miranda seemed able to speak to each other from the heart, and that was a precious thing. "I'm trying."

Miranda nodded. "Okay, then. Oh, I almost forgot why I'm here, besides my abundant curiosity." She thrust an envelope toward Tory. "This came to the inn for you. I thought it might be important."

"Thank you." She took the envelope, frowning at the return address. Why was *Glass Today* magazine writing to her?

Miranda gave her a quick hug. "Don't forget. Trust." She was gone before Tory could respond.

Trust. She looked at the window again. *I'm trying, Lord.*

She ripped open the envelope, pulled out the single sheet of paper and stared at it in disbelief. *Glass Today* magazine wanted to do a story about her work in the Caldwell Cove church. She'd mentioned the project when she'd run into the magazine's photographer at a glass show. He'd seemed interested, but she never expected this.

She blinked back the tears that threatened to spill over. This was an opportunity she hadn't had the nerve to dream of. If her work was featured in the magazine, she'd find the church commissions she longed for. She'd be able to create her own songs of praise in the windows she made, like the craftsmen who'd done the windows in this church so long ago.

Thank you. Thank you.

She looked around, feeling as if the news would explode from her if she didn't share it with someone. And then she realized she did have someone to share it with. She could tell Adam. Even if he wasn't ready yet to claim more than friendship between them, he'd be happy for her. They would celebrate together.

Did he have any idea what he was doing where Tory was concerned? Adam leaned against the workbench, absently running his hand along the planking for the new boat. The converted warehouse he used for construction was silent. Most of the crew had gone home already, making this a good time and place to think.

Except that thinking didn't seem to be getting him very far. Every time he tried to assess his relationship with Tory, his errant imagination presented him with an image of her face, tipped up to his in the moonlight. Her dark eyes seemed to promise love, comfort, understanding, faithfulness—all the things he'd believed he had once.

He seized the plane, feeling muscles flex as he ran it along the plank, the fresh smell of sawdust mingling with the salt air. He'd better concentrate on work, since he couldn't think about Tory without getting emotions tangled up in it.

Who was he kidding? Everything about Tory had to do with emotions. He'd asked her to stay, but he could hardly expect her to hang around here while he tried to decide if they had a future. She had a right to more than that.

He wanted to believe he could love again. But he'd run on autopilot for the last four years, telling himself he had enough in life with his family, his business and his responsibilities. He stopped planing, letting his palm rest on the warm wood. Since Tory came, he'd realized that wasn't enough. What he didn't know was whether he was ready for more.

Why not, some part of his mind demanded. Why can't you move on? Why can't you move on with Tory?

Tory wasn't Lila. She wasn't anything like Lila. Tory understood.

He heard the creak of the wooden door, and something told him it was Tory before he turned around. She stood in the doorway for a moment, the light behind her, and he couldn't make out her face.

Then she moved quickly toward him, and he read the joy in her expression.

"Hey." He rested a hip against the workbench, enjoying the sight of her. "It's good to see you."

"You almost didn't. The boatyard looks deserted.

I thought you'd gone home, but then I spotted your truck."

"I wanted to get in an hour on the hull of the new boat." He patted the smooth wood. "If I do it when people are here, they keep interrupting me."

"Like me?" She lifted those level brows.

"You're a welcome interruption." He reached for her, taking her hand and drawing her closer to lean against the workbench next to him. "I'm always glad to see you."

Funny, that she'd become such an important part of his life in such a short period of time. They'd had a head start, though. Maybe subconsciously he'd always remembered his Cinderella.

"That's good." She let her hand rest companionably in his, apparently content to enjoy the moment.

That was one of the things that drew him to her— that certain stillness. Maybe it was the artist in her, letting her look with appreciation at dust motes floating in a shaft of sunshine from the high windows.

"This is a nice place," she said finally. "It feels like good work is done here."

"I hope so." He shifted so he could look more fully in her face. Those strong bones of cheek and jaw would give her a distinctive beauty even when she was as old as Gran. And how far gone was he that he even thought such a thing? He brushed a lock of dark brown hair from her cheek. "Of course it's not quite as nice as working in the church, now, is it?"

She turned to look at him, her soft cheek moving

against his fingers. "That reminds me why I came. I got some exciting news. I wanted to share it with you."

Something vaguely uneasy touched him, like a cold chill on the back of his neck. "News about what?"

She pulled an envelope from the pocket of her denim jacket. "This came to the inn for me, and Miranda brought it over. It's from *Glass Today* magazine."

"The magazine that did that spread on your old boss?" He remembered as he said it that the man had also been her old fiancé. He hadn't deserved a woman like Tory.

She nodded, and happiness danced in her eyes as she filled him in on her good news. "I know one of their photographers, and I guess she suggested a story. It just came out of the blue."

The chill intensified. "A story? What kind of a story?"

If warning sounded in his voice, she obviously didn't hear it. She gestured, her hands opening an imaginary magazine. "A photo layout of the church, with pictures of the restored windows and a bit of information about the original artist, if they can find it. But mostly it will be about the new window—interviews, photos, everything."

"Interviews," he repeated. His stomach roiled. Interviews about Lila, probably.

She must have heard his tone. Caution dampened the excitement in her face.

"That's what they usually do." She eyed him as if trying to read his mind.

He pressed both hands hard against the wooden bench behind him. "Tory, you can't let them do that."

She blinked, looking at him without understanding. "What do you mean?"

"Just what I said." He used his hands to launch his body away from the bench, unable to stand still a moment longer. "No article, Tory."

"You can't be serious." She flung her hands out. "Don't you understand what this means to me? This will open the door to all sorts of church jobs for me. I can do what I've always dreamed of doing."

"You're the one who doesn't understand. They'll want to write about Lila. They'll want to interview us. Can you imagine what Mona would say? They'd probably even want a picture of Jenny. You can't let them do that. *I* can't!"

"But you agreed to the window. You said you could handle this."

His jaw clenched so tightly it was painful. "I guess I was wrong, then. Maybe I can cope with seeing that window in the church, but I can't cope with this. I won't have my family put on display in a magazine for all the world to see."

"It's not…"

"Tory—" He stopped, took a breath, tried to think through the maze of emotions that tumbled inside him. "Tory, I love you. If you love me, you'll give this up."

Chapter Sixteen

Adam's words echoed like a death knell. He loved her, but— The pain deepened, like a sliver of glass driving into Tory's heart. He would only love her if she did what he wanted, like her grandmother, like her mother, like Jason.

She looked at him. His usually laughing eyes were as hard as flint.

She could have what she wanted. She could have his love. All she had to do was accept the conditions that came with it. A longing swept over her to do just that.

"No." She didn't realize she was going to say it aloud until she heard the word echo in the still, cavernous space. It ricocheted from the high ceiling and clanged against the walls.

Adam looked taken aback. "No what?"

"No." She knew what she had to say, and her heart shattered with the knowledge. "It's not love if it comes with strings attached."

If that hurt him, he didn't show it. No feeling stirred in his usually expressive face. "You're going to go ahead with this, knowing how I feel."

She had to fight the wave of exhaustion that swept over her. Even shaking her head took an effort. She didn't want to fight any more. She wanted—oh, how she wanted—to pretend she could believe he truly loved her. But she couldn't. Real love wasn't preceded by the word *if*.

"I'll turn down the article."

He took a quick step toward her, his face lightening. "Tory, I'll make it up to you."

She stopped him with an outflung hand. "No." She pushed the word out, swimming against the tide of longing to be in his arms. "I'll give up the article not because I think it's right, but because it matters so much to you. But I don't want anything else from you."

He went still. "I don't understand."

She wouldn't let herself cry, not in front of him. She forced her voice to be steady. "I don't want love that comes with conditions, Adam. If I've learned anything, I've learned that."

"I'm just asking you not to do something that will hurt my family."

"We both know that's not what this is about." She breathed a prayer. *Please, Lord. Let me say what needs to be said.*

Anger sparked in his eyes. "You'd better tell me, because I don't know what you mean."

Somehow Adam's anger stiffened her spine.

"This isn't about family. It's about your bitterness toward Lila."

"All right, I can't forgive her." He almost shouted the words, then seemed to realize what he'd done and clamped his mouth closed. "I can't forgive her," he repeated quietly. "How could I?"

"I don't know. I haven't done so well in the forgiveness department myself." She closed her eyes for an instant, gathering strength. "But I know you can't love anyone else as long as you can't forgive Lila."

Adam's face tightened until it resembled a wooden mask, stiff and impenetrable. "Then I guess I'm not going to love anyone."

She wanted to cry out to him, wanted to tell him not to throw away what they might have together. But she couldn't. This was a battle he'd have to fight alone.

Help him, Lord, because I can't.

"Goodbye, Adam." She turned and moved blindly toward the door, feeling the hot tears spill onto her cheeks and knowing she'd lost him.

Adam accelerated until he could hear nothing but the roar of the boat's motor, feel nothing but the rush of wind against his body. He rounded the curve of the island and headed toward open water.

It didn't work. No noise was loud enough to drown out Tory's voice. He'd been trying to do that for nearly twenty-four hours, and he couldn't. If he ran the boat all the way to the Florida Keys, he wouldn't outrun Tory's words.

He eased back on the throttle, slowing until the boat bounced gently on the incoming tide, then cut the motor and let the boat drift. The endless, inexorable waves rolled toward him, gray and green as the waves in the church window of Jesus walking on the water. He'd looked at that image a thousand times without really seeing it until Tory, with her artist's eyes, had made him see.

Peter, drowning in his lack of faith. Something cold clutched Adam's heart. He looked at the waves and imagined what it would be like.

No, he didn't have to imagine. He knew. He'd been out of the boat himself—once in a fishing accident, once in a storm. He'd felt the current grab him, known his clothes were dragging him down, struggled in panic against the tide. He'd been in the place of all those islanders who'd been lost at sea.

But he hadn't drowned. Each time someone had been there to help him. Like Peter, he hadn't drowned.

Until now.

Peter had been sinking under the weight of his lack of faith. Adam was sinking under the weight of his lack of forgiveness.

Everything in him rose to reject that thought. He couldn't forgive. Anger and bitterness clutched his heart. What Lila had done to him was unforgivable.

Unforgivable? He saw, in his mind's eye, the face of Jesus in the window. Jesus looked at Peter without regard for Peter's failings—He looked at Peter with unconditional love.

Tory didn't deserve love that came with conditions. She was wise enough to know that wasn't love at all.

He had to free himself. But he couldn't. He stared at the rolling waves, tears salty as the ocean filling his eyes.

Please, Lord. I can't do it myself. Please, help me learn to forgive. Help me.

"Easy, easy." Tory held her breath as the workmen put the new window into its frame. It creaked as if in protest, and then settled into place.

She couldn't look at it. Her beautiful dolphin only gave her pain instead of joy.

She took a step back, letting the workmen secure the window. She wouldn't have to see it much longer. Her bags were packed. As soon as this was finished, she'd leave Caldwell Island. This time she wouldn't be back.

I failed. The thought haunted her. She hadn't found the dolphin, hadn't kept her promise to her mother.

She'd finished the commission, but at a cost she'd be feeling for the rest of her days.

She covered her eyes with her palms only to see the colored light from the windows against the darkness.

She dropped her hands and stared at the image of Jesus walking on the water. His loving gaze, directed at Peter, seemed to touch her, too. It was as if He spoke directly to her wounded heart.

You have unconditional love from Me, dear child. Forgive yourself, and be content.

Love flowed through her, easing the pain. She could see more clearly.

She couldn't erase the pain of her mother's life, no matter how much she longed to. She couldn't undo Emily's past. But she couldn't regret her time here, no matter how much it hurt. She'd done the right thing in coming back to Caldwell Island.

Tory looked at her dolphin, springing from the waves. She hadn't found the lost carving, but she'd done what she could. It had to be enough.

"I see it's finished."

At the sound of Adam's voice, her hands clenched, fingernails biting into the palms. How long would it be until she could think of him without pain?

She turned to watch as he came slowly down the center aisle. Through the pain, she stored up one more image of him to carry away with her. It would have to last a long time.

She was vaguely aware of the workmen gathering their tools. The moment they took to exchange a few words with Adam gave her time to armor herself. The door closed behind the workmen, and they were alone in the church. They'd come full circle.

"Yes. It's done." There didn't seem to be anything else to say. She'd already said it all. "I'll be leaving today."

"I don't think you should go so soon." Adam took a step closer. "The photographer won't be here until tomorrow."

It was hard to think with him so close. "Photographer?"

"From the magazine. I called them. They're going to do the story."

She looked at him, not quite able to believe what she was hearing. "You called them? But why? I told you I'd give up the story."

"You told me it wasn't love if it came with strings attached."

Her words came back to hurt her, and she swallowed hard. "I told you I'd give it up," she said again. "You didn't have to call them."

"Yes, I did."

She didn't dare to hope. "Why?"

His strong face grew bleak. "I wanted to take the easy way out. I thought I could accept the memorial and pretend that my life with Lila was behind me. That I could just forget."

His words pierced her heart. "Forgetting doesn't work, does it?" The Lord knew she'd tried that.

"No." He clenched his jaw. "I couldn't forget. You were right. I had to forgive first."

"I'm glad," she said carefully, not able to let herself hope. "If you're able to forgive Lila, I'm glad." The emotions roiling through her were too big, too scary.

"I had to forgive so I could free my heart to love again." He lifted his hand to touch her cheek gently. "It's the only way I could offer you my love. Unconditionally."

She searched his face, longing to believe and not quite daring to. But the steady light in his eyes told her the truth. He meant what he said. He loved her.

With a little sob, she stepped into his arms. "You mean it."

He held her close, his cheek against hers. "I love you, Tory Marlowe. Please say you can love me."

She'd come to Caldwell Cove to find the secrets of the past. God had shown her the secrets of the heart.

She looked at Adam, heart almost too full to speak. "I can," she managed to say. "I do."

Epilogue

A few weeks ago, Adam wouldn't have dreamed he'd be able to do this. He stood near the pulpit in the church, waiting his turn to speak at the dedication of the new window.

He hadn't thought he could even look at the window, but now his heart was drawn toward Tory's beautiful creation. The dolphin rose from the sea, even more dramatic seen as it should be, with the sunlight behind it and the colors streaming across the faces of the people he loved.

His brother, his cousins, their spouses and children—every Caldwell had come. His heart swelled as he looked at his father sitting next to Uncle Clayton. They'd taken another faltering step in finding a relationship, sitting together in church for the first time since they were boys. The joy in Gran's face was almost too intense to behold.

Music from the organ filled the sanctuary until it

seemed the walls must breathe with it. Soon the organist would finish, and it would be his turn to speak. He'd have to talk about Lila.

He could, now. Loving Tory had let him find his way to forgiveness and peace.

Tory sat in the front row, between Mona and his daughter. The engagement ring he'd given her sparkled in the light from the window, and it occurred to him how appropriate that was. The window had brought Tory back to him.

They'd settled so many things in the last few weeks. Tory would continue to create her stained glass in the larger studio he was building where she could have both a workroom and a display area. She'd travel when she had to, but most of the time she'd be on the island, where she belonged.

His heart filled with thankfulness as he looked at her serene profile. God had given them such a precious gift in their love for each other.

Tory turned her head, her gaze seeking his, and gave him a small, private smile. For an instant some trick of the light turned her into the young girl in the white dress with stars in her eyes.

His Cinderella. He'd found her and lost her fifteen years ago, but when the time was right, God had brought her home to him at last.

* * * * *

Dear Reader,

Thank you for choosing to pick up this book. I hope you've enjoyed the story of Adam and Tory. I've had such pleasure in writing the Caldwell clan stories that I'll hate to leave them when the stories are finished.

I began thinking about this story when I took a class in making stained glass a few years ago. Although I'll never be the artist that Tory is, learning about the glass has given me a new appreciation for the wonderful works that grace so many sanctuaries.

I love to hear from readers, and I'd be happy to send you a signed bookplate and let you know when my books are coming out. You can reach me c/o Steeple Hill Books, 233 Broadway, Suite 1001, New York, NY 10279 or visit me on the Web at www.martaperry.com.

Blessings,

Marta Perry

PROMISE FOREVER

Therefore, as God's chosen people, holy and dearly loved, clothe yourselves with compassion, kindness, humility, gentleness and patience.
—*Colossians* 3:12

This story is dedicated to my wonderful editor,
Ann Leslie Tuttle, with gratitude.
And, as always, to Brian.

Chapter One

❦

Tyler Winchester ripped open the pale blue envelope that had arrived in the morning mail. A photograph fluttered onto the polished mahogany desktop. No letter, just a photograph of a young boy, standing in the shade of a sprawling live oak.

He flipped it over. Two words had been scrawled on the back—two words that made his world shudder.

Your son.

For a moment he couldn't react at all. He shot a glance toward the office doorway, where his younger brother was trying to talk his way past Tyler's assistant. Turning his back on them, Tyler studied the envelope. Caldwell Cove. The envelope was postmarked Caldwell Cove, South Carolina.

Something deep inside him began to crack painfully open. The child's face in the picture was partly shadowed by the tree, but that didn't really matter.

He saw the resemblance anyway—the heart-shaped face, the pointed chin. Miranda.

The boy was Miranda's child, certainly. But his? How could that be? He'd have known. She'd have told him, wouldn't she?

The voices behind him faded into the dull murmur of ocean waves. A seabird called, and a slim figure came toward him from the water, green eyes laughing, bronze hair rippling over her shoulders.

His jaw clenched. No. He'd closed off that part of himself a long time ago, sealing it securely. He wouldn't let it break open.

The truth was, he didn't know what Miranda might do. It had been—what, eight years? He stared at the photo. The boy could be the right age.

He spun around, the movement startling both his brother and his assistant into silence. Josh took advantage of the moment to move past Henry Carmichael's bulk. He looked from Tyler's face to the photo in his hand, gaze curious. "Is something wrong?"

"Nothing." Nothing that he wanted to confide in Josh, in any event. He slid the photograph into his pocket.

"In that case…"

"Not now." He suspected he already knew what Josh wanted to talk about. Money. It was always money with Josh, just as it was with their mother and with the array of step and half siblings and relatives she'd brought into his life. The whole family saw Tyler as an inexhaustible account to fund their expensive tastes.

You can't count on anyone but yourself. His father's harsh voice echoed in his mind. *They all want something.*

"But Tyler," Josh began.

He shook his head, then looked at Henry. He could at least trust Henry to do what he was told without asking questions that Tyler had no intention of answering. "Have the jet ready for me in two hours. I'm flying to Savannah."

"Savannah?" Josh's voice suggested it might as well be the moon. "What about the Warren situation? I thought you were too involved in that contract negotiation to think about anything else."

He spared a thought for the multimillion-dollar deal he'd been chasing for months. "I'll be a phone call or a fax away. Henry will keep me posted on anything I need to know."

"Whatever you say." Henry's broad face was impassive as always. Henry was as unemotional as Tyler, which was probably why they worked so well together.

Tyler crossed the room quickly, pausing to pull his camel-hair coat from the mahogany coatrack. It had been a raw, chilly March day in Baltimore, although Caldwell Cove would be something else.

Again the image shimmered in his mind like a mirage. Surf. Sand. A laughing, sun-kissed face. His wife.

They all want something. What did Miranda want?

He shoved the thought away and strode to the door. He'd deal with this, just as he dealt with any project that went wrong. Then he'd bury the memory of his first love so deeply that it would never intrude again.

The bell on the registration desk jingled impatiently. Miranda Caldwell dusted flour from her hands as she hurried from the inn's kitchen toward the front hallway. The Dolphin Inn wasn't expecting any new guests today, and the rest of the family had taken advantage of that fact to scatter in various directions.

She'd thought she'd have an uninterrupted half-hour to bake some molasses cookies before Sammy got home from school. It looked as if she'd been wrong.

She shoved through the swinging door to the wide hallway that housed the inn's registration desk, along with whatever clutter of fishing poles and baseball bats her brothers had left on the wide-planked floor.

"May I help you?"

The tall stranger turned slowly. Afternoon sunlight through the front screen door lit broad shoulders, dark hair, an expensive suit that was far too formal for the island. Then he faced her, and her heart stopped entirely.

Tyler Winchester, the man she'd never expected to see again. The man who'd broken her eighteen-year-old heart when their marriage dissolved. The man who'd never known he'd fathered a son.

"Hello, Miranda. It's been a long time."

His voice was deeper than she remembered. More confident. Through a haze of dismay came the knowledge that Tyler didn't sound surprised. He'd known he was going to find her here.

"Tyler." Pain ripped through the numbness of shock when she said his name. She hadn't said it aloud in years. How could two syllables have such power to hurt?

He lifted his brows, eyes the color of rich chocolate expressing nothing at all. "Aren't you going to say you're surprised to see me?"

"I…yes, of course I'm surprised."

Tyler made no move to close the gap between them, thank goodness. If he attempted to shake hands with her, she'd probably turn to stone.

"What brings you to the island?" She managed to get the words out.

He seemed to move farther away from her, even though he didn't actually move at all. Maybe it was just the effect of the chill in his strong-boned face.

"Not a pleasure trip," he said crisply.

No, it wouldn't be that. Tyler probably vacationed in the south of France. He certainly wouldn't choose to come to Caldwell Cove after what had happened between them.

Maybe that didn't matter to him. After all, he'd had eight years to forget his youthful indiscretion. While she'd been looking at a reminder every day in Sammy—

Sammy. She sent a frantic, fearful glance at the clock. Her son would be walking in the door from school any minute now. As soon as he heard the name, he'd know who Tyler was.

But Tyler didn't know Sammy existed, and she had to keep it that way.

Oh, Lord, please. She sent up a fervent, desperate prayer. *Help me get rid of him before Sammy gets home.*

"You're here on business, then." She tried to sound as cool as he did, as if it were an everyday occurrence for the man who'd been her husband for one short month to walk back into her life. She moved behind the desk, putting an expanse of scarred oak between them. It wasn't enough of a barrier, but it was all she had.

"You might say that." Tyler leaned on the desk, the movement bringing him close enough that she caught the expensive aroma of his aftershave. "Maybe you'd better give me a room. I'll be here at least for one night."

Panic surged through her like a riptide. He couldn't stay here. "No. I mean, I'm sorry." She put both hands on the register to hide the pages. "We're all booked up."

His brows lifted again. "This early in the season? Try again, Miranda. I don't buy it."

When had Tyler become so sarcastic? That hadn't been part of the boy she'd married.

Her heart ripped a little. She didn't know him any longer. The boy who'd held her in his arms and promised to love her forever had turned into a man she didn't understand at all.

He was rich, of course. Winchesters had always been rich and successful. They were filled with the arrogance that came with always getting everything they wanted just by lifting a hand.

Once what Tyler wanted was her—shy little Miranda Caldwell, an island girl who hadn't had the least notion of the world he lived in. But that wanting hadn't lasted long. Just long enough to make the baby he'd never known about.

She swallowed hard, trying to come up with the words that would make him go away.

"I'm sorry, Tyler." She forced herself to meet his gaze. "I'm afraid we don't have room for you. I think you should leave now."

Some emotion she couldn't identify chased across his face, and the skin around his eyes seemed to tighten. "Leave? After you've gone to so much trouble to get me here? That doesn't make any sense."

"Get you here?" That was the last thing she'd ever do. "What on earth are you talking about?"

Tyler planted both fists on the desk, leaning so close their faces were scant inches apart. She felt the heat radiating from him—no, it was anger, so hot it threatened to singe her skin. His lips were a hard, bitter line.

"I'm talking about the little surprise package you sent me. Didn't you think I'd come down here as soon as I received it?"

She stared at him, baffled. "I didn't send you a package."

With a swift movement he took something from his pocket and tossed it to the desk between them. It fluttered onto the faded red blotter. She forced frozen fingers to pick it up.

Sammy. Her stomach twisted, making her feel as she had during those months of morning sickness. Tyler had a picture of Sammy.

No. He couldn't. Her mind moved slowly, struggling against the unthinkable reality.

With a quick, angry movement he turned it over in her hand. "Don't forget the inscription."

Your son.

The printed words struck her in the heart. They rang in her ears, mocking her. All these years of protecting her secret from him, only to have it blown apart by two simple words.

"Where did you get this?"

"You sent it to me."

"No!" The word nearly leaped from her mouth. "I didn't."

He made a quick, chopping motion with one hand, as if cutting her away from him. "Who else? I have to warn you, Miranda. If you want child support, you'd better be prepared to prove that boy is mine."

It took a moment for his words to penetrate, another for her brain to actually make sense of them. Then anger shot up, hot and bracing. How dare he imply she'd had someone else's child?

Common sense intervened. They hadn't seen each other in years. For all Tyler knew, she might have remarried, might have...

He doesn't know for sure Sammy is his.

Beneath the anger, beneath the pain, relief flowered. If Tyler wasn't sure Sammy was his son, she might still avert disaster. She wouldn't have to fear the nightmare of Tyler snatching Sammy away from her.

She stood up straight, trying to find the strength Gran always insisted was bred into generations of Caldwell women. "My son has nothing to do with you." She picked her words carefully. "I think it best if you leave now."

Furrows dug between his brows, and his angry gaze seemed to grasp her with the power that had swept her eighteen-year-old self along with whatever Tyler wanted. "I'll leave as soon as I'm satisfied, Miranda. I want to know why you sent this to me."

His words rattled around her brain. Who had sent it? None of this made any sense at all. She tried not to glance at the implacable round face of the clock, warning her Sammy could walk in on them.

Nothing else matters. Just get him out of here before Sammy comes in.

"I don't know who sent it. I didn't. I don't want anything from you." It took a fierce effort to look at him as coolly as if he were a stranger.

He is a stranger, a tiny voice sobbed in her ear. *He's not the man you loved.*

Tyler straightened, his shoulders stiff, his face a mask. "In that case, I'll—"

The creak of the screen door cut off the sentence, and fear obliterated her momentary relief.

"Hey, Momma, I'm home." Sammy's quick footsteps slowed when he saw that his mother wasn't alone. He glanced curiously at Tyler, then tossed a green spelling book on the desk. "Can I get a snack?"

"May I," she corrected automatically. Cool, careful. She could still get out of this in one piece. As long as Sammy didn't hear Tyler's name, she was all right. "Go on into the kitchen. I have some cookies started."

Sammy nodded, turned. She held her breath. Almost out of danger. There'd be time enough later to sort it all out. Get Sammy out, and...

"Just a minute." Tyler's voice had roughened. It carried a raw note of command.

She forced herself to move around the desk, grasp Sammy's shoulders, look at Tyler. The expression on his face chilled her to the bone.

He knew. He'd taken one look at Sammy, and her son's beautiful eyes, so like his father's, had given them away. Tyler knew Sammy was his son.

Tyler couldn't stop staring. At first he'd seen a child with Miranda's heart-shaped face, her pointed chin.

Then the boy looked at him, and Tyler had seen the child's eyes. Deep brown, with the slightest gold flecks in them when the light hit as it did in that moment, slanting through the wavy panes of the hall window. Eyes deeply fringed with curling lashes.

Winchester eyes—they were the same eyes he saw every time he looked at his brother and every morning in the mirror.

Stop, take a breath, think about this.

He didn't really need to think about it. Maybe the truth had been there all along, beneath his initial assumption that he couldn't have a child. He'd known, at some level, that if Miranda had a son, that boy was his.

She hadn't told him. Anger roared through his thoughts like a jet. Miranda had borne his child, and she hadn't told him.

The three of them stood, frozen in place, the old house quiet around them. From somewhere outside came the raucous squawk of a seagull, seeming to punctuate his anger. She hadn't told him.

He shifted his gaze to Miranda, furious words forming on his tongue. He'd tell her just what he thought—

He couldn't. Not with the boy standing there, looking at him with those innocent eyes. No matter how little he welcomed this news, how angry he was at the woman he'd once loved, he couldn't say anything in front of the child.

He took a breath. "We have to talk."

Miranda turned the child toward the swinging doors. "You go on back to the kitchen. I'll be with you in a little bit."

The boy nodded. After another curious glance at Tyler, he pushed through the door.

He gave the child—his child—another moment to get out of range. He heard the swish of the kitchen door closing. He could speak, if he could find the words.

"Well, Miranda?"

Her soft mouth tightened. "Not here. Anyone might walk in."

The fact that she was right didn't help. His son.

The words pounded in his blood. "There must be privacy somewhere in this place."

She gave a curt nod, then led the way to the room on the right of the hall.

Tyler shut the door firmly, glancing around at overstuffed, shabby chairs, walls covered with family photos, a couple of toy cars abandoned on a round pedestal table. He didn't remember being in this room before, but that wasn't surprising. Miranda's family had been as opposed to their relationship as his had been.

He swung toward Miranda.

"Well?" he repeated. "Why did it take you eight years to let me know I'm a father? Or didn't you want child support until now?"

She flinched, her eyes darkening. "I don't need or want anything from you, Tyler."

He suppressed the urge to rant at her. Tyler Winchester didn't lose control, no matter what the provocation. That was one of the keys to his success. "Then why send me that picture now?"

"I didn't!"

Even through his anger, he had to recognize the sincerity in her voice. And he couldn't deny the shock that had been written on her face when she'd first seen him.

"You mean that, don't you?"

She nodded.

"Then who?"

"I don't know. Does it really matter? You know."

"I should have known eight years ago." His anger spiked again. "Why didn't you tell me, Miranda?

Even if our marriage was a mistake, surely I deserved to know I had fathered a child."

She crossed her arms, hugging herself. He'd thought, when he first saw her, that she didn't look any older than she had at eighteen. Now he saw the faint lines around her eyes, the added maturity in the way she stood there, confronting him.

"Well?" He snapped the word, annoyed at himself for the weakness of noticing how she looked.

She spread her hands out. "I don't know what you want me to say, Tyler. By the time I knew I was pregnant, our marriage was over."

He'd told himself he barely remembered that one short month. That wasn't true. He remembered only too well—remembered the furious quarrel with his father over his involvement with a local girl, remembered storming out of the beach house intent on showing the old man that he could manage his own life.

A runaway marriage would do it. He hadn't found it difficult to persuade Miranda or himself that was their only option. They'd come back from their secret honeymoon to face the music—to tell both their families they were married.

Miranda's father had been disapproving but ready to accept the inevitable.

Not his. His father had ranted and raged at both of them, his emotions spilling out like bubbling acid. And then he'd had a heart attack. He'd died before the paramedics reached him.

Tyler slammed the door on that memory. He'd

better focus on the present. "You were having our baby. I should have been told."

Anger flared in her heart-shaped face. "You wanted the divorce."

"I had a right to know," he repeated stubbornly. He moved toward her a step, as if he could impel an explanation. But this wasn't the old Miranda, the sweet young woman who'd been so dazzled by love she'd gone along with anything he said.

"What was the point?" She brushed a strand of coppery hair away from her face impatiently. "You were busy taking your father's place and saving the company. You had a life mapped out that didn't include a child."

"And you figured you didn't need me." That was what rankled, he realized. She hadn't needed him then, didn't seem to need him now.

"I had my family."

She gestured toward the groupings of family photographs hung against the wallpaper, the movement sending a whiff of her scent toward him. Soap and sunshine, that was how Miranda had always smelled to him. She still did, and he was annoyed that he remembered.

"They thought you shouldn't tell me?" This branch of the Caldwell clan had never had much money, as he recalled. He'd have expected them to be lining up for child support long before this.

She glanced at him with an odd expression he couldn't quite pin down.

"They were as opposed to our marriage as your

family was, remember? They never held with marrying someone from a different world. My daddy said only grief could come from that."

"Looks like he was right, doesn't it?"

Her chin lifted, looking considerably more stubborn than he remembered. "I have Sammy. I don't consider that a source of grief, no matter what."

"Sammy." He didn't even know his son's full name. "What's the rest of it?"

She didn't look away. "Samuel Tyler Caldwell, like mine."

It struck him, then, a fist to the stomach. He had a son. Somehow, he had to figure out how to deal with that.

"Didn't he ask questions about his father?"

She winced. "Of course he asked. Any child would."

"And did you bother telling him the truth?"

"Sammy knows his father's name. He knows our marriage ended because we weren't suited to each other."

It was what he believed himself, but it annoyed him to hear her say it. "Why does he think I never came around?"

"When he asked, I told him you had to work far away." For an instant there was a flicker of uncertainty in her face. "Eventually he stopped asking. He gets plenty of masculine attention. My father, my brothers, my cousins—he doesn't lack male role models, if that's what you're thinking."

It hadn't been, but now that she said it, he knew the sprawling Caldwell clan would take care of its own.

But Sammy was his son. He didn't know what that was going to mean yet, but it had to mean something.

"I'm his father."

She crossed her arms again, as if she needed something to hang onto. "He doesn't have to know you were here. You can leave, and we'll go back to the way things were."

"I don't think so, Miranda."

"Why not? You don't want to have a son."

"Maybe not, but I have one. I'm not just going to walk away and pretend it never happened."

She took a breath, and he seemed to feel her gathering strength around her.

"If you mean that, then I'll have to tell him you're here."

His world shifted again. He had a son. Soon that son would know Tyler was his father.

Chapter Two

Had she ever felt quite this miserable? Miranda sat on the porch swing, staring across the width of the inland waterway at the sunset over the mainland. Maybe, when she was eighteen and discovering that she couldn't function in Tyler's world. And that her fairy-tale marriage wouldn't survive the strain.

At the sight of Tyler standing in the hallway that afternoon, all the pain of losing him had surged out of hiding. Tyler was back—Tyler knew about Sammy. Somehow she had to come to terms with that.

This old swing, on the porch that stretched comfortably across the front of the inn, had always been a refuge. It wasn't today.

She closed her eyes, letting the sunset paint itself on the inside of her lids. *Lord, I don't know what to do.*

No, that wasn't quite right. She knew what she had to do. She had to tell Sammy his father was here, before her son heard it from someone else. She just didn't know how.

Please, Lord, help me find the words to tell Sammy without hurting him. Panic gripped her heart. *Don't let Tyler's coming hurt him. He's so young.*

Certainly there weren't any easy words for this situation. Telling her family that Tyler was here had been difficult enough—telling her son would be infinitely worse.

Her mother had been comforting, her father rigidly fair, silencing the angry clamor of her three brothers, who wanted to dump Tyler into the deepest part of the channel. Her sister, Chloe, married now, hadn't been present, but she'd undoubtedly join them as soon as she heard.

Her father had been firm. Tyler had a right to see his son, Clayton Caldwell had said. They'd have to put up with it, for Sammy's sake.

That had been the only thing that would make the twins and Theo behave, she suspected. David and Daniel considered themselves substitute fathers, while Theo had always been a big brother to his ten-years-younger nephew. None of them would do anything to hurt Sammy.

She rubbed her forehead tiredly, then tilted her head to stare at the porch ceiling, painted blue as the sky. She cherished her family, but coping with their reactions had made it impossible for her to work through her own feelings about Tyler's reappearance.

Maybe she wouldn't have been able to, anyway.

Just the thought of him seemed to paralyze her with shock.

"Momma?" Sammy pushed through the screen door and let it bang behind him. "Grandma says you want to talk to me."

She forced down a spurt of panic and patted the chintz-cushioned seat next to her. *Please, Lord.*

"Come sit by me, sugar. We need to talk."

Sammy scooted onto the swing. Those jeans were getting too short already, she noticed automatically. He was going to have his father's height.

His face clouded. "I studied for my arithmetic test. Honest."

She was briefly diverted, wondering how Sammy had done on that test. What she had to tell him made arithmetic unimportant for the moment.

"I know you did." She ruffled his hair, and he dodged away from the caress as he'd been doing for the last year or so, aware of being a big kid now. For an instant she longed to have her baby back again, so that she could savor every single experience.

Tyler had missed all those moments. Tension clutched her stomach. Was he angry about that? Or just angry that she hadn't told him about his son?

Sammy wiggled. "Is somethin' wrong?"

"No. I just need to tell you something." She hesitated, searching for the words.

"Somethin' bad?"

Sammy must be picking up on her apprehension, and that was the last thing she wanted. She forced a smile. "No, not bad. Just sort of surprising."

Say it, she commanded.

"You know the man who was here this afternoon, when you got home from school?"

He nodded.

She took a breath. "Well, that was…Tyler Winchester."

Sammy jerked upright on the swing. "My father?"

"Your father. He came to see you."

Her son's small face tightened into an expression that reminded her of his grandfather's when faced with an unpalatable truth. "He never wanted to before."

"Sugar…" He didn't know about you. Her throat closed at the thought of saying that. She ought to, but she couldn't.

"He wants to see you," she said finally. "He wants to get to know you."

Sammy slid off the swing and stood rigidly in front of her, his solemn expression at odds with his cartoon-character T-shirt. "When?"

"Maybe tomorrow after school?" She made it a question. "If that's okay with you."

"I'll think on it." That was what her father always said when presented with a problem. *I'll think on it.*

"All right." She was afraid to say more.

He went to the door, his small shoulders held stiffly. Then he paused. "Will you come up and say good-night?"

She couldn't let her voice choke. "In a minute."

She watched him disappear into the house. He'd taken it quietly, as he did everything, but this was a bigger crisis than he'd ever had to cope with in his young life. And she was to blame.

Had it really been for Sammy's sake that she'd hidden his existence from Tyler? She struggled to say the truth, at least to herself.

She'd been so distraught when she'd come home from Baltimore, her marriage in tatters, that she hadn't even realized what was happening to her body. By the time she did, she'd already been served with the divorce papers. The trek she'd made to Baltimore in a futile effort to see Tyler and tell him had only convinced her that their marriage was over.

She crossed her arms, hugging herself against the breeze off the water. She'd made her choice. This was the world for her son—the secluded island, the patient pace of life, the shabby inn, the sprawling Caldwell clan who'd accepted him without question as one of them.

Now Tyler was back, with his money and his power and his high-pressure life. He wanted to see his son.

What if he tried to take Sammy away? The question ripped through her on a tidal wave of panic. She wasn't as naive now as she'd been at eighteen, but she still knew that power and money could sometimes overcome justice.

The Winchester wealth might dazzle Sammy. She couldn't compete with all the things Tyler could give him.

Worse, Sammy could risk loving him, as she had. What were the chances Tyler would walk away again, leaving broken hearts behind?

* * *

Tyler pulled into the shell-covered driveway of the Dolphin Inn that evening, his lights reflecting from the eyes of a shaggy yellow dog who looked at him as if deciding whether to sound an alarm. His son's dog?

That was one of the many things he didn't know about his child. Maybe that was why he hadn't been able to stay in his room at the island's only resort hotel.

He'd never intended to start a family. The example his parents had set would be enough to sour anyone on the prospect of parenthood. It was too late now. He'd fathered a child.

Deep inside a little voice said, Run. Go back to Baltimore, forget this ever happened.

Tempting, but impossible. Would he eliminate those days with Miranda if he could, even knowing how their relationship would end?

Of course. Their marriage had been a mistake, pure and simple, born out of sunshine and sultry breezes.

He got out of the car, his footsteps quiet on the shell-encrusted walk. The dog, apparently deciding he wasn't a threat, padded silently beside him. He rounded the building and had to force himself to keep walking.

Miranda's family waited on the wraparound porch, at least the masculine portion of it. She'd told them.

Tension grabbed his stomach. They had no reason to welcome him. They couldn't stop him, but they could make this more difficult if they chose.

"Evenin'." Clayton Caldwell didn't offer his

hand, but at least he didn't seem to be holding a shotgun.

"Mr. Caldwell." He stopped at the bottom of the porch steps. "Is Miranda here? I'd like to talk with her." Has she told our son about me?

Miranda's youngest brother shoved himself away from the porch railing. "Maybe she doesn't want to talk to you."

The kid's name floated up from the past. Theo. Theo had the height of all the Caldwell men, even at seventeen or so. Dislike emanated from him.

"That's enough, Theo." Clayton's soft Southern voice carried authority. He eyed Tyler for a moment. "Miranda's down at the dock."

Tyler jerked a nod, then spun away from their combined stares. He walked toward the dock that jutted into the channel between Caldwell Island and the mainland, aware of the men's gazes boring into his back.

Miranda stood with her hands braced against the railing, her jeans and white shirt blending into a background of water and sky. She must have heard his footsteps crossing the shell pathway, then thudding onto the weathered wooden boards. She didn't turn.

Caldwell boats curtseyed gently on the tide on either side of the dock as he approached Miranda. Her slim form was rigid.

Slim, yes, but there was a soft roundness to her figure. The bronze hair that had once rippled halfway down her back brushed her shoulders.

It's been eight years, he reminded himself irritably. Neither of us are kids any longer. If they hadn't been kids, fancying themselves Romeo and Juliet when their families tried to part them, maybe that hasty marriage would never have happened.

Then there'd be no Sammy. The thought hit him starkly. That would be a harsh trade for an untroubled conscience.

Miranda turned toward him, her reluctance palpable. He looked at her without the anger that had colored his image of her earlier.

Her shy eagerness had been replaced by maturity. She probably had a serene face for anyone but him.

That serenity had been the first thing that attracted him to her. She'd worn her serenity like a shield even while she waited tables at the yacht club, taking flak from spoiled little rich kids. Like he had been.

Just now her body was tight with apprehension, her face wary. She stood outlined against the darkening sky, and the breeze from the water ruffled her hair.

One of them had to break the awkward silence. "Should I have called before I came over?"

She shook her head, the movement sending strands of coppery hair across her cheek. "It's all right. I thought you'd probably come back tonight." A ghost of a smile touched her lips. "We have things to settle, I guess."

"Yes." He bit back the horde of questions he wanted to throw at her. Why didn't you tell me? She still hadn't answered that one to his satisfaction. "I take it you've told your family."

"I didn't have a choice. You can't come back to a small place like Caldwell Cove after all these years and not cause comment. You must remember what the grapevine is like."

"We were summer people. The island never included us."

Her face shadowed, and he almost regretted his words. Summer people. The wealthy visitors who owned or rented the big houses down by the yacht club had always maintained a clear division between themselves and the islanders.

"I guess not," she said carefully.

"Did you tell Sammy?"

She rubbed her arms, as if seeking warmth. "I told him."

"How did he take it?" He didn't know if he wanted his son to be glad or sorry he was here.

"He was upset. Confused." She shook her head, and he saw the stark pain in her eyes. "I tried to explain."

"I hope you did a better job of explaining it to him than you did to me."

"That's not fair."

"Funny, but I don't feel too much like being fair, Miranda." The anger he'd thought he had under control spurted out. "It isn't every day I find out a girl from my past had a baby she never bothered telling me about."

"I tried to tell you."

He raised an eyebrow. "Tried how? I wasn't that hard to find. A letter or phone call would have done it."

Some emotion he couldn't identify flickered across her face. Once he'd known the meaning of her every look, every gesture. At least he'd told himself he did. Maybe that had been an illusion.

"I came to Baltimore," she said slowly, not looking at him. "Not long after I'd gotten the papers."

He didn't need to ask what papers. His mother had wielded the Winchester clout as easily as his father. She'd pushed the divorce through in record time.

"You didn't oppose the divorce." That wasn't what he'd intended to say, but it just came out.

"No, I..." She stopped, seeming to censor whatever she'd been about to say. "That doesn't matter now."

He leaned against the weathered railing next to her, studying her down-tilted face and wishing he could see her eyes. "If you came to Baltimore, I didn't see you."

"I changed my mind," she said carefully. "I did what I thought was best for all of us. Maybe I was wrong, but it's too late now."

He stared at her, frowning. He wanted to push for answers, but maybe she had a point.

"All right, forget what we did or didn't do then." He didn't think he could, but he'd try. "Let's talk about now. Is Sammy angry about his father showing up after all this time?"

"Not angry, no." Her grip on the railing seemed to ease. "Confused, as I said, but he's a much-loved, secure child. He can deal with this."

None of that love and security in Sammy's life came from his father. Well, fair enough. Tyler hadn't had that from his father, either.

Again he had the urge to walk away. All he could offer this child was money. He'd lost the capacity to form close relationships a long time ago, if he'd ever had it.

He couldn't leave until he'd talked with Sammy. He owed both of them that much, at least.

"When can I meet him?" He threw the question at Miranda.

Her soft mouth tightened. "I suggested tomorrow, and he said he'd think about it. I'd like to let him agree without pressuring him."

Was she trying to get out of it? "I have a business to run, Miranda. Tomorrow after school. I'll be here."

Her head came up, and she glared at him, then jerked a nod. "I'll talk to him about it."

"Tomorrow after school. I'll see you then."

He pushed away from the railing. He'd gotten what he'd come for. He had no reason to linger.

Miranda took a quick step, stopping him. "I said I'd talk to him, Tyler. I'm not going to force him to do something he doesn't want to, just because you're in a hurry."

He swung toward her, and they stood only inches apart. He could read the expression in her eyes—she was wishing for distance between them. He reached out and caught her wrists in his hands, feeling smooth, warm skin and a pulse that thundered against his palms.

"It's already been his lifetime, Miranda. I won't wait."

"Fine." She jerked her hands free, and fierce

maternal love blazed in her face. "Just you be careful of what you say to him. If you hurt Sammy, I promise you, I'll make you regret you ever heard of Caldwell Cove."

"Chocolate, vanilla or something more exotic?" Tyler lifted his eyebrow as he asked the question, and Miranda tried not to let that simple movement affect her. She was immune to Tyler Winchester's charm—she'd gotten there the hard way.

She concentrated on the list of flavors posted behind the counter in the ice-cream shop. "I'll have the peanut-butter ripple."

Taking a walk through town with Sammy after school had been her idea. It seemed so much less intimidating than pushing the boy into a face-to-face interview with a father he didn't know.

She'd suggested to Sammy that they show Tyler around Caldwell Cove, not that there was much to see. The village still lay in a sedate crescent along the inland waterway, anchored by the inn at one end and Uncle Jeff's mansion at the other. The spire of St. Andrew's Church bisected the village. Little had changed since Tyler was here last, except for the new resort hotel down near the yacht club.

She had an ulterior motive for this walk. She wanted Tyler to understand that Sammy belonged here. Sammy's happiness didn't depend on anything his father could give him. Maybe when Tyler realized that, he could go away with a clear conscience.

Tyler handed Sammy a chocolate cone, then took a small vanilla for himself. Conservative, she thought. When had Tyler become conservative?

When he'd been drawn back into the Winchester way of life, probably. He'd slipped into his father's place as CEO of Winchester Industries, apparently forgetting that he'd ever had other dreams.

Concentrate on the present, she ordered herself. Don't succumb to the lure of the past.

They stepped onto the narrow street bordered by the docks, and she looked for an inspiration to give them something to talk about.

"Sammy, why don't you tell your father about the boatyard."

Her son didn't seem too enthusiastic about his role as tour guide. He licked, then pointed with an ice-cream daubed finger toward the docks and storage sheds lining the quay.

"That's Cousin Adam's boatyard. He fixed Grandpa's fishing boat when the motor died."

"Adam took all of us on the schooner for Pirate Days, remember?" she prompted.

Enthusiasm replaced the caution in Sammy's face as he turned to Tyler. "That was really cool. I got to help put up the sails and everything. Cousin Adam's going to give me sailing lessons this summer. He says me and Jenny are big enough to learn."

"Jenny is Adam's little girl," she explained. "You must remember Adam, don't you?"

"I remember Adam." His expression suggested the memory wasn't a happy one. "As I recall, he, um—" he glanced at Sammy "—suggested it would be better if I didn't see you."

She felt her cheeks grow warm and hoped he'd attribute it to the March sunshine. "I didn't know that." It made sense. Adam, Uncle Jefferson's older son, belonged to the rich branch of the family, the one that sometimes frequented the yacht club. He would have heard the rumors that his little cousin, who was supposed to be waiting tables at the club, was instead dating a wealthy summer visitor.

"Your ice cream is dripping." Tyler reached out with a napkin and dabbed at her chin just as she ducked away from his touch. His fingers brushed her cheek instead, and her skin seemed to burn where they touched.

"I'll get it," she said hurriedly, hoping the napkin she raised to her lips hid her confusion. She couldn't be reacting to Tyler. She was immune to him. Remember?

"Mine's getting away from me, too." Tyler licked around the top of the cone, where the ice cream had begun a slow trail toward his fingers. "I'd forgotten how hot it can be on the island in March."

"Summer's on its way," she said, then regretted that she'd mentioned the season. Tyler wasn't to know it, but summer always brought back memories of him. She glanced at his face involuntarily, then wondered how often this adult version of her first love indulged in something as simple as an ice-cream cone.

Tyler licked a froth of vanilla from his lips, drawing her gaze. He'd always had a well-shaped mouth. He didn't smile as easily now as he had when she'd known him, and she didn't think that was entirely due to current circumstances. Maybe Tyler didn't find much to smile about anymore.

It probably would be an excellent idea to stop looking at Tyler's lips. Next she'd be remembering how they felt on hers, and things could only get worse from there.

They strolled along the tabby sidewalk, uneven from the shells that formed part of the concrete, worn by a century or two of foot traffic. Live oaks shaded them, and Sammy hopped carefully over a crack in the walk.

Concentrate on what you're doing, she commanded herself. "Don't you want to tell your father about your school?" she asked.

Sammy flicked a faintly rebellious look toward her. "That's it." He waved at the white frame building, set in its grove of palmettos, that had served the island's children for over a hundred years. "I'm almost done with second grade."

"Looks as if the building's been there a hundred years." Tyler said just what she'd been thinking, but it didn't seem complimentary when he said it.

"It's a good school." She hoped she didn't sound defensive. What if Tyler thought his son should go away to some private academy? The idea turned her ice cream to ashes.

"Equipped with the latest in chalkboards, no doubt."

She felt diminished by his sarcasm, and that angered her. "Our classrooms have computers. We're not exactly living in the dark ages here."

"I like my school." Sammy stopped, frowning at Tyler with an expression so like his father's it nearly stopped her heart. "You shouldn't put it down just because it's not new and fancy."

Tyler looked baffled, and little wonder. He probably hadn't expected Sammy to pick up on the byplay between adults.

She was tempted to let him stew, but she couldn't. If she didn't take pity on Tyler's efforts with Sammy, she would only hurt her son.

"Why don't we have a game of catch." She nodded toward the playground where island children had played under the spreading branches of the live oaks for years. "I brought the ball." She pulled it from her bag and tossed it to Tyler, stepping onto the grass.

He caught it automatically. "I don't think…"

She frowned him to silence. Didn't he see she was trying to help him? "Sammy wants to play T-ball this summer. I'll bet he could use some practice."

"Sure. Right." He swallowed the last of his cone and threw the ball to Sammy, then patted an imaginary glove. "Throw it in here, Sammy."

Sammy lobbed it to Miranda instead. She didn't miss the quick flare of irritation on Tyler's face. Well, he couldn't expect this to be simple, could he?

Temptation whispered in her ear again. It would be so easy to be sure Sammy didn't warm up to his father. So easy, and so wrong. Even if it insured that Tyler would go away, she couldn't do it.

Her throw went a little high, and Sammy had to

reach for it. He wore a surprised look when he came down with the ball.

"Good catch, Sammy." Tyler's voice had just the right amount of enthusiasm. Sammy responded with a cautious smile.

Tyler blinked, his face softening with the effect of that smile. Her eyes stung with tears, and she was grateful for the sunglasses that shielded them. Tyler didn't need to know that it moved her to see Sammy playing with his father.

That wasn't the purpose of this little excursion, remember? You're supposed to be showing Tyler what a happy life Sammy has here so he'll soothe his conscience and go away.

Tyler's comments about getting back to his business had confirmed what she'd already suspected—he'd turned into the same driven businessman his father had been. She'd known that would happen when he'd insisted they move back to Baltimore after his father's death.

Their dreams of settling down on the island and starting a small business had vanished like the mist. Tyler hadn't had time for that. Now the CEO of Winchester Industries probably didn't like to take time for a simple game of catch.

"Try it this way." Tyler walked over to Sammy, reaching toward him to correct his throw.

Sammy jerked away. "I don't want to."

"Sammy," she began, but what could she say? Be polite to the father you've never seen before didn't seem to cover it.

Her son frowned, first at her, then at Tyler. "Why do you want to play ball now? You never even wanted to see me before."

Miranda's heart thudded. There it was, the question she didn't want to answer. But she didn't have a choice.

She couldn't look at Tyler. She didn't even want to meet her son's eyes, but she forced herself to. "Sammy, that's not fair."

"It is, too." His fists curled. "He could've come, but he didn't."

"No, he couldn't." She felt Tyler's gaze on her.

"Why not?" Sammy demanded.

Truth time was here, and she wasn't ready for it. She had to be. "Your daddy didn't know about you."

Her son stared at her.

She licked dry lips. "I never told your father about you." She reached a hand toward Sammy, but he took a step back. "Sugar, I thought it was best."

The words sounded feeble to her own ears. Hurt and accusation battled in Sammy's face. As for Tyler...she could almost think that was pity in Tyler's eyes.

Chapter Three

"I have a proposition for you." As soon as the words were out of her mouth, Miranda realized she could have phrased it better. Standing in the doorway to Tyler's hotel room that evening had rattled her so much that she didn't know what she was saying.

"A proposition?" Tyler looked as startled at her words as she probably did. "In that case, I guess you'd better come in."

Clutching her bag with cold fingers, she stepped inside. They could hardly discuss Sammy's relationship with his father at the house, where her son would wonder what they were talking about. Any public place was out of the question.

Tyler crossed the room to switch on another lamp against the darkness that pressed against the sliding glass balcony doors, giving her a moment to collect herself. She took in the sweep of plush, sand-colored carpet, the pale walls and the cream furniture with pastel floral upholstery. Dalton Resorts knew how to treat their wealthy guests.

"I haven't been in the hotel before. It's quite… elegant." It was certainly the antithesis of the Dolphin Inn, but people who could afford this wouldn't be staying at the inn anyway.

Tyler looked at her, hand still on the cream pottery lamp. He had traded the casual shirt and khakis he'd worn for the meeting with Sammy for a white dress shirt, open at the throat, and dark trousers. Maybe the dining room in the hotel required formal attire. Or maybe that was just how he felt comfortable now.

"I thought your brother-in-law worked for Dalton."

"Luke did start out with Dalton, and he helped pick the site for the hotel." Her brother-in-law had been a driven businessman, too, before her sister, Chloe, brought out a different side to him. "He and Chloe are running the youth center in Beaufort now."

"That's quite a change." He strolled toward her, and she had the sense that he wasn't in the least interested in what Chloe and Luke were doing. He was wondering what had brought her here tonight.

"Yes, well, they're happy." Chloe and Luke's love was so bright that it almost hurt to look at them.

Tyler stopped, a bit too close for comfort, and she glanced past him. He'd converted an oval glass-topped table to a makeshift desk. It was littered with papers and centered with a sleek laptop computer.

"I see you've been working."

He followed the direction of her gaze, frowning.

"Business doesn't stop just because I'm out of the office. We have an important deal coming up soon."

The fact that he couldn't even get away from Winchester Industries for two days gave her a surge of confidence. Her plan to deal with this situation was dangerous, but it would work. It had to.

Tyler turned to her, still frowning. A lock of dark brown hair had fallen over his forehead, the only thing even faintly disarranged about his appearance. Had he run his hand through his hair in frustration over being tied here when his business was in Baltimore?

"How is Sammy?"

She took a breath, trying to think of Sammy without pain. She'd let him down so badly.

"He's doing all right," she said carefully. "All this has been hard enough on him, without finding out—" She stopped, started again. "I should have told him the truth about you long ago. I was wrong."

She waited for him to say she should have told him, too, but he didn't. She could almost imagine she saw sympathy in his eyes.

"Do you think he understands why you didn't?"

"I don't know." Sammy's small face appeared in her mind's eye. "As much as an seven-year-old can, I guess. He forgives, even if he doesn't understand."

He studied her face for a long moment, his expression unreadable. "You wanted…" His tone made it a question.

She looked at him blankly, realizing that she'd been staring at him as if she'd never seen him before. Or as if she'd never see him again.

He lifted an eyebrow, something that might have been amusement flickering in his face. "You have a proposition for me, remember?"

"Oh. Yes."

He had to be deliberately attempting to make her nervous. There was no other reason for him to be standing so close, taking up all the air in the room.

Concentrate. This idea will work, won't it? *Please, Lord.*

"You said this afternoon that you want to be a part of Sammy's life." It frightened her just to say the words. "You must realize that you have to get to know Sammy before that can happen."

She expected him to bring up again the fact that it was her fault he didn't know Sammy, but he nodded. "I realize that. I don't want to rush him. But I'm not going to disappear."

She clasped her hands together, trying to find a core of strength inside. "This can't be a halfway thing, Tyler. I won't let Sammy be hurt by it."

"I'm not looking to hurt the boy." He sounded impatient. "So what is this idea of yours?"

Now or never. She had to say it.

"You stay here, on the island, for one month." She swept on before he could interrupt. "You can move into the inn, so you'll see Sammy every day. Then—" She breathed a silent prayer. "Then we can make arrangements together for you to be a real parent to him."

"Stay here?" He made Caldwell Island sound like the outermost reaches of the earth, and his firm mouth tightened even more. "I can't do that. I have a business to run."

That was what she'd thought he'd say, but even so, the words made her heart clench. Tyler would see how impossible this was, that was the important thing.

"I'm not trying to be unreasonable." She nodded toward the computer. "You can stay connected, go back to Baltimore for a day or two if you have to. Surely even the CEO gets some vacation time."

"I can't run a business that way, especially not now." His dismissal was quick. "Sammy can come to Baltimore to get to know me."

Fear flared and had to be extinguished. "Sammy isn't a package, to be sent back and forth when you have time for him. If you want to be his father, you have to realize that. You getting acquainted with him needs to happen here, where he feels safe."

His eyes narrowed. "Suppose I just start legal action. You can't keep me from my son."

The thought of facing a phalanx of ruthless Winchester lawyers made her quake, but she held her voice steady. "And have our private quarrel splashed all over the papers? I don't think you'd like that. And I don't think a family court judge would look favorably on a father who won't take a few weeks to get acquainted with his son."

Something that might have been surprise flickered in his eyes. "You've grown up, Miranda."

"I've had to."

"What you ask is impossible. You must know that."

It wouldn't have been impossible for the man he'd

been at twenty-one, but she couldn't say that, and maybe it wasn't even true. Maybe she hadn't really known the man she'd married.

She had to say the hard thing and end this now, before it damaged Sammy. Tyler's sense of duty to the child he'd fathered had brought him here, but his sense of duty to the company would take him away again.

"If you can't get away from your business for something this important, maybe you're not meant to be a father."

Tyler didn't answer. He couldn't. She had known all along how this would turn out, but still pain clenched her very soul. She turned away.

He grasped her arm, pulling her around to face him. At his touch, her treacherous heart faltered. She forced herself to look at him, her gaze tangling with his. Her breath caught in her throat, and for an instant she thought his eyes darkened.

"I know a challenge when I hear one, Miranda." His voice lowered to a baritone rumble. "I've managed too many business deals not to know when someone's making an offer they think I won't accept."

"I don't—"

His grip tightened. His intense gaze was implacable. "Get a room ready for me. I'm moving in tomorrow."

This was certainly a far cry from the elegance of the Dalton Resort Hotel. Tyler tossed his suitcase onto the patchwork quilt that adorned the four-poster bed in the room to which Miranda had shown him. He glanced around, wondering if he'd made a hasty decision the previous night. Did he really propose to run Winchester Industries from this small room on an island in the middle of nowhere?

He strode to the east window and snapped up the shade, letting sunlight stream across wide, uneven floorboards dotted with oval hooked rugs. Someone had put a milk-glass vase filled with dried flowers on the battered, rice-carved bureau, and the faint aroma seemed a ghost of last summer's flowers.

Well, there was a phone jack, at least. With that, something to use for a desk and enough electrical outlets, he ought to be able to make this work if he wanted to.

Maybe that was the question. Did he want to do this? He frowned at what seemed to be a kitchen garden. The small patch of lawn, crisscrossed with clotheslines, couldn't be intended for the use of guests. Beyond it was some sort of shed, then the pale green-gold of the marsh grasses. A white heron stood, knee-deep, waiting motionless for something.

Tyler assessed his options, trying to weigh them as if this were any business deal that had come up unexpectedly. In a business deal, the first step would be to research what was being offered. He grimaced. Miranda wasn't exactly offering him anything. As for research—well, he didn't need a DNA test to confirm what he knew in his bones. Sammy was his son.

He could stay. That meant subjecting himself to the uncertain welcome of Miranda's family and trying to figure out how to be a father under Miranda's no doubt critical gaze. Then, assuming he could gain Sammy's acceptance, he'd face the tricky task of working out long-distance custody arrangements between Baltimore and Caldwell Cove and he'd commit himself to being a significant part of Sammy's life for—well, forever.

He shoved the window up, letting the breeze that bent the marsh grasses billow the ruffled curtains. The alternative was to leave. Go back to Baltimore, take up life as it had been. He could afford generous child support, the best schools, anything material his son needed. He could satisfy his conscience without getting emotionally involved.

"Is everything all right?" Miranda paused in the doorway, clutching an armload of white towels against the front of a green T-shirt with a dolphin emblazoned on it.

No, Miranda, nothing's been all right since that photo of Sammy landed on my desk. Miranda was undoubtedly talking about the room, not his inner struggle.

"Fine."

"You looked as if you might be having second thoughts about this, now that you've seen the accommodations." She put the towels on the edge of the bureau.

"The accommodations are fine."

"If you want to change your mind—"

"I don't," he said shortly, trying to ignore the fact that he'd been thinking just that. He'd better concentrate on the room instead of noticing how well those faded jeans fit her slim figure. "I need something to use for a desk. A table would work, if you have one to spare. If not, I'll go out and buy one."

"No need. I'll find something."

She shoved a strand of hair from her eyes. He found himself thinking that its color was nearer mahogany than auburn and then told himself that it didn't matter in the least what color Miranda's hair was. She vanished before he could say anything, her quick footsteps receding down the hallway.

All right, he needed some rules if he were actually going to stay here. The first one had to be no staring at Miranda. And the second one better be no remembering the past.

He heard her coming before he could decide on rule three. Something thumped against the wall. He reached the door to see Miranda backing toward him, holding one end of a rectangular oak table. Her mother, wearing a dolphin T-shirt also, wrestled with the other end. He sprang to help them.

"Mrs. Caldwell, let me take that."

Sallie Caldwell surrendered her grip, giving him a smile too like her daughter's for comfort. "I'm afraid the table doesn't match the rest of the furniture, but Miranda said that didn't matter."

Miranda had probably said that if he didn't like it he could lump it.

"It'll work." He guided the heavy table through the doorway, finding it necessary to remind himself again not to let his gaze linger on Miranda's face. Her cheeks were slightly flushed, either from exertion or because she had indeed said what he imagined.

Miranda helped him position the makeshift desk near the window. Then, as if she thought she'd spent enough time in his company for one day, she retreated to the doorway where her mother waited.

"If there's anything else you need, just let us know." Sallie Caldwell put her arm around her daughter's waist with easy affection as she smiled at him. She had Miranda's bronze hair, streaked with gray.

"I will." He tried without success to imagine his mother letting gray appear in her hair or wearing faded jeans and a T-shirt.

"We'll try to make you comfortable while you're here."

They all knew there was nothing comfortable about any of this. Still, he sensed that Miranda's mother meant what she said. There was no artifice about her—just the same unselfconscious natural beauty her daughter had.

"Thank you, Mrs. Caldwell. The room will work just fine."

If I stay. The words whispered in his mind as the Caldwell women vanished down the hall.

His cell phone rang, and he flipped it open. Probably Henry, responding to the message he'd left at the office. But it wasn't his assistant—it was his brother.

"Henry's secretary passed your message on to me. He's out of the office. What's going on?" Curiosity filled Josh's voice.

"Out of the office where?" What was reliable Henry doing out of the office when he'd left him in charge?

"Didn't tell me." He could almost see Josh's shrug. "Something you want me to take care of before he gets back?"

His first instinct was a prompt no, but someone at the office had to know where he was. And why. And how long he intended to stay.

"Not exactly." He hesitated. His brother would have to know. As irresponsible as Josh was, he wouldn't spread the news if Tyler asked him not to. "I have a…situation here, and I don't want anyone else to know the whole story. You can tell Henry, but no one else. Understood?"

"Got it." He could almost see Josh leaning back, propping his feet on the desk. "What's up?"

"You remember Miranda Caldwell?"

A pause, but Josh would remember. After all, their father's death had rocked both their worlds.

"Your ex-wife."

"Yes. Turns out there was something she neglected to mention when we got divorced. I have a son." He waited for an explosion of questions.

Instead Josh whistled softly. "I assume you're sure he's yours."

"I'm sure."

"What are you going to do about it?"

The very question he'd been asking himself. Apparently he already knew the answer. "I'm going to stay here for a while to get to know him."

He expected an argument. He didn't get it. "Okay. I'll tell Henry. What about Mother?"

"Not yet." He thought uneasily of their mother,

honeymooning in Madrid with her new husband. She wouldn't be happy that Miranda was back in his life. "Thanks, Josh."

He hung up, realizing why he didn't want to tell anyone. The possession of a son had made him vulnerable. He didn't like to be vulnerable. Miranda's image presented itself in his mind and refused to be dismissed. Look where vulnerability had gotten him eight years ago.

Several hours later, he sat back in the chair and stretched, congratulating himself. He had a reasonable facsimile of an office set up, he'd been in touch with Henry about his plans and he'd contacted the Charleston subsidiary of Winchester Industries and arranged a meeting there, since it was only a couple of hours away. Almost as much as he might have accomplished in Baltimore.

At corporate headquarters, though, he wouldn't have been quite so distracted by the view from the window. There, he'd look out on the Inner Harbor. Here, he looked out at Miranda, busy putting sheets on the clotheslines strung across the yard.

He stood, frowning at the photo of Sammy he'd propped next to his computer. The reason had nothing to do with sentiment, he assured himself. He'd put it there to remind himself that he had to find out who'd sent it, and why.

He picked it up, gaze straying again to Miranda. The chances he'd learn the truth about that without her help were slim and none. Therefore he needed to enlist her aid. He glanced at his watch. He'd better do it now, before Sammy came home from school.

Tucking the photo into his shirt pocket, he headed for the backyard and Miranda.

When he pushed open the screen door, Miranda was bending over an oval wicker clothes basket. She looked up at the sound, and her face went still at the sight of him.

"I thought you were busy with work." She shook out a damp sheet and began pinning it to the line, as if to show him that she was busy, as well.

"I've made a good start." He approached her, then had to step back as she shook out another sheet. "Don't you have a dryer?"

"Of course we have a dryer." At his raised eyebrow, she shook her head as if in pity. "We like to sleep on air-dried sheets. So do our guests."

"Why?" He caught the end of the sheet she was manhandling. For a moment he thought she'd yank it free, but then she handed him a clothespin.

"They smell like sunshine."

You smell like sunshine. He dismissed the vagrant thought. "Wouldn't it be more efficient to use a laundry service?"

"That's not how we do things here." She snapped out the words as if he'd insulted her. Sunlight filtered through live oaks and dappled her face.

He reminded himself that he wanted her cooperation, not her enmity. "So you're helping to run the inn now."

"That's right." She pinned up another sheet. "My college plans were derailed."

She'd been saving money that summer, he remembered, waiting tables at the yacht club so she could attend the community college that fall. Both their lives had gone in an unexpected direction, but hers had obviously been skewed more than his.

"I'm sorry," he said, and meant it.

She looked at him for a long moment, then nodded in acceptance. "I don't regret anything." A smile blazed across her face. "I have Sammy."

He nodded, the photo seeming to burn a hole in his pocket. Maybe he'd better get to the point before he brought up any more touchy subjects. "I've been thinking about that picture of him."

"I've already told you, I didn't send it." She snatched the basket and ducked under flapping sheets to the other end of the yard.

He followed, evading damp linen. He needed her on his side in this. "I know you didn't send it. Don't you want to know who did?"

"Yes, of course." She stopped, eyes clouded. "I've worried and worried, and I still don't have an idea."

"There has to be a way to find out. Why don't we talk to Sammy about this?"

"Absolutely not." She shot the words at him, shoulders suddenly stiff.

"But he may have noticed who took the picture."

"I mean it, Tyler." Her soft mouth was firm. "I don't want him questioned about this."

"That's ridiculous. If we can find out—"

"It's not ridiculous," she snapped. It looked as if they were back on opposite sides. "If we talk to Sammy, he's going to ask how you got a picture of him."

"We can say—" He stopped. What would they say?

"I don't want him thinking that some stranger is going around taking pictures of him, manipulating his life." A shiver seemed to run through her. "It's bad enough thinking that myself."

"All right."

Miranda looked at him suspiciously, and he raised his hands in surrender.

"I promise. I won't say anything to him."

The tension went out of her, and she reached up to unpin a dry sheet. He caught the end of it, and she let him help her fold it.

"Why? That's what gets me," she said. "Why would anyone want to interfere in our lives like that?"

"I wish I knew." He had to hurry to keep up with the deft way she flipped the corners together. "No one's said anything to you about it?"

"Nothing."

He finished the last fold, then put the sheet into the basket as Miranda moved on to the next one. She was right—the sheet did smell like sunshine.

"Stop a minute and look at it again." He drew the photo from his pocket and handed it to her.

She studied the picture, absently twisting a strand of hair around her finger. Her gaze lifted, startled, to him. "This looks like—"

"What?"

"Come with me." She dropped a clothespin into the basket and started around the inn at a trot. He had to hurry to keep up with her.

"Look." She stopped at the corner of the veranda, pointing.

He stepped closer, looking over her shoulder at the photo, then at the scene in front of them. An ancient, gnarled live oak filled the corner of the yard, its branches so heavy they touched the ground in places. From this angle, they formed a kind of archway through which he saw a corner of the dock. It was exactly the same in the photograph.

"Whoever he was, he took the picture here," he said.

This time he was so close he felt the shiver that went through her.

"Here. And sometime within the last six months." She touched the photo with one fingertip. "I bought that polo shirt for Sammy when school started in September."

"Stands to reason it was fairly recent. If he wanted to send it to me, whoever he was, why wait?"

Miranda's breath seemed to catch. "Tyler, we have to find out who did this." She swung around, apparently not realizing how close he was. She was nearly in his arms.

He caught her arm as she bumped against him. Her smooth skin seemed alive with memories— visions of holding her close, of promising to love her forever. The fresh scent of her surrounded and over-powered him.

This was bad. This was very bad. He'd never dreamed those feelings still existed, ready to be awakened. It was as if the very cells of his body remembered her.

He'd wanted Miranda's cooperation. He'd gotten it, but in the process he'd found out something very unwelcome about himself. He was still attracted to her.

Chapter Four

Miranda couldn't move. Tyler held her elbows, steadying her, and her hands pressed against his chest. She felt his heartbeat through her palms, up her arms, driving straight to her heart. It had been years since they'd stood together like this. It might as well have been yesterday.

She curled her fingers, pulled her hands away from him. She couldn't look at his face. Instead she focused on the placket of his white knit shirt. Two of the three buttons were open, exposing a V of tanned skin against the white.

That wasn't any better than looking into his eyes. She took a hurried step back, and he released her instantly. If he guessed her reactions—

He wouldn't. Tyler was too focused on the task at hand to have time for any other considerations. At the moment he was totally consumed with finding out who'd taken the photo of Sammy.

She wanted to know that, too, but somehow she also had to find a way of keeping her balance where Tyler was concerned. That meant not finding herself in any more moments like that one.

Tyler glanced from the photo to the scene before him. He frowned, and she sensed that, as far as he was concerned, the moment when they'd touched might never have been.

Well, good. That was what she wanted, too.

"So, we know the picture was taken within the last six months, and by someone standing in just about this spot." He seemed to measure the distance from the driveway to the street. "How unusual would it be for someone you don't know to come this far onto the property?"

She steadied herself. Tyler didn't feel anything. She wouldn't feel anything, either.

"Not unusual at all, I'm afraid."

"Why not?" He shot the question at her with that intent, challenging stare of his. "If someone's not a guest at the inn, why would he be here?"

She pointed to the small placard attached to a post near the end of the driveway. "The historical society put those up a few years ago. I worked on the project, as a matter of fact. We designed a walking tour of historical houses. Visitors can pick up a brochure anywhere in town and follow it. In nice weather we often see people, brochure in hand, taking pictures."

"There's no way of tracing them?"

"None. People don't buy tickets or sign up. They just follow the map." A shiver ran along her arms, and she rubbed them. "Sammy wouldn't think anything about it, even if he noticed someone with a camera." She took another step away from him. "I should get back to the laundry."

"Wait a minute." His hand twitched as if he thought about touching her and changed his mind. "We haven't finished talking about this."

"I don't know how to find the person who took the picture. There's nothing else to say. I want to take down the sheets before it's time to start dinner." And I want to put a little distance between us.

"Fine." He seemed to grind his teeth. "I'll help you with the sheets, if that's what it takes. We can talk and fold at the same time."

She's forgotten how persistent he could be when he wanted something. "Sammy will be home in a few minutes. I don't want him to hear anything about this."

He slid the photo into his pocket. "I've already said he won't hear it from me, Miranda." He moved past her, then stopped and raised an eyebrow when she didn't follow. "Aren't we going to fold laundry?"

Without a word, she brushed past him and started around the house, aware of him on her heels. Persistent. Aggravating. Determined to have his own way. Tyler hadn't changed—those qualities had intensified, probably from years of surrounding himself with people who always agreed with the boss. Well, he'd have to get used to the fact that this situation was different.

She reached the dry sheets she'd hung out earlier

and began taking them down. Tyler let her get one more sheet into the basket before he started in again.

"There's no reason to suppose it was a stranger, anyway."

She frowned at him, not sure where he was going with this.

He frowned back. "Well, think about it, Miranda. Why would a stranger go to the trouble of taking a picture of Sammy? How would a stranger even know who he was? Or who his father was?"

Good questions, all of them. Unfortunately, she didn't have any good answers. She turned it over in her mind as she took a pillowcase off the line.

"I suppose it might be some bizarre string of co-incidences. Weird things do happen. Someone visiting the island to whom your name would be familiar, maybe, then finding out about Sammy."

It sounded weak to her. Judging from Tyler's expression, it sounded pitiful to him.

"I don't believe in that wild a coincidence." He unpinned a sheet and handed her one end, his fingers brushing hers. "How widely known is it that I'm Sammy's father?"

The only surprising thing was that he hadn't asked the question sooner. "Islanders know, for the most part." She carefully didn't look at him. "Our elopement was quite a sensation. People talk."

"Gossip." He sounded uncompromising.

"Talk," she said again. "But folks here are used to the situation. I don't think they'd mention it to outsiders, anyway. Islanders protect their own."

"Unless there's something in it for them."

She didn't know how to combat that kind of cynicism. "You're wrong, Tyler. No one here would deliberately set out to hurt me or Sammy."

"Then what's left?" His brows twitched, impatience returning. "I can't believe in some kind of random coincidence. You can't believe your neighbors would meddle. What are we left with? Your family?"

"No!" She planted her fists on her hips. "Tyler, that's ridiculous. No one in my family would do anything like that."

"According to you, no one would do it, but it happened." He ducked under the clothesline, and it brushed the top of his head. The movement brought him within inches of her, and her breath stuttered.

"Get rid of your rose-colored glasses for a minute, Miranda. Someone did this thing. Someone deliberately took a picture of Sammy and sent it to me. Someone who knew I was Sammy's father and knew how to reach me."

His words battered her like waves in rough surf. She brushed her hair from her eyes, looking at him.

"Why?" The word came out in a whisper. "Why, Tyler?"

He caught her hands, imprisoning them in his hard grip. "We'll find out, but you have to help me. We can't be on opposite sides in this."

Opposite sides. The only safe place for her was not opposite, but as far away from Tyler as possible.

His grip tightened, compelling a response. "You have to help me," he repeated.

The more she was near him, the more difficult and dangerous it would be to her heart. She didn't have a choice.

"All right. I'll help you."

"Tyler, would you like another piece of fried chicken?" Sallie Caldwell held the platter out to him. It had been piled high with golden chicken pieces when they sat down, but one trip around the table had diminished it considerably.

"No, thanks, Mrs. Caldwell. I have plenty." He'd already made his way through two pieces and a mound of mashed potatoes and gravy. He hadn't eaten like this since—well, he'd never eaten like this.

The long table, set in the center of the dining room, was used as a buffet for guests' breakfasts, but now light from the overhead fixture fell on seven Caldwells and one unwelcome guest.

Miranda's mother must have her hands full, cooking for this bunch every day. David and Daniel, seated opposite him, were a couple of years older than Miranda. Both tall and lean, they wore the same stamp their father did of men who worked hard in the outdoors. People like that didn't need to worry about getting to the gym to work off an extra serving of fried chicken.

Theo, the baby of the family, alternated between focusing on his plate and glaring at Tyler. He was clearly not reconciled to Tyler's presence at the family table.

Nobody was, he supposed. Sallie had a smile

for him, but that was either her natural expression or her idea of Southern hospitality. Sammy fidgeted in the ladder-back chair that was a little too big for him, probably eager for the Friday night movie Miranda had said he'd be attending with his cousins.

Tyler could feel Miranda's tension from across the table. He knew its cause. They'd agreed that once Sammy was off to the movies, she'd talk to her family about the photograph.

She didn't want to do it, didn't think it was necessary. He crumbled a feathery-light biscuit between his fingers. She'd only agreed because she'd known that if she didn't, he would.

Talk of the weather shifted to fishing. Tyler's gaze crossed Miranda's, and she glanced quickly away. Was she disappointed at his silence? She must realize that he didn't have much to say on either subject. He wasn't going to try to manufacture conversation with his son while all of them listened.

Not that Sammy seemed to notice. He avoided Tyler's eye, piping into the conversation about fishing once or twice. He said something teasing to one of his uncles about coming home with an empty net and earned a grin and a ruffle of his hair.

"Did I tell y'all I saw the pod today?" That was David, he thought, though the twins were so alike it was hard to tell.

"Sure that wasn't a sand shark?" His twin's voice was lazily teasing. "Or maybe an old inner tube?"

"Did you honest, Uncle David?" Sammy bounced

on his chair. "You should've taken me out with you. I'm good at spotting them."

"School first, then dolphins," David said easily. "How'd you do on that spelling quiz?"

Sammy sent an uneasy glance toward his mother. "Okay, I guess."

"Just okay? Maybe we better drill a bit more this week."

"My turn to help Sammy this week," his twin interrupted. "I'm a better speller than you ever thought of being. Isn't that right, Momma?"

Sallie turned that hundred-watt smile on him. "Funny, that's not how I remember it. Maybe I ought to get out your old report cards. Let Sammy see how his uncles did in school."

Good-humored protests from the men vied with Sammy's cheers at the idea. Tyler leaned back. He wasn't part of the circle of Caldwells around the table. Whether meaning to or not, they'd made that clear to him.

His childhood table hadn't borne much resemblance to this. His parents, before they divorced, dined in the elegant room with the crystal chandelier and the velvet drapes. He and Josh had a nursery supper, he supposed, but then he'd been shipped off to boarding school, where supper was a noisy affair with people who weren't related to you.

Was that the kind of childhood he wanted for Sammy? He looked at the boy, smiling at some quip his grandfather had aimed at the twins. The laughter in his son's eyes was for the Caldwells, not for him.

Something Miranda had said about Sammy being a well-loved child rang in his mind. Sammy had plenty of people to love him. Miranda had plenty of people to support her. It didn't look as if either of them had any need of him.

Headlights flashed against the windows, and a car horn sounded. Sammy was off his chair in a flash. "That's my cousins, Momma. Can I go now? Please?"

"Not with chicken on your mouth." Miranda handed him a napkin, and he mopped his face quickly.

"Now?" His feet moved as if he were already running.

"All right." Miranda grabbed him before he could dash. "But you say goodbye properly first, y'hear? And don't forget to mind Cousin Matt."

"I won't." Sammy planted a quick kiss on Miranda's cheek. "Bye, Momma. Bye, y'all." His gaze, rounding the table, came to Tyler and stopped.

Tyler could almost see the thought running through his son's mind. Sammy didn't know what to call him.

"G'night," he muttered. Then he dashed out the door.

Clayton's children, though grown, called him Daddy with open affection. Tyler's son didn't have a word for him. That mattered more than he'd have expected.

"Before y'all go, there's something I want to ask you." Miranda clearly didn't like it, but she intended to fulfill her promise.

David, who'd half stood, sat down again. "What's up, sugar?"

"Y'all know about the picture of Sammy someone sent to Tyler."

There was a murmur of assent and one or two hostile glances sent his way.

"We…I feel like I need to know how that happened. So I'm asking for the truth. Does anybody know anything about it?"

Tyler's fists clenched under the edge of the woven tablecloth. If they did, would they admit it?

For an instant her family stared at Miranda without speaking. Then Theo smacked his palm against the table. "No! You can't think we'd do anything to bring him here."

Clayton cleared his throat. "No need to get riled, Theo. The thing's worrying at her, and your sister's got a right to ask." He looked around the table, his clear glance seeming to measure each of them in turn. "Anybody know anything about this?"

The anger faded from Theo's face, leaving him looking young and vulnerable. "No, Daddy."

"No," the twins said together.

Sallie shook her head.

"Nor I," Clayton said. He reached across to clasp Miranda's hand. "I understand why you wanted to ask, sugar. Anybody thinks of anything that might help, you tell Miranda right off." He pushed his chair back. "Mind, now. Anything at all."

That seemed to be a sign of dismissal. The family filtered out of the room until only Tyler and Miranda were left. She began stacking plates on top of one another, as precisely as if it were crucial that they lined up evenly.

Finally she looked at him. "They were telling the truth."

"I know." He did know. Whoever had sent that photo, for whatever reason, it wasn't one of the people who'd sat around the table tonight.

"They'd never do anything to hurt me or Sammy." She said it as if she expected an argument.

He had none to make. They loved her. They'd supported her and Sammy for the past eight years, when he hadn't been a part of their lives.

They didn't need him. Neither the woman he'd once loved nor the son he hadn't known about needed anything he had to offer.

Had Tyler believed her family? Miranda shoved the tip of the spade into the soft earth at the corner of the front porch the next morning, her mind far from the azaleas she meant to plant.

He'd said he did. She frowned at the sandy earth she'd turned. Her people hadn't sent Tyler the photo of Sammy. They wouldn't. Probably next he'd want to ask her sister, then her cousins, then anyone else he could think of.

Her thoughts touched on an army of Caldwell second cousins and courtesy aunts. Everyone knew who Sammy's father was, but they'd all known for her son's entire life. If they'd wanted to make trouble, they could have done it any time in the last eight years.

She leaned on the shovel for a moment, glancing past the crepe myrtles that edged the yard. Sammy was at the dock, spending his Saturday morning helping David clean the boat. He could have been doing something with his father, but Tyler was upstairs in the room he'd turned into a branch office of Winchester Industries.

The really exasperating thing was the fluctuation of her feelings about that. One minute she wanted to pressure him into spending time with Sammy, the next she assured herself that it was better this way.

You're a mess, she told herself sternly. Decide what you want and stick to it.

That was certainly one of those things easier said than done. *Lord, maybe You'd better show me what I'm supposed to do in this situation, because I surely can't figure it out for myself.*

The screen door banged, and she heard footsteps on the porch.

"Are you digging or daydreaming?" Tyler leaned on the porch rail.

"Digging." She shoved the spade in and struck a root. "We had a lilac bush here, but it died, so I'm putting in some azaleas." She nodded toward the pots behind her. "My brothers have been promising to dig the bed for me, but they always have something more important to do."

Tyler came down from the porch as she spoke. Before she knew what he was about, he'd grasped the spade.

"What are you doing?" Her grip tightened.

He lifted an eyebrow. "Isn't that obvious? I'll do the digging for you."

"I can do it myself." Amazing how childish that sounded.

"I'm sure you can." The look he gave her suggested the words meant more than the obvious. "I'd like to help you, however, and you wouldn't be so impolite as to refuse."

She let go of the shovel and moved out of his way. "My momma taught me never to be rude."

Tyler shoved the spade into the earth, striking the same root she'd hit.

"I guess I should have mentioned that the old roots from the lilac were still there."

He maneuvered the blade underneath the root, prying it up. "Guess you might have."

He'd left her with nothing to do, but she could hardly walk away. It would be better if she didn't stare quite so obviously at the movement of his muscles under the white knit shirt he wore.

She picked up one of the potted azaleas. "Looks like that hole's about ready for the first one."

Tyler moved back to give her room, then knelt beside her to help slide the azalea from its pot into the hole. Together they pressed the earth around the plant.

"How long has it been since you've gotten your hands dirty like this?" She tamped the soil down with a trowel.

He shrugged, so close she felt the movement brush against her. "A while, I guess."

It was too bad Sammy wasn't here to see his parents working together on something. That might be better for him than constantly sensing their tension. But Sammy was off with his uncle because his father had had something more vital to do with his Saturday morning.

"Did you finish up whatever work was so important this morning?" She didn't mean her question to sound quite as condemning as she feared it did.

Tyler's expression told her he'd taken it that way. "I have a business to run, remember?"

"Don't you take Saturdays off?"

"Maybe, when I haven't spent Wednesday, Thursday and Friday on other things."

"Important things." *Like your son, for instance.*

He leaned on the shovel, studying her face for a moment. "Is it important for you to help your family run the inn?"

The question took her by surprise. "Yes, but… that's different." *It was, wasn't it?* "That still leaves me plenty of time for Sammy. Besides, my family depends on me."

"The people who work for Winchester Industries depend on me. I try not to let them down."

That was probably true, though she couldn't help but believe his devotion to his position was more consuming than it had to be.

"Can't your brother take some of the load?" Josh had still been in school when she and Tyler were married, but she remembered it had been assumed he'd go into the company, too. That was what Winchesters did.

"Josh doesn't handle responsibility very well."

Tyler began digging the second hole with unnecessary force.

She sat on her heels, watching him. "Doesn't he also work for the company?"

Tyler's face set. "If you call having a corner office with his name on the door working for the company, I suppose he does."

"Don't tell me there's a Winchester who'd rather do something else." She said the words lightly, but a chill touched her. Was Tyler thinking that now he had a son to fill the role Josh apparently didn't?

"Josh talks a good game." He grabbed an azalea and shoved it into the hole. "But when I trusted him with something important to do, he let me down. I won't make the same mistake again."

Tyler's expression was as impervious as granite. His brother had let him down, and he didn't forgive that.

Her chill intensified. Tyler didn't forgive. No matter how they managed to cooperate about Sammy, she'd best keep one thing in mind. Tyler would never forgive her for not telling him about their son.

Chapter Five

Tyler tamped the earth around the last of the shrubs, then stretched. His back felt tight from the unexpected labor, but it was a good sensation. He hadn't done any physical work outside the gym for a long time.

"Is that it? Or are you hiding some more plants somewhere, just waiting for someone to come along and help you?"

"That's it." Miranda sprinkled pine bark mulch around the bushes, then smiled at him. "Thanks, Tyler. I really didn't expect you to do this."

"I know. You could have done it yourself." He followed her to the hose. She sprayed sun-warmed water over his hands.

"I could have." A note of defensiveness touched her words. "You didn't have to leave your work on my account."

Was that a slap at him for working this morning instead of doing something with Sammy? He took the hose from her, holding it so she could wash her hands. She hesitated for a moment, then thrust her hands under the spray. Small hands, but strong and capable, like the rest of her.

He frowned, trying to look honestly at his actions over the last few hours. What he'd said to Miranda was true—he did have work to do, and he didn't trust his brother to take over for him.

Unfortunately, a niggling conscience suggested that hadn't been the only reason he'd hurried to his room after breakfast. Had he been backing off from spending time with his son, avoiding a possibly awkward encounter with Sammy?

If so, he had to do something about that, and quickly. His only reason for being here was to build some sort of relationship with his son.

Miranda turned off the hose, coiling it against the latticework beneath the porch. She had to be wondering what was going on with him. Trouble was, he didn't know.

"Is Sammy still down at the dock?" he asked abruptly.

She nodded, a question in her eyes. "He's helping David clean the boat."

"Maybe I'll see if he'd like to do something with me." Like what? He hadn't a clue.

"I'll walk down with you."

Miranda fell into step with him as he crossed the lawn, then the shell-covered path. Was she thinking he needed her intervention with Sammy?

Sunlight sparkled on the waterway between the

island and the mainland. A sailboat dipped and swayed in the wind as gracefully as a dancer. Gulls circled the mast, white against a sky that was bluer than it could ever be in the city.

The weathered wooden dock stretched into the water, lined with boats on either side. He stepped onto it, his gaze held by the sight of a small figure industriously polishing the chrome trim of a white catamaran. His son. A feeling he didn't recognize welled inside him.

"They're cleaning up the *Spyhop*. David uses her for the dolphin watch, and Daniel takes visitors out on her."

"Sammy likes doing that?"

The wind ruffled Miranda's hair into her face and fluttered her oversize blue T-shirt. "He loves it." Maternal pride blazed in her eyes. "He's turning into a real waterman, just like his grandfather and uncles."

Not like his father, in other words. She seemed determined to turn the boy into a complete Caldwell with no trace of Winchester to be found. That bothered him more than he'd expected.

Miranda stopped level with the boat. "Hey, guys. You've got the *Spyhop* looking like new."

"Not quite that." David ran a paper towel over the windscreen. "But I'd say she's ready for the season. Sammy's been a big help."

Sammy's gaze slanted off Tyler and landed on his mother. "I did all the polishing."

Tyler seemed to feel an invisible push from Miranda, demanding that he respond. "Good job."

"Thanks." Sammy hesitated, as if on the verge of saying his name, then let it trail off.

Tyler braced himself against the railing, the rough wood warm under his hands. He had absolutely no reason to be nervous about this. If he could walk into a multinational corporation's boardroom as if he owned the world, he could surely invite a seven-year-old to spend some time with him.

"Sammy, I thought maybe you'd like to run into town with me." He felt ridiculously like a teenager asking for a first date. "We could stop and get a hamburger for lunch if you want."

For a moment no one moved or spoke. A gull squawked above them, and he sensed Miranda holding her breath. What was she wishing for?

His son squared his shoulders as if facing something unpleasant. "I already promised to go on a dolphin watch with my uncle. But thank you."

Miranda's hand clenched on the railing next to his. "Sammy, you can go on the next trip. I'm sure Uncle David wouldn't mind."

"That's right," David began, but Sammy shook his head, his mouth setting stubbornly.

"We just got the boat ready. I want to go today."

"Fine." Tyler hoped that didn't sound as curt as he feared it did. "We'll do it another time."

"Maybe you'd like to go along on the boat," Miranda said quickly. "They have plenty of room."

"No, thanks."

Miranda meant well, but he had no desire to compete with David for Sammy's attention. He stepped back, watching as Sammy loosed the lines that held the *Spyhop* to the dock. His son moved around the boat easily, as if advertising the fact that he was at home there.

The catamaran nosed slowly through the water away from them. Sammy hopped onto the seat next to his uncle, and David let him put his hands on the wheel as they steered into the current.

"Tyler, I'm sorry."

Was she? "Leave it, Miranda. Sammy can do something with me another day."

Everyone wants something from you. Here was one case where his father's prediction had been wrong. Miranda hadn't wanted anything from him but out. It appeared Sammy was felt exactly the same way.

She should be glad Tyler wasn't fitting in. Miranda had been telling herself that for the past hour, but if it were true, why did her heart ache for both Tyler and Sammy?

She pulled the car into the drive next to the church, got out and unloaded the bucket of red tulips and yellow daffodils from the back seat. Maybe a little time spent alone in the sanctuary while she arranged the flowers for tomorrow's service would help calm her mind.

I don't know what to do, Lord. I don't even know how to pray in this situation. Maybe You'd best give me some direction, because I'm sure not doing very well on my own.

She straightened, closing the car door, and heard someone call her name. Gran Caldwell waved from the front porch of the white clapboard house next to the church where Caldwells had lived for the past hundred and fifty years or so.

"Miranda, come along over here. I've got some lilacs for the vases."

Miranda picked up the bucket and started toward her grandmother, her steps making little sound on the thick carpet of pine needles.

"Hey, Gran. I already have some of Momma's tulips and dafs." She hefted the bucket as she grew near, hoping she could keep the conversation on flowers instead of the tangle her life was in at the moment.

"No paperwhites?" Gran did love the pale, old-fashioned cream narcissus. "We'll cut some of those, too, with the lilacs."

Miranda followed the spare, erect figure in the faded print dress along the hedge of lilacs—deep purple, pale lavender, pure white. Her grandmother's green thumb was legendary. She inhaled, the perfume taking her back to playing under the lilac hedge with her sister, Chloe, on warm spring afternoons that seemed to last forever.

How long would it take Gran to bring up Tyler's arrival? Not long, she'd guess.

Gran cut a spray of purple blossoms with her shears and turned it in her hands as if assessing its worthiness to appear in the church vases. Then she looked at Miranda, her faded hazel eyes still sharp even though she'd soon celebrate her eighty-first birthday.

"I hear Tyler's back on the island."

"Yes." No sense trying to avoid discussing it with Gran, even if she wanted to. Gran always knew everything that happened on the island, and she generally knew what you should do before you did. "Someone sent him a photograph of Sammy."

"So he came. Well, I reckon that's what he ought to do."

"Ought to do?" She set the bucket down. "Gran, he's furious that I never told him about Sammy."

Her grandmother eyed her sternly. "I'm not saying his coming here is a good thing. I'm just saying if he's any kind of an honorable man, he'd have come once he found out about the boy."

Honorable. Tyler's face filled her mind, and she felt the jolt to her heart that she should be getting used to by now. Honorable wasn't a word she associated with Tyler, but maybe Gran had a point.

"I guess it might have been easier to toss the picture away and tell himself it was some sort of joke." But then, Tyler never had been one to do things the easy way.

Gran nodded. "He wouldn't do that, not if he was a man you could have fallen in love with." She snipped another stem of blossoms. "How is it going?"

Miranda thought about Tyler's rigid figure as he watched Sammy go off on the boat with David. "Not well." She tried to swallow, but there was a lump in her throat that wouldn't go away. "He and Sammy— they just seem to glance off each other instead of connecting. Maybe that's best, anyway."

"Best? Way I hear it, you were the one who asked Tyler to stay. Now you wanting him to leave?"

"I didn't think he'd agree." Her reasoning seemed vaguely shameful when she tried to explain it to her grandmother. "I thought he'd say he was too busy and that would make him see that he didn't have time for Sammy. I thought he'd go away, and we could go back to our lives."

"And now that he's staying, seems like everything's changed."

All the things she hadn't been able to say to anyone else began to pour out of her mouth. "Gran, I just don't know what to do. If they go on the way they are, Tyler and Sammy are never going to be anything to each other. But if I help them…"

Her voice choked. Gran folded strong arms around her, holding her close. Miranda inhaled the lavender scent that always meant Gran to her.

"There now, child. Did you take it to the Lord?"

Miranda nodded, trying to sniff back tears. "I've prayed about it and prayed about it. I don't know if it's better for Sammy to lose his father now or to try and divide his life between our world and Tyler's. I guess the truth is, I'm scared."

Gran took Miranda's face between her hands, her palms dry and cool against Miranda's flushed cheeks. "Seems to me you're trying to push God into choosing between your two options. How do you know the Lord doesn't have something else in mind entirely?"

"But—what else is there?"

"Miranda Jane Caldwell, you took vows before God

to love that man forever. Did you ever think maybe God wants the two of you back together again?"

For an instant she could only stare at Gran's face. The world narrowed to the question that hung in the air between them, Gran's challenging gaze, the faint buzz of a bee investigating the lilacs.

"That's impossible." The words came out forcefully. She took a step back. "Gran, that can never happen."

"Why not?"

"Isn't it obvious?" It certainly was to her. "Even if I wanted that, Tyler certainly doesn't. He's turned into a man just like his father, obsessed with business and making money. I can't ignore that, and even if I could, I still can't be the wife Tyler needs. I couldn't eight years ago, and I can't today."

"You stop that kind of talk." Gran shook her finger at Miranda as if she were six instead of twenty-six. "How do you know you're not the wife Tyler needs?"

"I tried!" Tears stung her eyes at the memory of those humiliating days. "I couldn't fit into Tyler's world. As soon as he saw me there, he must have known that."

"So you came back here, where you felt safe." There was no condemnation in her grandmother's voice, just concern. She took Miranda's hands in both of hers. "Child, you remember the verse I gave you?"

How could she forget? Gran gave each of her grandchildren a Bible verse to live by. Miranda's was embroidered on cream linen, framed and hanging on her bedroom wall.

Therefore, as God's chosen people, holy and dearly loved, clothe yourselves with compassion, kindness, humility, gentleness, and patience.

"I remember." She tried for a watery smile. "I'm not sure I do so well with the patience part."

Gran shook her hands as if she'd like to shake Miranda. "You're right good at humility, child. But it seems to me you're forgetting about how God dearly loves you. If you really believed that, you'd know you're worthy wherever you are, whether it's here or in that big house of Tyler's up north."

It was as if she'd looked straight into Miranda's heart. Gran patted her cheek. "You think on that. God will give you the answer. You just have to listen."

She managed to nod, hoping she could somehow hide her feelings from Gran's sharp eyes. She couldn't let herself believe that Gran's idea had any merit, because if she did, she might start hoping for something with Tyler that was never going to happen.

Miranda tucked a spray of white lilac into the vase with the tulips and assessed the effect. Yes, that was going to look lovely.

She took a breath, letting the peace of St. Andrew's seep into her troubled spirit. The small chapel had stood on this same spot for nearly two hundred years. She looked around at the simple wooden pews, the white walls, the stained-glass windows with their colors glowing in the afternoon sunlight. She could use a little peace after listening to Gran's upsetting ideas.

Her gaze was drawn to the image of the risen Christ looking at Mary Magdalene, kneeling before him in the garden. The Christ figure glowed with light, seeming to radiate peace and understanding.

Miranda slipped into a pew, putting her hands on the wooden seat back in front of her and leaning her face against her hands.

Father, I don't know what to think. Is Gran right? Have I been hiding?

She longed to reject the thought, but Gran knew her as well as anyone.

I want to be the person You expect me to be. If I have been hiding, please help me see what to do about it.

No immediate answer leaped into her mind, but that didn't matter. The answer would come. She had confidence in that.

She stood, feeling better than she had since the moment she'd seen Tyler standing in the hallway, and returned to the flowers.

Half an hour later, she'd finished the two vases that stood on either side of the communion table and begun work on the arrangement for the bracket behind the pulpit. One of the double doors at the rear of the sanctuary swung open, letting in a shaft of sunlight. Tyler walked toward her.

Please, Lord, she murmured silently.

"Your mother told me you'd be here." He came to a stop a few feet from her. "She said you were arranging the flowers for tomorrow's service."

Miranda gestured with the narcissus in her hand. "As you can see." She hesitated, not sure she wanted to ask him what he was doing here.

"Very nice." He touched the delicate blossoms of the white lilac. "Where will this one go?"

"There." She nodded. "On the dolphin shelf."

Anyone would think Tyler was here for no other reason than a casual conversation with her. Anyone would be wrong. Tyler never did anything casually.

He moved toward the shelf, his long stride bringing him within inches of her. "Wasn't there some old family legend about that?"

"Yes."

He stopped, looking at her with a raised eyebrow. "Just yes? You could tell me about it, you know."

He almost seemed to be teasing her, and she didn't know how to react. It didn't help that her heart was thumping at his nearness.

"A wooden statue of a dolphin once stood there, carved by the first Caldwell on the island." She mentally deleted all the references to the special blessings that were supposed to come to those wed under the dolphin's gaze. Tyler didn't need any reminder of weddings. "It disappeared a long time ago, when my father was a teenager." Tyler also didn't need to know how her father and uncle had been entangled with that disappearance.

"But you still put flowers on the shelf."

Unnerved by his closeness, she jammed a tulip into the arrangement too hard and broke the stem. "Yes, we do. And I need to get on with it."

Tyler shrugged. "Don't let me stop you."

She could hardly say the truth—that his very presence was enough to disrupt just about anything she might be doing. He moved away, and she could breathe again.

"I'd forgotten how peaceful this place is." He walked toward the side of the sanctuary.

She ought to be able to concentrate on the flowers now that he was at a safe distance. Instead her senses followed him, informing her when he stopped and what caught his attention.

With jerky movements she tucked the rest of the paperwhites into the vase and lifted it to the shelf. There, it would have to do. She could come in early in the morning and adjust it if she had to. At least then Tyler wouldn't be around to distract her.

"This is new, isn't it?" Tyler had stopped in front of the stained-glass window depicting a dolphin surging from the water.

"Yes."

Again he lifted his eyebrows, and again she knew she was being ungracious. It was a bad sign that Tyler brought out the worst in her. Unwillingly she crossed the sanctuary to stand on the opposite side of the window from him.

"It's the Caldwell dolphin. My cousin Adam's fiancée designed and made it."

Tyler touched the crest of a glass wave. "It's beautiful. She's a skilled artist."

"Tory brought back our dolphin, in a way." Things had come full circle. Tory's mother had caused the loss of the dolphin, but Tory had created this beautiful tribute in its place.

Miranda felt Tyler's gaze on her face as she stared at the dolphin. Why had he followed her to the church? She wasn't sure she wanted to know.

"Your family must be very pleased with this."

It was certainly easier to talk about the window than about the situation between them. "We are. Although I think Gran still believes the original dolphin will come back someday."

"Hardly likely after all this time, is it?"

"No, I guess not." *You came back, Tyler. What am I going to do about it?*

She took a breath, summoning her courage. Tyler had something on his mind besides the Caldwell dolphin. She'd better try to find out what.

"Why did you come here looking for me?" It sounded blunt, but it was the best she could do. "Did you want something?"

Tyler's chiseled features seemed to tighten. "I want to talk with you about Sammy."

She saw again his expression when Sammy had gone off with David that morning. Tyler probably didn't experience rejection very often. She suspected he didn't know how to cope with it.

"What about Sammy?"

He moved restlessly, the colored light from the window touching his cheek, then his shoulder. "The point of my staying here is for us to get acquainted. That's a little tough to do when he doesn't want to spend any time with me."

There were a lot of answers to that—that Sammy didn't want to, that she wasn't going to force him, that there wasn't anything she could do.

Gran's words echoed in her mind. If what Gran said was true, it was time she did something about it. No more hiding. She couldn't run from the pain of what she and Tyler had once had. She could only try to repair the damage she'd done when she'd kept Sammy from him.

"It's hard," she said, not sure whether she was talking about Sammy or herself.

"Most things that are worthwhile are hard." His face was uncompromising. "I don't plan to give up on this, Miranda."

Where was the courage Gran insisted all Caldwell women had? Maybe it had skipped her.

"I think it might be best if we planned to do some things with Sammy together." She didn't know she was going to say it until she heard the words come out of her mouth. She'd asked God to show her what to do, and He had immediately given her an opportunity to find out. She couldn't back out now.

Tyler's gaze seemed to probe for the truth beneath her skin. "The three of us together."

She forced herself to meet his eyes. "That will be easier for Sammy."

"It won't be easier for you, will it?"

For an instant she thought she saw sympathy in his face. She must be mistaken. Tyler could hardly feel sympathy for the woman who'd wronged him in such a fundamental way.

"Maybe not. But it's the right thing to do."

He gave a curt nod. "Very well, then." He seemed to slip into his businessman persona. The brief flicker of feeling vanished.

That was for the best. She was only going to get through this if she didn't have too many more disturbing glimpses of the man she'd once loved.

Chapter Six

This wasn't exactly what he'd thought Miranda meant about spending time together with their son. Tyler sat at the round oak table in the parlor on Sunday night with Sammy opposite him, homework spread out between them. Sammy looked as doubtful as Tyler felt about his ability to help with homework.

"How about a snack to help the studying along?" Miranda put a tray down between them. "Do you have a lot for tomorrow?"

Sammy brightened a bit at the sight of oatmeal cookies and milk. "Just my report."

Wonderful. What did Tyler know about the kind of report a second grader would write? He didn't even remember second grade. This evening was as out of tune with his normal life as the rest of the day had been, including sitting in church with the Caldwell clan and enduring a huge family dinner.

Sammy bit into an oatmeal cookie and smiled at

his mother. His son, it seemed, smiled at everyone but him. For Tyler he always had a wary look.

Well, maybe homework help was the route to a smile. "What's your report about?"

Sammy flattened a lined yellow sheet on the table. "I'm s'posed to write a whole page about the dolphin from the church. And draw a picture, too."

"That doesn't sound too hard. Your mother told me a little bit about the dolphin yesterday."

Sammy picked up his pencil, then put it down again. "I don't know what to put in and what to leave out."

"Why don't you just talk about it first," Miranda suggested. "Tell your father the story."

Sammy heaved a sigh, prompting an involuntary smile to Tyler's lips. Homework reluctance didn't seem so far away, after all.

"Gran says the first Caldwell on the island made the dolphin," Sammy began. He slanted a look at Tyler's face. "Did you know he was in a shipwreck?"

"I don't think I heard that part."

Sammy nodded. "Maybe it was even a pirate ship."

Miranda's eyebrows lifted. "Now, you know that's not true."

"It'd be a better story if it was a pirate ship."

"Maybe we ought to stick to the facts," Tyler said. "What did your great-grandmother tell you about it?"

"He was almost ready to drown when he was saved by Chloe and her dolphins." Sammy clearly thought a pirate ship would be more exciting. "Gran

always says he took one look at her and loved her."
He wrinkled his nose. "Mush."

"He took one look and knew he'd love her
forever," Miranda said, her mouth curving softly.

Tyler felt an unexpected, unwelcome tenderness
at the sight and had to beat it down. "I don't think
Sammy wants to include the mushy part."

"True love isn't mushy." Miranda looked ready
for a fight.

"It is when you're seven," he said.

They looked at each other over their son's head,
Miranda's eyes very bright. Then she shrugged, long
lashes sweeping down to hide the green. "I guess you
can just say he carved the dolphin for the church as
a way of thanking Chloe and the dolphins for saving
him."

Miranda obviously preferred the more romantic
version. Had she ever told him that story when they
were dating? Somehow he thought he'd have remembered if she had. He took one look and knew
he'd love her forever.

"Okay." Sammy picked up his pencil. "I can do
that."

Miranda crossed to the shelves that covered one
wall. "I'll find you a picture of the dolphin." She
knelt, sliding a fat leather album from a whole row
of similar albums. "It should be in here."

She brought the book to the table and began
looking through it. For a few minutes there was no
sound but the scratching of Sammy's pencil and the
ruffle of pages as Miranda leafed through the album.

It should have been boring, but instead Tyler felt oddly relaxed. Maybe this was the way he'd envisioned his life for those few summer weeks when he thought he'd found the love of a lifetime—the shabby, comfortable room, the boy's intent face, the gentle curve of Miranda's cheek.

"Here it is." Miranda shoved the album across the table to Tyler, and he and Sammy leaned close together to look at it.

The dolphin was pictured on the shelf he'd seen in the church, against a white wall. Probably an expert would say the carving was crude, but emotion radiated from the form as the dolphin arced upward.

"I can draw that." Sammy pulled a sheet of plain paper toward him. "I've seen lots of dolphins."

Tyler propped the album page in front of him, then slid a book behind it to give Sammy a better angle. His son glanced up with a tentative smile.

"Thanks."

The smile, slight though it was, reached straight for his heart. He glanced at Miranda to find her watching them. She looked down quickly but not before he caught a glimpse of tears in her eyes.

The image was oddly disturbing. Was Miranda that moved to see his son warming to him? Or was she upset at the thought that he and Sammy might find some common bond?

"You know what I think?" Sammy's crayon paused on the dolphin's back.

"What?"

"I think the dolphin's hidden someplace."

Tyler glanced uncertainly at Miranda. She'd said the dolphin disappeared. Tyler had the impression she didn't believe it would ever turn up again.

"Sammy, I don't think—" Miranda began.

"I do." Sammy touched the faded photograph. "Somebody hid it, and Gran would be really happy if we found it for her." He gave Tyler a questioning look. "I want to look for it. You wanna help me?"

He could practically hear Miranda's thoughts. She didn't want him to encourage Sammy's search. She thought it futile, and she was probably right. But the first time his son asked something of him, he wouldn't say no.

"I'd like that, Sammy. It sounds like fun. Almost like a treasure hunt."

Sammy's blazing smile grabbed his heart and squeezed it. "Okay. We'll find it. You'll see."

Miranda was undoubtedly going to tell him how wrong he was to encourage Sammy in this. He didn't care. Any amount of censure was worth it for that small step into his son's life.

"That's enough chapters for tonight." Miranda put the book on Sammy's bedside table. She knew stalling when she saw it. Even Tyler, standing behind her, probably recognized that. "Prayers now, and then into bed."

Sammy seemed to calculate whether he ought to push for more, then slid to his knees on the rag rug next to the brass single bed that had been his since he'd outgrown his crib. He folded his hands to recite the Lord's Prayer, proud that he'd outgrown the simpler prayers she'd taught him when he learned to talk.

"And please God, bless Momma, and Grandpa and Grandma and Gran, and my aunts and uncles and cousins." There was a hesitation, so slight she wondered if Tyler, lingering in the doorway, noticed it. "And my father. Amen."

Sammy hopped into bed, pulling up the patchwork quilt Gran had made for him. "'Night, Momma." He paused again, his gaze not quite meeting Tyler's. "'Night."

"Good night, sugar." She tucked the quilt over him and bent to kiss his forehead, glad he hadn't outgrown good-night stories and kisses yet. "Sweet dreams."

"Good night, Sammy." The low rumble of Tyler's voice set something vibrating inside her.

This was like those dreams she'd never shared with anyone—herself and Tyler looking at their son, telling him good-night. In that dream she could feel his solid presence near her, sense his support in all the troubling questions about how to raise a boy to be a good man.

A dream, just a dream. It was as unreal as all those other dreams she'd had over the years of Tyler holding her hand when Sammy was born, standing proudly beside her at the baptismal font, clapping when Sammy recited his verse at the Christmas pageant. None of them were real.

A spurt of panic touched her. Tyler must never

know she'd spent the past eight years dreaming he was here with her.

She walked from the room, hearing Tyler's footsteps behind her. Just dreams, except that now they were coming true in a skewed, hurtful way.

Tyler followed her into the parlor. It was still empty. The rest of the family had apparently decided she and Tyler needed time alone to settle things. They were right.

"About looking for the dolphin," she began, turning to face him.

His eyebrows lifted. "You don't like the idea. Why?"

There were too many answers to that. Maybe she'd best stick with the easiest one. "Because it's hopeless."

"Most treasure hunts are. That doesn't mean they're not fun."

"If Sammy sets his heart on finding the dolphin for Gran, he'll be disappointed."

Tyler frowned. "Being disappointed is part of life, Miranda. Sammy can learn to cope with that."

"Are you telling me how to be a mother?" Better to be angry with Tyler than think about foolish dreams that would never come true.

"I'm stating the obvious. No reward comes without risk."

Like the risk she'd taken when she fell in love with Tyler? She pushed the thought away. "That may be true, but there are things about the dolphin's disappearance you don't know."

Tyler propped his hip against the round table, folding his arms across his chest. "If it's something

Sammy knows, maybe you'd better tell me, unless it's a family secret."

You were my husband, Tyler. You had a right to know any of my family secrets.

She'd better tell him before he said something he shouldn't out of not knowing. "The dolphin disappeared when my daddy and his brother were teenagers. Turns out Uncle Jefferson took it from the church out to Angel Isle to impress a girl—a rich summer visitor. They were all at a party there. The girl's father and his friends raided it. I guess he didn't like his daughter associating with people like us."

That hit too close to home, and for a moment she couldn't go on. Did Tyler see the parallels between that old story and the way his family had reacted to their runaway wedding?

"What happened to the dolphin?" Tyler, frowning, seemed to be focused on the disappearance. Apparently she was the only one who related it to their personal story.

"There was a lot of confusion, and my daddy was hurt in an accident. By the time anyone looked for it, the dolphin was gone."

"So she took it away." Tyler came to the obvious conclusion.

"That's what Daddy always thought, until the woman's daughter came to the island. Tory—the one who made the dolphin window in the sanctuary. She says her mother never took it off the island. It just vanished that night."

"Sammy must think it's still on Angel Isle."

He said the name easily, as if it were just any spot, instead of the place where they'd spent their honeymoon before coming back to face the music with their families.

"I suppose so." She tried to say it with as much unconcern as he did. "I'm sure that's where he wants to look."

Tyler pushed himself away from the table, the movement bringing him close enough she could smell the musky aftershave that clung to him. "Nothing you've told me seems a good enough reason for denying Sammy the pleasure of hunting for it."

"All right. Fine." She turned away, picking up the photo album to return it to the shelf. Anything to put a few feet between her and Tyler. "We'll look for the dolphin." *And I'll try not to remember what Angel Isle once meant to us.*

"You have more of those."

She couldn't imagine what he was talking about. Then she realized he meant the photo album.

"A whole shelf of them."

"Including pictures of Sammy." There was an edge in his voice, but she thought it overlay longing.

"Yes. Of course." She slid the old album into its place and touched the ones that chronicled Sammy's life—three fat albums stuffed with photos of all the things Tyler had missed. Would they make him hate what she'd done even more? Maybe that wasn't possible.

She pulled the albums out and carried them to the table. "Here they are."

Tyler slid into the chair in front of them, then looked at her, a challenge in his dark eyes. "Don't I get a guided tour of my son's life?"

The lump in her throat threatened to choke her. She nodded, sat down and opened the first album.

"This is the day he was born." Her fingertips touched the picture of a red-faced infant, squalling his indignation at being thrust into the world. "It's a little blurry. Daddy took it through the glass of the nursery window."

Tyler pulled the album closer, his hand brushing hers and sending a shaft of awareness along her skin. "Your family was with you."

"Naturally." Did he think they'd have deserted her because she'd come home pregnant and divorced? "Momma was my labor coach. She said it was harder to do than to have all five of hers."

Tyler's hand stilled on the page. "I should have been there."

"You…" She caught the words that wanted to be spoken.

I dreamed you were there, Tyler. You held my hand, and I saw the incredible joy in your face when our son was born.

"What?" He turned, his face too close to hers.

"Nothing." Where was this going? Panic ricocheted through her. How could she ever get out of this situation without her heart shattering into a million pieces?

Tyler leaned forward on the bench seat of the catamaran the next afternoon, watching Miranda ease the boat to the dock at Angel Isle. She had suggested they wait until Saturday for this trip, but Sammy had been so eager she'd finally agreed to come today after school.

His son stood on the opposite seat, rope in hand, ready to tie up. Tyler resisted the impulse to grab the back of Sammy's shirt as he reached for the post. He wouldn't appreciate being treated like a baby.

Sammy made the rope fast, then scrambled off to loop the stern line around another post. His movements were as quick and efficient as any sailor's.

"Good job."

His son gave him a smile that seemed a little easier today. Because he was feeling more comfortable around Tyler or because he'd succeeded in getting them to take this trip to Angel Isle today? Tyler didn't know him well enough to be sure.

That added to the list of things he didn't know about this child of his. Resentment had bubbled beneath the surface since they'd looked at those photograph albums.

Sammy, tiny in his grandfather's hands, sitting up in a high chair, reaching for a rattle held by one of his uncles, showing two teeth in a proud grin. He'd missed his son's babyhood, his toddler years. All those landmarks would never come again.

Miranda climbed lightly out of the *Spyhop*, and he followed her, carrying the picnic basket her mother had thrust on them as they went out the door. Apparently Sallie thought they couldn't make the trip without sustenance, even though Miranda had insisted they'd be back for supper.

He patted the pocket where he'd put his cell phone and intercepted a quick glance from Miranda.

"Couldn't leave it behind?"

"Never," he said firmly. "It's permanently attached."

She started up the path, resting her hand on Sammy's shoulder. It was an automatic gesture, one he hadn't quite had nerve enough to make with the boy yet for fear Sammy would pull away.

The resentment burned again as he followed them. Only one thing had kept him from lashing out at Miranda the night before when he'd looked at the photographs of all he'd missed in his son's life. It continued to keep him silent.

Miranda's devotion to their child shone so brightly that a blind person could see it. She'd been wrong not to tell him about her pregnancy, but he had to admit, to himself if not to her, that she'd been trying to do what she thought was best for their son.

Miranda and Sammy paused at the bend in the path, waiting for him under a live oak, its branches festooned with Spanish moss. "Is something wrong?" She pushed bronze curls from her face.

"No." He couldn't tell her he'd lagged behind because he'd been trying to figure out what kind of relationship they could have after everything that had happened between them.

"We're almost there," Sammy said. He darted ahead. "Come on and see the cottage."

He heard the quick catch of Miranda's breath.

"He doesn't know I'm not a stranger here, does

he?" he said, and watched the color rise in her cheeks.

"I've never found it necessary to tell him we came here on our honeymoon, if that's what you mean." Her mouth was set firmly. "Did you think I should?"

For an instant he wanted to say something hurtful, something that would pay her back for all he'd missed. He shook his head. "I don't want to fight with you, Miranda."

Her chin came up. "Don't you?"

"No. Not that I'm not tempted, but I remember what it's like to have parents who hated each other. I won't show Sammy the kind of relationship they had."

She seemed to digest that for a moment. "I don't see any reason we can't try to be—" she paused as if searching for the right word "—friendly."

"Come on!" Sammy shouted impatiently. "Don't you want to start looking?"

"We're coming," Miranda called. She looked as if she would say something more, then turned and went quickly up the path.

He followed, rounded the bend and came to a halt. The cottage stretched in front of them, its porch reaching out welcoming arms across the front of the gray shingled building. He'd carried Miranda up those steps, across the porch, laughing and kissing at the same time.

Miranda glanced at him. "Is something wrong?"

"No." He hurried to catch up with her, and they went together up the steps to the porch where Sammy waited, dancing with impatience. Nothing was wrong except that he'd suddenly been slapped with a whole raft of memories he didn't know what to do with.

Miranda seemed oblivious to the effect the cottage had on him. She took the key from the nail above the door and unlocked it. Sammy rushed in, and she crossed to the windows to throw open the shutters, letting sunlight stream across the wide pine floorboards and touch the hooked rugs and faded chintzes.

"I'm going to look upstairs. Maybe it's hidden in one of the closets." Sammy scrambled up the open stairway.

Tyler stood in the doorway, watching Miranda. They'd married in a tiny church miles away on the mainland, and she'd wept a little afterward because she hadn't been married in her own church. He'd held her in his arms and kissed the tears away.

They'd rented a boat and come here, to the place she loved, for their stolen honeymoon. He'd carried her over the threshold he stood on now, laughing and triumphant. Had that triumph been for marrying the woman he loved or for outwitting their families? He tried to look rationally at the kid he'd been at twenty, but he couldn't.

Emotion had clouded his judgment then. He pushed away from the doorjamb and crossed the room to help her with the shutters. He wasn't a kid any longer. He had to concentrate on establishing, if not a friendship, at least a truce with Miranda. Maybe that was the best they could hope for.

Miranda thumped a recalcitrant shutter with her fist. "This one always sticks."

He grabbed the handle and pulled. With a creak of hinges, it grumbled open.

Sunlight crossed Miranda's face, bringing out the gold flecks in her eyes. She smiled, pushing back the opposite shutter. "You're just trying to make me look bad."

An answering smile touched his lips. "I'd never do that." He brushed her cheek with his fingertips. "Never."

Her hand was arrested on the shutter, as if she'd forgotten she held it. Her eyes met his, wide and questioning.

What was he doing? That had to be the question in her mind, just as it was in his. Surely his brain had a coherent answer somewhere, but it had gotten lost in a flood of memories and feelings brought on by this place, this woman.

"Tyler…"

His name came out on her breath. He cupped her cheek with his hand. Her lips were only inches away. And then he kissed her.

Crazy, crazy, something in his brain shouted, but he wouldn't listen to it. Miranda was as warm and sweet as he remembered, and he didn't want to listen to logic or reason, not now.

He released her mouth, pressed his cheek against her hair. The words came before he thought. "What happened, Miranda? What happened to us?"

Chapter Seven

All the wounded places in Miranda's heart were flooded with a warm, healing light. She'd waited for Tyler's kiss during the long, arid years. Now, with this one meeting of lips, hearts had met, too.

No, oh, no. She drew back, slowly and painfully, feeling as if she were wrenched away and had left her heart behind.

She couldn't make the same mistake again. They'd been down this road together before, and it had ended in unimaginable pain. They couldn't repeat that.

She took a step away from him, knowing the light from the window showed him every expression on her face. Her longing must be written there for him to see, but she couldn't let that matter.

"I'm sorry," he said at last, his dark eyes masking whatever he felt. "That shouldn't have happened."

"No." She cleared her throat and tried to steady

her voice. "You asked what happened to us, but we both know the answer to that. If we'd been right for each other, we wouldn't have parted. We'd have fought for our marriage instead of giving up at the first obstacle."

His mouth tightened. "We were certainly too young to make lifetime decisions."

"Yes." She tried to smile. "Very young, and in too much of a hurry." She thought of her younger self, crazy in love and longing to be Tyler's wife. She'd thought marriage was the one thing that would guarantee she'd never lose him. Instead, it had driven them apart.

"I would have stayed with you, you know." Tyler's dark brows drew down over his eyes, making him look formidable. "If I'd known about the baby, I'd have tried to make it work."

Because of Sammy, he'd have tried to make a go of something that would have made both of them miserable. Even knowing how badly things had turned out between them, she couldn't help but wince at that.

"I intended to. But when I came back to Baltimore—"

His mouth hardened. "I think I can guess. My mother intercepted you, didn't she?"

She nodded. Repeating the cruel things his mother had said wouldn't do any good.

"We can't go back and rewrite the past." She took a step back. "All we can do is try and make things as right as possible for our son."

He nodded, his face bleak. "Friends, I think you said. I guess we'd better try."

He didn't look as if the prospect gave him much joy, but then she could hardly expect that it would.

"Isn't anybody going to help me hunt?" Sammy's plaintive voice floated down from upstairs.

"I'll go," Tyler said. He crossed the room with quick strides and hurried up the steps as if he couldn't wait to be away from her.

She rubbed her arms, cold in spite of the warmth of the day. Tyler had taken all the sunshine out of the room with him, leaving only a gray, draining chill that seeped into her bones and made her feel as old as Gran.

She forced herself to walk across the room and unpack the picnic basket Tyler had left on the round oak table. Lemonade in a jug, red Delicious apples, a bag of oatmeal chocolate-chip cookies—comfort food, and she was certainly in need of comfort. Maybe her mother had guessed that was how it would be, coming back with Tyler to the place where they'd been so happy.

She glanced up when she heard thumps coming from upstairs. They must be pulling things out of the storage spaces beneath the eaves.

The light chatter of Sammy's voice mixed with the deeper chime of Tyler's answers. Sammy was getting past his reserve where his father was concerned. She closed her eyes, groping in prayer.

Lord, at first all I wanted was to get rid of Tyler, but now I see that's not right. Like it or not, Sammy needs to know his father. I'm trying not to be a coward about this, but I surely could use Your help.

Some of the tension eased out of her in the silence, and she could look at the situation with more clarity. At some level Tyler must still be attracted to her, but he obviously didn't feel that marriage was forever. If he did, he'd never have agreed to the quick divorce his mother had pushed through.

So she had to find a way, for Sammy's sake, to keep things at a calm, friendly level between them. Committed as they were to spending time together with Sammy, that wouldn't be easy, but it had to be done.

One thing she could never do was betray to Tyler the fact that, for her, marriage was forever. She'd never stopped feeling married to him, no matter how many legal documents or miles or years stood between them. She'd never stop feeling that, but it would be a disaster to let Tyler suspect such a thing.

By the time she'd found napkins and glasses and spread the red-and-white checked cloth over the table, Tyler and Sammy came down the open stairway. One look at Sammy's face told her they'd found nothing.

"No luck?"

He shook his head, his mouth set in a determined line. "But there's lots more places to look. We can't give up yet."

"How about a little snack before you search some more?"

"Sounds good," Tyler said, as easily as if he hadn't been kissing her only a little while earlier.

Sammy slid onto a chair and picked up a cookie. "We went way back under the eaves, Momma. I found a box of old cars. Do you think we could take them home?"

"Why don't you bring them down and put them in the game room closet instead. Then you can play with them when your cousins are here."

Sammy nodded reluctantly. "Guess that would be okay."

"You come out here a lot, do you?" Tyler glanced from her to Sammy as he asked the question. Was he remembering when they'd come alone to the cottage, heady with their new status as man and wife?

"Lots in the summer," Sammy answered. "Gran says when Great-grandpa was little, they used to stay out here all summer long. Wish we could do that."

"We have the inn to run now," she reminded him. "Besides, if we did that, you couldn't play T-ball in the summer."

Sammy nodded, then cast a sideways glance at his father. "First practice for T-ball is tomorrow after school. We're s'posed to bring a parent. You could go, if you want."

"I'd like that," Tyler said. He reached out a little tentatively to ruffle Sammy's hair. "I'd like that a lot."

She'd been right. Sammy was adjusting to Tyler. She blinked. Both of them would be embarrassed at the idea that they'd brought her to tears.

An electronic peal startled her. "What was that?"

Tyler reached for his pocket. "Cell phone. Never

go anywhere without it, remember?" He pulled the phone out, and with it came a square of paper that fluttered to lie, face up, on the floor. It was the photograph of Sammy.

For a moment Tyler froze, not sure what to do. He'd agreed to Miranda's decision that Sammy not be told about the photo. She'd probably assume he'd done this deliberately.

The phone buzzed again, and he snapped it off. He reached for the picture, but Sammy had already grabbed it. Over their son's head he met Miranda's gaze and mouthed a quick sorry.

"Hey, where'd you get this picture of me?"

Sammy looked at him, and the lie that had been tentatively forming in his mind died. Whatever he told his son, it couldn't be a falsehood.

"Well, I…" Okay, where were the words? He didn't have this much trouble dancing around an unpalatable truth in a business deal. Which just went to prove that he was better off avoiding emotional entanglements.

"Someone sent the picture to your father." Miranda didn't seem to have his difficulty in coming out with the truth now that she'd been forced into it. He could read the worry she was trying to hide.

Sammy frowned at the picture. "You mean that bird-watcher guy sent it to you?"

"What bird-watcher guy?" He addressed the question to Miranda, but she looked as perplexed as he felt.

"You know, Momma." Sammy dropped the

photo on the table. "That guy who stayed at the inn a while ago. He had those neat binoculars he let me look through."

"You mean Mr. Dawson."

"Yeah, him." Sammy turned away, losing interest. "I'm gonna look in the closets where the games are."

"Just a minute." Miranda touched his arm, stopping him. "Are you sure Mr. Dawson took this picture?"

He nodded. "One day when I got home from school. He said he wanted to finish up a roll or something." He shrugged. "He said he'd give me the pictures, but he never did. Can I go now?"

"Okay." Miranda managed a smile, but her eyes were troubled. "You put all those games back when you're done, though, hear?"

"I'll be there in a minute to help you." As soon as he'd found out what Miranda knew about this Dawson character.

But she got in with the first question as soon as Sammy had disappeared. "Do you know him?"

"I know a lot of people, but nobody called Dawson comes to mind. What did he look like?"

And why didn't anybody notice him taking pictures of our son? That probably wasn't a fair question. This was Caldwell Island, where no one thought twice about a visitor with a camera.

Miranda shrugged. "Average height, average looks. Forties, at a guess. He said he was a birder, and we get a fair number of them. He went out every day with a camera and binoculars. He didn't appear to take any particular interest in Sammy."

Tyler drummed his fingers on the table, mind moving rapidly through possibilities. "When exactly was he here? What do you know about him?"

"Last month some time." She frowned. "He stayed about a week, I think. When we get home, I can look him up on the computer and be more exact." She met Tyler's gaze, hers perplexed. "Why? Why would he take the picture and send it to you?"

"I don't know. But I think the sooner we find out, the better." He shoved back his chair and glanced at his watch. "Do you think another hour of this will satisfy Sammy?"

Miranda's smile erased some of the worry in her face. "Nothing short of finding the dolphin will satisfy Sammy, but I think he'll have to be content with that today."

"I'll go help him look." A very good idea, he told himself as he walked away from Miranda. Because the longer he stayed in the same room with her, the more he wanted to kiss her again.

He found Sammy burrowing into the depths of a large closet off the game room and set to work to move some of the folding tables and chairs that were stowed there. Unfortunately that didn't serve as enough of a distraction.

What had he been thinking, to let himself get that close to Miranda? He must have been crazy. One moment he'd been noticing how the sunlight through the window brought out the gold flecks in her eyes, and the next he'd been holding her.

He'd known it was a mistake while he was doing

it, but he couldn't stop himself. Kissing Miranda again had felt like water after thirst or food after hunger—something so elemental it couldn't be denied. It had felt like coming home after years of wandering.

But it wasn't, and they both knew it. Whatever the source of that lightning between them, it didn't translate into marriage. They'd tried that, and they'd both come away scarred.

Now there was Sammy to figure into the mix, making it even more difficult. They couldn't risk letting Sammy be hurt by their impossible attraction.

Don't count on anyone. They'll only let you down.

His father's words didn't quite fit in this situation. He and Miranda had let each other down.

Sammy sat on his heels and stared disconsolately into the empty closet. "Do you think maybe there's a secret hiding place?"

Tyler reached in to thump the walls with his fist. "Seems pretty solid to me. I'm sorry, son."

It was the first time he'd used the word to Sammy. He held his breath, waiting for a reaction.

But Sammy's mind seemed to be on the failure of his search, not on anything his father might say. "I thought it would be here." He straightened, seizing a stack of games to put back. "But I'm not giving up. I'm going to find it."

Had his son's stubbornness come from him or Miranda? They probably both had more than their fair share.

"Maybe we can look some more another time. I think your mother wants to start back soon."

He thought the boy would argue, but Sammy seemed to realize it would do no good. "We can come again some other day, okay?"

"Okay." Tyler hefted one of the folding tables. "Let's get these things put away."

Doing a simple job with his son was oddly satisfying. Had he and his father ever done anything so mundane together? Not that he could recall. His father had always been too busy with the company. Their rare times together had been scripted— business social events where he was supposed to occupy some colleague's children while his father closed a deal.

"I want to bring that box of cars down, then I'm ready." Sammy darted off.

Tyler went to the living room, but their snack had been cleared away and Miranda was nowhere in sight. He pushed through the front screen door and saw her.

She sat on a fallen log under the palmettos, perfectly still. A few feet from her, a deer nosed its way through the undergrowth.

He eased the door closed. If Miranda knew he was there, she gave no sign. Her entire being was concentrated on the graceful brown creature that moved closer and closer to her.

His throat tightened. Miranda fit into island life as surely as the deer in the woods or the dolphins at play in the sound. She moved to the rhythm of the tides and the seasons.

Little wonder she hadn't been able to adapt to the kind of life he offered her. He'd told himself at the time she hadn't tried, but that had been unfair. She couldn't. She belonged here.

Their son would have to bridge two worlds. That would be difficult enough, without adding uncertainty over the relationship between his mother and father.

Tyler and Miranda would have to step as carefully as the deer did. And no matter how hard they tried, there were no guarantees they could do this without damaging their son.

"What are you doing?"

The voice startled Miranda, and she inadvertently closed the file she'd been searching. She glanced up.

Tyler stood in the office doorway. The pool of light from her desk lamp didn't quite reach him, making him a dark silhouette against the hallway beyond.

"Looking for the records on our Mr. Dawson." She rolled her chair back from the desk. "I haven't been able to get him off my mind since Sammy told us about him this afternoon, but this is the first chance I've had to look through the records."

Family had surrounded them since they'd returned from Angel Isle. That should have made it easier for her to be near Tyler, but it hadn't. She'd been too aware of the necessity to hide her feelings both from him and from the family.

She'd asked her mother about Dawson, evading explanations for her interest. She hadn't wanted the outpouring of advice that story would have triggered.

All in all, she'd been happy to escape into the office once Sammy was in bed.

Tyler crossed the small office and leaned his hip against the desk. He still wore the khakis and dress shirt he'd donned for supper—apparently he wasn't convinced he could appear at the table in jeans.

He glanced at the monthly charts posted along one wall, the filing cabinets, the fax and copy machines. "This isn't what I expected."

"The office? Did you think we did it all with quill pens?"

"Not quite that." He smiled, and she appreciated the width of the desk between them. She needed something to safeguard her from the effect of that smile. "But the registration desk with the old-fashioned register sends a different message from this."

"People want old-fashioned, down-home charm when they come here. They don't need to know that all the records move from the register straight to my computer."

"Very nice. You probably even have a Web site."

"Thanks to Chloe. She set it up for us." She swiveled to face the computer. "I ought to be able to track everything we have about Dawson—his reservation, how he paid, credit card."

"Ought to be?" His voice came from directly behind her. He'd rounded the desk while she'd focused on the screen, and he stood close to her chair. She felt his hands brush her shoulders, then grip the chair back.

Breathe, she ordered herself. Concentrate. She

couldn't let Tyler guess his nearness reminded her vividly of that moment when they'd kissed. He'd obviously been able to dismiss it from his mind. So should she.

Her throat felt tight, and she swallowed. "The trouble is, he didn't make a reservation." She pulled up the relevant screen. Tyler leaned over her shoulder to look at it, and she had to remind herself to breathe again.

"He just walked in?" His question was sharp, and he wore the expression she'd always thought of as his business look—intent, determined, focused.

"Well, it was February. We weren't exactly busy." She frowned. "It's a little unusual that he didn't even call to ask if we had a room, but it does happen."

"What about his credit card?"

She clicked to the payment file, then shook her head. "He paid in cash."

Tyler's hand came down on her shoulder. "You're not going to tell me that's routine."

"No." She tried to ignore the warmth that trickled through her at his touch. "No, that's not routine. Most people use credit cards, a few pay by check. Cash is—strange."

"I'm beginning to find the mysterious Mr. Dawson a little too strange to believe." Tyler sounded grim. "Can you trace his address?"

"Let's have a look." She tried to manage a smile. "Theo showed me a Web site where you can check an address anywhere in the country. I don't think I want to know why teenagers know something like that."

"Power," he suggested.

"I suppose so." She clicked to the site, trying to ignore the pressure of Tyler's hand, the feel of his breath against her cheek as he leaned over. "Let's see if Alfred Dawson really is at 4423 Steeple Drive in Detroit."

The answer popped up in seconds, and Tyler saw it as quickly as she did.

"A phony address." His anger was communicated through his touch.

"It might not mean anything." She tried to come up with a logical reason and failed.

"Somehow I can't buy that."

"I guess I can't, either. I asked my mother what she remembered about him."

Tyler turned her swivel chair so she faced him. "And?"

"He didn't make much impression on her, either. But she was surprised when I said he was from Detroit."

"Why?" Tyler's habit of firing one-word questions was unnerving.

"She said she talked to him about things to see in the area, and Charleston was mentioned. He referred to it as the holy city. Nobody does that except died-in-the-wool Charlestonians."

That brought some reaction to his stern expression, so quick she couldn't quite decipher it.

"What is it?" Apprehension colored her voice.

"Winchester Industries has a branch office in Charleston."

"That could just be coincidence."

"That's a few too many coincidences for my

peace of mind. Maybe you can believe in this random visitor with the vanishing past who just happens to take a photo of Sammy that just happens to get sent to me, but I can't."

She battled a rush of fear. "If you weren't who you are—"

Tyler's face was set. "If I weren't Tyler Winchester, this wouldn't have happened, is that what you mean?"

"Well, would it?" She tried to push her chair away from him, but he gripped it firmly.

"You knew who I was when you married me."

Her brief flare of anger was extinguished by his tone. "Yes. I knew." She had to deal with the repercussions of that.

He straightened. "I'm going to the office in Charleston tomorrow. I'll find an investigations agency while I'm there and put them onto it. Give me everything you have on Dawson."

Her life was spinning out of control. "I'll get it ready for you."

"Good." He turned away, his mind obviously racing ahead to the next day.

"Tyler, don't forget about the T-ball practice. You promised Sammy you'd be there."

"I'll be back in plenty of time." He focused on her, his expression softening. "Don't worry so much." He touched her cheek lightly. "I'll get to the bottom of this, whatever it is. I'm not going to let anything hurt Sammy."

She nodded, pinning a smile on her face. All Tyler's concern was for their son, and that was the way it should be. Still, she couldn't quite suppress the rebellious little corner of her heart that wished some of his concern were for her.

Chapter Eight

"He's not coming." Sammy's lower lip came out, and Miranda suspected he was pouting to keep himself from crying.

Miranda glanced at her watch again, then down the street toward the center of the village. Tyler had promised to be back from Charleston in time for Sammy's T-ball practice. He wasn't.

"Come on, Momma." Sammy yanked the car door open and tossed Theo's old ball glove onto the seat. "We'll be late if we don't go now."

She felt like pouting herself. Or crying. Seeing Sammy's hurt was worse than her own. She slid into the car.

"Maybe he got stuck in traffic getting out of Charleston." She'd suggest anything that might wipe the pain from her son's face.

"He could've been here if he wanted to." Sammy clutched the glove, not looking at her as she pulled onto the street. "I knew he wouldn't come."

"Son, maybe you ought to wait and see what your father says before you decide that."

Sammy didn't answer. How could she blame him for his anger and disappointment when she was seething with it, too? This was just what she'd feared would happen when she let Tyler into their lives.

You couldn't keep him out, her conscience reminded her. *Once he knew about Sammy, that option wasn't open.*

Her eyes searched the bridge to the mainland as they passed it, looking without success for Tyler's burgundy rental car. *We agreed we weren't going to let Sammy be hurt. How could you let him down this way?*

There was little point in addressing the question to someone who wasn't there. But when Tyler arrived, he'd have to answer her.

Something prickled in her mind, refusing to go away until she looked at it.

You never confronted Tyler about anything when you were married.

She looked at the truth with dismay. Had she really been that young, that much in awe of him? Had she been that much of a doormat?

She drew up under the live oaks that ringed the practice field, clenching the steering wheel for a moment of prayer as Sammy darted from the car.

Lord, I'm angry right now with Tyler. I don't want

to confront him out of my own hurt. Help me to make
him understand his responsibility to his son.

She wouldn't let her feelings get in the way. She
wouldn't repeat the pattern she'd begun when they
were married. This time Tyler would be called to
account.

Practice was long over when the moment came to
put her resolution into action. Miranda sat alone on
the front porch when Tyler's car finally pulled into
the driveway after supper. The family was tactfully
avoiding the area to give her free rein with Tyler. She
would need it.

He mounted the porch steps, then put his briefcase
down. The suit jacket he'd worn when he left was
slung over his shoulder, but he still looked businesslike and intimidating in the dress shirt and striped tie
that announced his status.

"Waiting for me?"

"Yes." He obviously didn't remember. Anger for
her child burned along her veins. How long would it
take him to realize what he'd done? "We have to talk."

He nodded, leaning against the railing. "Dan Carpenter, who's in charge of the Charleston office, was
able to recommend a private investigations agency.
I talked with them, gave them all the information we
had. They hope to get a line on our Mr. Dawson
before long."

If he expected congratulations on that, he was
doomed to disappointment. "And did some disaster
hit the company this afternoon?"

He frowned. "No, of course not. Why?"

She shoved herself out of the rocking chair, letting it creak back and forth. "Why? Because I couldn't imagine that anything less would keep you from fulfilling your promise to your son." She planted her fists on her hips. "You don't even remember, do you?"

She watched him thinking it over, mentally checking his calendar. She saw the moment when it registered.

"T-ball practice."

"You told Sammy you'd be there."

Annoyance flared in his eyes at her tone, and he crossed his arms over his chest. "I had business to take care of." He was clearly not used to accounting for himself to anyone.

"More important business than keeping your promise?"

"Look, I forgot." His belligerent attitude eased, and he put his hands against the railing on either side of him. "I'm sorry. Was he upset?"

The sign of concern for Sammy heartened her. "Yes." She wouldn't pretend this wasn't important, because it was. "He was upset. He said he knew you wouldn't come."

Tyler winced at that. "What did you tell him?"

"I said he should wait and talk to you before he decided that. That maybe you had a good reason."

"I take it business isn't a good enough reason."

Please, Lord, help me make him see.

"Not for breaking a promise."

"Come on, Miranda. People break promises all the time."

Maybe the people in your life do, Tyler. Not the people in mine.

"A promise between parent and child is…well, it's sacred. You can't treat it lightly."

He frowned. "You make it sound like an article of faith."

"It is." She took a breath, searching for the words that would make him understand. "I can't separate faith out from parenting. I know I can't be as good a parent as God is, but I have to try."

Pain flickered in his eyes. "If I compared God to my father—" He stopped, shook his head. "Okay, I was wrong not to keep my promise. I don't have a good excuse. I'm still trying to figure out this parenting stuff."

Meaning it was her fault he didn't have much experience as a father. They'd never get past that.

"I know." She forced her voice to be steady. "This is one of those situations where you learn from your mistakes. But this one really hurt him."

His mouth tightened. "Where is Sammy? I owe him an apology."

"He's down at the dock. I'll go with you."

He lifted his eyebrows as they started down the steps. "Afraid I'll make a mess of it on my own?"

"Not if you're honest with him." How much should she push him? "Try to open up to him, Tyler. That's what he needs."

For a moment she thought he wouldn't reply.

There was no sound but the crunch of their footsteps on the shell-covered path and the distant cry of a gull. Sammy's small figure perched on the end of the dock, the channel beyond him turning purple in the setting sun.

"There's not much call for opening up in my life," Tyler said finally. His gaze was fixed on Sammy. "I'm probably not good at it. But I'll try."

Please, Lord, she prayed as they reached the dock. *Please let them hear each other.*

Tyler's movements were slow as they approached their son, as if Sammy were a wild creature, not to be startled. "Hi, Sammy." He squatted next to him.

Sammy pulled his knees up and wrapped his arms around them. "Hey," he mumbled.

"Okay if we sit down?"

He got a shrug of the shoulders in answer but seemed to take that for a yes. He sat on the dock next to Sammy, not quite close enough to touch.

Please, Lord. Miranda sat, folding her legs. *I'm not even sure where Tyler stands in relation to You now. I don't know if he's asking for Your help. But I'm asking. Please help him.*

"I'm sorry I missed your practice today."

Another shrug. "It's okay."

But it wasn't. Her heart hurt for him.

"I wanted to be there."

Sammy looked at him, his small face set. For a moment she saw the resemblance between them so clearly that she could hardly bear it.

"If you wanted to, you would have."

The logic of a seven-year-old was direct. To do him justice, Tyler didn't try to argue with it.

"I guess you've got a point there. I didn't set out to miss it, but I got busy talking to someone, and I forgot."

Open up to him, Tyler. She thought the words so strongly she almost felt he could hear them.

Tyler leaned forward, his elbows on his knees. She spared a brief thought for what the rough planks were probably doing to his dress trousers. He didn't seem to care.

"You know, Sammy, I guess I haven't quite figured out this father stuff yet. But I remember…"

He paused, glanced at her. She nodded, trying to look encouraging. He couldn't give up now, even though Sammy wasn't responding.

"I was probably a little older than you are. My school had this program where kids' parents came in and talked about their careers."

"Career day," Sammy muttered without raising his head. "We have that, too."

"I was at a boarding school, where you actually live at school. My father said he'd come for career day. It was the first time he'd ever promised something like that. He'd always been too busy before."

Tyler seemed to look into the past, to the boy he'd been. "I was really excited. I told all my friends he was coming. I remember the teacher even had me make a name sign for him."

The timbre of Tyler's voice had deepened. She heard it and knew she was hearing genuine emotion.

Sammy seemed to recognize it, too. He looked up, fixing his gaze on his father's face. "What happened?"

Tyler shrugged. "He didn't show up. The other parents came, and they sat at a long table with their name signs in front of them. I sat there the whole period and looked at my father's sign and his empty chair."

"You felt bad." Sammy's loving heart filled his voice.

"Yes."

She didn't think Tyler would say anything more. Then he cleared his throat.

"He hadn't forgotten. Something else just came up that he thought was more important. He never even said he was sorry."

His words pressed on her heart. She knew what Sammy didn't—that the story he'd told wasn't just an isolated incident. Tyler's father had never been there for his son.

Why hadn't she realized the effect of that on Tyler when they were married? Guilt swept over her.

No wonder it had been so important to him to take over after his father's heart attack. He'd still been trying to prove himself, and she hadn't understood that.

Did that lonely little boy still lurk inside Tyler? He'd built his life around not being emotionally involved with anyone, but maybe he needed family more than he thought he did.

"Sammy, I want to do better than my father did. I'm sorry I let you down. I hope you can forgive me."

Sammy's eyes were suspiciously bright with tears, but he wouldn't let them fall. He nodded, then stuck out his hand. They shook hands solemnly.

Her eyes were wet. Miranda blinked rapidly, trying not to make a fool of herself. Neither of them would thank her for crying over them. Seeing the two of them bond with each other wrenched her heart. This was the way it should have been from the beginning. Maybe it would have been, if she'd only had the courage to try harder.

Tyler hadn't felt this much relief when a risky business gamble had paid off. He smiled at his son, hoping he wasn't going to disgrace himself by tearing up. He wanted Sammy to like him, not to feel pity for him.

"Thank you, Sammy." The feel of his son's small hand in his gave him a visceral surge of totally unexpected love, knocking him completely off balance.

Of course he'd thought he'd love his son. He'd assumed it would come slowly, growing as they got to know each other.

He hadn't anticipated this overwhelming emotion, sweeping everything else aside with its power, so strong he didn't know what to do with it. Wherever this relationship was taking him, there was no turning back.

He put his hand lightly on Sammy's shoulder, afraid to give in to the longing to hug him. "You're a better person than I was. I guess we have to thank your mother for that."

He looked at Miranda. She leaned against the rough wooden post, her gray sweatshirt blending into it. The setting sun made her hair blaze like a flame, and her green eyes sparkled with unshed tears.

"Sammy's a good kid. I've had good stuff to work with." Her voice trembled just a little, and he knew she didn't want their son to hear that tremor.

His hand still rested on their son's shoulder, and he didn't want to let go. "What do you say, Sammy? You think I could make another try at going to T-ball practice with you?"

Sammy nodded. "Next practice is Thursday after school. Okay?"

"Sounds great. I'll be there, no matter what. I promise."

"Speaking of school…" Miranda sounded as if she had herself under control.

Sammy's nose wrinkled. "It can't be my bedtime already."

"It will be by the time you have your bath and your story. You scoot on up to the house, sugar. We'll be up in a few minutes."

The boy scrambled to his feet. "Okay, Momma." He turned toward Tyler. "Good night… Daddy."

Before Tyler could respond, he darted off, running full tilt toward the house.

He'd had the wind knocked out of him. "He called me Daddy."

"Yes, he did." Her smile shimmered on the edge of tears.

"That's a pretty decent reward for forgetting my promise."

"It wasn't for forgetting. Or even for apologizing. It was because you shared yourself with him."

He hadn't heard that gentle, loving note in Miranda's voice directed at him in a long time. It rocked him nearly as much as hearing Sammy call him Daddy, and it made him grope for something solid to hang on to.

"Believe me, it wasn't hard to come up with a time when my father let me down. They were too numerous to count."

"I'm sorry. I wish…"

"What do you wish, Miranda?"

He moved next to her, watching the way the light touched her skin with gold. On the waterway a boat arrowed toward the distant shore, darkening as the sun slipped lower. They were alone.

"I wish I'd understood, back then, about your relationship with your father. I could have done better if I had."

Regret and guilt showed on her expressive face— regret for the girl she'd been, guilt over whatever she imagined she could have done differently.

"It wasn't your fault." He tried to look at their marriage without the anger that had consumed him since he'd learned about her deception. "We were both too young to know what we were doing."

"We thought we did."

"You think you know everything at eighteen and twenty. It takes a few years to realize how wrong you are." Impelled by something he wasn't sure he understood, he smoothed a strand of auburn hair from her face, letting his fingertips linger against the smooth curve of her cheek.

Her gaze met his, startled and aware. Her lips softened, parting a little on a sigh that seemed to echo the soft shush of waves against the dock.

That sound had accompanied their first kiss. They'd walked barefoot along the beach in the afterglow of sunset, letting the warm waves wash over their feet. He'd stopped, turned her toward him and kissed her, sensing nothing was going to be the same again.

That was then, and this was now. Eight years later, and apparently not any wiser.

"Tyler." She said his name softly, so softly he seemed to sense it instead of hear it.

His hand moved of its own volition, cradling her cheek, tilting her face to his. Slowly he covered her lips with his.

She was soft, so soft. She turned more fully toward him, and his arms slid around her, holding her as closely as his lips held hers. A wave of longing and tenderness swept over him, strong enough to pull him under.

His heart beat in time with the waves, as if his blood moved to some eternal rhythm he hadn't ever been aware of. His lips moved to her temple. He felt the pulse that beat there, and it, like the waves, seemed to move in time with his.

Miranda settled against him as if she'd come home. Or maybe as if they'd never been apart.

"Tyler." She whispered his name against his chest.

Something swelled inside his heart, longing to break free. Emotions he'd denied for years beat against his control.

It's not safe, he warned himself. It's not wise. Don't get involved.

Don't count on anyone else. They'll only let you down.

Sluggishly, as if he moved through water, he drew away from her. He watched the light in Miranda's eyes die.

He couldn't do this. Not because of what his father had believed, but because of what he suddenly saw so clearly about himself.

This wasn't about anyone else letting him down. It was about him letting them down.

He'd have to struggle to be the man his son needed. It would be downright impossible to be the man Miranda needed.

Chapter Nine

Miranda pressed the rolling pin firmly, spreading the piecrust dough in a circle on the floured board. She found comfort in the familiar, soothing movements. Doing something routine was a relief from the tensions of the past week.

This old kitchen was equally comforting. At five or six she'd knelt on a stool at the counter, painstakingly rolling out the scraps of dough her mother had given her, trying to be just like Momma. Later, she and Chloe and the twins had sat at the scrubbed pine table in the evenings, doing homework while Momma and Daddy talked over the day's doings in soft, contented voices.

She looked at the large calendar posted on the kitchen wall. Crowded with notations, it kept track of who was where in the busy Caldwell clan. Today, Saturday, it showed that Tyler and Sammy were at T-ball practice. It also showed her that one week was gone from Tyler's month.

A burst of panic touched her—one week down, three to go. Tyler probably checked the days off in his engagement book or his electronic organizer, counting down the moments until he could leave Caldwell Cove and get back to his real life.

The life that had no place in it for her. She'd known that for years and had it reinforced since the night on the dock when he'd kissed her. His immediate withdrawal and the efforts he'd made in the days since to avoid her had shown how much he regretted that act.

He'd left for Charleston each day immediately after having breakfast with Sammy, returning scrupulously by the time Sammy got home from school. He'd been pleasant, polite and cooperative. He'd felt as distant from her as if he were already in Baltimore, living the life that didn't include her.

She fit the crust into the pie pan, fluting the edge with the quick twist of the fingers her mother had taught her when she'd been deemed old enough to start baking real pies instead of playing with the dough. Comforting or not, making pies for Sunday dinner wasn't enough to distract her mind from the treadmill it had walked since that night on the dock.

Tyler didn't want anything from her except cooperation in their joint parenting. His kisses had been a fluke, perhaps a reaction to some faded memory of the people they'd once been. He must have been horrified at the mistake he'd almost repeated.

Unfortunately those moments had shown her the truth she could no longer avoid. She still loved Tyler.

She'd buried those feelings in family and work and her son, but a few kisses and a moment in his arms had brought the flame blazing to life.

At some level, she'd known that would be inevitable from the moment she'd walked into the hall and seen him. She pressed a floury hand against the front of her T-shirt, as if that would ease the hurt. Her relationship with Tyler was beyond repair. All she could do was concentrate on making the changes in Sammy's life as smooth and easy as possible for all three of them.

The screen door slammed, and Sammy raced into the kitchen. He sported a streak of dirt on one cheek, and his T-shirt looked as if he'd rolled around in the grass, but he was smiling.

"Hey, Momma. I smell pies. Did you make some cinnamon crust for me?"

"What's cinnamon crust?" Tyler stopped inside the door.

Miranda swallowed, her mouth suddenly dry. It ought to be illegal for a man to look that good in jeans and a T-shirt.

"Leftover pieces of piecrust. We always bake them with cinnamon sugar for hungry little boys." She held the baking sheet out to Sammy, who grabbed one. "And big boys." She offered them to Tyler.

He dropped the ball glove he carried onto the kitchen table, broke off a piece and popped it into his mouth. His eyes widened.

"Wonderful. Why haven't America's baking

companies started putting these on the supermarket shelves?"

Tyler would be easier to ignore if he weren't there, filling up her kitchen, an errant crumb clinging to his lips.

"Because they're only good if they're homemade crusts, fresh from the oven. One of those things that can't be mass produced."

Would there be homemade goodies in Sammy's life when he went to visit his father in Baltimore?

Three weeks, a little voice in her head reminded her. Only three weeks, and then you'll have to make plans for your son to spend some of his days far away, living a life you can barely imagine.

Sammy grabbed another crust. "I'm going to find Granddaddy and tell him about practice." He got to the door, then glanced at Tyler. "Thanks, Daddy."

Then he was gone, and she was right where she didn't want to be—alone with Tyler.

"He enjoys saying that, you know." She picked up the bowl of apple slices and started filling crusts.

"I have to say it feels pretty good to me, too." He leaned against the counter, keeping a careful foot of space between them.

"You don't look very glad. What's wrong?" It was scary how well she could still read his expression after all this time. Something had put that brooding look in his dark eyes.

He shrugged, pointing toward the glove on the table. "I bought a new baseball glove for Sammy, gave it to him when we went to practice. He didn't want it."

She pressed her hands against the counter, not sure what to say. If only he'd asked her first, she might have foreseen the difficulty. "I hope he was polite."

"Oh, very polite." His eyes were stormy. "But very definite. He'd rather use his old one."

She heard the hurt under the annoyance in his voice. This was the first gift he'd given his son, and Sammy hadn't wanted it.

She had to try to make this right, if she could. "Did he tell you why?"

"No." He frowned at her. "What do you know about it?"

She wiped her hands on a tea towel, then turned to face him. "I'm sure he appreciated your thoughtfulness. It's just that the one he's been using was Theo's. And before that either David or Daniel's."

She smiled, remembering the squabble between her brothers. "One of them lost his, and they both claim the remaining glove is his."

"So Sammy would rather have an old glove because it belonged to Theo." He obviously didn't care which twin had lost his glove. He only cared that Sammy had rejected his gift.

"It's kind of a tradition. Your younger brother would feel that way about something you passed on to him."

Or didn't people like the Winchesters pass things on from one child to the next? Maybe she was making this worse by bringing up his family.

"I doubt it. My brother and I aren't very close.

And knowing Josh, I'm sure he'd prefer something new to something I'd already used."

She was probably getting in deeper, but she had to contest that.

"Younger brothers always look up to older ones. Josh probably feels that way about you, even if he's never said it. He followed your footsteps into the company, didn't he?"

"I suspect that had more to do with getting a large salary for doing very little than from any idea of being like me." He shook his head, an errant lock of dark hair tumbling onto his forehead. "Why are we talking about my brother, anyway?"

Did he really not understand?

"Because he is your brother. Sammy's uncle."

Tyler folded his arms across his chest. "Don't go running away with the idea that Josh will be the kind of uncle your brothers have been. He wouldn't know how."

"Sammy will see him when he comes to visit you, won't he?" She tried to make that eventuality sound as routine and everyday as a trip to the grocery.

"I suppose so." He searched her face. "Are you worrying about that?"

"Not about your brother, no. But about what Sammy's life will be like." A lump constricted her throat. "When he's away from here."

"I'll take good care of him." His voice softened. He reached toward her, almost but not quite touching. "You must know that."

"I know." Somehow that wasn't as reassuring as

it should be, not when she tried to imagine those spaces in her son's life that wouldn't include her. "What about church?"

"What about it?" The softness disappeared.

She lifted her chin. This was one thing she'd go toe-to-toe over if necessary. "Church is an important part of Sammy's life. I want your assurance that won't change when he's with you."

"I'll see that he goes," he said shortly.

"With you." She pressed the point. "You can't just drop him off as if he has to go but other things are more important to you."

A muscle twitched in his jaw. "Sounds as if you're making all the decisions about Sammy and expecting me to go along with them."

"About this I am." Standing fast in the face of Tyler's irritation wasn't as difficult as she'd expected. Maybe she'd grown up a bit.

"Fine. I promise I'll go to church with him when he stays with me." He stalked to the door, annoyance filling his voice and his movements. "Now if you'll excuse me, I have work to do."

An annoyed Tyler wasn't as much of a threat to her vulnerable heart as he was when he said her name in that soft, masculine rumble. Maybe, if she could annoy him enough, she could learn to harden her heart against him. But that didn't seem very likely.

If his church in Baltimore was like this one, he might be less reluctant to attend. Tyler leaned against a pew back the next morning, waiting for Miranda to finish talking with all the people who had something to say to her after the worship service.

What was it that felt so different about the Caldwell Cove church? He glanced around the sanctuary, small enough to fit four or five of them into the vast nave of the church he normally attended a few times a year.

This simple, whitewashed structure boasted plain oak pews and a slightly faded carpet runner down the center aisle. The sanctuary's only claim to elegance was the ancient stained-glass windows that glowed in the spring sunlight.

An old-fashioned church, it had an old-fashioned charm. The minister had been neither profound nor philosophical, but the love he projected to his parishioners glowed as much as the windows did. The warmth filling the small sanctuary had nothing to do with the temperature.

He didn't have to continue attending the same church in Baltimore just because his parents had been long-time members. He could find someplace else to go when Sammy stayed with him. Miranda had certainly made it clear that going to church wasn't negotiable.

Across the length of the pew, Miranda continued to talk, apparently in no hurry. She tilted her head in response to some comment, her hair brushing the shoulders of the cream dress she wore. Her profile was serene and lovely.

Beautiful, in fact. He suspected the simple dress

was several years out of date, and no professional stylist had touched her hair, but Miranda didn't need polishing to shine. Her light came from within.

Uncomfortable at the direction his thoughts had taken, he moved to the dolphin window.

"Pretty thing, isn't it?" Miranda's grandmother came toward him, nodding at the window.

"It's lovely." He tensed, half expecting her to take him to task for his presence on the island. Everyone knew Gran Caldwell was the matriarch of the clan. He was surprised she hadn't tackled him before this.

The elderly woman didn't seem to have battle in mind as she stared at the dolphin. Whatever she felt, no emotion showed. The clean, strong lines of her face had elegance, too, like the windows. She was what Miranda would be in fifty or sixty years.

"My grandson Adam's fiancée did that window. I reckon you heard that."

"Miranda told me."

"Told you the story of the first dolphin, too, I suppose." She nodded toward the bracket behind the pulpit where the wooden dolphin had once stood.

"Yes. Well, Sammy told me most of it. He wrote a story about it for school."

He thought of what Miranda had said—that her father and his brother had been at odds for years after the incident with the dolphin and her father's injury. That must have been hard on their mother.

"Should have the dolphin here for weddings, at least." She continued to stare at the shelf, filled with flowers.

"Why weddings?"

She switched her gaze to him, and he had the odd sensation that those wise old eyes saw right through him. "Thought you said you'd heard the story."

"Maybe Sammy left something out. I don't remember anything about weddings."

She shook her head. "That boy's at the stage where he thinks love and such is foolishness. That's probably why he didn't say anything. The first Caldwell carved the dolphin out of love for his bride. Folks always believed it brought special blessings on those who wed under its gaze."

An uneasy feeling prickled along the back of his neck. Special blessings? He and Miranda hadn't married under the eyes of the dolphin, and the only blessing that had come of their marriage was Sammy.

"Hasn't been right, having Caldwells marry without it," she said firmly, as if he'd argued.

"No, I guess not." Was she thinking of him and Miranda, their marriage broken before it began?

His uneasiness intensified. Was that what lay behind Sammy's determination to find the dolphin? Could he possibly imagine that restoring it would bring his parents together?

If Sammy thought that, he was setting himself up for disappointment. Tyler tried to tell himself the idea was nonsense, but the uneasiness clung like a burr.

"Reckon I'll see you over to Jeff's for dinner." Miranda's grandmother didn't offer to shake hands. "I'd best get my salad ready to go." With another glance toward the dolphin shelf, she made her way toward the door.

Trying to shake oppressive thoughts about the dolphin and Sammy from his mind, Tyler moved along the pew toward Miranda, who was concluding her conversation.

She gave him a quick smile. If appearing in church with him had bothered her, she wasn't letting it show.

"I guess we'd better get along over to Uncle Jeff's place." She started toward the door, and he followed. "You'll get to take on the whole Caldwell clan at once."

"Is this get-together for my benefit? Are they preparing tar and feathers?"

A smile tugged at her lips as she stepped into a shaft of sunlight. "Not that I know of, though I wouldn't put anything past those brothers of mine. No, we just all have Sunday dinner together at least once a month."

"Another tradition." To his surprise, the words came out sounding wistful. There'd been precious little tradition in his family, unless the predictable fact that his father would miss every celebration counted as one.

Miranda didn't seem to notice. She was glancing around the church lawn, apparently counting heads.

People still stood in small clusters, probably catching up on the events of the past week. Some of the children had started a game of tag under the swaying Spanish moss of the live oaks. The girls' pale dresses fluttered around their legs. Across the narrow street, a boat revved its motor at the dock—some Sunday sailor off for a ride, probably. What did a scene like this have to do with him?

"We'd best collect Sammy and get on our way," Miranda said.

"Just a moment." He stopped her with a hand on her arm.

She glanced up at his touch, something unguarded showing in her eyes for an instant. "What's wrong? If you don't want to go—"

"Of course I intend to go," he said impatiently. "I told Sammy I would. But there's something I need to talk with you about first."

He'd better tell Miranda what he feared was behind Sammy's search for the dolphin. Probably she'd laugh at the idea, and then he'd be able to forget it.

"What is it?" Apprehension colored her voice, as if she felt anything he wanted to discuss must be unpleasant.

"Your grandmother told me the rest of the story about the dolphin." An elderly couple moved slowly past them. He stepped off the walk and lowered his voice. "The part you left out. About how couples who marry under the dolphin's gaze are supposed to be especially blessed."

"That's how the story goes." Her cheeks grew pink. She was probably thinking, as he had, that there hadn't been anything particularly blessed about the painful brevity of their marriage.

"It made me wonder if that's what's behind this

treasure hunt of Sammy's." He couldn't think of any tactful way of saying this. "Do you think he's got some notion that finding the dolphin is going to fix his parents' marriage?"

The words sounded even more foolish said out loud than in his mind. He waited for Miranda to tell him how ridiculous that was.

Instead, dismay filled her face. "It never occurred to me. If that's what he's thinking, we've got to do something about it."

"You know him better than I do." For the first time, he didn't feel resentful at the thought. "If it never occurred to you, it probably didn't to him."

Worry lines crinkled her forehead. "He has been awfully obsessed with that story lately. I wish I could say the idea is impossible, but I can't." She met his gaze, her green eyes clouded. "Tyler, what are we going to do?"

We, she'd said. For the first time, she'd included him in a decision.

"We can't do anything right now." Sammy, abandoning his game, was running toward them. At the curb, Caldwells piled into various vehicles. "We've got Sunday dinner to attend. Let's give it some time. Maybe I'm wrong."

Sammy ran up and grabbed his hand, and it seemed natural to take Miranda's arm. Linked, they started down the walk. They might almost look like a family.

Miranda balanced the pie carrier with the apple crumb pies as she crossed the veranda of Twin Oaks,

Uncle Jefferson's house. Tyler came behind her, carrying two lemon meringues. If he felt any nervousness about encountering the entire Caldwell clan, he didn't show it. His face was perfectly composed.

They went through the open front door and into the spacious center hallway. She glanced at the graceful sweep of the curving staircase, the crystal chandelier, the rice-carved drop-leaf table surmounted by its Empire mirror, trying to see them through Tyler's eyes.

He lifted an eyebrow at her. "I take it this is the wealthy branch of the family."

"You might say that." Everyone knew Uncle Jeff put success ahead of everything else. He and Tyler might have a lot in common.

Except that Uncle Jeff had begun to change in the last year, seeming to want to make amends for the long breach between him and her father. She couldn't think of anything that was likely to make Tyler change.

She swept that unproductive thought from her mind. "We'll put the pies on the buffet."

He followed her into the dining room—more crystal, more rice-carved mahogany. The room's French doors stood open to the veranda overlooking the marsh. Most folks were gathered out there, except for a cluster of kids checking out the bounty on the long table.

"You young 'uns get out of my way now, y'heah?" Miz Becky, the Gullah housekeeper who kept Twin Oaks running smoothly, swept through the door from the kitchen with a steaming tureen in her hands.

She caught sight of them as she put the dish of sweet potatoes down, and her face broke into a broad smile. "Miranda, child, it's good to see you. This here must be Sammy's daddy."

Tyler put the pies he carried on the sideboard and shook hands.

"This is Miz Becky. She takes care of everyone at Twin Oaks."

Miranda didn't say what else she was thinking— that Miz Becky was a fount of knowledge where people were concerned. She'd be happy to be on the back porch right now, snapping beans into a bowl with Miz Becky, listening to her wise counsel about the difficult art of raising children.

Tyler nodded toward the laden table. "You must be a gourmet cook, as well, if you produced all that."

"It's nothing. Everybody bring something, it's not too much for anybody." Miz Becky raised her voice. "Jenny, you go on and tell your granddaddy the food is up now. Somebody better ask the blessing 'fore it gets cold."

The group on the veranda must have heard her, because Caldwells started streaming into the dining room. Her cousin Adam held hands with his fiancée, Tory, and the sight touched her heart. For so long it had seemed Adam would never find his true love, but now happiness shone in their faces. In June, dolphin or no, they'd be wed at St. Andrew's.

Should she point out to Sammy the happy marriages that had taken place even without the dolphin? Not until she'd discussed it with Tyler. She glanced at his strong face, familiar yet somehow hiding thoughts and beliefs she knew nothing of.

From now on, she had to take his opinions into account in every decision she made for Sammy. She wasn't a single parent any longer. Tyler had as much to say in raising their son as she did. The idea sent a shiver sliding along her arms.

I'm not ready. She sent up an almost involuntary prayer. *I don't want to share, and I don't want Sammy to accept Tyler's values.*

That was at the core of her resistance, she knew suddenly. She'd loved Tyler, married him in spite of common sense. She loved him still, as hopeless as that was.

But that love didn't keep her from looking at Tyler honestly. Every now and then, she'd get glimpses of the boy she'd fallen for, think she saw the man he could be. Then he'd turn back into Tyler the business tycoon, and she was afraid that could never change.

Chapter Ten

Tyler snapped the phone shut with a quick movement and slid it into his pocket. He stood on the inn's porch, looking at the fishing boats moving down the channel. Josh's early morning call probably meant nothing at all, but he couldn't shake off the uneasiness that gripped him.

The fact that Josh, of all people, was in the office this early on a Monday morning was startling enough. The fact that Josh was concerned about business was downright astonishing.

Tyler planted his hands on the porch railing, wishing it were the polished surface of his desk. He'd talked with Henry several times over the last few days, and his assistant had assured him all was fine with the Warren deal. Henry had years of experience to back him up. Nevertheless—

In view of Josh's concern it wouldn't be a bad idea to go to the office for a couple of days. Sammy would understand if he explained it to him, wouldn't he?

Miranda was another story. Instinct told him she wouldn't look favorably on his leaving just when Sammy was warming up to him. Still, she'd been the one to mention the possibility that first night, when she'd brought her proposition to him.

That night had been a little over a week ago, but it felt like forever. In such a short time his life had changed beyond recognition. Would he go back, if he could, to a time before the photo of Sammy arrived on his desk?

A cold hand gripped his heart at the thought. If it hadn't been for that mysterious visitor who'd mailed the picture to him, he might never have known he had a son.

Now that he did, his business success had become more meaningful. He had a son to inherit what he'd built, instead of just hordes of eager relatives with their hands out.

He didn't intend to let anything sour this deal. If that meant a few days away from the island, so be it. Miranda would have to understand. He went quickly into the house.

He poked his head into the office, then walked through the dining room and the kitchen. No Miranda, but Sallie was pouring a cup of coffee.

"Miranda?" He raised his eyebrows.

She gestured with her mug toward the back door. "She's out at the shed, working on Mary Lou."

Mary Lou? He pushed through the screen door,

then crossed the lawn to the weathered shed that sat on the edge of the marsh.

He paused in the doorway, letting his eyes adjust to the dim interior. Wearing her usual uniform of jeans and T-shirt, Miranda bent over an elderly bicycle, a can of oil in her hand. She'd tied her hair back with a yellow ribbon, but curls escaped to cluster against her neck.

"Performing surgery on that thing?" The bike in question was an old-fashioned girl's bike with coaster brakes and a wicker basket attached to the handlebars. "It looks terminal."

She looked up at his approach, giving him the smile that had once twisted his heart out of shape. Not any longer, he assured himself.

"How can you talk that way about Mary Lou? She's one of my oldest friends."

"I can believe the old part." He squatted next to her. "Did someone take away your car keys?"

"No." Her heart-shaped face took on a wary look. "Sammy's getting a two-wheeler for his birthday, and I thought I'd get Mary Lou in shape so I can ride with him. Just until I'm sure he knows how to handle himself."

"His birthday." He repeated her words slowly. "When is it?"

"Thursday." Miranda's look turned defensive. "You knew the date. I showed you his birth certificate."

Clearly something he should have remembered. He wasn't very good at this father business. "You might have reminded me."

Miranda stood, dusting off the knees of her jeans. She lifted the bike to spin the front wheel.

"I guess you know now." Her voice was carefully neutral, as if she was determined not to betray whatever she thought about a father who didn't remember his son's birthday.

He stood, too, frowning. "About this bicycle…"

"I know she doesn't look like much, but she'll do for what I have in mind," Miranda said quickly.

"Not this one, although I think you're wrong about that. The bicycle Sammy is getting for his birthday. You've bought it already?"

"Not exactly." The wariness was back in her eyes. "I ordered it. I have to go pick it up tomorrow."

Resentment pricked him. "You're giving Sammy a new bicycle for his birthday. What do I get to give him that could possibly be more exciting than that?"

She leaned the bike against a workbench. "We're not in a competition, Tyler. Sammy will love whatever you give him."

"I haven't done very well so far." Like the baseball glove, for instance.

She studied him for a moment, as if assessing how much it bothered him. "Well, how about if we go in on the bike together? Trust me, this is a gift he won't turn down. He's been wanting a new bike for ages."

He'd like to find something even bigger than a bicycle, but he recognized how foolish that would be. He and Miranda weren't competing, as she'd said. Little as he knew about parenting, he knew that wouldn't be good for Sammy.

"Okay. The bike is from both of Sammy's parents. Where do we pick it up?"

"You don't have to go with me. I can manage it myself."

That was predictable. "I'm sure you can, but you're not going to."

Her lips twitched. "Has anybody mentioned to you lately how stubborn you are?"

"Seems to me I've heard that a time or two. I don't think I have a monopoly on it."

Her smile took over, making her green eyes sparkle. "You may have a point there. Okay. I ordered it from a bike shop out on the highway near Savannah. They said I could pick it up tomorrow morning."

"We'll pick it up."

He wasn't sure how this had happened. Hadn't he come out here to tell Miranda he had to run up to Baltimore tomorrow? Well, it didn't have to be tomorrow, necessarily.

"By the way, I might need to go to the office for a couple of days soon."

He almost imagined he saw regret in her eyes before her lashes swept down to hide her reaction. "Is that really necessary?"

Was it? He thought again of Josh's call and of Henry's reassurances. "I don't know." The uncharacteristic uncertainty made his voice sharp. "It may be. It was part of our agreement that I'd go back for a few days if I had to, remember?"

"I'm not the one you need to convince. If you're going away, you'd best tell Sammy ahead of time."

Amazing how difficult a simple thing like that sounded. "I thought maybe you'd do that," he said, knowing what her answer would be.

Her smile flickered again. "Sorry. Breaking bad news is part of being a parent. You may as well start getting into practice."

Oddly enough, he liked the fact that she expected something of him. "Meaning I don't get to just do the fun stuff."

"No way." She wiped her hands with a paper towel from the workbench. "Do you really have to go to Baltimore? Can't you take care of whatever it is from the Charleston office?"

He shook his head. "It's an entirely different division."

She looked at him blankly, and he realized he'd never talked to her about the changes that had taken place in the corporation over the past few years.

"Charleston is the home office for a group of textile mills in Georgia and South Carolina. We acquired them a couple of years ago. They fit in well with the rest of our holdings."

"And this problem doesn't have anything to do with textiles." If she wondered why he'd decided to expand into her part of the world, she didn't mention it.

"Right." He rubbed the back of his neck, realizing that the familiar tension had taken up residence there since the talk with Josh. He hadn't noticed it had all but disappeared during the past week. "We have an important meeting coming up soon over a contract to supply compressors for a company that could be a major new customer for us."

She leaned against the workbench, looking for all the world as if she really was interested. "Are there problems with it?"

"There shouldn't be." Again that edge of tension pricked him. "The deal was completely in place when I left. Henry—my assistant, Henry Carmichael—should be able to handle everything without a hitch."

"Then why do you feel you need to go back?"

It was a fair question, but he wasn't used to explaining his actions to anyone. Parenthood changed that, too, it seemed.

"I had a call from Josh this morning. For some reason, he's got the wind up. He can't even tell me why. Just a feeling." He shrugged. "Maybe he's belatedly developing a sense of responsibility. He knows how important this is. Without this contract, we could be facing extensive layoffs. Nobody wants that."

"I didn't realize." Miranda's expressive eyes mirrored guilt. "I didn't think about the people who might be affected by what you do."

"It's not something I can ever forget." He shook his head. "I wish—"

"That you were there," she finished for him.

He looked up, startled. "No. Actually, I was wishing I thought I could count on Josh the way you count on your family."

"That's what families are for. Counting on. And driving you crazy, of course."

He liked the way her face softened when she talked about her family. Liked the way the Caldwells trusted each other, relied on each other.

"My father always said you can't count on anyone but yourself," he said abruptly, surprising himself. "That was his philosophy."

She turned her soft look on him. "That doesn't mean it has to be yours."

"No." He looked at that thought in some surprise. "I guess it doesn't."

The unaccustomed understanding seemed to weave strands of connection between them. He thought Miranda's cheeks flushed a little.

"If you feel you have to go, I'm sure Sammy will understand."

Will you, Miranda? This wasn't about Miranda. This was about his commitment to his son.

"I won't miss his birthday." He said the words with a sureness that surprised him.

Priorities. His father had always put business first. That wasn't the kind of father he wanted to be.

Approval shone in her eyes. "I'm glad you feel that way."

"I'll have Henry go over everything again, just to be on the safe side. It'll be all right."

If he did end up explaining to Sammy that he had to go away, he'd make very sure it was necessary.

He smiled wryly. Maybe the secret to this father business was to do the opposite of everything his father had done. That, and make sure what he did earned that soft look of approval from Miranda.

* * *

Had she handled that conversation with Tyler about business correctly? Miranda sat in the porch swing that evening, looking across the inland waterway. This situation was so difficult that, at every step, she felt she risked making an irrevocable move.

Tyler would probably have to figure out for himself where the balance was between business and parenting. No one else could determine that for him.

Her initial reaction, when she'd believed Tyler couldn't hang around long enough to be any kind of a father, had certainly been easier to live with. But each day, Tyler continued to prove her wrong.

Lord, I confess I never really thought about the people who depend upon Tyler's business. I've been so focused on the personal that I never looked beyond that. Forgive me for being so shortsighted.

A few feet away from her, Tyler and her father sat in matching rocking chairs, talking a little, then falling silent, then talking again. Their conversation wasn't strained any longer, and she thanked God for that fact. If Tyler was to be a true father to Sammy, he had to be on cordial terms, at least, with the man who'd been both father and grandfather to Sammy since he was born.

What did Daddy think about all this? He'd maintained a careful silence on the subject, and she thought she knew why. Clayton Caldwell was an honorable man. He would never want to betray that he had a negative thought about the man who was Sammy's father.

If Tyler wanted a model of what a father should be, he obviously couldn't use his own. Her heart hurt when she thought of what Tyler had betrayed about his relationship with his father. Given that model, it was a wonder he was even trying.

He *was* trying, and she had to help him. The better a father Tyler was by the time he left the island, the safer she could feel about sending Sammy to spend time with him.

Tyler was leaning forward, arguing some point with her father in a friendly way. She let her gaze linger on the stubborn line of his jaw, the flash of interest in his eyes, the vigor of his movement when he gestured. The same determination to succeed that had fueled twenty-year-old Tyler's will to take over the company when his father died could make him succeed at fatherhood.

She had to help him, and that meant she had to let him take equal responsibility for both the joys and difficulties of raising Sammy. That meant no more unilateral decisions about her son. She suspected Tyler could never guess just how difficult that was for her.

Help me with this one, Lord. I'm not good at sharing where Sammy is concerned. Next to You, Daddy will be the best model of a father Tyler is likely to find. Please, open his heart to Daddy and to You.

The screen door creaked, and Sammy bounded onto the porch. He made a beeline for Tyler, who stopped what he was saying to smile at him.

"What's up?"

Sammy grabbed the arm of the rocker. "Well, I was thinking about when we could go back to Angel Isle to look for the dolphin again. You and Momma said we'd go again, remember?"

"I remember." Tyler tousled Sammy's hair, and their son grinned. "And if I'd forgotten, I'm sure you'd remind me."

"I was thinking we could go this weekend. If we went on Saturday, we'd have lots of time."

She'd half hoped Sammy had forgotten about this. Clearly her son had inherited his father's single-minded determination.

"Sammy, you know that folks have looked for the dolphin for a long time without finding it," her father said. "Seems like maybe we'll have to get used to doing without it."

Sammy shook his head. "I just think maybe I'm going to be the one to find it. And think how happy Great-Gran will be."

Sadness touched her father's eyes. "I guess she would be, at that."

"So could we go on Saturday?" He rocked back and forth on his toes, all energy and stubbornness.

"I suppose—" she began.

"Maybe we can find some day other than this Saturday," Tyler said.

Startled, she met his eyes and realized she'd just done what she'd promised herself she wouldn't do— she'd started to make a decision without consulting him. She'd have to unlearn the habits of the past eight years to make this work.

"Do you have something else planned for Saturday?" She hoped he could see the apology in her eyes.

"Actually, I was hoping you and Sammy would spend Saturday and Sunday in Charleston with me."

"Charleston?" In all the days he'd gone off to the city, it had never occurred to her that he'd want them to go along.

Tyler looked from her to their son. "The manager of our Charleston subsidiary invited us to come and spend the weekend. He has a boy just about your age." He touched Sammy lightly. "Sammy could stay with him and his sitter while we go with Dan and Sheila to a charity concert. It's to raise money for Habitat for Humanity." He waited for Miranda's response.

She sat immobile for a moment. It was a good thing she hadn't blurted her first reaction, because that would have been a resounding no.

Part of the problem was that she knew exactly what benefit concert Tyler was talking about—a huge, expensive, dressy affair for the cream of Charleston society. People with whom Tyler would feel right at home. And she would feel about as welcome as a skunk at a picnic.

She couldn't say any of the things she was thinking in front of her father and Sammy. She summoned a smile. "Let me think about it, okay?"

Eyes questioning, he nodded.

She turned to Sammy, who didn't look thrilled at the idea, either. "Sugar, you have next Monday off from school for a teacher in-service day. Why don't we plan to go then? We can take a picnic lunch, and we'll have all afternoon to do a good search."

The pout that hovered on Sammy's face disappeared. "Can we build a fire and cook hot dogs on it?"

"I don't see why not." The way to a growing boy's heart must be through his stomach.

"Okay. I'm going to tell Theo. I'll bet he'll wish the high school had a day off, too." He darted inside, the screen door slamming.

Before she could muster a reasonable excuse for delaying an answer on the trip to Charleston, her father leaned forward, pressing his palms against the rocker's arms.

"I thought for sure that boy would forget about looking for the dolphin with all the other things that are going on."

"He's certainly obsessed with it." Tyler's gaze met hers, and she knew what he was thinking. He was afraid Sammy had a reason besides pleasing Gran for his search.

"The dolphin's brought us enough sorrow." The lines deepened in her father's face. "I hate to see another generation get caught up in the trouble my brother and I caused."

"It wasn't your fault," she said quickly. "You didn't take the dolphin, Uncle Jeff did."

"He took it, but I'm just as much to blame for what followed."

"But—"

"Hush, Miranda. I mean what I say. I took that grievance against my brother and added it to all the other things I thought he'd done wrong. Told myself I'd bailed him out for the last time."

"That's understandable." She hated that Tyler was hearing this. "You were the one who was hurt."

He shook his head. "I never really gave Jeff a chance after that. I judged him without even realizing I was doing it. And every time he did something I thought was wrong, I just added it to that scale I was making."

"Daddy, it's not your fault that Uncle Jeff is the way he is." He was expressing feelings she'd never guessed at, and doing it in front of Tyler, of all people. "Anyway, things are better between you now, aren't they?"

"Better." He stood. "Maybe that's what helped me see that I'd done as much wrong in judging him as he'd ever done." He smacked the bad leg he'd had ever since the night the dolphin vanished. "My attitude toward my brother hurt me as much as this leg ever did."

She could feel the tears sparkle in her eyes, and she blinked them back. "I never knew you felt that way. I just thought—"

"You just thought your uncle Jeff was a man without honor, 'cause that's what you've heard me say. But if Jeff was at fault, I was, too. Maybe if I'd stayed his friend and brother like I should have, I'd have helped him to be a man our momma and daddy would have been proud of."

Before she could say anything else, he stalked into the house.

She wiped an errant tear away with her fingers.

Not speaking, Tyler got up from his chair and came to sit on the swing next to her. It rocked with his movement, then settled.

"All these years, and I never knew he felt that way," she said softly.

Tyler stretched his arm along the swing behind her. It felt strong and secure.

"Your father's an honest man. Not many people would hold themselves to that standard of conduct."

"No, they wouldn't." Did she dare believe he admired her father's character?

"About the dolphin." He hesitated, frowning. "We probably ought to talk about this. About what's behind Sammy's determination to find it."

Was Sammy hoping the dolphin could bring his parents together again? She'd wrestled with it, and she didn't have an answer.

If that was what Sammy wanted, he would think the dolphin was already working if he saw them sitting so close to each other.

She tried to discern Tyler's expression in the dusk. How awkward he must find this situation. It would be even more awkward if he knew what her heart was telling her.

"Maybe we ought to talk to him about the whole thing," she said.

"That's what I thought at first," he said slowly. An expression she couldn't identify crossed his face. "Now I'm thinking that might be a mistake."

"But if he's imagining we're going to get back together if he finds the dolphin—"

"What if he's not thinking anything of the kind? What if this is a complication we've imagined that's never even occurred to him?"

She stared at her hands, twisted together in her lap. "If we bring it up, he'll certainly think about it then."

"Exactly. We might be starting a problem instead of solving it."

"So what do you suggest we do about it?" She looked at him, troubled.

"Let's not say anything for the moment."

His hand rested lightly on her shoulder, and she could feel the weight of his arm across her back. She let herself imagine he was sending out messages of protection and caring.

"If that is what he's thinking, maybe he'll bring it up himself when we go back to the cottage," he went on. "If not, well, we'll have to deal with it once he's convinced the dolphin is gone for good."

She wanted to argue, but she hesitated. She'd promised herself she'd share responsibility for decisions involving Sammy. Now she had a chance to prove she meant it.

"All right," she said reluctantly. "We'll do it your way."

Chapter Eleven

If someone had told him three weeks ago he'd be driving a rattletrap van down a Georgia back road to buy a bicycle for his son's birthday, he'd have thought that person was hallucinating. Tyler stretched, pressing his hands against the steering wheel.

"This thing isn't exactly built for comfort, is it?"

Miranda smiled, as if at some level she enjoyed his fish-out-of-water discomfort. "We couldn't have fit the bike in your rental car very easily, could we?"

"Guess you have a point there." At least he'd been able to convince her to let him drive. He gave her a sideways glance. Miranda looked less wary today, as if she might almost enjoy this trek with him to buy their son's birthday present.

She hadn't given him an answer yet on going to Charleston on the weekend. He sensed her reluctance without understanding it. With a little luck and tact, on today's expedition he could prove to her that they could be in each other's company for two days without coming to blows, especially since Sammy would be with them.

"The shop is just ahead there." Miranda pointed to a bright blue cement-block building.

Tyler pushed aside thoughts of the weekend. He'd better concentrate on getting into the bike shop parking lot without hitting any of the numerous potholes. Each one made the van shiver as if it had a bad case of the flu.

Miranda should have better transportation than this. He took a cautious look at that idea, surprised. It wasn't his business or his responsibility what Miranda drove. So where had that impulse come from to buy her a nice, safe vehicle?

She slipped out of the van without waiting for him to open the door and scurried to the shop. He followed, a little amused. She obviously intended to keep him from paying his share if she could.

That had to be a first in his adult life. Most people were only too ready to let the Winchester bank account foot any bill.

Not Miranda. All those years of raising Sammy without his support—how on earth had she managed? Her family had helped, obviously, but as far as he could tell, Clayton and Sallie were just getting by.

By the time he reached Miranda, the salesman was showing her a bright red bicycle, and she was reaching for her bag.

He caught her hand, stilling the movement. "Let's have a look first."

For an instant she pulled against his grip. Then she stopped, maybe realizing how childish that was. She nodded toward the shiny bike. "What do you think of it?"

He surveyed the two-wheeler, wondering how many years it had been since he'd ridden one and what exactly they should look for in a bike for a just-turned-eight-year-old. "Are you sure the wider tires are what he wants?"

"That question proves you haven't ridden a bike on the island lately. You have to have wide tires to make it through the sand." She grinned. "That's why old Mary Lou works so well. You could take back those disparaging remarks about her any time now."

That lighthearted smile reminded him of the younger Miranda. "I'll have to take your word for it. I haven't done much bicycling lately. What about a helmet?"

The salesman jumped in immediately. "We have a nice selection of children's helmets right over here."

Miranda hesitated. "I think there's an old one in the garage he could use."

He saw into her mind so clearly. She was counting up how much money was in her bag, wondering if she had enough to pay for it.

"I'm getting the helmet, and anything else he needs to go with it."

Her mouth was set. "I just agreed to let you go halves on the bike."

"I have a lot of birthdays to make up for, remember?" he said softly. Her betraying flush told him the shot had gone home. He took her arm. "Let's go look at the helmets."

He hadn't intended to remind her of that today, not when he was trying to persuade her to go to Charleston for the weekend. They followed the clerk past racks of bicycles. But he could be just as stubborn as she could, and he had a right to get his son whatever he wanted for his birthday.

The salesman, apparently sensing a customer who intended to spend money, got into the spirit of the thing. By the time they'd finished, they'd added not just the helmet but also a biking jersey, water bottle and cage and a pack that fit on the handlebars, just in case Sammy wanted to carry anything with him.

"Will that be all?" The salesman sounded hopeful.

Tyler looked at Miranda. "Sure you won't let me get a new bike for you?"

"My old one is fine." Apparently deciding not to take offense, she let an impish twinkle appear in her eyes. It made her look like Sammy. "What about you? We ought to get a bike for you, so you can ride with Sammy."

She was challenging him, he suspected, but if she thought she'd throw him off track, she was going to be disappointed.

"Good idea." He looked at the salesman. "Let's see something for me."

The salesman practically rubbed his hands together.

He had never known buying a bike could be so complicated. After measurements, consultations with another clerk and Miranda's insistence on a bike suitable for beach riding, they finally had him outfitted. He slapped his credit card on the counter before Miranda could reach for her wallet.

"Put it on this one."

Miranda's jaw set, and she pulled a wallet from her overstuffed shoulder bag. "I'm paying my half."

"Let this be on me." He couldn't help trying to persuade her.

She held out the bills to him, arm stiff. "Take it."

He tried to remember the last time a member of his family had repaid him for something. He couldn't, and he knew suddenly that he'd have been disappointed if Miranda had given in.

Besides, if he wanted her cooperation on the weekend trip, he'd better let her have her way.

"I'll take it, but only if you let me get lunch."

"We don't have to stop for lunch."

"Maybe we don't have to, but I'm hungry. Deal?"

She nodded, pushing the bills into his hand. "If that's what you want."

They each wheeled a bike out to the van. He had to admit, as they loaded their purchases, that it was good they'd brought the van, no matter how decrepit it looked.

"Okay." He slammed the door. "Where's a good place for lunch around here?"

"There are some fast-food places along the highway on the way home."

He opened the door for her before she could grab the handle. "I might settle for fast food if Sammy were along, but I'd prefer something up a step or two."

She smiled suddenly, as if deciding that she didn't have a choice so she might as well get into the spirit of it. "A couple of miles down the road there's a good seafood place."

"Done." He held her elbow while she climbed into the van. "I could eat a horse."

A half-hour later, Tyler looked dubiously at the concoction of pink shrimp in creamy sauce atop a roll the waitress had just put down in front of him. "So this is a shrimp roll."

"Hey, you said you didn't want a fast-food burger." Miranda bit into her sandwich with every sign of pleasure. "Shrimp rolls and sweet potato fries aren't on most fast-food menus."

He took a bite, nodded appreciatively and took another. At least Miranda had lost the mulish look she'd worn while insisting he take the money she offered.

He'd like to insist she accept all the support he'd missed out on the past eight years, but he was getting to know this grown-up version of the girl he'd married, and he knew she wouldn't accept. One step at a time, that was the way to get what he wanted.

Now if he could just be sure what that was, he'd be all right.

Miranda set her iced tea glass on the blue-and-white checked tablecloth. Sweet tea, she'd called it.

Another low-country thing, like shrimp rolls and sweet potato fries, he assumed.

"Did you manage to get things settled back at the office?" she said.

Are you going away? That was probably what she really wanted to ask him.

"I had a long conversation with Henry. He seems to think Josh is just nervous because he's not used to my being out of the office, especially when a big deal is pending."

She paused, roll halfway to her mouth. "Do you trust Henry's opinions?"

That startled him. He wasn't sure Henry, the perfect subordinate, *had* opinions.

"I trust Henry to do what I've instructed him to do. I've gone over every step of the deal with him, and I see no reason anything should go wrong."

"It's all right, then."

"Yes." He tried to ignore the niggling feeling of doubt. "I'll talk with both Henry and Josh every day. By next Thursday it'll be settled. The deal we're offering is a good one. The buyers won't get the quality of product we supply at a better price from anyone else."

He glanced out the window at the marsh grasses bending in the breeze. What was he doing here when he had a deal pending? The Tyler Winchester he'd been a month ago wouldn't have been caught dead anywhere but in the office, personally supervising every step of the deal.

But that Tyler Winchester hadn't known he had a

child. Sammy changed things, and Tyler was still trying to understand how.

Which reminded him of the answer he wanted. "Have you made a decision about going to Charleston with me on Saturday?"

Her lashes swept down, hiding her eyes. "Why is it so important to you?"

He reached across the table to grasp her hands, making her look at him. "This is for Sammy. I want him to see that I have another existence besides that of visiting dad. That's a reasonable request, isn't it?"

She looked as if she'd like to say no. "I suppose so. But we wouldn't have to go to that benefit concert to show Sammy that. All of Charleston society will be there."

"Is that what's bothering you?" Why hadn't he realized that? "You'll do fine. You'll probably be the prettiest woman there."

"I won't fit in." She looked startled that she'd said it to him. "That sounds silly to you, I guess, but it's true."

He didn't understand the emotion that lay beneath her words, but it warned him to proceed carefully.

"Not silly," he said, clasping her hands. "But it is surprising. I haven't seen you lacking any confidence in dealing with strangers. That's what you do all the time at the inn, after all."

"That's different." Her hands twisted in his, but she didn't seem aware of the convulsive movement. "The inn is home. Believe me, I have vivid memories of how I didn't fit in when we were married. It's not an experience I'd care to repeat."

It was the first time she'd spoken willingly of their marriage. He forced his mind to the couple of months that had changed both of their lives.

"I'm sorry," he said slowly. "Maybe I was oblivious, but I didn't realize the social side of things bothered you that much."

"I was eighteen." She yanked her hands free, anger flaring in her eyes. "I'd never been farther from home than Savannah. Of course it bothered me. I felt like a failure the whole time I was in Baltimore."

"Miranda—" She obviously had painful memories he hadn't even guessed at. "I didn't realize. I'm sorry I was so blind to what you felt."

Her brief flash of anger went out. "Forget it."

He didn't want to forget. He wanted to explain it in some way that would get both of them off the hook.

"My father's death pitched both of us into something we weren't ready for."

She tried an unconvincing smile. "There's no point in going over something that happened a lifetime ago. We were different people then."

"That's my point. You're not eighteen now. You have enough poise and maturity to run the inn and raise our son. You can take on a few of my business associates, can't you?"

Her smile turned a bit more genuine. "You sound like Gran."

That seemed highly unlikely. "What did your grandmother say?"

"That I was a Caldwell woman, and they're not afraid of anything. They took on the island and tamed it back when it was the wild frontier." She gave a little laugh. "I told her I'd rather tackle an alligator than a society party, and she said that was the point. That the thing I feared was my frontier."

"Your grandmother's a wise woman."

"She is." Miranda's gaze swept up to touch his face. "I don't want to disappoint her. So I guess I'll be going on Saturday."

His fingers closed over hers again. "I'm glad."

He felt unreasonably exhilarated at having gotten his way. But if Miranda was this skittish about a weekend in Charleston, what would she say if he broached the subject that had been hovering in the back of his mind for the past day or two?

What would Miranda say if he told her he thought the best way of taking care of Sammy was for them to get married again?

Tyler should look as out of place as a duck at a wedding, and instead he looked perfectly at ease as he guided her cousin Matt's blindfolded youngest toward the piñata they'd hung from the dining room archway.

Well, she'd wanted him to be comfortable with the whole family here for Sammy's birthday party. She just hadn't expected him to find it that easy.

After their trip the day before to pick up the bicycle, they seemed to have moved to a different level of understanding. She was still trying to figure out what it was.

"You've got to give the man credit." Her sister, Chloe, stopped pouring lemonade long enough to nod toward Tyler. "He's trying."

"Tyler doesn't just try," she said. He was holding the toddler up so she could get in a good swing with the plastic bat. "He stayed off the phone and away from the computer all day, he helped me decorate, he even gave Daddy a hand with the pork barbecue. He's being so perfect it makes me want to scream."

Chloe laughed, her lively face filled with the serenity it had acquired since her marriage to Luke Hunter. "Honey, perfection is usually considered a good thing in a man."

"I keep trying to remind myself why I'm no longer Mrs. Tyler Winchester," she said with mock severity. "It doesn't help to have everyone singing his praises all of a sudden."

"Singing his praises?" Chloe raised her eyebrows. "Sugar, that doesn't sound like the brothers I know and love."

"Well, maybe not the twins," she admitted. "But even they said he wasn't half bad after he took over hanging the decorations so they didn't have to."

"So what's wrong?" Chloe slipped an arm around Miranda's waist. "Don't you want Sammy's dad to get along with everyone?"

Was she really being that selfish? "I suppose so," she said. "It just makes me wonder what he's up to."

Chloe gave her a squeeze. "Never look a helpful man or a gift horse in the mouth." She picked up the tray of glasses. "I never do."

But Chloe was secure in the love of the man who'd been meant for her. And Miranda was... nervous.

Nervous about this suddenly charming and cooperative Tyler. Nervous about the weekend in Charleston she'd committed herself to. And nervous about what the future held.

Please. She snatched a moment for what Gran always called a prayer on the run. *Let this family gathering show Tyler what Sammy has here. Let him understand that he can't make big changes in Sammy's life.*

That sounded like she was telling God what to do rather than asking for His guidance. Still, she clung to her plea stubbornly. She did know what was best for Sammy, didn't she?

She batted away one of the helium-filled balloons that floated around the room, bumping on the ceiling. A huge balloon bouquet had arrived unexpectedly that morning with a card signed Uncle Josh. Sammy had looked astonished.

"Do I have an uncle Josh?"

"That's my brother," Tyler had explained.

Now that she thought of it, Tyler had looked almost as surprised as Sammy. Apparently he hadn't expected this of his brother.

The piñata split open. Candy and small toys scattered on the floor. Tyler stood back, watching with a smile as the kids rushed to snatch them up.

Then he looked at her, the smile lingering, growing softer, more personal.

It was as if he'd reached across the room and touched her cheek. A wave of warmth swept over Miranda, and her fingers fumbled with the candles she was putting on the cake.

Tyler worked his way through the horde of small children to her side. "Can I help you with that?"

She handed him the candles. "You do it. I seem to be all thumbs."

He arranged candles on the huge sheet cake decorated with dolphins and seashells. "Quite a party. Do you always go all out for birthdays?"

"Well, only the kids get piñatas, but everyone gets a party. It's a good excuse for cake and ice cream."

He frowned, adjusting the position of one candle as if it displeased him. "Another tradition, in fact."

"I guess so. All families have birthday traditions, don't they?"

"I don't know. I was always away at boarding school on my birthday. My mother sent a gift, but that was about all."

At Tyler's mention of boarding school, she felt as if a cold draft had blown through the room, extinguishing the candles.

"You…you're not thinking of boarding school for Sammy, are you?" She could never agree to that.

He straightened, the smile wiped from his face. "I did think that at first. It's what seems natural to me. My brother and I never questioned that we'd go off to boarding school when we were eight."

Her heart cramped at the thought of the boy he'd been. "I couldn't let you do that to Sammy."

"Relax. I've given up that idea." He glanced around the room. "Sammy shouldn't be away from family."

She could breathe again. "I'm glad you see that."

He frowned, his dark eyes serious. "That doesn't mean I'll let you have everything your way. Sammy has to learn to be a part of the outside world, too."

"Is that what this trip to Charleston is?" Fear made her voice sharp. "Some kind of test to see how Sammy does there?"

"Of course not." His voice was even sharper than hers, and the cooperative Tyler who'd been around all day seemed to vanish. "Don't put words in my mouth, Miranda. I've already told you—I just want Sammy to see the world I function in, because someday he'll have to function there, too."

"It didn't work very well when I tried it." Apprehension about the weekend forced the words out.

That reminder seemed to rattle him. For a moment she didn't think he'd reply, but then he shook his head, face somber.

"I admit I didn't do a good job of introducing you to my world, Miranda. But then, you never really tried to fit in, did you?"

"That's not fair." She lowered her voice to a furious whisper. "I didn't have the least idea what I was getting into, and you didn't help."

"We both made mistakes." He spoke quietly, although no one in the chattering crowd could possibly hear them. "We were both too young to do it right." His hand closed around her wrist, and her pulse thundered against his palm. "I won't make the same mistake with our son. I promise you that."

She wasn't sure whether to consider that a promise or a threat.

Chapter Twelve

"Miranda looks upset." Gran Caldwell planted herself in front of Tyler, letting the party swirl around them. Her voice was tart, and her eyes snapped at Tyler.

He glanced toward the table where Miranda and her sister were rapidly cutting cake and passing pieces out. He could protest that she was busy with the birthday party, but he suspected a half-truth wouldn't sit well with Miranda's grandmother.

"We had a misunderstanding." He tried not to let exasperation show in his voice. Didn't Miranda see that he had a right to expose their son to the wider world?

"Be better for Sammy if his parents understood each other."

Miranda's grandmother certainly had a point there. It was what he believed, too. Unfortunately, every time he thought he and Miranda were reaching that point, some unwary remark opened a chasm between them.

The buzz of conversation and the high voices of the children effectively masked anything he and Mrs. Caldwell might say to each other. Still, he wasn't sure he wanted to be having this talk with her.

"We're still trying to figure out how to deal with this situation," he said. How impolite would it be to slip away from the lecture Miranda's grandmother undoubtedly had in mind?

The frilly pink party hat that sat atop Gran's coronet of gray hair bobbed. "I reckon it's not easy. But then, change never is."

He glanced at her, a little surprised by the comment. "I wouldn't have thought change was something that came very often to Caldwell Island. Everywhere I turn, I trip over one tradition or another."

"Change comes to everybody, no matter where they live." She patted a child who ran by, but her gaze was still focused on him. "Caldwell Island might look the same to you as it did eight years ago, but it's changed beyond all recognition since I was a girl."

"I suppose it has." This elderly woman couldn't imagine the changes that took place daily in the world he lived in.

"You're thinking I don't know a thing about how you live."

Her perception startled him again, and he could see she knew that and enjoyed it.

"I didn't mean to offend you."

She patted his arm, her heavily veined hand surprisingly strong. "You don't have to worry about being polite to me, son. You just have to worry about doing your best for Sammy and Miranda."

"The tricky part is deciding just what the best is." That was the thought that haunted him, but he surprised himself by saying it to her.

"Our Miranda has strong feelings about raising her son."

Gran Caldwell looked across the room, and he followed her gaze to where Miranda was seating children around the oval wooden table they'd covered with a bright red birthday cloth. She was passing out plates of cake and simultaneously refereeing some dispute.

The denim skirt and aqua shirt Miranda wore outlined her slender figure. Come to think of it, he hadn't seen her wear anything that didn't look good on her. Not stylish, maybe, and certainly not expensive, but that didn't seem to matter.

"She comes from a long line of strong women." Gran's eyes twinkled. "Opinionated, too."

"I've noticed that." His lips creased in an unwilling smile. The woman had him, and she knew it.

She patted his arm again with what he might imagine was affection. "Talk to her. She'll listen if she knows you respect her opinion. You can't understand each other if you're not willing to do that."

Apparently having said what she intended to, Miranda's grandmother moved off. He let his gaze drift to Miranda again.

She had stepped back a little from the table,

letting her father snap a photo of Sammy with his cake. Her gaze rested on their son, and he saw a vulnerability in her expression that he hadn't recognized before.

Strong, yes. Her grandmother was right about that. But Miranda was vulnerable, too, in spite of being surrounded by people who loved her. Whether she knew it or not, she needed a man to share things with, a man she could depend on.

And how exactly did that fit into the idea he had been struggling with for the last few days—the thought that he and Miranda should marry again?

That would be best for Sammy, wouldn't it? He'd have both his parents, and he wouldn't have to feel split between them.

They'd need to work something out so that Sammy and Miranda still spent plenty of time on the island. He knew Miranda would never agree to anything else. Besides, he'd grown to respect the heritage his son had here.

Marriage would affect him and Miranda, too, obviously, as well as Sammy. As for himself, he'd decided a long time ago that marriage wasn't for him. He'd never settle for the kind of relationship his parents had had, and his attempt to create something different with Miranda had ended in a dismal failure.

He couldn't offer Miranda that fairy-tale romance they'd once thought they could have. He wasn't even sure such a thing existed.

Probably even happily married people like Miranda's parents eventually settled for mutual respect and friendship. Wasn't it reasonable for him and Miranda to start out that way the second time around?

This could be right for all three of them, but he had to move cautiously. Miranda's grandmother had it right—he and Miranda had to understand each other before they could forge a new relationship. He had to be patient.

Unfortunately, patience wasn't one of his better qualities. He was used to choosing a goal and charging toward it, pushing aside anything that stood in his way.

He imagined the weekend trip to Charleston as a positive step toward making Miranda see that they should be together as a family. If that were going to happen, he had to make peace with her right now.

He worked his way across the room, dodging the sticky hands of several small Caldwell cousins who'd escaped from the cake table. Miranda was trying to make room for a tray of glasses.

"Let me take that." He grasped the metal tray and put it down on the space she cleared. She shot him a glance of thanks, followed by instant wariness.

She was still thinking about their last conversation, obviously. If he wanted this to work, he had to clear that up.

"Can we talk?"

Her steady gaze assessed him, then she nodded. "Yes, if you can talk while carrying the coffee in."

"I can do that."

He followed her through the door to the kitchen. It swung shut, cutting off the party clamor. The ensuing quiet was so startling his ears rang.

Miranda picked up another tray, this one filled with cups. "I'll take this in, if you can bring the coffee urn."

He put his hands over hers, setting the tray on the scrubbed pine table. "Wait just a second. Please," he added.

"Whatever it is, can't it wait?" She tried to pull away, but he held her hands fast.

"Nobody's in that much of a hurry for coffee. You can give me a minute."

Her green eyes turned stormy, but she nodded. "All right. A minute."

"I'm sorry."

Her hands stilled in his. "For what?"

"That conversation we had about going to Charleston—I said it all wrong."

She was listening to him. He could let go of her hands. He didn't want to.

"I understand. You want Sammy to go so he can see what kind of circles you move in." Again that hint of vulnerability showed.

"I want the two of you to come so we can have a good time together," he said firmly. "And I suppose I do want Sammy to see me on my own turf. That's not such a bad thing, is it?"

"Are you saying I overreacted?" Her lips curved in the beginning of a reluctant smile.

The tension inside him eased. She was going to listen. "Maybe just a little."

"Okay." She let out a breath that was almost a sigh. "You're right. Sammy should see you in a situation where you feel comfortable."

Her comment startled him. Had he been acting uncomfortable?

"I like it here, Miranda. But we are kind of surrounded by family."

"Especially today." The corners of her eyes crinkled. "I know. You deserve some alone time with Sammy off the island and away from hordes of Caldwells."

He smoothed his thumb over her knuckles. "So we'll go?"

Her lashes swept down to hide her eyes, but she nodded.

"We'll have a good time, I promise." They would. He'd make sure of that.

Miranda would begin to see that they belonged together as a family. Maybe what he had to offer wasn't a fairy-tale romance, but it would be good enough.

She had to learn to cope with Tyler's world, or Sammy wouldn't feel comfortable there. So this weekend was the challenge she had to face, no matter how she dreaded it. Miranda looked out the car window, watching signs and consulting the map as Tyler negotiated the narrow streets of downtown Charleston.

"Turning left at the next corner will take us toward the Battery."

Tyler nodded, his face, in profile, relaxed. City traffic clearly wasn't the monster to him that it had always been to her.

"I want to take a picture of the cannons." Sammy

leaned as far forward in the back seat as his seat belt would permit, brandishing the disposable camera his father had bought him for the trip. "I can take my pictures to school, can't I?"

"Sure you can," Tyler said. "We'll make sure we get lots of them."

Everything about him seemed at ease. As he'd said, he was on his own turf here. Charleston might not be that familiar to him, but it was a city, and the people they'd encounter were his colleagues.

They'd arranged to sightsee during the day, then go to Dan and Sheila Carpenter's house in time to dress for dinner and the charity concert. Her stomach clenched at the thought, and she chastised herself for being such a wimp. The Carpenters were just people, after all.

The truth was, she was still a daughter in her father's house, still living the simple life she'd always known. Gran had been right about that— Caldwell Island wasn't a frontier for her.

She would find a way to adapt to this situation. She had to, for Sammy's sake. It didn't have anything to do with her relationship with Tyler, just Sammy. She sat up a little straighter. She could do anything for her son.

"There's a parking lot." She pointed. "I'm sure we can walk down to the Battery from here."

Tyler pulled into the gravel lot, taking a ticket from the automatic dispenser. He gave her a quick smile. "Good navigating, Miranda."

She folded the city map and slipped it into her

bag. "I don't mind reading the map, but I surely don't like driving in the city."

"Charleston is a challenge. These streets must not have been widened since horse-and-carriage days."

"No, I suppose they haven't." The narrow streets, lined with elegant antebellum houses and pocket gardens tucked behind wrought-iron fences, seemed to take them a step back in time.

They got out, Sammy checking to be sure he had his camera and baseball cap.

"Did you know the War Between the States started at Fort Sumter?" Sammy fell in step with his father.

Tyler smiled at him. "I assume you mean the Civil War?"

Sammy grinned. "Don't let Gran hear you call it that."

The ease of their exchange warmed Miranda's heart. Whatever the future held, this was how the relationship should be between Sammy and his daddy. Her son deserved what she had with her father. It had never been right to try to keep Sammy and Tyler apart.

I thought I was doing the right thing, Lord. Teach me how to look at myself more clearly. Show me how to make up for my mistakes.

She caught a glimpse of water ahead, and in a few minutes they'd emerged onto the wide walk and wall of the Battery. Out in the harbor, the twin forts that once protected the city had, no doubt, been invaded by tourists. The breeze from the water lifted her hair.

"Cannons," Sammy said with satisfaction,

pointing to the black cannons that lined the Battery. "I knew there'd be cannons."

"Looks like there are some soldiers, too." Tyler nodded to two young men in gray uniforms who leaned against the wall.

"They're Citadel cadets," Sammy said knowledgeably. "I thought I'd like to go to the Citadel when I get big enough, but Uncle David says if I want to study dolphins, like he does, I should go where he went to school in Florida. Then I can be an…an oceanographer." He said the long word carefully.

They reached the wall, and Tyler leaned against it, looking at their son. "Is that what you want to be, an oceanographer?"

Was that disapproval in his voice? She couldn't be sure. It might be, if Tyler envisioned Sammy taking over the company for him one day.

Sammy shrugged. "I dunno. Maybe." He swung the camera up. "I'm going to take a picture of the cannon." He darted off.

Tyler watched him run along the walkway. "That is one smart kid we have."

"Of course he is." She leaned against the wall next to him. She didn't know whether or not to be offended that Tyler would even think he had to say it.

He focused on her, smiling. "Don't get huffy. I just meant I'd probably never heard the word oceanographer when I was his age."

"Well, Sammy's grown up with the sea. You had other interests."

Tyler shook his head, the smile fading a little as he stared at the water. He'd rolled back his sleeves, and his forearms were tanned against the cream-colored shirt. Seagulls swooped, wings sparkling in the sunlight.

"You mean my father had other interests. My future was predetermined. I had to take over the company. He just never thought it would happen as soon as it did."

"Is that what you hope for Sammy?" She forced her voice to be steady. "That he'll take over the company one day?"

"I confess the thought crossed my mind when I met him. Why wouldn't it?"

Before she could protest, he touched her hand where it rested on the wall.

"I know what you're going to say, and you needn't bother. Sammy gets to determine his own future. Whatever he wants to be is all right with me."

"I'm glad you feel that way." *Thank you, Lord. That was one battle I didn't want to fight.*

"I don't want to be the kind of father mine was." His fingers closed over hers, and she felt the warmth all the way up her arm. "Unfortunately I don't have any other models."

"You'll learn by doing," she said, knowing it was true. "That's all any of us can do."

Just as she would learn to cope with his world by doing—beginning by staying with his friends and attending a social event. That was the only way she could help Sammy in the difficult adjustments he'd have to make when he started living with Tyler part of the time.

"Daddy, come see the cannon," Sammy called. "I want to take your picture."

"You've got it." Tyler pushed away from the wall. He caught her hand as they walked toward their son, and she steeled herself for the inevitable tingle as their hands swung, palm to palm.

It doesn't mean anything, she told herself desperately. Tyler has made that clear.

"You stand there with Momma." Sammy pushed them into place next to the cannon. "I'll take a picture."

The cadets strolled by, and one of them stopped, smiling at Sammy. "Would you like me to take it so you can be in it, too?"

Sammy gave him an awestruck look, then nodded. "Thank you, sir. That would be very nice."

He handed over the camera and scurried to pose next to his father. Tyler put his hand on their son's shoulder, linking them.

A family portrait, she thought as the cadet snapped one picture, then another. We might be any happy family out for the day.

Her smile faltered at the pain in her heart. Her goal—learning to function in Tyler's world to help Sammy—suddenly seemed a poor substitute for what she really wanted. For what she knew she'd never have.

They'd never be the happy family of the photo, because that wasn't what Tyler wanted any longer.

"This is the house." Tyler parked at the curb on the cobblestone street. "You'll like the Carpenters."

At least, he hoped she would. He could feel Miranda's nervousness from across the front seat.

He clasped her hand for an instant, telling himself he was only trying to convey assurance that this visit would be all right. He seemed to be doing that often lately—making an excuse to himself to touch her.

He got out, and Sammy came quickly to help him as he unloaded the bags.

"Look, Sammy. It's a genuine Charleston historic home." Miranda nodded at the bronze plaque set into the faded brick wall.

Tyler pushed open the filigree wrought-iron gate in the brick wall, and they stepped into a lush green garden with azaleas in full bloom. The house ran along the left side of the garden, and the brick walls lined the other sides, creating an oasis in the midst of the city.

A fountain with a graceful seahorse spout sprayed water in an arc, catching and reflecting a ray of sunshine that filtered through the sheltering live oaks.

"I've never seen anything quite like this." Tyler set down the bags on the brick walk to close the gate. "It's beautiful."

Miranda's face had tightened. "Yes. Your friends have a lovely home."

Sammy had run ahead to peer into the fountain, but Tyler lowered his voice anyway. "Why does it bother you? Your uncle's house is probably just as big."

"It's not the same. People don't live in a house like this unless they're part of Charleston society."

"Maybe Dan is from an old Charleston family. It doesn't matter. This is just business."

What was she thinking? That this would be as difficult as those weeks in Baltimore had been?

She nodded, but the tense line of her jaw told him that his rationalization didn't really help.

He clasped her elbow as they moved up the walk, hoping she knew he was on her side. But then, why would she feel any assurance of that? He should have been on her side when he'd taken her to Baltimore as his bride, and he hadn't been able to help her then.

No, that was letting himself off too easy. He looked back with disgust at the callow boy he'd been then. He'd been so obsessed with filling his father's shoes that he hadn't given a thought to how his decisions affected Miranda. He should have known, he should have done better, he should have been smarter.

They'd both been too young when they fell in love, and they hadn't known how to make it work. Now it was too late. He couldn't offer her what he should have then, but he certainly could make an effort to see that she felt comfortable here.

"It's business," he said again as they stepped onto the piazza. "You'll find both Dan and Sheila eager to make us welcome."

She glanced up with a flicker of a smile. "Because you're the big boss, you mean."

The smile encouraged him. "Oh, I'm an important person, all right." He lifted an eyebrow, holding her arm in a firm clasp. "Ready?"

She nodded, and he reached out to let the brass knocker fall.

Sheila Carpenter opened the door at once. "Come in, come in." Her wide smile swept them into a cool, elegant hallway. "We've been waiting for you."

"It's good to see you again, Sheila."

He glanced around, trying to see what Miranda might find intimidating about the place. The spiral staircase that swirled upward without apparent support might take his breath away, and the portraits on the walls might be antebellum ancestors, but otherwise it was just a house.

"We're just so happy to have y'all here." Sheila clasped Miranda's hand. Tall and blond, she was as elegant as her home, but genuine welcome shone in her wide blue eyes.

"It's very kind of you to invite us." There was no trace of nervousness showing in the warmth of her response.

"Our boy, Todd, is looking forward to having a guest." Sheila smiled at Sammy. "This must be Sammy."

Sammy shook hands with a grave courtesy that seemed inborn.

Tyler glanced from his son to Miranda. They both had that innate courtesy and dignity. With that and her native intelligence, Miranda could fit in anywhere. She just didn't seem to have confidence in that fact.

She'd had it, once upon a time. His memory flashed him an image of the girl Miranda had been when he'd met her. She'd had such natural grace and such bright confidence. She'd been willing to take on anything. She'd lost that somewhere along the way.

No, not somewhere. She'd lost it when he'd swept her into a marriage neither of them had been ready for.

The guilt he'd denied for years burst out of hiding. Their marriage and what had happened to her as a result had robbed Miranda of her girlhood, her college education, her chance at the happy family she deserved.

What could he offer her that would make up for that?

Chapter Thirteen

Miranda took a deep breath, opened the bedroom door and stepped into the upstairs hall of the Carpenters' house. She sank almost to her ankles, it seemed, in plush carpet.

Tyler waited under the amber glow of the wall sconces. He looked at her, not speaking, a portrait in black and white with his dark hair and dark eyes, his white shirtfront and black tuxedo.

She smoothed her hands nervously down the black silk of the evening pantsuit her sister had insisted she borrow.

"Well? Is this outfit all right?" Pitiful, a tiny voice in her mind taunted. You're begging for a compliment from him.

"Very all right." Tyler reached out to touch the curl she'd let fall to her shoulder from her swept-back hair. "You look beautiful."

Begged for or not, his words were good to hear.

"It's not me—it's the clothes. Chloe got this outfit for the kickoff party when Dalton Resorts broke ground for the new hotel. She said it would be just right for tonight's concert, but I wasn't sure."

"Chloe has good taste, but you're wrong." His fingertips trailed from her hair to her cheek, and she had to fight the longing to lean against him.

"I'm wrong about what?" How had her voice gotten so breathless?

"You are beautiful no matter what you wear." He pressed his palm against her cheek, and heat rose to her skin where he touched. "Now just say thank-you instead of arguing."

"Thank you," she whispered, her senses swimming.

This was what she wanted—this kind of relationship with Tyler. She'd been kidding herself to think she could be happy with any less.

"What do you think? Are we all ready to go?" Dan asked the question as he and Sheila came out of a door farther along the hallway.

Sheila looked elegant in cream lace shot through with gold thread. Dan, like Tyler, wore a tuxedo, but to Miranda's eyes he couldn't hold a candle to Tyler's dark good looks.

Tyler nodded. "We're ready, and you and I are lucky. We'll be the envy of every man there."

Sheila laughed as she started down the open spiral staircase. "That's what I like—a man who knows how to turn a compliment."

Tyler took Miranda's hand, slipping it into the crook of his arm. Her fingers closed on hard muscle.

"Smile," he whispered as they reached the top of the staircase. "This evening will be fun."

Fun, she thought, trailing her hand along the polished mahogany railing. This evening with Tyler wasn't fun. It was magical.

She had seen no reason to change her mind by the time they arrived at the restaurant Dan had chosen on Bay Street. Tyler helped her from the car, and she felt like Cinderella alighting from her coach.

He clasped her hand in his, waiting while Dan gave his keys to the valet. "Relax," he murmured softly, his breath brushing her ear as he bent close to her.

Was it conceivable that he thought she could relax when every nerve in her body was on edge at his nearness?

Dan and Sheila led the way through a wrought-iron archway, and they followed the hostess across a cobblestone patio surrounded by gaslights on black iron posts. The lights flickered on boxwood hedges and white tablecloths. String music from some hidden source muted the echo of conversation.

Magical, she thought as they reached a table set for four.

Tyler pulled out her chair. When she sat down, his fingers caressed her shoulders as lightly as the aroma of the flowers caressed her senses. The bowl of camellias in the center of the table seemed to waver for a moment.

"Good choice." Tyler sat next to her, glancing across the linen-covered table at Dan. "You know how to pick a restaurant."

Sheila looked around with satisfaction. "We thought you'd like it. They're known for doing great things with local fare like shrimp and black-eyed peas, so be sure you try something unique to Charleston."

The conversation moved to food, giving Miranda a respite to catch her breath and try to slow her tumultuous pulse. What was Tyler up to?

The touches, the sultry glances—they weren't accidental. It was as if he'd set out tonight to remind her of what they'd once had.

She slanted a look at him from behind the protective cover of the menu, and her heart trembled. She didn't need reminders. All she had to do was look at him, and she saw again the husband she'd never stopped loving.

The strong bones of his face were more pronounced, and there were fine lines around his eyes that spoke of the stress of the past years. But one thing hadn't changed—the way her heart stopped when he smiled at her.

"What do you think?" Tyler lowered his menu. "Sullivan Island crab cakes for a starter, followed by pecan-crusted fried shrimp with apricot chutney?"

"Sounds wonderful," she said, trying for normalcy. "I've never met a fried shrimp I didn't like."

"That's it, then." Tyler closed the menu. "We think alike tonight."

He gave her a small, private smile, as if the two of them shared a secret.

Her heart swelled with love. Hopeless, to try to

keep her feelings a secret. Her love for Tyler must be shining in her eyes for everyone to see.

This was the way he'd once imagined their lives would be, Tyler realized as they drove to the house after the concert.

He glanced at Miranda, seated next to him in the back seat of Dan's car. He'd pictured them doing this sort of thing, had envisioned Miranda looking elegant, beautiful and perfectly at ease. Pictured them coming home to their own house with their children asleep in their beds.

It was too late now to think about what might have been once upon a time. He had to concentrate on the present, and the present included a Miranda who'd fit in perfectly and had seemed to enjoy the evening.

At the moment she continued a lively conversation with Sheila about the community's youth center. Apparently the volunteer work she did at the center in Beaufort was similar to what Sheila did in Charleston, and the two of them had been exchanging war stories.

He captured her hand where it lay between them on the leather seat. Her fingers curled around his, and he thought she nearly tripped over a word.

This was working—he was sure of it. Miranda had begun to see that she could function perfectly well in the world he moved in. It would be a small step from that to convincing her that a marital partnership was best for all of them.

"Here we are." Dan pulled into the converted

carriage house that served as his garage. "We'll walk in through the garden. Sheila's done a wonderful job with it."

"You're only saying that because you know it's true," Sheila teased.

Tyler kept Miranda's hand securely enclosed in his as they went through a gate in the brick wall that rimmed the back and side of the enclosed garden. He heard her breath catch as they stepped into the garden.

He could understand her response. Tiny white lights, hidden in the shrubbery, picked out the gleam of a camellia here, the blush of an azalea blossom there. Lights illuminated the fountain, making the water glitter like crystal.

"It is perfectly lovely, Sheila." Miranda's voice was soft, as if she didn't want to disturb the night. "I can't imagine anything more charming."

"Well, now, y'all just stay out here and enjoy it for a bit." She grasped Dan's arm and whisked him toward the door. "We'll go up and make sure those boys are asleep, and we'll leave the door unlatched for you. Stay as long as you want."

The door closed behind them, cutting off Dan's surprised comment.

"Sheila's being tactful." He guided Miranda toward a wrought-iron bench that faced the fountain. "She's giving us a chance to be alone."

"I don't think...that is, we've been alone plenty of times." She rushed the words, as if tension danced along her nerves, and sat down abruptly.

"Not in such a romantic setting." He sat next to her, stretching his arm along the seat behind her and letting his hand cup her shoulder.

She sat very straight. "It sounded as if you and Dan were talking business at the intermission."

Obviously Miranda didn't want to discuss how romantic the setting was, though he suspected she couldn't ignore the heavy scent of flowers that perfumed the air. But if it made her feel more comfortable, they'd talk business.

"Dan has ideas about our acquiring some other companies in the southeast. I guess he thought this evening was his best chance to air them."

"Are they good ideas?" She sounded relieved that she'd successfully turned the conversation.

"Fairly good." He tilted his head, staring absently at the spray of water glistening in the light as he considered. "Maybe a little too ambitious for us right now. We have the other deal I told you about pending."

"So you don't intend to go along with his suggestions?" She made it a question.

"He's a good man with a lot of talent," he said slowly.

Funny. He wasn't used to discussing the decisions he made with anyone. That wasn't his style.

But Miranda had her gaze fixed on his face as if this was the most natural thing in the world, and at the moment, it seemed so.

"You don't want to discourage him," she said.

"That's exactly right. Maybe his idea isn't best for us at the moment, but I'd never want to dampen his ingenuity." He drew her a little closer. "You'd make a good manager."

"That comes of being a middle child in a big family," she said lightly. "You learn to manage people or you fight all the time."

"And you don't like to fight."

"I'm not good at it." She sobered suddenly. "Maybe if—"

"Maybe if what?" He wanted to know what had set that frown between her brows.

She gave him a solemn look that was very like Sammy's. "Maybe if I'd been better at fighting, things would have worked out better between us."

He was startled, not so much at the truth of the statement but that she knew both of them well enough to say it to him. "You ran away instead."

"And you didn't chase me."

He caressed the smooth skin of her shoulder. "I should have. I wasn't smart enough to understand what was happening."

Did he understand what was happening now?

The question annoyed him. Of course he did. He was showing Miranda that they had a chance to put their lives together again, the way they should be. They could have a marriage based on common interests and mutual respect.

Somehow the moonlit garden didn't seem the right place to be thinking about common interests. And the sensations he felt at having Miranda in the circle of his arm didn't have anything to do with mutual respect.

"We were too young." She said the words softly, mournfully, as if grieving for someone who'd died.

We're not too young now.

The words hovered on his lips, ready to be spoken, but something held him back. He didn't want to embark on a discussion of the businesslike marriage he envisioned, not here in the moonlight, not in someone else's garden with Dan and Sheila inside wondering what they were doing.

"It doesn't matter now." He turned her face toward him, hand cradling her cheek. "There's no point in dwelling on the past."

His thumb brushed her lips, and he felt them tremble.

"There is a point." Her lashes swept down, then up, unveiling the troubled expression in her eyes. "If you can't forgive me for not telling you about our son, it matters quite a lot."

Her words arrowed straight into his heart and lodged there. "Is that what you think? That I'm still angry with you?"

"Aren't you?"

"No!" Suddenly it seemed the most important thing in the world that she believe him. "I *was* angry at first, but I understand now. Even if I didn't understand, I couldn't have gone on being angry when I saw how much you love our son."

A tear spilled over, glistening on her cheek until he wiped it away with his fingertip.

"Thank you, Tyler. I'm glad."

The soft words, the perfumed air, the warm

familiar body next to him wiped away whatever armor he had left against her. He ought to tell her, ought to explain his plans for their future, but all of that was swamped in the need to have her in his arms.

He lowered his head, and his lips found hers. He pulled her close against him.

Miranda settled into his arms as if she'd never left them. Her mouth was warm and sweet and alive against his, and he never intended to let her get away from him again.

This is going to work. He buried his face in the curve of her neck and felt her arms clasp him tightly. He'd find the right time, he'd explain it all to her, and Miranda would understand.

The fact that they still had such a powerful attraction to each other—well, that made it all the better, didn't it?

Miranda could only wish she knew where they were going. She looked out the car window the next afternoon, watching the thick pine forest slide past. Geographically they were on their way to Caldwell Island. But emotionally where were they headed?

She slid a sideways glance at Tyler. He looked simultaneously relaxed and in control when he drove, as if the mechanical actions freed him from some internal tension that was otherwise present.

He caught her glance and smiled, and her heart turned over in her chest. Well, her emotions certainly weren't in question.

But Tyler's remained a mystery. Even in the turbulent wake of last night's kisses, she wasn't sure of him. The only thing she was sure of, as a result of this weekend, was that she'd faced something she feared and come out okay. Gran had been right, it seemed. She'd grown up.

"Is Sammy still sleeping?" he murmured.

She glanced to the back seat, where Sammy leaned against his seat belt, eyes closed. She nodded. "Those two boys must have stayed up late last night playing."

"Guess so. They both looked as if they had a hard time staying awake in church this morning."

She'd been a little surprised when Dan and Sheila had taken it for granted that they'd attend church together. She'd been more surprised when Tyler had agreed without a murmur.

The huge antebellum brick church with its magnificent pulpit and professional choir had been quite a contrast to St. Andrew's, but she'd felt at home there. The message had been just as clear, just as loving as any she'd ever heard.

"I liked the service," she ventured, wondering what he was thinking. "It was nice of Dan and Sheila to invite us to go with them."

He nodded, frowning. "I don't think I've ever heard a sermon before on Joseph and his brothers. Or on brothers at all, for that matter."

Was he thinking about his relationship with his brother? She couldn't be sure, but she felt compelled to keep him talking.

"The pastor did have a good point. The deepest hurt as well as the deepest love happens in families."

"Maybe so."

Tyler sounded noncommittal, and it pained her. Could anything ever repair the damage his family had done to him?

She'd be kidding herself if she imagined she might be able to do that. Perhaps his love for Sammy would be enough to heal his pain, as it had once healed hers.

"I've always liked the story of Joseph." She didn't want to let him lapse into silence. "The verse about the brothers intending what happened for evil but God intending it for good—that speaks to me. I guess I need to know that God can bring good out of even the worst of circumstances."

For a moment she thought he wouldn't respond. Then he glanced across at her with a slight smile.

"Your faith must be contagious, you know that? I've thought more about what I believe in the last couple of weeks than I have in a lot of years."

"Coming to any conclusions?" She held her breath, wanting to encourage, not wanting to push.

"Only that I need to do some more thinking."

She smiled, glancing at Sammy as he stirred and pushed himself upright. "That's a good start, don't you think?"

"Maybe so." He looked at Sammy in the rearview mirror. "Hey, sleepyhead. We're almost home."

Sammy blinked and stretched. "I'm glad we went to Charleston. I had a good time, didn't you, Momma?"

"I sure did." Possibly the best part had been the past few minutes. They swept onto the bridge, and as the island came into view, a prayer formed in her heart.

He's questioning, Lord. Please, draw him back to You for his answers. He'll be a better man and a better father when he grows to know You.

Whether anything could restore the love Tyler had once felt for her, she didn't know. She did know that restoring his relationship with God was the best thing that could happen to him.

They pulled into the driveway at the inn, and Tyler's cell phone began to ring. Well, they'd had a little time without business. He couldn't seem to get away from it entirely, even on a Sunday.

He put the phone to his ear, taking on what she always thought of as his business expression—absorbed, grave, intent.

She glanced at Sammy. "Grab your bag before you run inside, okay?"

He nodded, then slid quickly out, duffel bag in hand. He looked eager to tell the whole family about his big weekend. She started to follow him, intending to let Tyler take his call in peace.

Tyler caught her arm to stop her, tension communicated through the pressure of his fingers. The monosyllables of his conversation didn't tell her anything, but apprehension slid through her.

Finally he disconnected the call, still frowning.

"What is it? What's wrong?" Unpleasant possibilities chased each other through her mind like black clouds before a storm.

Tyler focused on her, his eyes very dark. "That was the private investigator I hired to find the man who took the picture of Sammy."

Her heart thudded uncomfortably. Whatever the answer was to that mystery, it was bound to create still more questions, maybe more problems. But they couldn't hide from it.

"Did he learn anything?"

"It turns out your mysterious bird-watcher was a bit more than that." Tyler looked angry and perplexed. "He was a private investigator himself."

She stared at him blankly. "A private investigator?" She could only echo his words, trying to get her mind around the concept. "But what— I don't understand. Does that mean someone actually hired him to come here and spy on us? On Sammy?"

"Unless you believe in a huge string of coincidences, that's the most likely thing." Tyler slammed the palm of his hand on the steering wheel. "If I could get my hands on him—"

"Don't, Tyler, don't." Some corner of her heart mourned the disappearance of the peace and hope she'd been feeling since those moments in the moonlit garden the night before.

"Don't what?" He bit off the words.

"I know it's upsetting, but you've got to let the professionals handle it."

He glared for a moment, then gave her a wry smile. "I've always said you should hire the best person for a job and then stay out of the way and let them do it. But in this case—"

"In this case it's too personal," she finished for him. "But we don't really have a choice, do we?"

"No. No matter how much I might want to rampage around Charleston looking for answers, you're right." He clenched his jaw. "He says he should know the rest of it in a day or two."

Apprehension seemed to dig a hole in her heart. "What do you plan to do then?"

"Once I know who's been interfering in our lives, I'll know what to do." His knuckles whitened on the steering wheel. "Whoever he is, he'll be called to account. He's going to regret doing anything to my son."

Tyler seemed to turn inward, his expression bleak. It was almost as if he'd forgotten she was there.

She ought to be glad one piece of the mystery that surrounded the photograph would be unraveled soon. She shouldn't be thinking about how it was going to affect her relationship with Tyler. But she couldn't seem to help it.

Chapter Fourteen

Tyler frowned at himself in the bedroom mirror the next morning, then transferred the frown to his cell phone, lying atop the dresser. It was probably irrational, but he'd somehow expected to hear from the private investigator this morning. For the amount of money he was paying the firm, he should see faster results than this.

Miranda's face, her eyes troubled, rose in his mind. She'd been as upset as he at learning that someone had apparently hired a private investigator to look into Sammy's parentage. Probably it had hit her harder because in her safe, peaceful little world things like that didn't happen.

If he persuaded her to marry him again, she'd have to learn to expect the unexpected. He knew as well as anyone that the prospect of large amounts of money brought out the worst in most people. There would be money at the bottom of this business with the photograph. He was sure of it.

Miranda didn't think that way, of course. Still, even her bright innocence had been damaged by their brief marriage. How much would she have to change to fit into his world? Would she consider marriage worth what she'd have to sacrifice?

He clutched the cell phone and slid it into his pocket. He wasn't used to doubting himself or his decisions. He most definitely wasn't used to letting someone else take care of something as crucial as finding out the motive behind sending him that photograph.

His edginess could be attributed to that fact, he realized. He hated waiting for someone to call and tell him. He wanted to be involved.

Well, why not? He could go to Charleston, get on the private investigator's back, keep after him until they found out the truth.

Just the idea of doing something positive in this situation energized him. He grabbed a tie and knotted it automatically as he headed out the door. He'd have to let Miranda know what he intended, and then he could be on his way.

His mind raced ahead to the road to Charleston as he trotted down the stairs. He glanced into the dining room. Sallie Caldwell was clearing tables, but Miranda was nowhere in sight.

She was probably in the office. She often used these morning hours to catch up on her book work after the flurry of getting breakfast.

He pushed open the office door. Miranda looked

up from a stack of envelopes on the desk, her mouth softening in a smile at the sight of him. The green shirt she wore accentuated the sparkle of her eyes. If she'd lain wakeful after what they'd learned, it didn't show.

"Good morning. Did you sleep well?"

He didn't want to tell her he'd been unable to oust the private investigator's call from his mind long enough to get a good night's sleep.

"Okay." He crossed to the desk and leaned one hip against it. "What are you working on?"

"Sorting through the bills." She wrinkled her nose. "I have to confess, it's not my favorite chore, but it has to be done."

"Speaking of chores, I've decided to go to Charleston today. I want to push the private investigator for results." The need to take action pricked at his nerves, demanding movement.

Miranda's face clouded at his words. "You can't do that."

"Why not?" Everything in him steeled at her opposition. "I can't just sit around and wait, Miranda. I'd think you'd be as eager as I am to get this thing cleared up."

"Of course I am." Her voice was tart. "But you're forgetting what day this is."

His gaze sought the large calendar posted on the wall behind the desk. Had he missed a holiday?

"Sammy's off from school today, and we promised to take him to Angel Isle, remember?"

The realization that he'd let something so important to Sammy slip hit a sore spot. It might be more difficult than he'd expected to avoid repeating his father's mistakes.

He pushed himself erect. "I didn't remember we'd planned that trip for today, that's true. That doesn't mean I don't care."

"I didn't mean to imply—" She stopped, shook her head. "Sorry. Just because I keep Sammy's calendar in my head doesn't mean that you have to. I'm used to juggling what everyone's doing."

If they married, they'd have to find a way to get past this kind of misunderstanding. Again he wondered if she'd find the benefits of marriage worth the cost.

He shook off the thought. One thing at a time. He had to get this business of the photo resolved.

"Look, can't we postpone the trip to another day?" He gestured toward the window. "Cloudy as it is, it's not a nice day for an outing, anyway."

"Sammy's not going to think a few clouds are a good enough excuse not to take the boat out. If you want to change the plans, you'd better talk to him."

She picked up an envelope and slit it open. Apparently she was ready to get on with her work, no matter what her attitude was.

"I thought maybe you'd tell him for me." He leaned forward persuasively. "You could explain I had to go in to work."

"Not a chance." She glanced at him, and he saw the amusement in her eyes. "Nice try, but I'm not going to be the bearer of bad news for you. I've already told you that. You'll have to do it yourself."

Apparently Miranda had been giving some thought to how this whole parenting thing worked out between them, too.

"So Daddy doesn't just get to be the giver of gifts and leave the unpopular stuff to Mommy."

"That's right. Breaking bad news is equal opportunity. If you want—" She stopped abruptly.

The smile slid from his face. Miranda was staring at the paper she'd pulled out of an envelope, and her face had grown pale under the tan.

"Miranda? What is it?" He went quickly around the desk to put his hand on her shoulder. "Bad news?"

"I don't know." She looked at him, her expression apprehensive. "I'm not sure what this means."

"What is it?" He leaned over, focusing on the paper in her hand. A phone bill, he realized. "Bell South make a costly mistake?"

"It's last month's itemized long-distance calls." She pointed to a line. "That's a call he made—the man who took the picture of Sammy. I recognize the area code." She looked at him, eyes wide. "He called someone in Baltimore."

"What?" He snatched the page from her, running his gaze along the column to find the call, anticipation mounting. This was an unexpected stroke of luck. Maybe he wouldn't have to wait for the investigator to pry loose the information. The telephone number would be a shortcut.

He stared, his mind unwillingly processing the information in front of him.

"Tyler?" Miranda pushed her chair back to stand very close to him, her hair brushing his shoulder as she leaned over to look at the bill. "Why are you looking that way?"

"Because I know the number." Certainty hardened in him. "It happens to be the private number of a man I'd have said I could trust with almost anything. My assistant, Henry Carmichael."

"Your assistant? I don't understand." She leaned against his arm as she studied the bill. "How can that be? Are you sure?"

"I'm sure, all right." Already the shock was passing, to be replaced with anger that ate its way along his veins. "Good old Henry has sold me out."

"You can't know that." Miranda's response was swift. "There might be a dozen explanations."

"Name one." He shot the words at her, annoyed at her naiveté.

"Well, suppose he found out about Sammy somehow and just thought you should know. He could have been trying to do a good thing."

"If he thought that, he'd have told me."

"But—"

"Forget it, Miranda. I know exactly what happened. I could practically write the script. Henry's doing something he doesn't want me to find out about, and he looked for something that would distract me." Bitterness edged his words. If there was anyone he thought he could rely on, it was Henry. He'd been wrong.

"Why would he do that? I don't understand."

No, she wouldn't. The people she knew didn't do things like that.

"At a guess, it's something to do with this deal we've been working on. There's a lot of money at stake. Possibly someone from a rival firm made Henry an offer too good to pass up. It might be worth a lot to be sure I was otherwise occupied at the crucial time."

Conviction formed even as he said the words. That had to be it.

"How can you be so sure?" Miranda obviously thought he was jumping to conclusions.

"The timing's too perfect. They'd think with me out of the way and only Josh left in the office from the family, they'd have clear sailing. Well, they're going to find they're wrong." Fury hardened to implacable determination.

"What are you going to do?" Apprehension filled her voice. Because she was worried about him? He wasn't sure.

"I'm going to Baltimore." He spun, the telltale bill clutched in his hand. "Henry's going to regret this to his dying day, I can promise you that."

"Tyler, please listen for a moment."

"Maybe my father had a point, after all. Don't rely on anyone else, that's what he always said. They'll let you down every time." He stalked to the doorway. "Well, this time they're not going to get away with it."

She took a step toward him. "Please, don't go into this angry. Don't do something you'll regret later."

He shook his head, making an effort to focus on Miranda's face. "This is business."

Funny. That was the phrase he'd heard all his life, always said meaning that this was more important than anything else.

"Maybe you should let Josh handle it."

"No."

He saw the hurt in her eyes at his abrupt tone. He was sorry for it, but he couldn't do anything else. This was something he had to take care of himself.

Miranda didn't understand that. The truth was, she probably never would.

Miranda sank into her chair, staring at the closed door. Tyler was leaving. From the moment she'd shown him that bill, his path was as irreversible as a tidal wave. He hadn't given a thought to Sammy or to her once his decision was made.

Please, Lord. The prayer came automatically, then she realized she didn't know what to pray for.

Please, Father, be with Tyler. He's angry, but he's hurting, too. Someone he trusted has betrayed him, and he's not even going to admit how painful it is.

Tyler's face formed in her mind, hard and implacable. He looked like the man he'd been when he arrived on the island. She hadn't realized how much he'd changed in the past weeks until that moment.

Don't let him turn back into that person, Lord. How can he be the father Sammy needs if all he thinks of is business?

She sat for a long time, her head bent to her folded hands, trying to see her path. Finally she stood.

She probably couldn't change his decision to go to

Baltimore and handle the situation himself. Maybe he did have to. But perhaps she *could* help him see that revenge wasn't the answer. For his sake, she had to try.

She walked up the steps slowly, running her hand along the rail that had been worn smooth by generations of hands. Where were the words that would reach him?

Tyler had made so much progress with Sammy. She couldn't let that slip away in his obsession with punishing the man he'd trusted. At the very least, he should talk with Sammy. If he explained why he had to go away, Sammy would understand. He could have confidence that his father would be back.

If he'd be back. The thought chilled her. She'd been making assumptions about his time here, about what his relationship with Sammy would be.

Maybe she'd been making assumptions about his relationship with her. Hadn't those kisses meant anything? Didn't they mean she was a part of his life, to be included in the decisions he made?

Maybe not. She forced herself to beat down the whimpering little voice that wanted to cry about her needs, her longings. She couldn't do anything about that. She had to try to do something about Tyler's role as Sammy's father.

The door to his room stood ajar, and when she knocked on it, it swung open. Tyler turned, and she realized he was simultaneously talking on the phone and packing a bag.

His frown lightened as he motioned her in.

"Look, everything you say is true." He spoke into the phone. "I'm sorry I didn't pay attention to your concerns earlier."

He was talking to his brother, obviously. Well, if Tyler was able to admit to Josh that he hadn't been perfect, that was an encouraging sign.

She took the shirt he'd been trying to fold one-handed and folded it neatly, then put it into the open case on the bed. She looked at him, raising her eyebrows in a question.

He nodded and pointed to a heap of clothing at the foot of the bed. She began packing it, a small measure of relief filtering through her concern. At least he wasn't packing everything. He must intend to come back.

"No, I don't want you to do that."

For a moment she thought he meant her, and her hands stilled. Then she realized he was talking to Josh.

"Look, I know you mean well, but don't do anything until I get there. I'll call you the minute I reach the city. In the meantime, just keep an eye on him." His voice hardened to implacability. "I don't want Henry to suspect a thing."

He snapped the phone shut and paced to the table, where he began sorting through papers. "Thanks, Miranda." He sounded a thousand miles away already. "I want to get on the road to the airport as quickly as possible."

Could she say anything that would deflect his obvious desire for revenge against the person who'd wronged him? "It sounded as if your brother wanted to handle this."

"He wanted to. He's not going to." His tone told her that any discussion of that subject would be useless.

She switched gears. "Before you go, you need to explain to Sammy why you're leaving."

He slanted a look at her, his expression harassed. "I'm kind of in a hurry here, Miranda. Can't you explain it to him?"

"No, I can't." She had to make Tyler understand. "This isn't just a matter of postponing the trip we planned to take today. The fact that you're leaving will upset him. You have to be the one to reassure him."

The stern lines of his face softened, and she knew she'd reached him.

"Okay. You're right. I don't want my son getting the message from someone else that I've left."

He was comparing himself with his father again, she supposed. Maybe that was a good thing, if it meant he was determined not to make the same mistakes.

"Thank you, Tyler. When you're talking to him I hope you won't—"

He lifted his eyebrows "Won't what?"

This was difficult. "I think it's better if he doesn't feel that you're out for revenge against your assistant, no matter what he's done to you."

"A matter of values?" His voice was soft, and she couldn't tell whether he was angry or not.

"He's been taught that seeking revenge is wrong,"

she said firmly. "I don't want him getting mixed messages about that."

Their gazes clashed for a moment. Then he nodded. "All right. I won't promise to change how I deal with Henry, but I certainly won't discuss it with Sammy. Still, he's going to have to understand that sometimes business has to take priority. That doesn't mean I love him any less."

That was probably the best she was going to get from him on that subject.

"I think Sammy will understand that." She put the last shirt in the suitcase. "Do you want anything else packed?" She gestured toward the closet.

"No." He stepped away from the desk, putting out his hand toward her. "Stay a minute, Miranda. There's something else I want to talk with you about."

To her surprise he looked uncertain. That wasn't an expression she was used to seeing on Tyler's face, and it sent a shiver of apprehension through her.

"Is anything wrong?"

"Not exactly. I've just been giving a lot of thought to what our lives are going to be like in the future—Sammy's, yours, mine. I'm sure you've been doing the same thing."

She nodded. Tyler didn't need to know she had been cherishing some totally unreasonable hopes about that life.

"We'll have to work out some kind of schedule so that he sees you often."

"You said once that he wasn't a package to be

shipped back and forth. I didn't understand what you meant then, but I do now."

She wasn't sure where he was headed. "If Sammy's going to spend time with you in Baltimore, I guess he'll have to get used to traveling. That's the only option."

"It's not the best one." He crossed the few feet between them and took both of her hands in his. "I've given this a lot of thought. I think I know what's best for Sammy. He needs to have his parents together. We need to be a real family."

Her knees went suddenly weak. "Wh—what do you mean?" He couldn't mean what she thought he did.

"I want you to marry me, Miranda." His grasp tightened, sending a thousand unspoken messages along her skin. "Will you marry me again?"

Her heart swelled until she thought it would burst out of her chest and float to the ceiling. Tyler loved her. After all that had happened, after all this time, Tyler loved her. They were going to have the marriage she'd always dreamed about.

Apparently taking her stunned silence for doubt, he rubbed his fingers over her knuckles. "I wanted to bring this up now so you can think it over while I'm away."

Think it over? Some caution sounded through the singing in her soul.

"Look, I know this won't be the romantic fairy tale we once thought we'd have, but we're not those young kids anymore, are we?"

It took a moment to process his words. I am, she wanted to cry, but she couldn't. She could only look at him, feeling the hope drain out of her.

"You must see that marriage is the sensible solution. It's not as though either of us is involved with anyone else. We both want to put Sammy first, and getting married is the best way to do that, don't you agree?"

A business deal. Obviously that was all this was to him. He didn't imagine marriage could mean anything else to her.

He was waiting for her answer. He'd said he wanted to give her time to consider, but he obviously didn't think it was necessary. He expected her to agree with him.

The longing to do just that overwhelmed her. She wanted—oh, how much she wanted—to say yes. To be Tyler's wife again, the way she longed to be.

It wasn't right. She knew that deep in her soul. God wanted more for His dearly loved children than that. Whether Tyler knew it or not, they both deserved better from marriage.

"Miranda?" He was smiling, confident.

"I'm sorry, Tyler." How much it cost to pull her hands away from his, knowing she might never feel his touch again. "I don't think that would work."

His expression was stunned, disbelieving. "Not work? Why wouldn't it work? You can't deny it would be best for Sammy."

She took a deep breath, willing herself not to cry in front of him. "I don't agree with you. Sammy won't benefit from seeing his parents in a marriage that isn't real."

Anger flared in his eyes and declared itself in the

taut lines of his face. "I'm offering you a marriage that's real in every way I can make it. I'm not suggesting we pretend anything."

"You're asking that we pretend the most important thing of all." Couldn't he see that? Her head throbbed. "Tyler, you're asking me to take vows before God to love and cherish—vows that you don't mean. I can't do that."

"Grow up, Miranda. Half the marriages that are based on romantic love end up in the divorce court. We're the living proof of that, aren't we?" He gripped her hands tighter, as if he could pressure the answer he wanted from her. "We'd have caring and respect between us. And the attraction is still there. We both know that. Isn't that enough?"

Again she felt the insidious temptation to say yes—to have as much of Tyler as he was willing to offer. But she couldn't.

"No." Her voice trembled on the verge of tears, and she held them back with a fierce effort. "I'm sorry, Tyler. It's not enough."

She could almost imagine she saw something die in his eyes.

"Fine." He flung her hands away from him, then snatched his bag. "If that's what you want, that's how it will be."

He was walking away. She wanted to stop him, whatever the cost. She couldn't. She could only watch him disappear out the door.

She sank onto the edge of the bed, letting the hot, salty tears spill once he wasn't there to see. She'd had everything she wanted there in her hands, and she'd let it go.

No. She wiped the tears away with an impatient hand, but they persisted. Tyler hadn't offered what she really wanted and needed. He hadn't proposed a marriage based on love and blessed by God.

Ironic that, once she'd finally seen she could cope with his world, he'd made her the one offer she couldn't accept. If God's love made her fit for any society, it also made her deserving of a real love.

Tyler couldn't see she offered what he needed so desperately to fill that aching void inside him left by his loveless childhood. He needed her love, but he couldn't admit it. He was trying to cheat. He wanted to fake a solution that didn't require risking his heart.

She couldn't help him do that. Even if it meant a lifetime of grieving for what they might have had, she couldn't.

She'd have to trust that God could see a way out of this, because she couldn't.

Chapter Fifteen

Could this day get any worse? Tyler sat in the corporate jet that was supposed to rush him anywhere he needed to be. He stared at sullen clouds and rain spattering against the window.

Sat was the operative word here. Even the best transport money could buy didn't argue with the weather.

First this day had brought the stunning news about Henry. Then had come the utter fiasco with Miranda. Then a series of storms had come up seemingly from nowhere, grounding flights and throwing his plans into disarray.

He picked up the phone. He'd better let Josh know what was happening. He didn't want his brother getting nervous and blowing everything.

"I thought you'd be on your way by now." Josh sounded as jittery as he'd feared.

"That's because you haven't checked the weather

in Savannah. I can't go anywhere until they let us take off. What's happening there?"

"Henry's been closeted in his office all day, making calls. Do you want me to try and find out who he's calling?"

"I don't want you to do anything!"

His brother's silence told him that his reaction had come out a lot more explosively than he'd intended.

"Sorry." It wasn't fair to take his frustrations out on the one person who was trying to help him. "I didn't mean to blow up at you."

"Is something wrong? Besides the obvious, I mean." Josh sounded as if he really wanted to know.

Tyler realized in a moment of surprise that he wanted to confide in his brother. He had to talk to someone, and there wasn't anyone else. He looked at that fact bleakly. It was a sad comment on his life.

"Things aren't going well here right now, and the timing of this situation didn't help any."

"Things aren't going well with Sammy or with Miranda?"

Josh's perception startled him.

"How did you get so smart about relationships all of a sudden?"

"Lots of observation," Josh said. He chuckled. "Not personal experience, I assure you."

"I guess not." Maybe that was the point of his brother's habit of never appearing with the same woman twice. Josh was as wary of relationships as Tyler was. "Our family life didn't prepare us for anything most people would call normal, did it?"

"Hardly." Josh hesitated a moment, and Tyler listened to the spatter of the rain and the static on the phone. "You know, our family to the contrary, plenty of people manage to create real marriages for themselves. Maybe even a Winchester could do that."

"Maybe." There didn't seem much else to say. "Hold the fort. I'll be there as soon as I can."

He put the phone away, but Josh's words seemed to hang in the air. *Some people manage to create real marriages for themselves.*

Real? The word lodged in his mind, resisting his effort to ignore it.

Real wasn't what he'd offered Miranda. She'd been wise enough to see that.

If he'd really proposed, if he'd told her he didn't know if he had it in him to love someone but he wanted to try, what would she have said then?

You'll never know, because you don't have guts enough to risk it.

The thought came out of nowhere, shaking him. Was that it? Was he really too afraid?

He took a hard look at the possibilities. The alternative seemed to be living his father's life over again, relying on no one, substituting business success for personal success, having no decent relationships with any of the people he loved.

Love. The word terrified him, and that was the truth of it. He'd been determined to love no one. Then Sammy came along.

He hadn't had a choice about being Sammy's

father. Loving him had been inevitable and irrevocable. Miranda was another story.

He'd played it safe. Disgust at himself welled up suddenly. He'd made a halfhearted offer of a half-baked marriage, and he'd expected Miranda to jump at the chance. Was it any wonder she'd been revolted? He hadn't even taken the time to do it right, trying to sandwich in asking her to be his wife between business calls and rushing off to Baltimore.

He saw what he had to do, and it scared him. If he wanted to make things work with Miranda and Sammy, he had to be honest with them. He had to show them that he would put them first. There was a way to do that, if he could.

For a long moment he stared at the phone in his hand. Then he punched in his brother's number.

"Josh Winchester speaking."

"I want you to handle this situation with Henry," Tyler said, not bothering with the pleasantries.

"What?" Josh's voice sounded far away, as if he'd removed the phone from his ear to stare at it, incredulous. "Are you sure about that?"

"I'm sure." Suddenly he was smiling. "You're not any less prepared to take over than I was when Dad died. You can do it."

"But what if Warren doesn't want to go through with the deal? You know the competition has probably lowballed us, based on whatever info Henry sold them."

He could see only one way to handle this, and Josh could do it as well as he could.

"Go in there prepared to sell them all over again. The bottom line is, we can give them the best product at the best price, regardless of what Henry's done." He hoped Josh could hear the conviction in his voice. "You can do this. And when the meeting's over, either way, you can have the pleasure of firing Henry, with my compliments."

"If you say so."

Through the doubt, Tyler heard a new sense of responsibility in his brother's voice. For some reason it made him think of Miranda's father talking about how he'd let his brother down by not forgiving him for his mistakes and trusting him again.

"I say so," he said firmly.

"What are you going to be doing while I'm playing chief?"

"Trying to put my family back together again, if I can."

"You can." Josh sounded confident. "Good luck."

If. He hung up, trying not to think how iffy this really was. Whatever the chance, he was doing the right thing.

He ran through the drizzle to the rental car. Josh deserved the chance to see what he could do. And Tyler—well, deserve it or not, he wanted a chance to convince Miranda that they could build a life together.

Eager to hear her voice, he called the inn as he drove toward the island. It was her father, not Miranda, who answered.

"Thought you were on your way north." Clayton sounded wary.

"I made a mistake," he said. "I'm on my way back now. Where is Miranda?"

"Well, Sammy was right disappointed about not going to Angel Isle today, so Miranda decided to take him."

"In this weather?" Fear gripped him.

Clayton must have heard it. "Now, there's no cause to be upset. They left in plenty of time to be there before these storms come up. Miranda will have them snug in the cottage until the weather clears, count on it."

"You're sure they'd have gotten there?"

"Certain sure. You just come on back home. These storms will blow off before you know it."

Relieved, he put the phone down and put both hands on the wheel. Fierce wind buffeted the car, and the drainage ditches on either side of the road showed an alarming tendency to spill over onto the surface. Clayton said the storms would blow over soon, and he certainly knew the weather on the islands as well as anyone. They'd be okay.

That assurance was growing thin by the time he battled his way across the bridge. Each line of thunderstorms was succeeded by another, equally bad. Impelled by fear for Miranda and Sammy that grew with each rumble of thunder and crack of lightning, he pulled to a stop at the dock in front of Adam's boatyard. He spotted Adam tying up a small motorboat.

He stepped into a downpour that soaked him through in seconds and ran toward the dock. The fear that rode him quadrupled. He had to get to them. He couldn't explain it logically, but he knew in his bones he had to get to them.

"Now we'll be warm in no time at all." Shivering, Miranda touched a match to the paper she'd crumpled under the kindling in the fireplace. She smiled at Sammy, hoping she sounded calm and confident.

A blast of wind rattled the windows in spite of the storm shutters they'd closed, and apprehension widened Sammy's eyes. "D'you think it's going to last a long time, Momma?"

"Oh, I don't think so." Flames licked around the pine knots, catching quickly. She held out her hands to the welcome warmth. "Even if it does, we're okay, aren't we? We've got a fire to keep us warm, a roof to keep us dry, and we can probably find something to eat in the kitchen if we need it. It's an adventure."

He grinned at her with his father's smile, shattering her heart yet again. "I'll bet none of the cousins got stuck here in such a bad storm."

"You can tell them all about it, can't you?" She put her arm around his shoulder.

He leaned against her, relaxing. "I hope the storm lasts till suppertime, so we can cook hot dogs over the fire. And marshmallows."

Apparently her words had calmed his fears. Now if only she could calm her own, she'd be all right.

Where was Tyler? She suppressed a shiver. He'd

set off to fly to Baltimore. Would the plane be safely above the storms by now? Or was he stuck on the ground in Savannah, raging against the freak weather that kept him from being where he wanted to be?

Her heart ached so strongly she rubbed her hand against her chest, as if that would ease the burden. Sammy had taken the news that his father had to go away with disappointment but no doubts that he would be back. He'd probably talk Tyler into another trip to Angel Isle, based on the argument that this trip was supposed to involve all three of them.

All three of them. The image made her heartache worse. If she'd said yes to Tyler, they'd have looked forward to a lifetime of all three of them.

No, not a lifetime. Sammy would grow up, go off to college, have a life of his own. That was the way it should be. What would she and Tyler have done then, tied in a marriage that wasn't real?

She'd dreamed, often enough, of growing old with Tyler, but not that way. Not living as two separate individuals trapped in the same house, existing politely in a vacuum.

As God's dearly beloved children...

God had something better in mind for those He loved. She had to believe that.

Sammy stirred. "You think we could make some popcorn in the fireplace?"

"Hungry already?" she teased, ruffling his hair. "Sure, I guess so. You go pick out a game you'd like to play, and I'll get the popcorn and popper out."

He was up in an instant. Another boom of thunder

sounded, very close, and she saw the flicker of fear in his eyes, quickly masked.

"I'll get Monopoly, okay? Then it'll be okay if the storm lasts a long time."

She gave him a reassuring smile, and he ran through the kitchen toward the game room they'd added years ago to the cottage. She followed, hoping the popcorn jars in the kitchen were full. Sammy would be disappointed if his adventure didn't include popcorn, and probably hot dogs, as well. Since the storm didn't show any signs of letting up, he'd probably get his wish.

She pushed through the kitchen door, looking through the opposite door to the game room. They'd never bothered to put storm shutters on those windows, since the wind didn't come from that direction. That seemed small comfort in a storm like this. Sheets of rain drove against the exposed panes, and the wind whipped the palmettos and live oaks into a frenzy of ripping leaves and torn Spanish moss.

She paused, hand reaching for the popcorn jar on the shelf above the stove. Sammy was safe enough in the walk-in closet where the games were stored, but the turmoil outside the windows still made her uneasy.

"Sammy, grab the game and hurry in here," she called. "Let's get back to the fireplace where it's warm."

"Okay, Momma, I'm coming."

She heard the game hit the floor, then Sammy muttering something about dropping it. Lightning cracked again, illuminating the wild scene outside the windows in an eerie light. The clap of thunder followed so closely they were almost simultaneous. Apprehension skittered along her skin, and she put the jar down.

"Come on, sugar. I'll get it." She stepped into the game room, heading for the closet.

Lightning cracked again, so close the acrid scent filled the air. Another crack burst on her ears, even louder than the thunder. The hundred-year-old live oak outside the windows shuddered. Before she could move, it fell. The room collapsed around her in a kaleidoscope of shattering walls and flying debris.

She was on the floor, a chair lying across her legs. She struggled to her feet. Sammy. She had to get to her son.

"Sammy, where are you?" She looked around, completely disoriented. The room was a shambles of broken siding and shattered glass. "Sammy!"

"I'm okay, Momma." His voice was reassuringly near. "But I can't get up."

"Hold on, sugar. I'm coming." She battled a few steps, shoving debris aside. A blast of wind drove a sheet of rain into her face, and the cold shock cleared her head.

Please, Lord. "Sammy, say something!"

"I'm here. In the closet."

Thank You, Lord.

She stumbled across the room, dashing the water from her eyes so she could see. The door-frame was still there, the walls surrounding it still upright. She clambered over a fallen beam and made it through the door.

"I'm okay, Momma, but I can't get out." Sammy's anxious face peered at her through a tangle of boards. The shelves had come down, boxing him into a small den behind them.

"I'll get you out. Don't you worry." She forced her voice to remain steady while panic ripped along her nerves. She grabbed the nearest board, yanking it free.

Please, God, please, God, give me the strength to get him out.

"I'll help," Sammy said, but when he pushed on a board, the wall above him swayed ominously.

"Don't, honey, don't. We have to take them away carefully." She fought for calm. "Like playing jack-straws. We don't want them to topple over."

Cautiously she lifted out one board, then another. She could reach through the hole and touch him, and she stroked his cheek.

"Just one more, then you can wiggle out."

She grasped the heavy beam. It wouldn't move. She braced her feet against a pile of rubble and pulled again. It remained stubbornly immovable. Another crack of lightning lit the room, showing her Sammy's scared face.

She had to get him out. If another piece of the roof fell, they could both be buried. She tugged again, hands tearing against the rough wood, muscles screaming.

Help me, Lord, help me. I'm not strong enough. Help me!

"Miranda! Sammy!"

She recognized his voice even while her logical mind told her there was no way on earth Tyler could be there. He climbed into the closet beside her, running his hands down her arms, trying to pull her away from the beam.

"No, I have to—"

"I'll get it, love." His voice was deep, reassuring. "Just move back a little."

She couldn't. He had to unclasp her hands, lift her away. She felt his strength as he maneuvered past her, wedging himself into the space she'd occupied.

"How are you doing, son?"

He was so calm he might have been asking how Sammy's day at school had been, but she had glimpsed the anguish in his eyes.

"I'm okay, Daddy." Sammy's voice trembled a little. "I'm glad you're here."

"Me, too, son." Tyler gave an experimental tug at the beam, then nodded to Miranda. "It's wedged too tightly to pull out," he said softly. "I'll have to push it up. As soon as I clear enough space, you pull him out."

She nodded, not sure she trusted her voice to speak. Tyler stooped and wedged his back under the beam, bracing his hands against the wall. With another glance at her, he began to push.

The beam remained stubbornly immobile. Lightning cracked again, seeming to give Tyler more strength. He pushed harder, face taut, muscles tight. The beam creaked, groaned, then began to inch upward.

The hole through which she'd touched Sammy's face widened a little, then a little more. She reached through, her legs pressing against Tyler's. His were solid as rock, holding danger away from their son.

She got both hands around Sammy's shoulders. "Almost enough," she breathed. "Just a little more."

The veins in Tyler's temples stood out. Eyes closed, he pushed harder—surely beyond the limit of his human strength.

Help him, Lord. Help us.

She clutched their son, began pulling him through the space made by his father's strength.

"It's okay, sugar. Just a little more."

She had him out far enough that he could clasp her around the neck. She tugged, and he was free.

She hugged him tight. "He's all right. I've got him. You can let go now."

Tyler shook his head, sweat pouring off his face. "Get him out before I let go."

What would the whole precarious stack do when he let go? It could come down on him.

"I'll help you—"

"Out!" It was nearly a shout, and it propelled her backward out of the closet, into the rain again. She clutched Sammy close, breathing a frightened prayer.

Protect him, Lord. Don't let me lose him now, please.

The remaining walls seemed to shudder, and a cloud of dust erupted from the closet.

"Tyler!"

Even as she cried his name, he emerged from the smoke. His arms circled both of them. They stumbled to the shelter of the kitchen.

Safe. God be praised, they were safe.

Chapter Sixteen

They weren't safe yet. Gasping from the pain in his back and shoulders, Tyler grabbed Miranda and Sammy, hustling them through the kitchen and into the large living room. Closing the door behind them instantly muted the roar of the storm, and he saw with relief that storm shutters protected the windows.

"Are you all right?" Miranda pulled free from his arms, her attention on Sammy. She took his face between her hands, then ran her fingers through his hair. "Does it hurt anywhere?"

Sammy wiggled, impatient at being held. "I'm okay, Momma. Don't fuss."

Tyler caressed his son's face as he set him on his feet. "That's what mothers do, son. Be glad of it."

"What about you?" Miranda was looking at Tyler with an expression he couldn't interpret. "Are you hurt?"

He stretched cautiously. "Nothing permanently damaged."

He saw her hands then, and caught them in his, turning the palms up to reveal the abrasions. Something winced inside him at the thought of Miranda struggling alone, without him, ripping her hands trying to free their son.

Thank You, Lord. The passion in his prayer caught him unaware. *Thank You.*

"It's nothing." She tried to pull her hands away, but he held them fast.

"We need to get those cleaned up." He glanced around. "Is there water somewhere?"

"Should be jugs under the kitchen sink." She shivered as thunder boomed, and he caressed her wrists lightly.

"Sounds like it's moving off."

She nodded, and he thought she drew on some reserve of strength to speak naturally. "Even if it gets worse again, this part of the original building will be safe. It's gone through a couple of hurricanes without falling."

He turned her toward the sofa. "You relax. I'll get the water."

He opened the door to the kitchen cautiously, but the room seemed secure. The room beyond, the addition Miranda said they'd built when her father was a teenager, had taken the brunt of the damage. He found a water jug and hurried back to Miranda and Sammy.

They were snuggled close together on the sofa, and he stood for a moment, looking at them, his heart overflowing. They were safe and together. At the moment nothing else seemed significant.

"Here we go." He set the water jug on the coffee table, then dampened the dish towel he'd found on the counter.

"I can manage," Miranda protested, but he clasped her hands and began to sponge her palms gently.

"Let Daddy," Sammy said. He looked at Tyler with something that might have been awe in his eyes. "I knew you'd come."

It was what he'd said when he was trapped in the closet and Tyler had been terrified he wouldn't be able to get him out.

"I came," he said. "But how did you know?"

"Cause I prayed." Sammy wiggled a little closer to his mother. "When I was scared, I asked God to help us. And I asked Him to send you. And He did."

"You know what?" Tyler smiled at his son. "I prayed the same thing. God must have heard both of us."

He sensed Miranda's measuring gaze on him as he cradled her hand in his to clean her cuts. She must be wondering whether he meant what he said.

She couldn't know how the past weeks had gradually opened the long-closed doors of his soul. He hadn't known it himself until he'd instinctively turned to God when he'd been afraid for them.

Whatever Miranda saw must have satisfied her, because she nodded. "All three of us," she said softly. "He heard all of us."

He held her hands, his gaze meeting hers.

Probably the question he wanted to ask showed in his face. Could she see that?

She moved a little, drawing her hands away, glancing at Sammy. "Maybe—" She sounded a little breathless. "Maybe we ought to try to get through to the family. They'll be worried." She smiled suddenly. "You do have your cell phone, don't you?"

He pulled it from his pocket and handed it over, wondering what she was thinking. Did she know how much he longed for a private moment with her, so he could try to repair the damage he'd done with his clumsy proposal?

He studied her face as she spoke with her father, cherishing the curve of her cheek, the generous mouth, the love in her eyes. He hoped he heard caring in her voice when she told her father that Tyler was there, that thanks to Tyler they were safe.

Was it selfish to want more than safety? He had to find a way to let her know how much he cared— to convince her that he didn't want a fake marriage. He wanted the real thing.

Miranda tucked an afghan over Sammy, who was curled up asleep in the big easy chair. The storm had ended, but not before they'd dined on hot dogs and marshmallows. Then, suddenly exhausted, Sammy had fallen asleep in the middle of a sentence.

Tyler added another log to the fire, then leaned his elbow on the mantel. He'd lost his tie somewhere along the line, and he'd pulled on an old flannel shirt of her father's in place of the dress shirt that had been ripped and filthy. The mismatched clothing, the shadow of a beard, his tousled hair only served to make him more handsome.

He glanced at Sammy. "He's wiped out."

She sank onto the sofa. "So am I. It's just as well we decided to stay here until morning. I'd probably have run the boat aground if we tried to go back tonight."

The rain spattered gently against the windows as Tyler came to sit next to her. Her nerves jumped. With Sammy asleep, they were alone.

The hurtful words they'd spoken to each other when they parted returned to haunt her. What if he intended to repeat his proposal? How would she ever summon the strength to say no again?

He touched her wrist, and her pulse fluttered.

"How—how could you come to the island today?" Any question would do to keep him from knowing how she felt when he was near. "What happened to the deal?"

For an instant he looked blank, then he shook his head, smiling. "Hard as it is to believe, I'd actually forgotten all about it. I put Josh in charge." His gaze lingered on her face, so warm he might as well have been touching her skin. "I had other things on my mind."

She swallowed. She had to remember that nothing had really changed. He still wanted a sham of a marriage that she couldn't accept.

"Maybe you ought to call him and find out what happened." Anything to put off the moment when he'd ask her again, when she'd have to try to find the courage to refuse again.

She felt his gaze on her face and stubbornly refused to look at him. Finally he drew away a few inches and picked up the phone.

While he talked, she studied her hands, folded in her lap, and tried not to let herself think about what it would be like to be Tyler's wife again.

"Good job, Josh. I knew you could do it."

The warmth in his voice pleased her. Apparently he and his brother had found some common ground at last.

"No, I don't want to prosecute. Just let him leave. He can't hurt us any longer."

He exchanged a few more words, then hung up. She looked at him questioningly. "It went all right?"

"Very much so. Josh handled everything perfectly." He gave her a rueful smile. "Maybe better than I would have. Seems I've been underestimating my little brother."

"You trusted him today."

His hand closed over hers, setting her pulse thudding. "Thanks to you."

"Me?"

"Your family," he amended. "If I hadn't been here, seen how all of you rely on each other, I might never have taken the risk." His gaze, very serious, rested on her. "I remembered something your father said about how he'd never trusted his brother again after that business when the dolphin was lost, that maybe his distrust kept his brother from being the man he should have been. I didn't want to wake up and feel that about Josh twenty years from now."

"I'm glad," she said, wondering if he could hear the joy she felt that he'd made peace with his brother. "And I'm glad you decided not to prosecute Henry."

He squeezed her hand. "'You meant it for evil, but God meant it for good.' You quoted that verse to me, remember? Henry sent that photograph for his own ends, but it brought me Sammy. I couldn't punish him for that."

Thank you, Lord. The prayer was whispered in her heart. Tyler was becoming the man God intended him to be. Whatever happened between them, he'd be a better father for that.

"You know, you didn't ask the right question."

She looked at him, startled. "What right question?"

"You asked how I could come back. You didn't ask why I came back."

She was suddenly breathless, and her heart seemed to be beating in her throat. She managed a whisper. "Why did you?"

He lifted her hand gently to his lips. "Because I did it all wrong when I asked you to marry me." His voice was husky, and she felt his breath against her fingers as he spoke. "I tried to cheat. I tried to get what I wanted without risking my heart."

She couldn't speak to save herself, but he didn't seem to expect it.

"I was kidding myself, you know that, don't you? You already had my heart right here." He turned her hand over, dropped the lightest of kisses in her bruised palm. "I love you, Miranda, with all my heart. Please marry me again. Let us have a real marriage—the one that God intended for us."

Joy bubbled inside her until she thought it would lift her right into the air. In spite of the darkness outside, she could almost hear a bird singing, giving wings to her heart.

She reached to touch his dear face. "Don't you know I've never stopped loving you?" She traced the outline of his lips with her fingertip. "Yes, Tyler. I've never stopped being your wife."

She saw the sheen of tears in his eyes through a haze of joy. His lips claimed hers, and she thought her heart would burst with loving him.

What was meant to be from the beginning was coming true. Their love had been broken. Now it was mended, and it would be all the stronger.

A clatter on the porch woke Miranda. For an instant she thought the house was coming down around them. Then she sat up and smiled at Tyler, waking on the sofa.

"Time to get up. Sounds as if the family has arrived."

Sammy had already jumped up and run to the door. In a moment the room was filled with Caldwells, all of them talking at once. All exclaiming, hugging, kissing. Tyler looked embarrassed at all the emotion, but he was smiling.

"Not much left but matchsticks out there," her father said, coming in from the kitchen. "Still, we may as well start clearing up. Jeff and his boys just pulled in, and Adam's brought equipment from the boatyard."

Tyler stretched. "I'll come and help you."

"No need, son." Her father clapped his shoulder. "You've done more than your share already. Get some breakfast and coffee in you first. I reckon Sallie brought some clothes for y'all, too."

"That I did." Sallie handed him a bag, then enveloped him in a hug. "God bless you, Tyler. Thank you."

He drew back, as if not sure how to react, but Miranda saw pleasure in his eyes. "Just thank God," he said. "That's enough."

Miranda disengaged herself from Chloe's hug, wondering whether the happiness in their faces had already given away the announcement they'd need to make once they'd told Sammy. Her heart clenched. Would he be as happy as she hoped?

From outside, one of the twins yelled at the kids to stay away from the wreckage. "Let's go upstairs and change." She took Tyler's arm. "Maybe by that time they'll have stopped making so much noise."

Tyler grinned as he followed her. "I don't think it'll get any better."

She showed him into one of the bedrooms, then started for the other side of the hall to change. Realizing she hadn't taken her clothes from the bag, she turned back.

"Tyler, I forgot—" She stopped. He'd taken his shirt off, revealing the dark bruise the beam had left clear across his back.

She went to him, touching him with a murmur of distress. When he'd been tending her hands, he must have been in pain. "Why didn't you tell me you were hurting? We ought to get you to a doctor."

He took her hands in his. "I don't need a doctor. But I could use a kiss."

She smiled at him, still troubled. "You can always have that."

He'd barely touched her lips when the door creaked. Which of her kin had decided to interrupt them now?

Their son stood in the doorway. She wasn't sure what to say, and she suspected Tyler didn't have a clue, either.

Sammy solved it for them. "Are you going to get married again?"

"We want to." Tyler spoke before Miranda could. "Would that be okay with you?"

Sammy surveyed them solemnly, then nodded. Suddenly he rushed across the room and threw himself at them. That three-way hug was probably the best thing she had ever felt in her life.

Too soon, Sammy wiggled free. Uncertainty clouded his eyes. "Will we have to live up north?"

"I've been thinking about that." Tyler glanced at her, as if measuring her approval. "We've got some ideas for expanding our companies in the southeast, so I thought maybe we could live in Charleston. That way we could have a house on the island, too, and come over as much as we wanted to."

She could hardly believe what she heard. Tyler must have been thinking about this half the night, and she knew what it cost him to make this change in his life.

"Cool," Sammy pronounced, and then darted from the room, shouting. "Hey, Gran. Guess what?"

"Somehow I don't think we'll have to tell anyone else." Tyler put his arm around Miranda again.

She searched his face. "Do you really want to do this? Because I'd live anywhere with you." She wasn't afraid any more.

"I know you would, but this is what I want. Developing something new will be a challenge for me, and Josh can be in charge in Baltimore without me looking over his shoulder all the time. Now, about that kiss—"

This time the interruption came in the form of a shout from outside. A ripple of fear told her she hadn't totally recovered from yesterday's terror. "We'd best see what's happening."

Tyler clasped her hand in his as they went quickly down the stairs and out the door. Everyone seemed to be gathered around the wreckage next to the kitchen.

Miranda hurried to Gran. "What is it? What's Daddy doing?"

Her father squatted in the midst of the fallen wall next to the kitchen, carefully unearthing something.

"It was in between the uprights where they put the addition on that summer." Gran looked as if she were talking in a dream. "Your daddy just spotted the tip of it."

"What, Gran?" She clutched her grandmother's arm, frightened at the strained look on her face. "What did he find?"

"The dolphin," someone said in a whisper. "It must be the dolphin."

Her father looked up, seeming to search until he found the face he wanted. "Jeff," he called to his brother. "Come help me get it out."

Uncle Jeff clambered over the wreckage, his face taut.

Miranda clung to Tyler with one hand, to Gran with the other. They'd mourned the loss of the dolphin for so long. If they found it now, only to discover it broken to bits as a result of the storm—

Daddy and Uncle Jeff stood up. In their upraised hands the Caldwell dolphin soared upward, as if it leaped toward the sky.

Tears spilled onto her cheeks. "We found it." She turned into Tyler's arms. "After all this time, we found it."

"That poor girl must have hidden it in the wall that night and never had a chance to tell anyone." Gran's eyes were bright with tears. "It's lain there all these years, waiting to be found in God's own time."

Miranda leaned her forehead against Tyler's chest. "Suppose you think we're foolish, to get so excited over an old carving."

He tipped her face up. "Nothing foolish about it. Like your grandmother said, what was lost is found again. Nobody knows that better than we do."

She smiled through her tears, understanding. They'd lost each other, too, but finally, in God's own time, they'd found each other again, for keeps.

Epilogue

Tyler stood at the chancel of St. Andrew's Church, waiting for his bride. He took a steadying breath and glanced across the few feet that separated him from Miranda's cousin Adam.

It had been Gran's idea that this be a double wedding—Adam and Tory, Tyler and Miranda. He hadn't been sure at first about sharing this day, but he'd come to see that this was about more than their wedding. It was about family, joined together and extending into the past and into the future.

Josh, perfectly at ease in his best-man role, leaned close. "You're acquiring a lot of family today."

"Yes." He looked across the church, packed with those who'd come to wish them well. He'd once thought family meant only people who wanted something from him. Now he knew better.

Even his mother was there, all the way from Madrid and her new husband, looking dazed at the fact of being a grandmother. He still had to smile at the thought of the gracious way Miranda had welcomed her. She'd found again all the confidence she'd ever need.

His gaze intersected with Gran's, and she nodded solemnly, then looked past him to where the dolphin stood. He didn't need much imagination to know what she was thinking. Once again things had been restored to the way God intended them. The lost had been found.

The organ music swelled, and Sammy appeared at the head of the aisle next to Adam's daughter. Jenny carried a basket of flowers. Sammy stared intently at the rings he bore, then looked up and flashed a smile at his father as he began to walk toward him.

Tyler's heart lifted with the music. All this had begun with a picture of Sammy sliding onto his desk, interrupting the life he'd thought he wanted. He couldn't have guessed then that it would end this way, with wholeness restored and a richer future than he'd ever dreamed of.

The matrons of honor came next—Miranda's sister, Chloe, and Tory's new sister-in-law, Sarah. Then a rustle went through the church as the music rose triumphantly.

Miranda came toward him, radiant in the ivory gown that had been her grandmother's and the lace veil that had been handed down to generations of Caldwell brides. His throat was so tight he had a moment of panic, thinking he wouldn't be able to voice his vows.

Then she reached him, and he took her hand in his and knew he could do anything, be anything, as long as he had her love. Together they turned to face the minister.

Behind the pulpit, the Caldwell dolphin, back where it belonged, arched upward in prayer, its smile a reminder of God's eternal love and blessing.

* * * * *

Dear Reader,

I'm so glad you decided to read this book. The love story of Miranda and Tyler brings the Caldwell Kin stories to a close. I've loved writing this series on the power of family, and I hate to see it end. So this has been a bittersweet story for me to write.

Maybe it was fitting that Miranda and Tyler's story closes out the family series, because their story is a tale of a broken family brought back to wholeness through the power of God's love. My prayer is that you've experienced that love in your own life.

Please let me know how you liked this story. You can reach me c/o Steeple Hill Books, 233 Broadway, New York, NY 10279, or visit me on the Web at www.martaperry.com.

Blessings,

Marta Perry